The Apollo Illusion
A Novel
By Shari Lopatin

BookBooks Publishing LLC

This is a work of fiction. Names, characters, places, and incidents either are the products of the author's imagination or are used fictitiously. Any resemblance to actual persons, living or dead, businesses, companies, events, or locales is entirely coincidental.

The Apollo Illusion. Copyright © 2018
by Shari Lopatin. All rights reserved.

Requests for copyright permissions or bulk orders should be sent in writing to the publisher, BookBooks Publishing LLC, at 2550 E. Rose Garden Ln. #72258, Phoenix, AZ 85050; or to the author, Shari Lopatin, at shari.lopatin@gmail.com.

Published by: BookBooks Publishing LLC, Phoenix, Arizona
Edited by: Hilary Dartt of Darttboard Creative Writing, and Megan Yakovich
Cover Art by: Rebecca Lopatin
Cover Design by: Ryan Quackenbush
Formatted by: Diane Serpa of GreyCatDot Digital Design
Author Photograph by: Oscar Barrascouth

(E-Book) ISBN-13: 978-0-9997827-0-5

(Paperback) ISBN-13: 978-0-9997827-1-2

Library of Congress Control Number: 2018902058

First Edition
Printed in the United States

Visit the author's website at www.ShariLopatin.com

Contents

PART ONE......................................1

The Wall 3

World History 5

The Log Cabin................................9

The Anniversary 13

Oak Creek Canyon 17

The Hike..21

The Journal 27

The Morgue....................................31

The Event 35

Dolores..37

The Book 41

A-Search.. 43

Strike Two 45

The Confession 47

The Visitors 51

The Number..................................59

The First Date 63

The Dream 67

The Question 73

Sophie 77

Government Class 81

The News 85

Death Sentence 87

Losing It 91

The Phone Call..............................95

Don's House..................................99

The Tunnel 101

PART TWO..............................105

The Scent of Freedom 107

The Transport...............................111

The Black-and-White Leggings 117

Dr. Thompson..............................121

Diagnosis 125

The Contacts................................129

Socialization Hour 135

Therapy Session..........................139

The Patient....................................143

Deceived..147

The Mail 151

The Meeting..................................155

Lunch Date 163

The Way Out................................167

The Museum................................171

Lockdown 177

EMP 183

Hallway to Hell............................ 189

Jaron 195

HELL's Hole................................201

The Real City................................205

Dr. Hollister Wesson.................. 209

The Virtual Revolution 215

Return to HELL 221

The Name......................................225

PART THREE........................... 229

Poison Ivy 231

The Surprise 235

Reunion.. 237

Getting Out.................................. 241

The Safe House............................245

The Plan 251

Hacking War 255

The Light...................................... 259

Moment of Truth........................ 263

The Return..................................267

The Little Stunt 271

Lymphocytes 275

Secrets.. 279

The Choice 283

Home..287

Be the Light................................ 291

A NOTE TO MY READERS........ 295

ABOUT THE AUTHOR.............. 297

Acknowledgments

Where do I begin? I finished the first draft of this book in September 2014 (four years before publication), but I could not have reached this point without an army of supporters by my side.

First off, no writer can survive the cruel world of critics without a ruthless editor to ensure her prose is sharp, and her story tight. I was lucky to have a team of two talented editors work on this book for me: Hilary Dartt of Darttboard Creative Writing, and Megan Yakovich. Thank you both for helping this novel be the best it could be! I could not have reached this level without your guidance and support.

Secondly: design. I've heard publishing professionals say the cover sells a book, not the description. I was honored to have the accomplished and talented fine artist, Rebecca Lopatin, classically hand-paint my book's beautiful and striking cover art. Additionally, digital artist Ryan Quackenbush did a slam-dunk job of turning the art into a stunning cover design. Finally, Diane Serpa of GreyCatDot Digital Design formatted my book with precision to ensure professionalism and class. Thank you, Rebecca, Ryan, and Diane for your amazing work and your partnership!

Furthermore, a writer needs a solid, professional head shot for book covers and marketing purposes. I want to thank Oscar Barrascouth for the amazing portrait he took of me that brought out what he saw, yet I could not: my "feminine empowerment." Thank you, Oscar!

Next up, my family and friends, all of whom spent time reading this book and offering their feedback. Thank you to my mom and dad, Jill and Jerry Lopatin, for always believing in me, supporting my writing, and feeding my imagination. Thank you to my love, Oscar Barrascouth, for being my greatest fan, my brainstorming partner, and my writer's block smasher. Thank you to my sister, Rebecca Lopatin, for being my first audience (ever!) and still listening to my stories with enthusiasm today.

Thank you to my friends, Richard Gray, Megan Janas, and Hilary Dartt (before I hired you as an editor), for reading my book and offering your opinions during your precious, free time. And of course, I have numerous family members and friends who have supported me through this writing journey—too many to name, but you know who you are. I also want to thank my high school English teacher, Rachel Prince, for detecting my potential early on, and once telling me I was a leader; I just didn't know it yet.

Finally, I could not have written this book without the love and companionship of my snowshoe cat, Chance "Mr. Man" Lopatin (may you rest in peace, my little love), and my gray tabby cat, Chester "Plumperton" Lopatin.

For my family, Jill, Jerry, and Becca
And for my love, Oscar

The
Apollo
Illusion

Part One

Apollo

The Wall

FLORA

Its presence has loomed over me since birth, but my eyes have never looked upon it—until today. The moment feels surreal, like it's happening to someone else, and I find myself consumed by disbelief.

My bike is parked against the tree beside me, and I tilt my head toward the sky until the soaring Ponderosa pines disappear. The Wall towers over them all, far surpassing the woods surrounding it like some dark lord overlooking its peasants, and it mesmerizes me.

I could reach out and touch it, feel what mysteries are hidden within, the secrets I've been drawn to discover since I was a child—what's on The Other Side—but the Wall's authority stops and reminds me: *You're forbidden to venture beyond this point.*

"Flora!"

Andrew. I hear his voice calling my name, floating between Aspen and Ponderosa branches. "I'm over here!" I yell.

We are mountain biking together through the forest in Apollo, like we do almost every Saturday when the weather warms enough to melt the snow and ice. I've been pushing our starting point further each week, asking Andrew to drive an extra ten miles here, five miles there, before pulling our bikes from the back of his car and pedaling into adventure. Today, my efforts paid off.

I hear Andrew's tires cracking over broken branches and the gentle panting of his breath as he swoops in behind me. I turn around and smile, watching him swing a long leg off the mountain bike and lean it against a tree.

"I thought we agreed not to go off-course," he says, approaching me in a slow stride, his dark eyes piercing through mine in that evocative way. A thrilling chill grips my core and I try to concentrate on anything but Andrew's delicious looks.

"I thought you knew me better than that," I say. "Since when do I follow the rules?"

I try to ignore the wistful pit developing in my gut, and I worry my face reveals too much. Andrew has been my friend since we were eight years old. He was my only friend then, and is my only friend today, at nineteen. I don't intend on ruining our history because of some stupid, fleeting attraction.

Andrew smirks and approaches me, playful but intense—too intense, and I realize I've stopped breathing. He leans against the tree trunk, trapping me, and lowers his gaze to meet mine.

"Now, how will you get away?" His voice grows deeper and I smell the mixture of sweat and cologne; we're so close now, only inches apart. Worried that my rapid breath might reveal too much, I yank away and spin around.

"Like that," I say.

As I'm staring at Andrew—admiring his thick, disheveled hair—I notice his gaze rests on something behind me. I turn around, only to confront the Wall once again. While joking with him, I'd almost forgotten what I had come across.

"You found it?" he asks.

"Not on purpose."

"Bullshit." Andrew pauses for a moment, lifting an eyebrow. I know he doesn't believe me.

"Flora, you ask about the Wall too much."

I reach into my back pocket and pull out a crumpled map littered with red squiggles and black Xs. "I swear to you, Andrew, I didn't find it on purpose," I tell him. A little white lie never hurt anyone. "Do you have a pen?"

Andrew winces—I can tell from the nervous twitch in his hand that he's uncomfortable here—but he pulls a pen from inside his jacket anyway.

"Here," he says, handing it to me. "Where's yours?"

"I'm not the writer."

I stand still and absorb our position for a few moments, taking in the possible location of our morning ride, and I lower my eyes toward the map, estimating where we had drifted. Andrew watches me in silence as I draw a solid black circle around the southern edge of Apollo.

"Do you really think it's a good idea to mark it?" he asks.

"We mark *everything*," I tell him. "It's our map, Andrew. We've never omitted one of our discoveries before. Why should we start now?"

Andrew lets out a laugh, but it's forced. "You know why, Flora." He begins to back away from the Wall, looking like an intruder who encroached upon enemy land. "We should get out of here."

"Who's going to know?"

But Andrew shakes his head. "We need to leave. Now."

He jogs back to his bike and swings that long leg over the seat. I sigh, disappointment washing over me like a flash flood in the mountains. Reluctantly, I fold our map and shove it into my back pocket before following Andrew's lead and grabbing my bike.

As I'm pedaling away, however, the Wall seems to beckon me. I glance back over my shoulder, and I swear I see the thing smiling.

World History

FLORA

Andrew made me promise I wouldn't say a word—not a freakin' *word*—about the Wall and our encounter. So now, as I sit in my World History class, I'm frustrated.

It's a boring general requirement course at the University of Apollo, but on the up side, we're reviewing the history of the Wall for our final exam. I always found it ironic that merely discussing the Wall with friends or family is a misdemeanor crime, but the moment you're within the confines of a classroom, it's free reign.

"The Wall was built in 2075, to do what?" my professor asks.

The Asian girl to my right raises her hand, and the professor calls on her.

"To protect us," she says.

I don't know her name, but I've seen her somewhere before—perhaps in my Spanish Literature class? I think this somewhat odd, since most of the students I meet of Asian descent prefer to study a language such as Korean, Chinese, or Japanese. Usually, their great-grandparents spoke one of those languages when they immigrated to Apollo, long ago.

"That's correct," the professor says. "And what else of note happened in 2075?"

I'm staring at the classic novel resting on my desk, which I plan to begin reading during lunch: *The Kite Runner*. I'd give anything for this class to finish so I can lose myself in yet another story, one which challenges me to imagine a world other than *this*.

"The State of Apollo was established," I answer, without raising my hand.

The professor glances my way, visibly annoyed at my refusal to follow protocol. "Very good, Flora," he says, his voice flat.

I know the whole story. It's something every Apolloan learns in grade school, because that's when they teach you how "the Wall is forbidden to discuss, or venture beyond."

Of course, they never tell you *why*.

Their response usually resembles something like, "There's evil on The Other Side." For my entire life, it has been the elephant in the room, and I sometimes wonder if I'm the only person who wants to scream, deck someone in the face, and shriek, "C'mon, *think!*"

Perhaps this is where my love for books stems: the urge to seek truth or to explore other realms beyond my own. One can often find me wandering like a ghost through the towering shelves of the Apollo Library. The library is filled with ancient books, yellowed pages and decaying leather-bound covers; I'm fascinated by them.

My professor continues reviewing the history of Apollo, and I force myself to stop my mind from wandering, instead following the familiar plotline inside my head:

Long ago, before our "Great State" was established, the Central Commerce Hub of Apollo was known as Flagstaff—a quaint college town in the northern mountains of Arizona, a state from the former United States of America. Although the majority of citizens live within the Central Commerce Hub today, Apollo's territory stretches across the entire northern part of Arizona's former terrain, including the Grand Canyon and Oak Creek Canyon.

In 2075, that land was incorporated into the newly formed state of Apollo, and two years later, the Wall was completed to protect us from evil. Now that it's 2150, we are celebrating Apollo's seventy-fifth birthday.

"Who knows the origin of our state's name?" my professor asks the class.

I know the answer to this question too, but decide to let someone else respond. The professor glances around, and I catch him eyeing me, but I refuse to my raise my hand, so he answers. "It's named after the Greek god, Apollo, who was the god of light, truth, and knowledge."

There is a momentary silence in the class, before a deep and noticeably angry voice breaks it. "Because that's what we're all about, right professor?"

The remark comes from a shadow stuffed into the back corner of the classroom. My professor saunters toward the half-hidden desk, and a boy about my age reveals himself. I've seen him in class, but he's never spoken until now. His dark, black-rimmed eyes challenge our instructor, and after further observation, I realize he wears eyeliner.

"Excuse me, Donald?" my professor says.

"Yeah, it's Don." The kid's voice is snide, sarcastic. I can tell it riles the professor. "I said, because that's what we're all about, right? Sharing truth and knowledge with the world?"

The professor pauses and pulls a white handkerchief from his front pocket, coughs like a gentleman into it, and returns his attention to the boy.

"Well Don," he says, his voice cool, "I think any historian would agree, that yes, the State of Apollo was established to represent just that."

"Then how come they never talk about what's beyond that damned Wall?"

My head and ears perk up at this. My professor pauses again. I can see him trying to collect his thoughts and re-gain his position as leader of the class. He adjusts his glasses, and I lean in, paying keener attention.

"Because what's beyond the Wall is not important to Apollo and its movement forward in the world," he says.

The boy follows his nod with a smirk. "Then how can we call ourselves the leaders of light, truth, and knowledge?"

The professor shifts his weight, and I can tell he's ready to let this kid have it. "Because, *we are*," he says. "Apollo requires its students to study everything from Shakespeare, to a musical instrument, to calculus, and to master a second language. It provides free education for all its citizens, all the way through college. We believe in knowledge and community for all. And knowledge, my friend, is power."

***

Class couldn't finish fast enough. The moment we're set free, I hurry outside, dashing through chatty cliques of students and flocks of boys and girls, trying to find this *Don* character—the mysterious recluse who sports black eyeliner and challenges professors during lectures.

As I travel down the university's massive hallways, the words, "Light, Truth, and Knowledge" loom over the swarming pools of students below. The hallways seem infinite, broken only by periodic, circular courtyards that wind around central statues of the infamous Greek god for which we're named. He is always holding a torch toward the sky, much like the famed Statue of Liberty in ancient New York.

Lose yourself in discovery. My mother's words flash through my mind unexpectedly as I seek to find Don among the crowds. *Don't let those girls steal it from you, Flora. Your curiosity makes you unique. There's no fun in normal.*

For a moment, I can feel it again—the sticky hair spray gluing together my eyelids and stiffening my hair, dripping down my arms as they laugh, standing in a circle around me, all ten of them. *Need some hairspray, Flora? Maybe this will help!* Never so humiliated, I'd stopped my recess treasure hunts after that, until my mom reminded me why I shouldn't.

Today feels like another hunt, I realize, and I revel in it. When I glimpse a black ball of grease scurrying toward the corridor that leads to the university's mess hall, I grab my backpack and jog to catch up to Don.

"Excuse me!" I say, but he doesn't respond, so I call his name. This time, the boy stops and turns around, scanning my features from nose to foot with a flicker of his black eyes. They remind me of obsidian stones: cold.

"What do you want?" he asks. His eyes briefly meet mine before jetting toward the ground again.

"Hi, I'm sorry to bother you. My name is Flora."

"So?"

I'm rather shocked at his lack of manners. *So?* What kind of way is that to greet a friendly introduction? But I decide to let it slide this time. I'm too curious.

"So, I'm in your World History class. And I found your question about the Wall quite fascinating."

For a moment, his mood seems to lighten. "You did?"

"What do you know about it? Have you actually *seen* it?"

Now he turns away and begins walking, as fast as he can. "No one has ever seen the Wall. You know that."

I refuse to let him slip away so quickly, and begin pacing him. "But *you've* seen it, haven't you?"

He shakes his head, and I can tell from the cornered look crossing his face that he's hiding something. "No," he says. "I haven't. No one has."

He's lying, and I feel my heart leap. I imagine this is the way detectives must feel when they find a solid lead that could finally solve an elusive murder.

"You *have* seen it!" I quicken my pace as he speeds his steps and tries to lose me. "What do you know?"

Don's head continues shaking, and he's obviously growing more agitated. "I don't know anything," he says.

His refusal triggers a tinge of frustration inside me—what gives him the right to keep something this significant from a fellow explorer, a fellow outsider? But the frustration quickly transforms into something else: an urgency. Without thinking, I grab his shoulder, spinning him around to face me and our noses nearly collide. He smells of cigarette smoke, and the odor floats into my nostrils.

"I've seen it," I whisper, and I can feel my hands grasping his shoulders.

He places a palm atop mine, and for a moment, we connect; I can sense he wants to talk and with my eyes, I coax him to speak.

"I—I'm sorry," he says, and shoves my hand from his shoulder, turns around, and races down the corridor. As I watch him disappear into the crowds of hungry students, I know I must get through to Don. I must know what he knows.

This kid has definitely seen *something*.

The Log Cabin

FLORA

When I approach the front door to my log cabin after school, piano notes are dancing through the compacted wood. I pause before inserting the key, close my eyes and smile while absorbing my dad's music into every crevice of my being. His tunes often greet me before he does.

Ernest, our three-year-old golden retriever, is the first to welcome me, as usual. Mom gave Ernest his name, after the great author and World War I veteran, Ernest Hemingway. She introduced me to Hemingway when I was twelve; she adores all his books and tries to style her own writing after his.

Since I don't see her relaxing on the couch and enjoying my dad's music, I'm sure she's currently locked upstairs in her room, working on her latest article for *The Apollo Times*.

The tantalizing aroma of my favorite dish, sweet potato casserole—warm marshmallows and cinnamon—lures me further inside. I stroll into the living room and plop onto the couch, petting Ernest as he rests his head on my lap.

The music stops momentarily. My father is seated at the piano bench across from me, his eyebrows drawn together in thought as he scribbles music notes onto blank sheets of paper. He's in the midst of his next great composition.

But the moment I sit down, his mood changes. He knows something is wrong, and *the look* surfaces.

"How was school?" he asks, setting down his pen and paper while trying to sound matter-of-fact. My dad has these big brown eyes—real soft, like a teddy bear—and this scruffy mustache that makes him resemble a sheriff from the Old West.

"Ehhh," I say, leaning over to scratch Ernest under his floppy ears. I smirk as his lips curl to reveal miniature sharp fangs. Ernest is perhaps the only dog I know who smiles.

"Your mother and I were thinking of going on a camping trip this weekend, down by Oak Creek Canyon. Do you and Andrew want to come?"

Diversion. My dad loves using diversions to distract me when I'm feeling upset. He started this habit after the hairspray incident when I was eight. We thought the "incidents" would end after that, but they continued for years, and so did my father's diversions.

"Of course," I say. "I'll message Andrew."

I smile at the thought of taking another camping trip with my parents and Andrew. They've treated him like my brother since we met as children, the same year the group of girls started their torture. In fact, it was Andrew who found me crying under the slide on the playground the day of the hairspray. Rather than laugh at me, he sat next to me, and has been my only friend since.

My parents love inviting Andrew for camping trips. For them, I think it creates the feeling of a complete family. They'd always wanted to have another child, and I know secretly, they would have wanted a little boy.

The laws of Apollo don't allow it, though. Each family is permitted only one child, to prevent overpopulation of our treasured State.

I pull my cell phone from my backpack and send a quick text message to Andrew, a technology most of us know is dated, but still preferred for its simplicity. *Camping with my parents for the weekend? Oak Creek?* Within moments, my phone chimes with his enthusiastic response, and I tell my dad we're on.

"Why don't you go check on the garden?" he says, and I know his suggestion is meant as another distraction.

I obey my dad, as I almost always do, and walk toward the backyard garden, Ernest trotting loyally behind. I stare into the rows of sprouting tomatoes, lettuce, and strawberries.

My parents are the epitome of naturalists, like the majority of Apolloans. Almost everyone I know grows their own garden, but my parents tell me it wasn't always like this. In fact, when Apollo was established, most of its citizens didn't know how to grow anything.

"But everyone knows agriculture," I'd said, in complete disbelief. *"It's like knowing how to read, or add two plus two."*

I couldn't comprehend that the average Apolloan didn't understand the concept of companion plants, nevertheless know that peanuts and watermelon are two of them. Nor could I fathom that older adults, thrice my age, were never taught how lavender flowers ward away unwanted, plant-eating bugs. *Didn't everyone know that?*

My parents had to drag me to the Apollo Library to prove they weren't lying. I didn't believe them until I saw the history books flipped open, words and images spitting truth back into my face. And even then, I still openly questioned the sources of such perilous information.

Now, of course, I know the truth. But every so often, another inconvenient reality will surface, and I have to trick my brain into believing it. Otherwise, I might find myself living in denial.

"Are finals done, yet?" my dad asks, calling from inside the cabin. I know he's probing.

I shake my head and walk back into our house. "No, today was Spanish Literature and Advanced Biochemistry. Tomorrow I still have World History."

I collapse back into the warm embrace of the living room couch, letting its soft cushions engulf me. I grew up in this house and absolutely adore it. The place is old—I mean *ancient*—so much that the wood still smells of last century. The stairs to the second level creak, and I sometimes get the sense that ghosts of past owners linger within the walls, refusing to leave such an inviting atmosphere.

"Well kiddo, take it easy, and let your mother and I worry about dinner."

My dad usually requests I help contribute to the house in some fashion. He doesn't make me work; both my parents prefer I concentrate on my studies, as nothing is more important in Apollo than a well-rounded education. However, my dad does like me to help cook, clean, and tend to the garden.

This is how I know he's sensing my uneasiness. I want to open up, to tell him about the Wall and Don, but I don't dare. As much as my parents have been my source of comfort, my safety net when walking on a tightrope, I know when it comes to this one topic, he'd side against me.

My parents would *never* turn me in. Hell no.

But they'd lecture. And perhaps they wouldn't trust me anymore. Quite frankly, the thought of losing my parents' trust kills me.

And so, I smile at my father, grateful for his comfort, and keep everything else to myself.

The Anniversary

FLORA

Before Andrew and I take our weekly bike ride through the forest on Saturday morning, we decide to meet at our favorite coffee house, La Experiencia Maya, or The Mayan Experience. The owner claims to order his coffee straight from the tropics where the former city of Antigua, Guatemala used to be.

I assume this is untrue, because coffee shop owners need to purchase their beans from the Apollo government. Coffee doesn't naturally grow in the mountains up here. The same goes for other goods, such as sugar and cacao beans. It's a mystery where the government gets its stash because no one has contact with The Other Side.

Andrew and I lock our bikes onto a light pole just outside of La Experiencia Maya, right near the old railroad tracks. Trains have become obsolete over the past fifty years, but I find the tracks still hold a romantic nostalgia.

This area used to be the central section of downtown Flagstaff, and I love its decaying buildings. Some of them stretch all the way back to days of the Old West, when cowboys and outlaws roamed the streets on horses. Several shop owners—patisserie chefs and chocolate connoisseurs—managed to revive certain buildings, and today, run their businesses from them, thus starting the northern tip of the Central Commerce Hub. The remaining structures are abandoned and preserved as historical sites or museums.

Sprinkled among the old buildings, however, are bright and new billboards, courtesy of the Apollo government, proclaiming the words "Light, Truth, and Knowledge." I sometimes cringe at these monumental messages, which mess with the purity of the area's history.

"I know what you want," Andrew says to me, after we wander into the coffee shop and take a seat. The morning sun is beaming through tall glass windows and illuminating the cream-colored tabletops.

"Oh yeah?"

"Yeah." He stands and places one arm on the back of his chair, leaning over with a silly grin on his face. "Chai tea latte, with vanilla soy milk."

I laugh at his giddy demeanor. "You got me," I tell him, standing and joining him behind my chair to order our drinks.

I've never cared for coffee; it's too bitter for me. Andrew on the other hand is a religious coffee drinker, as is my mom. I've come to the conclusion that coffee must be a writer thing. I'm always teasing Andrew about his teeth, how someday he'll be an old, wrinkly man with yellow choppers from all the coffee.

Andrew stops me from walking toward the barista, though. "Tea's on me," he says.

"You don't have to do that. I can pay for—"

"Flora, I've got it. It's cool."

Before I can argue further, Andrew steps away to place our order and I watch him with a sense of longing. In the past, I've caught myself wondering what it feels like to be one of Andrew's girlfriends. I never allow my thoughts to drift further though, reminding myself that in the end, he chooses our friendship over them. They hate it, but I know Andrew is a special soul—kind and deep and real—and I never want to lose our friendship.

I sit down and lean back in the chair, letting the sun's early rays warm my skin. The mornings are still chilly in Apollo, so I hug my sweater closer around my chest. I watch Andrew order our drinks and then remember today marks one full week since I've seen it.

The Wall.

I can still remember the first time I asked about it in class as a kid, wondering what was so evil on The Other Side, and the teacher scoffed. I paid the price for my innocent question on my way home that day, when that same group of girls cornered me in the alley and called me a dirty globalist. I was ten and had no idea what "globalist" even meant, but looking back, I assume they heard the term from their parents.

Don't you know Apollo is the leader of light, truth, and knowledge? Why would you care what's behind that stupid Wall? Dirty globalist traitor. We should report you to the ABI.

I returned home with mud in my hair and vowed to myself that someday, I'd learn what's on The Other Side. *Why don't you stand up to them, Flora?* Andrew had asked, but I didn't have an answer. The truth is, the more I tried, the worse it got. I didn't have the courage to confront those girls, so eventually, I surrendered to the inevitable: coping. That's when Andrew and I started our map of uncharted Apollo territory, but when I'd told him I wanted to explore beyond, fear fell into his eyes and he begged me to forget it.

This is why, as much as I love him, I can't tell Andrew about the decision I came to after meeting Don.

I'm going to start a research project on the history of the Wall. This project won't cover the vague facts they feed us in school. That's the boring stuff. I'm going to dive deeper, into *why* the Wall was built—what "evil" it's protecting us from. I'll begin with the Apollo Library and slowly work on Don, pecking away at his angry boy façade until eventually, he'll crack and tell me what he knows.

How I wish I could bring Andrew along—I've never sought a new discovery without him—but for his own well-being...

"Do you know what today is?" Andrew's voice surprises me. I didn't notice him sit back down, or place the Chai tea latte in front of me.

When I answer with a mere, "huh?" annoyance crosses his face.

"Today, Flora. Geez, where were you just now?"

I lower my eyes. Is he thinking about the Wall, too? Instead of telling Andrew what I'm sure he wants to hear, I play dumb. "No, what is today?" I ask.

"It's the eleven-year anniversary of the day my dad left."

His words slam into me like a meat hammer. I can't believe I forgot. In the eleven years we've been friends, I've *never* neglected this day. In fact, every year, I've prepared a small gift to help Andrew cope.

"Andrew..."

"You were thinking about it again, weren't you?" His voice is accusing.

"No."

"C'mon Flora, I can tell you're lying."

I feel like the bacteria clinging to dirt on the bottom of my shoes. Andrew's father left when he was eight years old, never to be heard from again. No notes, no mail, no money... nothing, leaving Andrew's mother to raise a young boy in a community that prides itself on families.

"I can't believe you forgot," he mumbles under his breath, and the knife twists deeper. "You—of all people—the only friend who actually met my dad."

I wince, recalling the brief meeting during my first playdate at Andrew's house. Three days later, his father disappeared. And now, here I am, lost in my selfish thoughts.

"I'm so sorry," I tell him, unable to meet his eyes.

Andrew sighs. "Y'know, I never told you this," he says, and his voice lowers, "but I blame my dad's obsession for his disappearance."

Caught off-guard, I ask, "What obsession?"

Andrew pauses for a moment, and I can feel his gaze boring into me. He lifts his coffee mug to his lips, sips a minuscule amount, and I shamefully guide my eyes to meet with his. His expression is serious, intent.

"The same one you have," he says.

I gulp. And I feel riddled with guilt. Unable to speak, I allow Andrew to continue.

"It's not worth it. It's led to nothing but pain. You're better off forgetting about it."

I want to believe him, and I wish—so *desperately* wish—I had the willpower to simply forget and play dumb like everyone else, to just accept what the history books tell us. But instead, I find myself wondering something else entirely:

I want to know what Andrew's dad discovered.

Oak Creek Canyon

FLORA

It's probably about one o'clock in the afternoon, and we're finally on our way to Oak Creek Canyon, the four of us stuffed into an old 2130 model car with Ernest drooling on our laps. It's rare that my family uses our car; most Apolloans don't drive unless it's necessary, but when we do, our cars run off hydrogen fuel cells and emit nothing but water vapor.

"How's your mom, sweetheart?"

My mother turns around from the passenger seat and peers over her shoulder. Since Andrew's father left, my mom has made it her mission to help his mother in whatever way she can. Even though we're both nineteen now, nothing has changed, and I smile internally.

"She's good," Andrew answers. "Today is a little hard for her."

I hear my mom gasp. "Oh that's right," she says. "You should have invited her to come along. We would have loved to have her."

"Trust me, it wouldn't have made a difference."

Ever since this morning, Andrew hasn't been as friendly toward me. While conversing with my mom, he shoots me a cool glance, reminding me how much I screwed up.

My dad, feeling adventurous today, maneuvers the car onto a random dirt road and drives us another five to ten miles into the forest. By the time we park, hike further into the wilderness and reach a secluded spot by Oak Creek, only another two hours of sunlight remain.

Our spot is surrounded by Cottonwood trees and Arizona Sycamores, and the fresh mountain water streams like music in the background. Overwhelmed with boyish giddiness, my dad begins setting up the tent. He always gets this way at the beginning of a camping trip, loving nothing more than music and s'mores over an open campfire.

"I think Andrew and I will go swimming while you set up the camp," I announce.

My dad, in his altered state of elation, simply nods while my mom calls out, "Take Ernest with you!"

***

I always feel silly in a bikini and sneakers, but the shores of Oak Creek are rocky. I step into the water, only ankle-deep at first, and shiver as the freezing liquid surrounds my ankles like a bucket of ice.

"How is it?" Andrew is calling to me from behind a tree trunk, changing into his swim shorts.

"Cold! But refreshing."

A small bead of sweat dribbles down my forehead; it's warmer than normal today. Ernest races in from behind me and bounds right into the water, splashing droplets all over my body. I stiffen from the shock.

"Apparently, he doesn't think it's too bad," I say under my breath.

I lower myself into the frosty water a little more, cringing as the coldness hugs my calves, then my thighs, then creeps up my hips. I hate jumping into the mountain's streams; I always have to enter them gradually.

The red sandstone formations lining the creek soar over me on either side, offering a sense of protection and comfort from the rest of the world. My body is growing accustomed to the water now, and it's starting to feel warmer. I lift my head toward the sky—a few potential rain clouds are hovering nearby—and I close my eyes, letting the sun's afternoon rays sink into my skin.

I wish I could tan as easily as Andrew, but both my parents are of Eastern European descent. Therefore, I tend to morph into this horrific shade of red before my skin's melatonin decides to make its yearly appearance.

"You might want to take it easy in the sun," Andrew says from behind, startling me. "Remember what happened last year?"

I open my eyes and turn around. "I thought you were still getting changed."

He ignores me, though. "Flora, remember what happened?"

Of course I do. I'd been determined to get a nice summer tan, and thus spent all day lying outside under the sun. By nighttime, I'd turned purple. Yes, *purple*. I'd burned so badly, I developed a fever and my parents insisted I douse myself in Aloe Vera for the next week, not to mention, I'd craved nothing but bread and butter for seven days and gained two pounds.

"Don't worry," I say. "I'll be more careful this time."

Andrew dives into the water without testing its temperature before pushing up through the surface, slicking his dark hair back from his face. I admire his chiseled jaw line, his solid build, and quickly pull my eyes away before my thoughts drift where they shouldn't.

When we go swimming, Andrew usually sneaks up and yanks me into the water with him, inducing my scream. But today, he remains in the middle of the swimming hole, and I feel a sense of melancholy.

"Aren't you coming in?" he asks.

"Aren't you going to come and get me?"

Instead of answering, he just dips under the water again, the outline of his body remaining stationary. Guilt washes over me and I wait until he re-surfaces, then call out, "Andrew, I'm really, *really* sorry."

He shrugs. "Why are you apologizing?"

"C'mon. I'm serious. I feel horrible."

Andrew opens his mouth, about to say something, but Ernest paddles between us, his head lifted elegantly above the water. I watch my dog make his way toward Andrew and back to me, benevolent in his charming interruption. Growing tired, he decides to push himself toward the rocky shore and out of the water, his golden coat sopping wet, and he showers the trees surrounding us as he shakes the water from his fur. Andrew, a smirk crossing his face, soon follows him and takes a seat next to me.

He rests in silence and I watch the smirk disappear. I can feel his presence beside me, hear the gentle rhythm of his breath, and a yearning rises from inside me. I want to comfort him, to run my hands through his hair and over his muscles, acknowledging my mistake, but instead, I remain quiet.

Andrew speaks. "Did you know that no one wanted to listen—you know—to what it's like?"

I pause before responding. "What it's like to do what?"

Andrew looks over his shoulder at me. "To grow up without a father."

I gulp, unable to offer a response, so I sit quietly as he continues.

"I remember the sound of his voice, still, when he used to read me bedtime stories—these really adventurous ones. He'd change his voice to resemble the different characters; he was so animated."

"That's why you like to write," I say, moving my gaze to the ground.

Andrew lowers his head and sighs. "Yes, that's why I like to write."

We both continue sitting in silence and staring over the water, wondering who should speak next. It's Andrew who breaks the spell.

"When he left, it was literally overnight," he says, and I detect a quiver in his voice. "You remember, don't you?"

"Of course. I couldn't believe it. Your dad seemed so..."

"Happy," Andrew says. "I know. I was dumbfounded. Our neighbors brought us food, the local mechanic fixed a car for my mom. But no one wanted to listen. Their help was genuine, but it was also shallow."

He pauses for a moment, and turns to face me. "You were the only one to really care, Flora. You and your parents."

My breath catches in my throat, and for a moment, his eyes embrace every part of me, and I want to give in. But the doubt pushes it away. "Well... I'm sure I wasn't the *only one*," I say. "All of your girlfriends eventually—"

But Andrew shakes his head, his conviction unwavering. "It's always been you. Remember freshman year of high school, when my mom had her... event... and they locked her in the mental hospital for two weeks?"

I nod my head. "Of course I remember."

"You stayed by my side every night. Not even my guy buddies called to check on me. I would have been alone otherwise."

Of all the years we've been friends, Andrew trusted me the most to be there today, and I wasn't. Never have I felt so underserving of his friendship, and I watch as he buries his hands into his wet hair. When he turns away, water droplets slip down his bare back, glistening on brilliantly tanned skin.

"It was unfair for me to have expected so much," he says. "That's my fault. I'm sorry."

I tell him no, he shouldn't have to apologize; I'm the one who doesn't deserve his friendship. Andrew snickers at my comment, but it's snide, almost jeering.

"This damned Wall," he says. "It keeps me from leaving, from getting the hell out and finding somewhere else to go, where I belong."

His words surprise me, even jab with betrayal. "You want to leave?" I say. "What about your mom, and me? Do you really want to leave us behind?"

His back still facing me, Andrew's voice grows stiff. "And what happens if *you* leave *me*? Huh, Flora?"

I'm struck silent for a moment, staring at him in bewilderment before finding my voice again. "What are you talking about? Why would I leave you?"

"Never mind." He shakes his head and waves me off, dismissing me. "Let's just go swimming and enjoy the water. Your parents will be expecting us back soon."

Baffled, I watch as he dips into the creek again, and it takes a moment before the realization hits: Andrew is worried I'll disappear from his life, just like his dad.

The Hike

ANDREW

I've had girlfriends. A few, in fact. The first girl was this hot Latin chick, Luciana, with a rack the size of two basketballs. For a fifteen-year-old, she was mature, but Luciana was also Catholic—just my luck. Almost no one follows a religion anymore, but Luciana *had* to be one of them, and therefore, she teased the juice out of me. I maybe got to stroke those basketballs twice in the whole year we dated.

Then there was Nancy, who only lasted a few months, and Kim, an Asian girl who today is studying Spanish literature.

But Flora is different.

She was never just some girl. She's my best friend, my confidant. For God's sake, she's the only one who met my father, who saw my face the day after he left. We started that crazy map together, ran all over Apollo and marked it with our discoveries. It became our shared escape—me from my reality at home, and her from those witches who tormented her. *"What's knowledge without curiosity?"* Flora always says.

But most of all, when they threw my mom into the mental hospital, Flora was my savior. No girlfriend could have been a better shoulder to lean on during those torturous nights.

My girlfriends usually grow jealous of Flora. In fact, Nancy had threatened to break up with me if I didn't stop seeing her all the time. That girl was an idiot for not realizing whom I'd choose, and was in tears by my decision. Bros over hoes, you know?

This is why today, it's like someone stomped on my foot, then kneed me in the balls. For the first time, Flora became *just any girl*.

"Did you see that, up toward the top of the canyon?"

Flora's soft voice startles me. We are sitting around the campfire in the dark. She's holding a branch over the flames, watching her marshmallow slowly blacken into an oversized crisp, her almond-shaped blue eyes glowing from campfire flames.

"See what?" I ask.

"That building. I saw it while we were swimming. It's on the top of the canyon. I'd never noticed it before."

Here she goes again, I think, wishing she would stop and just let it go. I love our discovery expeditions, but lately, Flora has been taking it too far. She worries me.

I glance at the tent nearby. Her parents already fell asleep, cuddled close under extra-padded sleeping bags with Ernest curled at their feet. Her father brought along his guitar, and only thirty minutes ago, we were singing songs around the campfire.

"No, I didn't see any building," I lie.

"Oh."

She drops her gaze from mine, blonde waves tumbling over her face. For some reason, I feel like I'd just let her down. "But if you want, I'll go hiking with you tomorrow and we can check it out," I say.

At this, she perks up and smiles, her teeth glowing brilliantly white against the night's surrounding blackness.

"Seriously?"

I simply grin and nod my head. Flora stands, pulls her marshmallow off her stick, blows on it, plops it into her mouth, and walks around to lower herself onto the log next to me. We both stare into the fire, refusing to look at one another, but she nudges me with her elbow.

"Thanks," she says.

***

We begin hiking right after sunrise. Flora's dad tells us to be back within two hours for a full breakfast.

I am munching on a granola bar as we trek up the canyon, climbing sandstone boulders and cracking dead branches underneath our soles. For the moment, I forget about my concerns last night and feel like Lewis and Clark, or perhaps Ponce de Leon. Quite frankly, I'm loving this. I've never met anyone with Flora's sense of adventure, and I remind myself this is what I adore about her.

She is leading the way and I watch as her ponytail swings from side to side while she walks along the trail. It amazes me how girls can hike deep into the forest and still appear graceful. I'm pissed at Flora, but I can't hold a grudge against her for too long. Especially when she stops, turns around and flashes me that innocent smile, like a little kid watching cartoons for the first time.

"Isn't this exciting?" she asks, whipping out her water bottle and taking a swig like it's a beer.

"Hell yeah," I say. "How much longer, do you think?"

Flora takes a deep breath and looks yonder. "Well, from my observations yesterday, it should be just beyond that hill and those trees."

"Do you have our map?"

Flora shoots me a mischievous smile, reaches into the back pocket of her khaki shorts, and pulls out a folded piece of paper. "You bet. What's knowledge without curiosity, right?"

Propped atop a rouged boulder, I watch as she grins from ear-to-ear, holding our map with the same pride I imagine on the face of Cortes when he conquered Mexico. She swings herself around, her back facing me again, and begins climbing.

After another few minutes, we approach the clearing atop the canyon, and a building stretches across it, just as Flora had anticipated. I motion for us to stay behind the trees surrounding the area and we squat down, using the forest's undergrowth to hide our presence. As I scan the premises before us, I can't believe my eyes; the building is painted red—the same tone as the sandstone surrounding it.

Camouflaged.

It's two stories tall, but square-shaped, like building blocks. I count about six sectors.

"I knew it," Flora says. "I knew I wasn't going crazy. Look."

She points to her right, motioning toward a towering electric fence, clearly indicated by the "Danger: High Voltage" signs posted every few yards. Underneath them, I see another sign: "GOVERNMENT PROPERTY. Do Not Venture Beyond This Point, Under Penalty of Law."

"Flora," I whisper, leaning close to her ear. "I think we found what you were looking for. Now we should go."

"Go? We just got here. Don't you want to find out what this place *is*?"

No, I think, *actually I don't.* As I stare at the unmarked building and its boxed sectors, my father's face flashes through my mind, and I feel the need to run. "I think we've learned enough," I say.

"Well, you leave if you want. But I'm going to poke around a little longer."

Fuck. There is no way I'm leaving her here. What if something happens, if she gets hurt, if she needs me to pull her away, or run for help? I think of her parents, benevolently preparing breakfast for us back at the camp, and a pang of guilt flashes through me.

I turn toward Flora to say something else, but she's no longer here. I pause for a moment, and it takes a second for the realization to sink in. *She's not here...* completely vanished from sight.

"Flora!" I call in a hushed tone, suddenly panicked. "Flora!"

I swing my head to the left. Nothing. Then I look behind me. Only trees and undergrowth. My heart begins pounding, thundering into my ears, and my mouth goes dry. I realize I haven't taken a sip of water for nearly thirty minutes. I try to swallow, but my throat is sticky.

Keeping myself lowered toward the ground, I push through the undergrowth closer to the fence, defying every instinct in my body to run. *She owes me big time for this. Big time.*

Like a hawk, my eyes scan the grounds. I catch a glimpse of a guard tower at the top of the main building block, and a man dressed in military garb strolling back and forth—armed with an AK47. He's scanning as meticulously as I am.

But no sign of Flora.

I cannot decide if she snuck away while I was drowning in my own thoughts, and something happened to her, or if she slipped from my sight specifically so I can't stop her exploration.

Flora reminds me of a cat I used to have growing up named Misho. He was this white Turkish Angora that I adopted as a kitten, but because he grew up around my German shepherd, he never feared dogs. One day, I took him to the vet, and while we were sitting in the waiting room surrounded by canines, he somehow slipped out of his carrier.

I barely noticed he'd escaped until I heard a chorus of growls and barks, and some dude was yelling, "Hey! Get your cat outta there before my dog tears him up!"

I looked toward the middle of the room, and there, surrounded by five angry dogs, was Misho—quietly licking his paw and walking in circles, completely unaware of the danger surrounding him.

That's Flora.

And now, we're surrounded by a pack of hungry wolves.

I'm sweating. My palms are slick with anxiety and I realize I'm clutching the side of my pants, white knuckles and all. Nevertheless, I push myself to slide through the underbrush, looking... looking... and I see her.

She's wandered up to the electric fence, like it's some display in a museum. I know Flora is too smart to actually touch it, but she's examining it closely and I realize she's looking for weaknesses.

"Psst!" I call out. She doesn't hear me; or if she does, she doesn't acknowledge me. I shuffle closer to the fence, nudging out of the undergrowth. "Psst! Flora!"

Crouched low to the ground, she turns around and waves me away, placing her finger to her lips to shush me. I motion with my hands, urging her to get back over here. But she turns around and keeps examining the fence, remaining close to the ground.

I don't know what else to do. I feel helpless, so I continue squatting and watching. She's being quiet, so I decide she must have seen the watch tower. Flora backs away from the fence and tiptoes toward a nearby tree, using its trunk to avoid detection. She remains hidden and peers around the bark, waiting until the guard's eyes are turned away, and sprints further to the left, along the fence. I follow her, hidden in the brush.

And now I notice the gate, with a latch. Sly little Flora, she actually found a way inside. She turns around and smiles at me—I can tell she's proud of herself—and she bends down. *What is she doing?*

When she stands again, I see she's holding a small tree branch. Flora faces the fence and tosses the branch against it. The branch smacks the enclosure before falling down, unscathed. *Smart girl*, I think, and can't help but smile. She's testing the gate to see if it too is electrified.

Unexpectedly, an alarm pierces the peaceful silence. It echoes against the canyon walls, wailing so loud, I jump off my knees and slam my hip against the ground. *Shit!*

Pushing myself up with my elbows, I fly to my feet and sprint from the forest toward Flora. I grab her elbow and yank her away from the fence.

"C'mon!" I yell over the alarm.

Flora drops her water bottle as I drag her back into the forest, and we start running.

"Why would they do that?" she calls as we hurdle boulders and race down the canyon's walls.

"Why do you think?"

My heart feels like it's beating out of my chest in painful palpitations, but my legs won't stop; I'm like a cheetah. *We've got to get into the water*, I realize, *in case they have dogs. We can't let them track us.*

I look back and realize Flora is slowing down. I stop and climb back up, reaching for her. "Flora, c'mon, we've got to keep going!"

I hear footsteps further up the path.

"I twisted my ankle on the rocks," she says, and I see it in her eyes; she's worried.

I reach out my hand, encouraging. "Just to the water. C'mon!"

We zigzag around trees, navigating crooked rocks, and I finally see the water. It's only a few yards away. I grab Flora's arm again and yank her before me, throwing her body into the creek. She splashes in with a small shriek—Flora hates jumping into the cold mountain water—and I follow. By now, sweat is pouring down my forehead and stinging my eyes.

Wading through the water, we fight the gentle current upstream toward a fallen tree acting as a natural bridge. "Up there," I say, in between panting breaths, and I hear Flora inhaling just as hard. We approach the log bridge and slip under, my arm wrapping around Flora's waist.

She coughs, and I shush her as voices and footsteps approach from above. Vertigo overwhelms my head, but I fight to remain lucid. *They're not going to find us. They're not going to find us.*

"I thought I saw them go somewhere near the creek," a male voice calls.

Following his voice are several barks, and I know I was right about the dogs—their prying noses sniff the ground. "They went into the creek," another voice says. "I bet they knew we had dogs. Not the first time this has happened."

Not the first time? I wonder who else has stumbled upon this building.

Just as I'd hoped, they begin following the creek downstream, rather than upward. Flora is shivering in my arms, and I hear her teeth chattering. Once the voices and footsteps disappear, I ask if she's scared.

"No," she says. "Just cold."

We sit under the log for a few more moments, waist-deep in water, before Flora speaks up. "Why would they care so much if we saw their building?"

I shake my head. "You just don't know when to stop sometimes, do you? What did you think was going to happen?"

I feel her shrug against my chest. "What happens whenever the cops catch someone trespassing in town: they'd call our parents and we'd get a warning."

Such an innocent cat.

"My mom always says to never screw with the government," I tell her. "You can screw with people, with businesses, but *never* with the government."

I pause for a moment and pull myself above the log, looking around. "Do you think you can travel a little further upstream, before we hike back to camp?" I ask.

Flora nods her head, and looks me in the eyes. "I'm so sorry, Andrew."

I tell her it's fine, that I'm just glad we're both OK.

"Do you mind if we keep this between us?" she asks me. "You know, not tell our parents or anything?"

Oh, she can bet I'm *more* than fine with that. In fact, I'd prefer to convince myself this never even happened, so I smirk at her. "Let's get back and eat some breakfast."

The Journal

ANDREW

I'm relieved to see my mom up and about when I arrive home from the weekend trip. She refused to leave the couch the day I'd left, which is typical of The Anniversary. I've learned to just leave her alone and wait until she returns to normal again.

As I'm unpacking, she walks into my room and leans against the threshold. "That girl is turning into a beauty," she says, referring to Flora. "A clone of her mother."

"She is pretty," I say, but still hope to avoid the next question, which I know is coming.

"You should ask her on a date, Andrew. She'd be better for you than all those other girls you bring into my house."

I sigh. "Ma, it's not like that with Flora. You know this."

She shrugs and walks back into the kitchen. "A mother is allowed to dream," she calls over her shoulder.

I hear her clanking around with pots and pans in the other room, so I decide to close my door. I can't stop thinking about what I heard while Flora and I were hiding in the creek.

"I bet they knew we had dogs. Not the first time this has happened."

Like a broken record, those stupid words won't leave my mind. Flora's reaction to the guards was too genuine for me to think she'd confronted them before. And besides, I can usually smell her lies from two miles away.

So who else has been there?

I stop unpacking for a moment and flop onto my bed, staring out the window. I can see why Flora gets obsessed with mysteries like this. Constant contemplations can drive a person crazy.

The sudden urge to hunt down my old journal—the one I'd started when I was eight—overwhelms me, and I jump to my feet, opening my closet doors. It's like a dam of junk in here.

Carefully, I begin prodding through the stacks of boxes, old T-shirts, books, and, an ancient LEGO set? I'd forgotten about it. LEGO sets were a favorite toy for children nearly one hundred years ago. An *artifact*. This LEGO set was a gift from my dad.

Just months before he left, he found it while rummaging through a swap meet and bought it for me. I'll never forget how my mother laid into him, like a tiger ripping apart its prey, demanding to know why he spent so much money on a toy no one has wanted for a century.

Then, a few months later, he left. And I started writing in my first journal.

I place the LEGO set aside, and keep digging. I'm searching, and searching, and like the sun appearing from behind rainclouds, I finally see it: the box entitled, "Writings."

I rip the duct tape from its top, fumbling through my life's worth of journals, and midway down, I find it—ripped edges and pages falling from the binding. I reach into the box and slip my fingers underneath its leather exterior, pulling it out with a surgeon's care.

I know what's on the first page, and part of me warns to refrain from reading it. Do I really want to re-experience that moment? I contemplate for a second, but the pull becomes too great, and I flip open the cover.

May 29, 2139

Jornal,

    I'm at home right now. We can't find my dad. My mom is making a very big deal. Last nite, she was screaming her lungs out. My dad did not yell back. He never yells. But my mom yells when she gets mad.

    I told my mom that Dad will come home. Maybe he just got mad from her yelling. But my mom did not listan to me. She started to cry. I hate when my mom cries. It makes me sad, I hope my dad is all right. Flora brot me a flower. She said she hopes my dad comes back.

    I have a feeling in my stomach. It hurts and makes me want to throw up. I hate throwing up. I wish I can just fall asleep. I do not want to wake up for 5 days. May be when I wake up, my dad will be back.

    I wonder why my mom yelled so much last nite?

Andrew

I stop reading for a moment as the incident rushes back to me. I feel generous warmth for Flora, for the memory of her comfort, before my thoughts switch back to my dad. I'd always remembered him as happy, but maybe I had been wrong all these years. I recall him leaving, but had forgotten about that specific fight. Now that I'm reading this entry, I remember the night more clearly. My parents had fought—hard—over *something*. But I was only eight, and I had no idea what that "something" was.

I continue reading the next entry:

May 31, 2139

Jornal,

> *My dad is still gone. I do not know where he is. I wonder why he left me? May be I made him mad. What did I do wrong? May be Mom got mad at the new toy. Dad said it is very old. I wish my dad never gave me the toy.*
> *My mom called the Police. They came to the house yesterday. My mom did not let me talk to them. She looked scared. Why is mom scared of the Police?*
> *They are allways nice to me. I hope my dad comes home soon.*

Andrew

As I hold the journal filled with my eight-year-old thoughts, I ask myself the same question: why *did* my mom fear the Apollo police?

I flip through the next few pages, all of them mere ramblings about the same thing: wondering where my dad went, wondering when he'll come back home, my mom's increasing agitation.

Question after question riddles my brain until it hits me; I need to take a quick trip to the Apollo Library. I want to look through the newspaper archives and read the headlines between May 29 and May 31 that year.

I consider calling Flora to see if she wants to join me—she loves the library—but I decide against it. This is something I need to do alone.

"Ma, I'm running to the library! I'll be back in an hour," I call over my shoulder as I leave the house. I hear her respond and tell me to hurry home before dinner.

I grab my bike and start pedaling. The library is only a ten-minute ride from my house, just down the street from the Apollo Hospital. I bike hard, my old, leather-bound journal tucked away in my back pocket.

The Morgue

ANDREW

The library is overflowing with young students, college kids, and retired adults scattered amongst the various computer stations, mostly surfing the Internet or talking into A-Search. A few are reading books. Overlooking them, positioned in the center of the library, is a statue of Apollo encircled by the words, "Light, Truth, and Knowledge."

I locate the newspaper morgue toward the back of the library and begin walking toward it, when my attention becomes laser-focused on something else:

Flora, and *some guy*.

I see them standing together toward the back of the library, and suddenly, I'm irritated. I can feel the heat rushing to my cheeks, my heart pumping inside my chest. I don't know why the sight of her with *this guy* pricks at my brain like an icepick, but the scene of them together—him speaking into her ear like they're sharing an intimate secret—drives me senseless. And what's worse: she looks *fascinated* by him.

I pull myself behind a shelf and peek around the corner, not wanting Flora to see me. The guy is a grease ball, I realize, with oily black hair that falls into his face and ragged dark clothes. He even wears... black eyeliner? What is he trying to be, a raccoon?

They're poring over the contents of a book together. Maybe they're working on an assignment, but I remind myself that school finished last week, just before our camping trip. What could they be whispering about?

She's your friend, Andrew, I think. *You have no reason to feel this way. Get over it.*

Taking a deep breath, I'm about to reveal myself from behind the shelf, when I notice a group of four college girls approaching Flora and the guy. A couple of them are giggling, while the others are sneering. A blonde, who looks like the leader, invites herself to sit down at Flora's table. The guy begins to stand and leave, but Flora tells him to stay.

"From screwing a hot writer to screwing a skinny loser, huh?" the girl says to Flora. "Or maybe you're just sleeping with them both."

I watch as Flora drops her head toward the floor, and I know she's waiting for the verbal assault to pass. *C'mon Flora, stand up for yourself*, I compel her. I never understand why girls choose Flora to bully, but the pattern has continued throughout her life. Maybe it's her sense of curiosity, or her sometimes-awkward optimism.

As she's grown older, I know some girls have grown jealous of our friendship and spread rumors, which feeds the cruelty. I just wish Flora knew she doesn't have to take this crap.

The girl smirks, like a snake, before leaning into Flora. "You know Andrew just uses you for sex. Have fun being his whore, and tell him Abby says hi."

I don't know this girl, Abby, and if I ever run into her, I'd like to pull that smug ponytail off her head. The clique of girls leaves Flora alone, and I have to take an extra breath to calm down. It amazes me what some girls think happens between Flora and me. Over the years, Flora has managed to build a wall against the bullying, and I'm amazed as she lifts her head and appears unaffected.

My blood pressure rises, however, when I see her smile and begin talking again with *that guy*.

I remind myself why I came to the library in the first place—to research—and I leave my spot behind the shelf. I stroll toward an open computer station before remembering I'm not here for the computer; I'm here for the newspaper morgue. As I begin heading in the opposite direction, Flora's voice stops me.

"Andrew?"

I pause and turn around to find Flora standing before me. "Hey," I say, somewhat nervous, but my eyes quickly drift to the shadowed recluse behind her.

"Are you feeling OK?" she says. "You look flushed."

"Well..."

"I hope you didn't catch a cold from our swim in the creek yesterday." I can hear the concern in her voice, and I draw my eyes back to hers. They are scanning my face.

"I'm fine," I say. "What are you doing here?"

Now it's her turn to act peculiar. Flora never keeps secrets from me, but her demeanor appears evasive. Rather than answering me, she turns around and motions for her new "friend" to join us.

"Andrew, do you know Don?"

I watch as this sorry excuse for a human being approaches. He reminds me of a sloth, and the closer he moves, the more I can smell the odor of cigarette smoke. Doesn't he realize that smoking went out of style, like, seventy years ago? He refuses to meet my eyes, and when he reaches his position in front of me, he appears... sad. His eyes are dark, but much blacker than any I've ever seen, as if life somehow sucked the color from his soul. I can't help but wonder what dwells deep inside his head.

"I've heard a lot about you," Don says to me, as he reaches out a hand.

I shake it, noticing his weak grip and slimy fingers, and I force a smile for Flora's sake. "Is that so?" I ask, looking over at her.

"Don's helping me on a research project," Flora says. "I'm getting a head start, for next school year."

"About what?"

"Just some history," Don interrupts. "You know, on Apollo."

Flora is looking agitated. I can't tell if she's mad at me, or just uncomfortable.

"We should probably get back to work," she says. "Call you later?"

Before I can answer, Flora smiles and wraps her arms around me, giving me a quick hug. I'm hesitant to return the sudden gesture, wondering about her odd actions.

"Sure," I say.

When she pulls away, she lifts her head and plucks a quick kiss on my cheek before turning around. I'm left standing alone, completely bewildered. Flora has never kissed me before, not even a friendly kiss on the cheek. However, with her innate sense of curiosity, it's unlike Flora to walk away without asking me why *I'm* at the library.

Maybe it's better, I tell myself. Now I can go about sifting through the morgue, alone.

***

The morgue is dark, and exceedingly dry, with a musty scent that falls heavy on my senses. I'm not sure if the darkness is to preserve the ink on the newspaper, or just because, well, it's *the morgue*. When I told the librarian the dates I was searching for, she showed me the shelves I'd need to explore.

After she left, I settled down, and now I'm staring at an old edition of the *Apollo Times* from May 29, 2139—the same day I'd awoken to find my dad gone. The pages are stiff, like the time passed, and slightly yellowed. "Unseasonably late snow covers Apollo Friday night," the front-page headline reads, accompanied by a photo of some kid building a snowman after dark.

I strain my mind to remember, and vaguely recall the snow. My mom and I had been so distracted by my dad's disappearance, I barely even noticed, let alone cared.

I begin flipping through the pages. Articles on water shortages. Fire season coming soon. The completion of the Apollo Hospital.

The Apollo Hospital? That catches my interest; according to the article, The Apollo Hospital is only eleven years old, but I'd thought the building was older. I begin reading:

> State officials said the new building for The Apollo Hospital came to completion Friday afternoon, ensuring full access to a wide range of healthcare services for all Apolloans in times of need.
>
> Before opening today in the Central Commerce Hub, The Apollo Hospital

operated in the rural area of North Apollo, but officials said the new location is more accessible and offers a wider variety of services.

"We've been striving for universal health care for several decades now, and the new Apollo Hospital really represents the completion of that dream," said Chairman of State Health Care Alexander Dubois. "We will be hiring a total of 100 new doctors, nurses and specialists."

I stop reading. The article is interesting, but nothing spectacular, so I keep flipping through. As I approach the middle of the paper, I begin wondering if I'm just wasting my time. I turn the page once more and scan the local briefs section.

Wallet with ancient dollar coin found at Apollo Library
Naked man arrested for public intoxication
Dog dressed as lion scares neighborhood
Cause of brief power outage still unknown

Something about that last headline catches my attention and I squint my eyes, trying to read the small print.

Local officials said the cause of a brief, five-minute statewide power outage Friday night is still under investigation. The brief outage also caused the state's primary Internet service provider to lose power. State officials said they received nearly 200 calls from customers in less than five minutes asking why the Internet was down. No serious damage resulted from the outage, they said.

Instinctually, I know the brief is important in some way to my father's disappearance. I grab the paper, approach the librarian again, and ask to make a copy of it. The librarian looks at me with suspicion and tells me she can't trust some kid running around with the library's delicate newspapers.

Frustrated, I hand the paper to her and watch as she disappears into the back room to make a copy for me. While I'm waiting, I scan the library to see if Flora is still here, with *that guy*. What was his name again? Dan? Don?

But I don't see her anywhere.

"Here you go." The librarian's voice startles me, and I must have flinched, because she asks, "Jumpy much?"

I just look her in the eyes and grab my photocopy. Gently folding it, I reach into my back pocket and pull out my journal. I place the news brief inside before glancing at my watch. It's been well over an hour.

I'd better get back home, before my mom has one of her events.

The Event

ANDREW

When I walk through the door of my house, it occurs to me I haven't satisfied my body's daily need for caffeine yet, and my head is beginning to pound. Coffee is out of the question, since that's only available from local coffee shops, so tea is the alternative. As I advance further into my house, the aroma of roasted chicken, sweet grilled onions, and Italian seasoning sweep into my senses, and my mouth begins to water with anticipation.

"Ma!" I call. "I'm gonna make some tea! Want any?"

I hear clanging noises from the kitchen before my mom dashes around the corner into the living room—her brown hair clipped back from her face—and scans my features from top to bottom. "Where have you been?" she demands.

"The library. I told you —"

"I told you to be back in an hour."

I stiffen, a seed of caution growing in my gut. My mom's eyes are wild and I cannot tell if she's lucid and just upset, or something else. I swallow my concern and continue acting like everything is normal.

"Look Ma, I'm sorry. I got caught up over there," I say.

"Doing what?"

"Nothing. Just some research." I start walking past her toward the kitchen. "I'm going to make some tea. Do you want any?"

"It's nearly six o'clock, Andrew. You'll never sleep."

"I'll sleep."

"You won't sleep."

I walk to the kitchen counter and fill a pot with water to begin boiling, when I notice the five other pots already steaming on the stove. The oven is on, too.

"Ma, Jesus," I say. "Who are you cooking for, the Roman Army?"

"I just felt like cooking."

I look around: chopped carrots, fresh potatoes, piles of parsley, spilled flour. I switch my attention to my mother, to *really* look at her, and notice a splotch of flour highlighting her right cheek. Her hair looks like she's been electrocuted.

"What's going on?" I ask.

She begins pacing the kitchen floor. "You said you'd be back in an hour."

"So?"

"It's been almost two hours!"

My mom's voice is on the verge of hysterics, and with a wave of anxiety, I realize I've walked into one of her episodes. The "events," as I call them, started a few weeks after my father left and increased in frequency and intensity over the years. Then one day, when I was a freshman in high school, she lost it completely—talking to her dead parents in the living room and crying to them about my father, about me, and I called the police, scared and unsure how to react. That's when they committed her, and Flora came to live with me those two weeks my mother was gone.

I often try to remind myself that my mother never understood dealing with adversity, never learned how to cope with life's curveballs. She grew up in a happy home with two parents, attended school, started a career, and married my father. She never worried about anything, so the moment my dad left, it became too much for her to bear.

Now, as the only family she has left, it's my job to de-escalate my mother. Burying the angst that storms within my own mind during her events, I inch closer to her, take her hand, and place it between my palms. She's shaking, and I allow my breath to soothe my nerves. I guide my mother toward the kitchen table and we sit down together. I can hear her rapid breathing.

"It's OK, Ma," I say, rubbing her hand between mine. Her skin is growing coarser with age. "I'm back now. I'm not going anywhere."

She doesn't say anything, so I keep talking. "This house smells like a restaurant. I can't wait to eat. Thanks for cooking me dinner."

Her eyes, jetting back and forth before, now begin to focus again and I see her start to return. She wiggles her fingers inside mine and peers into my face. My mother smiles—that sincere, heartfelt grin I remember so well from the days before my dad left. And she places her other hand over mine.

"You're such a good kid," she says. "You'll make a great father someday."

The pots from the kitchen are bubbling over, and the noise distracts us from the moment. My mom pulls her hand from mine and stands, her head tilted to the side, and staggers back into the kitchen. I want to follow her and continue making tea, but I feel weak.

Sometimes, I miss my dad. But times like these, I truly loathe his actions, because this moment—well, it's *his* responsibility. Not mine.

Dolores

ANDREW

It's morning, and I can't help but think of my dad. He worked at the state's Internet service provider. I never knew much about his daily tasks, but my mom says he was involved with I.T. Because of people like my dad, everyone in Apollo has free access to the Internet.

I also recall a man named Joe from my younger years; he was a friend of my father's from work. Joe always came to our house for weekend neighborhood football games and afterward, he and my dad would tinker on the computer for hours.

Right after my dad left us, Joe stopped by almost every weekend, checking on my mom and me, but as time passed, we saw less and less of him until eventually, his visits ceased completely.

I don't know what made me think of Joe just now, but I realize the police never mentioned Joe's name when telling my mom who they questioned about my father's disappearance. Suddenly curious, I open my laptop and the bright blue "A-Search" blinks at me.

"Hello Andrew," the computer says. "What can I do for you today?"

I ask A-Search to find the phone number to the state's Internet service provider.

"Of course, Andrew. Right away." The computer pauses for a moment while A-Search seeks the number. "The phone number to the state's Internet service provider is 555-734-5555."

I'm somewhat doubtful that Joe still works there; after all, it has been eleven years and I don't even know the guy's last name. But I call anyway. Some lady who sounds like she's smoked half her life answers the phone, asking where to direct my call.

"I'm not sure," I say. "Perhaps you can help me. I'm looking for a man named Joe who works in your I.T. department."

The woman tells me Joe could be one of several people and asks for a last name. Disappointment teases me and I ask myself why I thought this would be simple. I respond to the woman, telling her I don't have a last name, but I know the man worked there eleven years ago.

"Eleven years?" she says. "You probably mean Joe Marino, then."

Shocked, I tell her it's possible, but her voice grows sorrowful. "How do you know him?" she asks.

"My dad. They were close friends."

"Who's your father?"

"Andrew Goldsmith." Not many people know I have the same name as my dad. Flora is one of the few.

I hear the woman sigh on the other line. "You're Andrew's son," she says. "Why don't you come down during my lunch break, kiddo. It starts in thirty minutes. My name's Dolores. I'll be up front."

Confused, I hang up the phone and look at the time, realizing I'd better hurry if I want to catch Dolores on her break. I wonder what she could possibly want to tell me.

***

Dolores reminds me of an old car: rundown, but proud and durable. She's about ten years older than my mom, and she looks *tired*.

We're sitting on the patio of a local sandwich shop, surrounded by a mixture of suited professionals, moms with their children, and off-season college students and their dogs. Dolores pulls a cigarette from her purse and looks to me.

"You don't mind, do you?"

Smoking does bother me, but if this woman is willing to meet me for lunch and offer information about my dad, then I'm OK with it. She lights up and begins puffing.

"You're starting to look like him," she says. "Your dad."

"You knew my dad?"

"Oh honey, *everyone* knew your dad. I'm so sorry, about, well, you know. How's your mom doing?"

"She's working. I'm in college."

"Oh, that's good to hear."

I don't want to be an asshole, but the small talk prompts me to feel impatient. I swallow it, though, and wait for her to begin the conversation. The waiter approaches, asking for our orders, and I request coffee with hazelnut-flavored creamer and a turkey sandwich on a challah roll. After he leaves, Dolores looks at me again, squinting her eyes.

"What made you want to call Joe now, after all these years?" she asks.

I shrug, telling her I don't know. "I guess I started getting curious why my dad left, and I figured maybe Joe knows something."

"It's the big mystery." She pauses, takes another drag while scanning me top to bottom, and sighs. "Your dad must have had, like, ten photos of you plastered all over his desk. I remember when he bought this LEGO set, bragged how his son would be the only kid in Apollo with something so cool."

The waiter returns with my coffee and I whisk the caffeinated drink to my lips before pouring any creamer, craving the bitter aroma and refreshing calm.

Dolores continues watching me closely and sits straighter before leaning over the table. "I'm sorry to tell you this, Andrew, but I felt you should hear it in-person. Not over the phone."

The curiosity swells, and I ask her what I need to hear.

"Your dad's friend, Joe?"

"Yes..."

"He died about two years after your father left. I thought maybe your mom knew."

My hopes drop through the floor, and I fall back against the rim of my chair. *Died?* It all seems so... final. My hands reach to grab my coffee again, its warmth helping to ground me in the reality of her answer.

"How?" I ask.

"Cancer. A brain tumor, actually. Very rare, in today's day and age. It was quite tragic."

I have no idea if my mom ever knew this. She certainly never told me, but now it all makes sense, why Joe's visits to our home stopped.

"How could that happen?" I say, and search Dolores' face for answers, but she offers none. I can't seem to comprehend this news. We have the Apollo Hospital, the best medical care. And yet, and yet...

Dolores leans over and places her hand on top of mine. "Oh sweetie, I'm sorry. You're such a good kid; I can tell you just want some answers. I wish I had better news for you."

So do I, I think. *So do I.*

The Book

Don lives alone. He's my age, in college, and lives all by himself; I can't get over it. I wonder why his parents kicked him out, if that's even what happened. Then again, I've never heard Don mention his mother or father.

For the past two weeks, we've met at the Apollo Library because Don refuses to meet elsewhere, especially his house. The first time we talked, I'd started to use A-Search, but Don nearly tore my arm from its socket stopping me. When I asked him what's wrong, he said he doesn't trust A-Search, which made me wonder if Don has paranoid schizophrenic tendencies.

I did, however, trick him into admitting he's seen the Wall.

"I don't think your friend Andrew likes me very much," he says, as we settle into our third weekly meeting at the library. As usual, he's looking down when he speaks.

"Oh, he's just being a boy," I tell him. "Andrew is like a brother, really. He acts like I'm some little sister who can't fend for herself." I cringe at how nonchalant I sound, when inside, I want Andrew to care—in *that* way.

"That's good, I guess. I'm used to it, though," Don says.

"Used to what?"

This time, he lifts his gaze toward my face, staring at me with those cold, black eyes. "Being judged. Dismissed."

I know how he feels when he says this, and recognize his defiance within myself. I watch as Don drops his head into a slump and begins scribbling on a random piece of paper with a broken pencil. His mannerisms are so *odd*.

"Well, I think your story is fascinating," I say, trying to lighten the mood. "I love stories, especially good ones. Plus, I really appreciate you helping me with my research project."

Don just shakes his head. "I don't know how I got sucked into this."

He does that sometimes: brutal bluntness. It bothers me—comes across as rude—but Don doesn't strike me as the type who would be malicious on purpose. "Can I ask you a question?" I ask him.

"I guess."

"Back in World History class, when you challenged the professor about the Wall—"

"Yes."

"Why were you so angry?"

Don stiffens, and I watch while his hands stop scribbling. He drops the pencil and begins tapping his fingers against the table instead. "Because," he says, slowly, "it's hypocritical. This whole state is filled with fucking hypocrites."

His anger startles me, but also makes me question why he would consider our World History professor a hypocrite. My theory is the man didn't know any better than me, or Don, or Andrew, or anyone else in Apollo for that matter.

"Do you mean," I say, "because they preach light, truth, and knowledge, but refuse to talk about what's beyond—"

"Shhh!" Don cuts me off and looks around us, paranoid. "Keep your voice down."

He's growing too agitated for my comfort level, so I decide to change the topic of discussion. "I began reading that book you told me about," I say. "*1984*, by George Orwell."

"And?"

"It's good, but I'm surprised they never had us read it in school," I tell him. "In my opinion, it's right up there with classics such as *Great Expectations*, *For Whom the Bell Tolls*, and *The Odyssey*."

Don is still staring at the table. "Do you think, perhaps, there's a reason for that?"

His question pushes me into discomfort, and I squirm in my chair. "What do you mean?" I ask.

From his shadowy hulk, Don lifts his torso and for the first time, looks me straight in the eyes. "I think you know *exactly* what I mean, Flora. Don't play dumb. You're smarter than that."

He has this way of looking at me, like he can read my thoughts, know my deepest fears. "But, we're *free* here," I say. "And happy. This isn't totalitarianism. Apollo is a democracy. We *vote*."

Don looks away from me again and switches his gaze toward the looming statue of Apollo resting in the center of the library. "You have a point," he admits, and lowers his voice even more, still staring at the statue in a dreamlike state. "The world is such a fucked-up place."

I'm quiet, not sure what to make of this unexplained intensity. Before I can say another word, Don speaks again.

"I need to go," he says.

"But, we just got here."

"Keep reading *1984*," he tells me, as he climbs to his feet. "And think. Think about more than what they teach us, here."

A-Search

FLORA

Don leaves me bereft at the library, in utter confusion. The novel he lent me, *1984*, is back home atop a pile of books next to my bed. Thinking of it, I'm seized by a sudden urge to research totalitarianism, and I spring from my seat to wander the library's towering shelves of knowledge.

I can imagine Andrew's voice from behind me, *"Let it go, Flora."* He means well, but sometimes he doesn't fully grasp my *need* to know. To discover. I know I'm not the only one with the drive, but others seem to have learned to suppress it.

Not me. My mother, an esteemed Apolloan journalist, fed it, encouraged it, turned it into the lifeline that's carried me through the cruelty I've been forced to endure. At first, it wasn't enough, but over the years, my urge to discover became the cushion against those who sought to do me harm. I could never live my life like the other girls in Apollo, their heads filled with facts and figures and science and literature, but never asking the hard questions, never striving to *understand*.

What's knowledge without curiosity?

I weave through the aisles, my fingers scanning book titles, my senses absorbing the scents of mothballs and wisdom. I whisk through titles on fascism, communism, capitalism, and utilitarianism, but surprisingly, nothing on totalitarianism.

That's when I glance at the computers, at A-Search—its bright blue "A" blinking at me. A-Search is Apollo's artificial intelligence search engine—an amazing technological invention—but I still prefer the texture of a book in my hand. I can't pinpoint why, but I don't trust technology.

Since I can't find any books on my topic of interest, I decide to give A-Search a try. I approach the nearest computer and plop down into its chair, hunching over the keyboard.

"Hello, welcome to Apollo Library," the computer says. "What is your name?"

I hesitate, but when A-Search refuses to continue, I answer it. "Flora."

"Hello, Flora. What can I do for you today?"

Talking to a computer makes me feel somewhat silly, I must admit, but I push away the discomfort. "I'm looking for some examples of totalitarianism."

"Certainly. Let me search that for you." The computer pauses for a moment while it scans the vast compounds of the Internet. "I have found three excellent examples for you, Flora. Please let me know if you require any further assistance."

The screen changes from the blinking A to three findings. The first title reads, "Former North Korean Three-Generation Prisons." I click and begin reading.

Kaechon Internment Camp, a slave labor camp for political prisoners in the former empire of North Korea, forced prisoners into hard labor until death. Many prisoners were born at Kaechon under North Korea's "three generations of punishment" law, which held that anyone found guilty of a crime against the government, such as trying to escape the country, would be sent to the camp along with his/her entire family. The next two generations of family members would then be born in the camp, where they remained until death. Work days consisted of highly dangerous labor that often lasted from 5:30 a.m. until midnight, even for children as young as 10. Prisoners were provided only enough food to sustain them.

The primary goal of the Kaechon Internment Camp was to keep politically unreliable individuals who were classified as "unredeemable" isolated from society. Prisoners were completely isolated from the outside world.

I stop reading for a moment, stunned by the last sentence. I'm not sure if I want to admit the thought coursing through my mind, but the harder I repress it, the stronger it pushes forth.

Isolated from the outside world... like Apollo.

I peer over my shoulder and scan the quiet crowds of citizens swarming throughout the library. I turn back to the computer, the pulse of my breath quickening against the screen, and my hand tightens against the chair.

"Sickening," I say aloud, to no one in particular. "I'm glad I wasn't alive back then."

But as I close the web page and pull myself from A-Search, a new emotion tugs at me for the first time in years. I realize it's fear.

Strike Two

FLORA

The Wall is separating us. I can hear Andrew on the other side, banging his fists against it like a gorilla, screaming my name, pleading.

"Flora! Come back! Don't do it!"

His voice is echoing in the wind as it mounts, whipping tiny strands of hair against my face that feel like barbed wire. In one hand, I grip the straps of a backpack, and in the other I hold—*something*. I can't distinguish what, but I know it's important.

I begin walking away from the Wall, Andrew's cries fading into the distance. The sky is glowing red, the way it looks when the forest is ablaze, and I push my body against the frantic wind toward the fire-lit horizon.

Abruptly, Don is beside me. He's crying, yanking at his hair as if it were poison to his skin. He turns and looks me directly in the eyes, his black eyeliner streaming down his cheeks.

"The world is such a fucked-up place," he says.

I open my mouth, wanting to ask him what he means, but realize I can't speak. Panic grips my throat as I attempt to talk, but my vocal cords are gone. Vanished.

Don seems to understand what I'm asking and points toward the enflamed sky beyond. Taking my first step, nervous and uncertain, I begin following his direction, still hearing Andrew's screams from behind, but the Wall holds him back, and I move further and further away, into the unknown.

"Flora!" His calls continue. "Flora!"

The earth trembles as the cries grow louder. "Flora! Flora, wake up!"

It's Ernest's tongue that finally forces me fully awake, and when I open my eyes, I see my dad standing overhead, gently shaking my shoulder and whispering my name. He's smiling at me.

"Hi sweetie," he says, standing up straight. "Are you OK? You were moaning in your sleep."

Ernest shoves his fluffy head under my arm and nuzzles into the crevice between my neck and chin. I scratch his head, trying to force myself into full consciousness. "I'm alright. Just a weird dream."

"Well, Andrew is here looking for you."

Confused, I look at my clock. "What time is it?"

"Almost noon," my dad says. "I should have woken you hours ago."

My dad leaves my room after that, and Ernest trots loyally behind him. Piano music begins floating through the hallways from our living room and I realize it's Saturday—I missed my weekly bike ride with Andrew.

My friend's head pops around the corner from behind my room's threshold and I feel another wave of guilt rise through me. This is strike two.

"I'm so sorry," I say, struggling to sit up, and the scent of sweet potato casserole wafts to my nose. I'm sure my hair looks like something from a horror book. "You officially have the right to punch me, now."

"I don't punch girls."

"Pretend I'm a guy."

"Most guys I know don't have tits." Andrew walks all the way into my room and begins poking at the stacks of books swamping my shelves. "You really can be a selfish asshole, though," he says, before approaching my nightstand. He drops down on my bed, right next to my feet. "Say it."

"C'mon, Andrew."

"Say it, Flora. I can't punch you, so say it instead."

I push myself to a full sitting position, cross my legs, and look at him with reserved resentment. "I can be a selfish asshole."

I watch as Andrew's face relaxes, and everything returns to normal. "I discovered something about my father," he says, abruptly changing the subject.

I'm intrigued immediately. "I thought you were done looking," I say.

"Well, this kind of found me. I haven't told anyone, but I need you to know."

I feel relieved Andrew is confiding in me again; maybe the remnants of our fight are over, and I want to be here for him. Looking at Andrew with affection, I say, "Let's take a walk."

The Confession

FLORA

The families of Apollo are out in full force today, and the Central Commerce Hub's sidewalks are streaming with them. I see a mother, father, and child, all smiling and holding hands. Tiny trilogies shopping and eating ice-cream and laughing with other tiny trilogies.

I can feel the uneasiness emanating from Andrew; around here, it's rare to see single parents, or orphans, which I know has forced Andrew into isolation in the past. I'm positive it's also the reason no one checked on him when his mother was committed to the mental hospital.

As we wait in line to order truffles, Andrew grimaces at something outside and buries his head into his arm, turning away from the window. When I ask what's wrong, he groans.

"Outside. It's Nancy, my ex," he says.

I glance over his shoulder and see her chattering away with a group of five girls. I look back to Andrew. "So?" I ask.

"She *hated* you. Please don't let them see us. I'm not in the mood today."

The hostess behind the counter motions for us to approach and we order chocolate truffles sprinkled with house-made salt, which is a treat, because house-made salt is a rarity. Even though mass production is not common in Apollo (most people cook with the food they grow), certain items are manufactured in large quantities to be bought at local grocery stores, like salt.

As we leave the shop with smooth chocolate melting in our mouths, Nancy still lingers nearby, and Andrew takes my hand to lead me away from the crowds, trying to avoid detection.

"Maybe we should find somewhere quiet," he says, guiding me toward the woods. I feel the warmth of his fingers encasing mine, sending electric shocks up my arm and into my heart. I feel giddy, but quickly remind myself I shouldn't, and follow him toward the trees. I hear Nancy and her clan call from behind, but we're already far enough away that their voices are whispers.

The crowds begin to fade, and Andrew keeps winding deeper and deeper into the forest. He doesn't want anyone to hear us talking, he tells me, until finally, he decides we're isolated enough.

"Sit down," he says as we approach a small clearing among the trees. "I have a lot to explain."

***

Andrew is staring at me, waiting for my reaction to his story. About Dolores. And Joe. And a brain tumor.

But I don't know what to say. What can I say? We're sitting in the middle of nowhere, cross-legged and facing each other. The sun is beginning to droop lower into the sky, casting ominous shadows all around us.

"So that's it," Andrew says.

I continue staring at him for another moment, struck silent by the bewildering nature of his discovery. "Did he have a family history of aneurysms, maybe?" I finally ask, and deep down, I know the likely answer, but hope Andrew will say something different.

"I have no idea," he responds.

We both continue sitting in the dirt, but restlessness grips my body and I bounce my knee against the ground. "Do you think he *really* died of a brain tumor?" I ask.

Andrew's gaze bores into me, no doubt questioning why I would consider anything other than the medical records report. At the same time, I know he knows my inquiry is justified, but instead of responding, he changes the subject.

"You ask more questions than anyone I know," he says.

I shrug my shoulders. "That's what happens when your mom is a journalist. You read between the lines."

"Your eyes look green in this light. Not blue. Very pretty."

His compliment catches me by surprise, and I blush. It's stupid and even a little cliché, so I quickly look toward the ground and stand.

"Stop being ridiculous," I say. "I might be your best friend, but that doesn't mean you can practice your petty pick-up lines on me."

"First of all, they're not petty. They're tenacious. And they work. And second of all..." Andrew joins me in standing. "... it made you blush, so it worked."

"I blushed because no one's ever talked to me like that, especially *you*." I playfully nudge his shoulder, trying to slip away, but this time he won't let me.

Gradually, I start to realize this is different than our Saturday morning games during bike rides. Something about the way Andrew is looking at me is *different*.

"Right," he says. "I never understood why you've never had a boyfriend."

I smirk, but smiling is becoming harder and harder with each passing second. "Probably because we're always hanging out, and let's face it, girls *love* you. It's intimidating for other guys to see us together."

"Do you love me?"

The question shocks him almost as much as it shocks me. Apprehension sweeps across his face and he pulls himself away. "I'm sorry," he says. "I have no clue why I said that."

I'm left leaning against a tree trunk, staring at Andrew's back, conflicting emotions warring within me. I want to tell him yes, I've loved him for years. He's the most caring, sensitive, empathetic, adventurous person I've ever known. I can't trust anyone like I trust him.

"You're my best friend," I tell him. "You're the only one who would risk getting arrested to follow me down some crazy adventure because I got too curious. You're the only one who has stood up for me when other people called me names."

At this, Andrew turns around to face me and his eyes are full of hope. But I don't want to ruin things, to become just another girl.

"No brother could be better," I add. "Of course I love you."

Andrew grins, but it's a sad smile, and my stomach falls through the ground. I've hurt him, I've hurt us, and I've lied about something too precious.

Lowering his head, Andrew walks over, reaches down, and slips his hand into mine. "C'mon," he says, and his voice hints at defeat. "Let's get back."

I take his hand and allow him to lead me toward the Central Commerce Hub again. As we walk in silence, I feel like I'm wandering deeper and deeper into some dark pit of the unknown.

My answer is not what Andrew wanted to hear. And worst of all, it's not the one I wanted to give.

The Visitors

FLORA

When I enter my house, I'm still frazzled after hearing the news about Andrew's father. The moment I turn the key and open the door, Ernest jumps all over me. My dad's music stops, and my mom, who was relaxing on the couch listening to my father play, loses her smile as I walk through the threshold.

"Flora!" my dad calls, walking over to help calm Ernest. "What's going on?" My mom is only inches behind him, a mix of concern and anger coloring her expression.

"What are you talking about?" I say. "I was just out with Andrew. You guys knew that."

"Then why were the police here looking for you, with an ABI agent?" my mom asks.

ABI is the Apollo Bureau of Investigation. They become involved only when the crime is serious, and the penalty, if convicted, usually starts at ten years in prison and strips the felon of all educational accolades, condemning him or her to a life of struggle and judgment. In the worst cases, the government has sentenced the perpetrator to death.

It takes a moment for my mom's question to sink in, for me to truly understand what she's asking. "I—I have no clue," I say, concern starting to grip my chest. "What did they want?"

"We thought maybe you could tell us." It's my dad who speaks this time. He's looking at me like a delinquent. *Like he can't trust me.*

"I don't know," I say. "I have no idea why they'd want to talk to me."

"Flora, we love you," my mom says. "I know I've always encouraged you to satisfy your curiosity, and if I played any role in what's happening because of it, I'm sorry. We want you to know that if you did something wrong, even if by accident, you can tell us. We'll do whatever we can to help. But please, just be honest."

Horrified that my parents think I would lie, I can't stop the tears from breaking through. "I *am* being honest!"

The fear begins rushing to my face and I push past my parents, running to my room. Ernest—thinking it's a game—barks and paces alongside me, his tongue hanging from his mouth as he gallops near my hip. The mere sight of his excitement makes me feel worse.

I gain speed and pass Ernest, wind around the door to my room and slam it before he can follow me inside. His claws paw at my door handle, his barks questioning why I'd shut him out, and I begin weeping.

Images of the Wall flash before my closed eyes, and I think of my lifelong obsession, of my map with Andrew. Until now, it all seemed so innocent, like a game. Maybe a part of me was acting out of defiance, but I never thought the ABI would show up.

As my vision blurs from tears, I allow myself to collapse onto my bed, wondering what they said to my parents, trying to think what I could have done. Stumbling upon the Wall might be forbidden, but if it's by accident, it's certainly not serious enough to warrant a visit from the ABI. As I slide my hands over my bed sheets, my fingers grip a book binding. Starting to calm down, I wipe the tears from my eyes and slowly focus on the title:

1984.

It suddenly occurs to me that everything was fine—perfect—until I started reading this book. This book that Don recommended. Is this the reason they wanted to talk with me? Surely, there's no law against reading a book, a classic novel, at that.

There's a loud knock at my bedroom door, and I hear my dad's voice. "Flora? Will you open this door, please?"

I realize that, in my frenzy, I'd locked the door. Overheated from the crying, I climb to my feet and let my dad inside. Ernest is standing next to him, his ears floppy, looking at me with big, curious eyes.

"What is going on in here?" he asks.

"Dad," I say, my voice small, "I have no idea why they came here. Honest."

My dad slips into my room and sits down on the bed next to me. He nods his head—a mixture of denial and understanding—and tucks his lower lip into his mouth. He does this when he's conflicted; I've seen him do it during arguments with my mom before.

"I believe you," he says, through a heavy sigh. "I don't think you'd act this way if you were lying."

Ernest places his head on my lap, asking for a pat. Gently, I begin scratching behind his mopey ears, and the softness of his golden coat helps calm my nerves. It's familiar. It's safe. "Dad?"

"Yes, sweetie?"

"I'm scared."

For the first time, I realize my dad doesn't have any wise or comforting words to say to me. No diversions. Instead, he merely places his hand, warm and firm, onto the nape of my neck. He gently squeezes and looks over at me.

"Tomorrow, we'll go into the station so we can see what they want. You won't be alone, OK?" His voice grows firm, and almost indomitable. "Your mother and I will be by your side the whole time."

***

I am dressed in white—the color of innocence, according to my mom. I'm wearing a knee-length skirt and loose blouse lined with buttons down the center. Even my conservative pumps are white.

"Minimal makeup, OK?" my mom had told me earlier, as I was preparing for my visit to the station. I'd felt like she was priming me for a trial.

The ABI Headquarters look and feel sterile, like a hospital, only colder. The walls are gray and bare, the words "Light, Truth, and Knowledge" are painted in bold black over the entranceway, and the floor is a stained concrete. We're sitting on a wooden bench that's painted white with the corners chipping away, the center grayed from years of wear. The whole place smells of hand sanitizer and old metal.

My mom is sitting to my left, my dad to my right. Each of them is holding one of my hands, squeezing a little too tight for my comfort. This is how I know they're just as nervous as I am, and the three of us stare straight ahead with blank expressions on our faces.

"I'm sure it's nothing," my mom says. "Probably a misunderstanding of some sort."

But my dad remains silent. I can feel his heartbeat pumping in the palm of his hand. Every few minutes, I find myself trying to catch my breath, and realize I'd stopped breathing. I keep blinking my eyes to prevent the ceiling from spinning around my head. *I wish Andrew were here.*

"Flora Loban!"

The lady who'd taken my name at the front desk calls me back. I rise, and my parents continue to hold my hands, remaining beside me. As we approach the woman, she stops the three of us.

"Which one of you is Flora?" she asks.

"Me," I say.

"Only you are allowed to come back."

My dad steps forward, his stance surprisingly authoritative. "Now hold on here," he says. "We're her parents. Flora is a minor, according to the laws of Apollo. She's younger than twenty-one. She will not speak to the authorities without her parents present."

The lady studies my dad for a few moments through suspicious eyes before allowing the three of us to proceed together. We follow her down a long, bare corridor, also painted jail-cell gray and lined with infinite florescent lights. Finally, we turn right and continue down another hallway to the end. It reminds me of a mousetrap.

The woman gestures for us to enter an empty room, other than two metal chairs.

"The detective will be with you in a few minutes," she says before walking out of the room and closing the door.

I hear my dad breathe with unease. "You take the chair, sweetie," he says, and his voice echoes against every corner of the room.

I listen to him and squint as I take a seat; the room's single fluorescent light burns into my corneas from above. The seriousness of the situation becomes real. *Too real.*

My mom starts pacing from one end of the room to the other. Each footstep echoes, doubling the pangs of noise vibrating in and out of my ears, but neither my dad nor I have the heart to ask her to stop.

After three suspenseful minutes, the door creeps open and a stout, bald man enters. He's middle-aged, wearing glasses and khaki pants. For some reason, he reminds me of a family doctor.

"Hello," he says, scanning my mom, my dad, and me. "I'm Agent Jackson of the ABI."

I stand from my chair and smooth my clothes. I realize my hands are trembling.

"You must be Flora?" Agent Jackson says to me.

"Yes sir," I say, reaching my hand to shake his. But before I can complete the action, my dad steps between the agent and me.

"I'm Flora's father, Randy Loban," he says, and shakes the agent's hand on my behalf. "And this is Flora's mom, April Loban. You're not the same agent who came to our house a day ago."

Agent Jackson smiles, but I can tell it's the sort intended to appease my father—the smile of a two-faced politician or snake lawyer.

"Yes, that's correct, Mr. Loban," Agent Jackson says. "You met my partner, Agent Garcia. He's busy right now, so I'm attending on his behalf."

"I see," my dad says. "Well, Agent Jackson, maybe you can fill us in here. My daughter was taken by surprise when she came home yesterday to learn the ABI had been looking for her."

"Oh, I can imagine."

"Yes, well, she—*we* don't have any reason to believe Flora did anything that would require questioning from the ABI."

"Have you asked your daughter?"

I watch as a slight shade of red flushes my father's cheeks, and his jaw grows firm. "Yes, several times," he says. "I stand by what I said. We'd like you to explain why we're here. We've come on good faith, as good citizens of Apollo."

I've *never* seen my dad like this before, and for the first time since yesterday evening, some of the fear begins to fade away. It's replaced by something else: admiration, and a sense of safety.

Agent Jackson doesn't answer my father immediately. I am expecting him to grow frustrated, or even threatening. Rather, he steps back from my dad's impeding posture, nods his head in apparent submission, and adjusts his glasses with the touch of his chubby index finger.

"I completely understand your concern, Mr. Loban. You know, I have a daughter myself." He pauses for a moment and looks over my dad's shoulder, at me. "She's actually about your age, Flora." He turns his attention back to my dad. "I admire your tenacity. In all honesty, I'd be concerned if you showed anything less."

The compliment, I notice, catches my father off guard, and a small smile creeps into the corner of his mouth. "You have a daughter?" he asks.

"Oh yes." Agent Jackson smiles. "She's at the university right now, studying history."

"Oh! Flora is also taking classes there," my mom says, cutting into the conversation. "Flora, I wonder if you knew her in high school."

I want to remind her I don't care, that I don't get along with girls anyway, that *this man wants to question me*, and I don't even know why.

"It's very possible," Agent Jackson says. "I believe you graduated last summer, Flora?"

My eyes dart back and forth between my mother and father, but both are staring at me, waiting for my answer, so I comply.

"Yes," I say.

Agent Jackson smiles brilliantly, revealing perfectly lined and bleached teeth. "Well that settles it," he says, cheerfully. "My daughter's name is Samantha, Samantha Jackson. Sound familiar?"

It doesn't, but something inside tells me to go along with this ridiculous story, so I nod and my parents seem delighted.

"Now I deeply apologize for the alarm," Agent Jackson says. "Truly. Our only concern, as you can imagine, is to keep Apollo in proper order, so good and contributing citizens, such as yourselves, can go on living in peace. We're simply investigating a small, possible security breach of A-Search at the Apollo Library on a day your daughter might have been there. She is not a suspect, but we want to question her, in case she saw anything that might aid in our investigation."

I watch as the relief washes over my parents' faces, the worry slipping off their expressions like oil off water.

"Well, that's good news," my mom says, looking toward my dad.

"Most certainly," Agent Jackson says. "There's one more thing, though. The contents of this investigation are considered State Classified, and as such, under ARS 13-6 Section A of the Apollo Revised Statues, I will need to talk with Flora alone as a possible witness."

"But she's a minor," my dad says.

"We are aware, but ARS 13-6 Section A excludes the definition of minor for a witness, due to the classified status of the information we need to share. As a witness, Flora is entitled to hear this information, but no one else—not even her parents. It will only take five minutes, I promise."

My parents are reluctant, I can tell, but how can they argue with the law? My nerves had calmed a bit, but now they begin firing again as I watch Agent Jackson gently guide my parents toward the exit, usher them outside and to another room, and return and close the door, trapping us inside.

Just the two of us.

He smiles that stale, stiff grin and motions for me to take a seat before lowering himself into the chair opposite me.

"What day did the breach happen?" I ask. "I doubt I saw anything, but I'll do my best to try and help."

Agent Jackson simply sits there, his leg crossed in self-righteous satisfaction over the other, and watches me. But he doesn't answer my question, and slowly, I begin to understand.

"There was no breach, was there?" I say.

His lips still tight, Agent Jackson shakes his head: to the left, to the right, mocking me and my parents, our naiveté. Anxiety grips my body, and I must remind myself to breathe.

"Why did you lie to us?" I say, my voice barely above a whisper.

"I didn't lie, completely. The investigation *is* classified."

"But you don't have a daughter."

Agent Jackson sighs. "Have a seat, Flora."

I sit, not because he told me to, but because I'm so nervous, I feel off-balance. Agent Jackson adjusts himself in the chair and leans forward, resting his elbows on his knees. His laser-sharp concentration pierces my brain.

"Why were you trying to sneak onto forbidden government property at Oak Creek Canyon two weeks ago on Sunday morning?" he says.

My voice drops away. And my throat squeezes shut, turns dry. I open my mouth to speak, but no words form.

"We found your water bottle, the one you probably dropped when you ran after setting off the alarm," he says. "I know you're wondering; I can see it on your face.

Yes, we checked, and the fingerprints on the bottle are yours."

After another moment, I manage to garner enough strength to say something. "But, isn't that invasion of privacy?"

"You discarded it as trash. Perfectly admissible as evidence."

How? Why? So many thoughts rushing through my brain, jumbled and confused and scared. I was being stupid. I was exploring. I stumbled upon it during a hike. I—I...

"I was just curious," I finally say. "Look, I'm sorry. I didn't go inside, and I'll never go back. It was a mistake."

Agent Jackson agrees and nods his head, this time crossing his arms over his chest. "I understand you're probably just a curious kid. We've all been there. I'm willing to let this one slide and drop any potential charges."

I watch as he climbs to his feet, appearing much taller than when he first entered the room, and walks closer to me. He lowers his body to kneel before my legs, until our noses are nearly aligned. His breath smells of old coffee disguised by spearmint gum.

"But all this research," he says, "on the Wall and totalitarianism? It needs to stop. Understand?"

"How do you know—"

"A-Search, Flora."

I gulp, trying to keep myself lucid and calm. "I thought Apollo encouraged the pursuit of knowledge," I say.

At this, something changes underneath the surface of Agent Jackson's collected exterior. I watch as his eyes grow callous, and I swear his pupils dilate. Any remnants of the grin he once wore are gone.

"Discussing and seeking out the Wall, except within the confines of a classroom, is a State crime worthy of ten years in a maximum-security prison," he says, his voice stiff. "And that's the minimum sentence."

His words slam into me with the power of a hammer, and when he steps back, I feel a small sense of relief to be rid of his intrusive glare. But that disappears as he smiles, his grin chilling.

"Besides," he continues, "I'd hate to see someone you love, like your mother, suddenly come down with an incurable disease, like pancreatic cancer. Or a brain tumor."

My head snaps up.

"Your parents are not to know *anything* about this classified conversation. Do you understand?"

I stare at him, infuriated, but I think back to my run-ins with the girls, to the hairspray incident, to all the names and the whispers. The intimidation of this moment feels the same, and like the times before, I want to say something, but I can't—speaking up always makes things worse—so I remain silent.

"Flora, do you understand what may happen if you refuse to comply with the State's request?"

Feeling defeated, desperate for this visit to end and for Agent Jackson to leave me alone, I stand and smooth my white clothes before him. Lowering my voice, I respond. "Yes, I do understand, Agent Jackson."

The Number

FLORA

I feel trapped, suffocating between the car windows and doors. I've stuffed myself into the backseat, my parents chattering up front about "what a relief" the visit was and how "nicely Agent Jackson treated us."

"Maybe it's because he knew you are a reporter for the *Apollo Times*," my dad teases my mom.

"Oh, Randy." She playfully slaps his arm and laughs in that light, high-pitched tone that surfaces when she's giddy. She sounds mirthful.

"Flora," my dad calls over the driver's seat, glancing into the rearview mirror, "I'm very proud of you. I want you to know that. This was not an easy situation today, and you handled it like such a respectable young lady."

I see a prideful smile overtake my dad's face as he looks at me from the rearview mirror, and my stomach curls. If only he knew...

"Yes, I agree," my mom says. "I'm glad it wasn't what we thought. That Agent Jackson, he reminds me of your pediatrician growing up, doesn't he?"

"Which one?" I ask.

"You know, the one who always brought you a lollipop. The sweet gentleman."

Sweet gentleman. Who threatened your life. A sharp, piercing sensation fires up my wrist from the palm of my hand. Shocked from the sudden pain, I look down and notice my fingers are clenched into a fist, my nails digging a groove into my skin. And I'm bleeding.

"What was his daughter's name again? Sammy? Samantha?"

I stare at the white knuckles of my fist and remind myself to breathe.

"Flora?"

I don't want to answer. I want out of this car, *right now*. "What, Mom?"

"You should try and call Samantha, if you knew her back in high school."

"I didn't know her."

Why isn't the air conditioning blowing back here? It's getting increasingly hot; I feel the sweat trickling down my temples.

"Then why did you say you did?" my dad says, cutting into the conversation.

I release my fist and stare at the drops of blood slipping down the palm of my hand, like paint. I wipe the red liquid away and press my thumb onto the wound to stop the bleeding.

"Because," I say, "I knew *of* her. She wasn't a friend."

"Did you want to stop and grab some lunch?" my mom asks, and I can tell she's trying to lighten the mood.

"No!" I realize my reaction is extreme, and I allow my nerves to subside before speaking again. "I mean, not right now. Andrew was really concerned about what happened, and I promised to call him when I get home. I just need some rest. Is that OK?"

My parents exchange puzzled looks in the front of the car, and my mom shrugs her shoulders. "OK, sweetie," she says.

In truth, I haven't told Andrew anything. Nor will I say anything after what happened today. But there is one person who I need to see, and it's not Andrew.

***

As I stare at the giant tower of Apollo in the middle of the library, I don't feel so proud anymore. In fact, I feel contentious. I'd left my house in a hurry, leaving my parents visibly concerned and perplexed. But I can't think about that, now.

My eyes scan the crowds of tiny trilogies among the Apollo Library, searching for Don. I can't help but notice all the pairs of parents reading to their young children. Teaching them. Primping them. Bestowing knowledge and thought and analysis upon them.

Without worry or care, in the open.

And why *should* they worry? Every person I've met knows about world history, ancient cultures, music, art, science, philosophy. But now that I consider more carefully, I realize not one person has mentioned the author George Orwell, or his book *1984*, or the term totalitarianism. Until Don.

"Were you looking for me?"

Don's voice startles me so much, I fall off my chair.

"Right," he says, sitting across from me, his eyes still plastered to the floor.

"How could you tell?" I ask.

"Tell what?"

"That I was looking for you."

Don's gaze floats toward the same statue I was studying moments ago. "I pay attention."

The guy barely ever looks at me, and yet he's trying to convince me he *pays attention?* "I need to talk to you," I say.

"What else is new?"

I can usually tolerate his snide remarks and offensive attitude, but not today. Not now.

"What's up with you?" I say. "Didn't your mother ever teach you to treat others with respect?"

The sharp tone of my voice surprises me, and clearly shocks him. I can't stop myself from continuing. "I want to know something, and don't bullshit me. Why did you give me that book, *1984*?"

"You wanted to learn. I'm teaching you."

"Well, I don't want it anymore." I reach deep into my purse and pull out the classic novel, plop it on the table, and slide it across until the binding rests against Don's fingers.

He stares at it for a few moments, the giant eye on the cover following his face, observing every move.

"They got to you, didn't they?" he says.

His words interrupt my thoughts and for a moment, I'm not sure how to respond. "I don't know what you're talking about," I say.

"Oh, yes you do." An eerie smile creeps into the corners of his mouth—the first I've seen from Don. "You're starting to learn."

I'm void of speech, and all I can do is sit and watch as he climbs to his feet and sweeps the book into his embrace, like a sacred child. After placing it inside his coat, he glances at me and whips out a pen with a small piece of paper. Intent with concentration, he leans down and scribbles a phone number, folds the paper, and slides it across the table.

"If you ever find yourself caught in a trap, call this number. It's safe."

And with that, Don turns around and walks away, through the crowds of smiling parents and their curious children.

The First Date

ANDREW

Her name is Sophie, and she's asking about my father—*already*. It's the first freakin' date, and I can't tell if she has Florence Nightingale syndrome... "poor, disturbed writer, I need to save him"... or if she just gets off on the fact that I'm one of the only fatherless offspring in Apollo.

Maybe I can get a hand job out of this. Lord knows I could use a few soft strokes.

"Do you ever think about him?" she asks, her promising pout growing fuller and fuller with each question, each inquiry designed to delve deeper into my psyche.

I decide to play this angle to my advantage. "Sometimes, late at night, yeah I do," I say. "It's hard being alone, just me and my mom, having to care for her, listen to her troubles. But what am I supposed to do? She's my *mom*, and I love her."

Heaving breasts. Just a hint of cleavage spilling over the dinner table, the restaurant's dimmed candlelight softly illuminating the curvature of smooth, golden skin. Yup, she wants me.

"That's so sweet," Sophie says.

I lean over the table, drawing her near with my eyes, soaking in the moment's intensity through her studious cherry wood frames. "I love how I can talk to you about this," I say. "You're such a great listener."

She giggles. Giggles! "Well, I am studying psychology."

"Doesn't surprise me," I respond. "Someone as observant as you... I'd trust you with my mother's care."

I may want to slip my hands under that gloriously snug sweater of hers, sure, but Sophie really does know how to listen (in an academic sort of way), and I'm sure she'd be great with my mom. I flash a quick smile at her, and can practically smell the desire emanating from her skin, mixed with the gentle scent of her rose and vanilla perfume. I feel my own pulse quicken.

"That's *right*. Your mom was in the crazy house for a while," she says, and I immediately regret mentioning my mother, pulling my elbows off the table and jerking my head back.

"She was," I say, a little grimmer now.

"I remember when all the kids were talking about it in school. God, that must've been hard."

I feel myself stiffen—and not in the good way. "Yes."

Sophie furrows her dark eyebrows in thought for a moment, and I can tell she's trying to recall some memory. She pushes her glasses back up the bridge of her nose and looks at me again.

"Weren't you sleeping with that girl back then?"

Even if she does evoke cravings for fruit and cream and sex, maybe Sophie isn't so different after all. I'm suddenly reconsidering that hand job.

"Flora," I say, confirming her suspicions. "My best friend."

"Oh, you guys stayed friends?" Her voice drips with disappointment.

"We were never anything more than friends." I'm beginning to grow defensive now. I can feel it. But I tell myself to let this go; I'll regret it later if I don't.

Her demeanor softens when I reveal this tidbit of information, but I'm positive it's only a matter of time before the jealousy starts. Give it another three dates, and she'll start questioning what's "really going on" between me and Flora.

Not that my constant contact with Flora would affect Sophie as much as it mattered to past girlfriends, because Flora has obviously decided to spend the remainder of summer as a hermit. I've barely seen her twice in three weeks.

"What about you?" Sophie asks me, drawing my mind away from Flora. "What are you studying at the University?"

"Writing."

"What kind of writing? Journalism? Marketing?"

"Just, writing."

Sophie appears stumped at my answer, but this doesn't surprise me; the only girl who ever understood what I mean by true writing, the sort done by greats like Charles Dickens or Herman Melville or Alexandre Dumas, is Flora. Many love to read in Apollo, whether classic or contemporary, but not many new authors are born into our society.

"Here, let me show you what I mean," I tell Sophie, reaching across the table to caress a lock of her black hair in the palm of my hand. The impulsive gesture startles her.

"Her hair flows through my palm like silk quenching the thirst of a desolate man," I say, in full improvisation. "Its dark waves whispering secrets of desires gone long unfulfilled. And I wonder, how can I make this angel's heart sing again?"

Sophie's chest is bulging once more, breathy gulps of air slipping in and out of those blossoming lips. She's ready to jump on my lap and straddle me; I can feel it. Normally, I'd seize any opportunity with a girl as smokin' hot as Sophie, but for some reason, I find myself thinking of someone else amidst the wave of intensity.

And that's when it hits me, like a bat to the head: it wasn't Sophie I was speaking poetry to just now. It was Flora.

***

Sophie's goodnight kiss reminds me of a cool autumn evening spent indoors by the warm fire. The only aspect it lacked was a sense of home. And now, as I'm driving back to my house, I find myself wondering what Flora's lips would taste like.

To my knowledge, she has never been kissed—*truly* kissed—and deep down, I know it's partly my fault. I've watched with disgust as our perfect little community bestowed upon her a ridiculous reputation.

And yet, as we've grown older, Flora began to skip through life, unscathed, like that old cat of mine who never feared dogs. Her parents are the epitome of happiness, in that sweet log cabin with Ernest. I suppose with that sort of safety net, resiliency is easier to attain.

But this—*this* is why Flora's obvious attempt at avoidance worries me.

I pull into the driveway when I arrive home. The moon is new tonight, and therefore, I can't see much after I've climbed from my car, except maybe the sprinkle of stars in the dark dome encompassing our neighborhood. Our house backs against the forest, and sometimes, I'll leave carrots in the backyard for the deer to eat.

When I enter the house, I flip on a light and hear the gentle muttering of the television from my mom's room. She probably fell asleep early again; it's barely nine o'clock on Saturday night.

I begin debating whether I should try to call Flora. I don't want to bother her, but her face, her name, her odd reactions lately won't leave my mind. Is she stuck in my head because of her avoidance, or because I now know I could never be more than a friend to her?

Screw it. Something tells me Flora needs me tonight, so I don't hesitate. Standing in the middle of the kitchen, I pick up the phone.

The Dream

ANDREW

Her voice is breaking when she answers the phone, and I know immediately she's been crying. *Crying? But Flora almost never cries.*

"Why are you calling so late?" she says to me. "Are you OK? Is your mom alright?"

"It's barely after nine o'clock on Saturday," I tell her. "I didn't realize Flora the Fearless had turned into an eighty-year-old grandma."

My attempt at playfulness fails, however. "You're OK then," she says, more as a statement than a question.

"I had that date with Sophie tonight, the girl I told you about."

Flora feigns interest; I can tell because when she truly cares, her voice lights up like a child laughing for the first time. So I finally cut the bullshit.

"What the heck is going on with you?" I ask. "You haven't met me for our Saturday bike rides in weeks, you're not returning my phone calls, we've barely hung out. And now you don't want to talk, because it's too late?"

God, now who sounds like a crazy, controlling girlfriend?

"I'm fine, Andrew."

"No, you're not fine. Maybe you can trick everyone else in Apollo, even your own parents, but not me."

I hear her sigh on the other end, and she sniffles. That's when I remember Flora's new "friend," Don. Had she started seeing him without telling me? *If he did anything to her...*

"I've been having these weird dreams," Flora says on the other line, cutting off my thoughts and forcing me to focus. "Eerie."

"How so?" I ask.

"Like, the sky is red. And, well, you're there, too."

At this, a small seed of hope rises from within. *Flora's been dreaming about me?*

"Your voice," she corrects. "Your voice is there, and in the dream, I'm standing on The Other Side of the Wall, and I'm walking, and walking, like on a cloud, and I can hear you screaming from behind, begging me not to leave. But this strange force, something outside of my control, keeps pushing me forward, further and further away from your voice, until I can't hear you anymore. And I wander into the redness, blind to what lies beyond."

She takes a long pause, but I don't know what to say. How can I possibly respond to something like that?

"What do you think it means?" she asks, breaking the silence after a few moments. My first thought is of my mother. Years ago, this is how she started with her events. Dreams. As I remember the darker days, a wave of apprehension swells up from my core. *Not Flora, too.*

"I don't know what it could mean," I tell her. "You've been so obsessed with the Wall, maybe you're starting to dream about it."

A muffled scrape drifts through the phone, and I envision Flora shaking her head from side to side. "No, this is different. It's like that place where dreams meet reality, between death and life. I feel like I'm witnessing a past that hasn't taken place yet."

As Flora talks, I reach into the depth of my psyche and scan my memories like library catalogs, searching for the name of that doctor who helped my mother long ago. *What was his name?*

"Andrew, how come you're not saying anything?"

I jerk myself back into the moment. "Sorry," I say. "Listen, do you want me to come over? I can stay the night, and we can visit La Experiencia Maya for some so-called Guatemalan coffee in the morning."

"That does sound nice," she says, her voice trailing off.

"I'll be right over then."

"But I think I just need some time alone, Andrew."

Never more certain I *need* to be by Flora's side, I throw words at her before processing them through my brain. "We can go check out that weird building again, by Oak Creek Canyon."

"No!" Her anxiety emanates through the phone, and the severity of her reaction stuns me, amplifies my questions to all new levels.

"I'm coming over. And that's final."

I hang up the phone before she can protest and grab my car keys, leaving a note for my mom.

***

When Flora meets me out front, a shadow stands before me: dark bags drooping under weary eyes, ragged hair stripped of its brilliance, and pale cheeks devoid of life—at one with the darkness. I almost drop my extra T-shirt, pair of boxers, and toothbrush in my surprise.

"You look like you haven't seen the sun in weeks," I say.

"I told you it wasn't a good idea for you to come over right now."

I approach her and grasp her arm; my fingers easily close around the circumference of her bicep. "Have you eaten?"

Flora doesn't answer.

"Let's get you inside. This is ridiculous." Gently, I lead her into the warmth of her cabin, like a parent guiding a child, and questions begin racing through my mind. Was she raped? Was she beaten? Did someone threaten her? And now I wonder about her parents. Haven't they noticed this dramatic change in their daughter?

"I'm an embarrassment, I know," Flora says as we enter the house and close the door behind us.

"Where's your mom and dad?"

"My dad's playing at the hotel tonight. My mom is with him."

Ernest comes trotting toward me and nudges his soft, golden head under my palm, begging to be pet. As I start scratching the tender spot behind his floppy ears, his tongue rolls out and hangs there, like a ribbon in the wind.

"So, how was Sophie?" Flora says.

"How *was* she?"

A forced smile spreads across Flora's face, and she playfully nudges me with her elbow—a hint of the girl I know. "C'mon, Romeo. I've heard Sophie talking about you before. Don't tell me she wasn't ready to give it up on date one?"

Such a perverted thought from someone so innocent. "Oh. Well, I just kissed her."

"That's it?" The look on Flora's face is genuine shock and awe.

"Yes, *that's it*. Did it ever occur to you that perhaps I'm not easy, either?"

At this, Flora chuckles. Not laughs, but chuckles. And I feel borderline insulted. "You know, I didn't drive all the way over here after nine o'clock on a Saturday night to be called names and laughed at," I say. "Now maybe we can turn the conversation back to you? I'm not the one who looks like a skeleton."

Flora's demeanor grows dark again, and I immediately regret killing what may have been her first sign of laughter in weeks. I apologize, but it doesn't seem to affect her. When I reach out to offer a hug, she retreats, and I sigh, defeated. "OK then, have you showered today?" I ask.

"Does it matter?"

This means the answer is no, so I tell Flora to get cleaned up and I'll pull together some sandwiches from her fridge.

***

I was never much of a cook. Blame it on my mother, I suppose, and her over-compensation for the other parent who I'd missed growing up. The guilt complex, I call it.

But as I work in Flora's kitchen—toasting the bread, spreading the mayo, carefully layering the turkey, cheese, tomatoes and onions and lettuce—I find myself hypnotized by the repetitiveness of food preparation. I wonder if this is why some people bake to de-stress.

I sporadically throw Ernest a small slice of turkey as I'm pulling together my pathetic attempt at a home-cooked meal. But when Flora reappears, damp golden hair slicked back from her forehead and subtle hints of lavender floating toward my nose, the look of relief on her face makes my attempts worthwhile.

"That actually smells delicious," she says. "Thanks for doing this."

I realize, even when food- and sleep-deprived, Flora looks stunning. She's not overflowing with sexuality like Sophie, but rather has the beauty of a fine silk scarf. All of a sudden, I no longer know how to act, or what to say. "I'm glad," is all I can muster, along with a smile, and I place the plate of food before her after she takes a seat at the kitchen table.

I settle myself opposite her, and we both begin eating in silence. I can tell the first few bites are a struggle for Flora, but soon she begins ripping into the sandwich like she hasn't eaten in days. I want to ask her again what's going on, but I keep quiet. *Let the girl eat, Andrew.*

"I'm sorry I've been so... absent... lately," Flora says, after devouring her sandwich. "God, that tasted good."

I just look at her, wanting to ask, wanting to read her thoughts, to understand her fears, but all I can read through those sky-blue eyes is sadness. Perhaps, regret?

"I guess sometimes you realize something about yourself that—well, can be hard to swallow," she says. Her voice is soft, lacking that luster for life I'm so used to hearing.

"What did you learn?" I ask, hoping she may finally open up.

"It's not important."

"It is to me."

Flora's head lifts and for a moment, we're suspended in time, entombed in a moment. Images flash through my mind: the nights she spent by my side while my mother was locked away, the hikes and the bike rides and the adventures... our map.

"Aren't you always the one who says, 'What's knowledge without curiosity?'" I say, offering a warm smile, reflecting my genuine hope to rescue her from whatever darkness has engulfed her.

A smirk creeps into the corner of her mouth. "Without curiosity, knowledge is empty," she says, finishing the thought.

"So satisfy my curiosity tonight, Flora." And I borrow a line from my earlier poem performed before Sophie. "Help quench the thirst of a desolate man."

She wants to tell me. Every feature across her face—from her parted lips, to her raised eyebrows, to her flittering fingers—secures this fact in my mind. I'm waiting for an answer.

"I can't talk about it, Andrew," she says, and disappointment washes over me.

"Why not?" The worries start to turn somewhere else now. Flora and I share everything with each other. If she was raped, or beaten, or threatened, that wouldn't stop her from revealing it to me, which leaves only one possibility.

"It's something with me, isn't it?" I ask.

"What?"

I push my plate away, my appetite suddenly gone. "I get it. It all makes sense now."

Flora stiffens as her eyes grow wide. "Andrew, what are you talking about?"

I shake my head, barely able to find the willpower to look her straight in the eyes. "Did your parents say something to you? 'Oh Flora, you need to stop hanging around that boy so much. It doesn't look good. We let it slide for too long, but enough is enough.'"

Flora shoots to her feet, pushing her body over the table. "Andrew, no! Of course not."

"Then why can't you tell me?"

"I—"

But her voice trails off. The clues fly together in my head, like puzzle pieces finally making sense. She's been avoiding *me*. She can't tell *me*. She says it's not a good idea for *me* to come over tonight. How could I have been so blind? And really, can I blame her? No boy will go near her because they all think I've claimed her as my own personal whore. And girls hate her because, because...

"That's what I thought," I say, my voice dry and cold now. "Look, I'm sorry I'm causing such a ripple in your life. My problems are my problems. They shouldn't bleed over to anyone else."

"Andrew, don't say that. Please. I loved having you come over tonight."

"Sure you did," I say, and look up at her, rejection filling my veins. "I'll do you the favor, without you having to ask. I'll walk out and leave you the hell alone."

Flora's eyes begin overflowing now, the tears streaming down her cheeks. "Please don't leave me," she says.

"You realized something about yourself that can be hard to swallow, huh? Save it, Flora. The last thing I need is anyone's pity."

Regretting my visit tonight, I grab my boxers, my T-shirt, my toothbrush, and I flee from her house. I want to run as far away from that cabin before it haunts me into delirium.

The Question

ANDREW

The chill air is crisp against my cheeks as I sit outside on the patio of La Experiencia Maya the next morning, drinking my cup of coffee. Even during summer, the mornings in Apollo are cold.

I'm supposed to be sitting here with Flora, but instead, I'm alone. As I glare far past the horizon, I know somewhere beyond those Ponderosa pines is the Wall. I can't see it from where I sit, but I sense its impeding presence, as I have my entire life. The Wall may not be visible, but it is *always* felt.

For the first time in my life, I desperately want to escape, to leave and never come back. It's selfish, I know, as my mother would probably die from loneliness without me nearby. However, even with the clear air and openness of the mountains, I've never felt more claustrophobic.

I take another sip of coffee and stand for a moment, reaching into my back pocket. I pull out a folded piece of paper and sit again, opening the document and staring at its contents. *Cause of brief power outage still mysterious.* It's the newspaper brief I copied from the Apollo Library last month, and I regularly find myself searching its contents for a new meaning. I read and re-read the brief, trying to decipher how it ties into my father's disappearance, wondering if it offers some hidden key for my escape, as well.

"I remember you." The words are spoken in a male voice from behind my chair, pulling me from my concentration, but before I turn around, I know exactly who it is; I'd remember that smell of cigarettes anywhere.

"Don," I say, and stand and turn to face black eyes outlined with women's makeup. The very sight of him makes me cringe in revulsion.

"Andrew," he responds, but doesn't look at me. I've noticed Don never looks anyone in the eyes; he always stares downward.

"Good morning," I say, not sure what else is appropriate.

"If you say so." He continues to stand there, and for the next few minutes we linger, motionless and awkward. "Flora OK?" he finally asks, and his question catches me off-guard.

"Why wouldn't she be?"

"You tell me."

Something warns me to proceed with caution, and I study his face intently. Expressionless. This kid is either a sociopath, or one heck of a poker player in some secret, underground life.

"You two not having your library dates anymore?" I ask, ignoring his inquiry.

I watch as the corner of his mouth jerks upward—an attempt at a smile? But he immediately scratches his nose, almost as if to wipe away the smirk, and his face once again falls vacant. Impossible to read.

"You think they were dates?" he asks.

"I don't know; you tell me." I throw the words back, but he doesn't flinch. God, I'd love to deck this kid in the nose, squeeze that slimy little hand until bones begin cracking...

"Tell Flora hi," he says before turning around and walking away, disappearing into the coffee shop. I'm left standing in the cold.

***

I don't know if it was the fight with Flora last night, or the two hours of broken sleep, but I know it's time to ask my mom about that fight she had with my dad when I was eight, and the next day, when he disappeared.

I'm standing outside my house like some roaming stranger about to knock on the door and ask for bread. I know my mom is inside; it's evening now and she's probably cooking dinner. I've spent the day wandering the streets of Apollo, my hair disheveled and my body unwashed. I haven't showered since yesterday and my five o'clock shadow is beginning to itch like millions of ants.

What if I trigger my mother into another event? What if I have to call for help, and they lock her away again? Or, worst of all, what if I discover something about my father that will transform my resentment into hatred?

I scratch my scalp—it's beginning to crawl too—and push open the door. I find my mother sitting under dimmed lights at the round kitchen table, reading today's newspaper, *The Apollo Times*. The paper is flipped open so I catch a glimpse of the front-page headlines.

"I made some potato soup for dinner tonight, fresh from the garden," my mom says without lifting her eyes from the newspaper. "There's leftovers in the fridge."

Relief washes over my body when I realize she's normal. I thank my mom, but at the sound of my voice, she pulls her eyes from the story and narrows her gaze at me. "What's wrong?"

I stop walking toward her and allow my mother to pause and soak in my appearance. "Andrew, you look like a car ran you over."

"Ma, can I ask you something?"

Unsure of what to say, my mom nods her head, and I tell her my question is about Dad.

"I see," she responds, the soft light revealing rounded cheeks that once glowed with life, but now are ridden with tired creases.

"You don't have to answer if you don't want," I say, sensing her uneasiness.

"Andrew, just ask, and let's get this over with."

I take a deep breath, preparing for the worst, and ask the question. My mother's entire body stiffens like hardening concrete.

"You remember that fight?" she asks, her voice growing smaller, thinner.

"I wrote about it. Yes, I do."

Her fingers begin tapping the table, her eyes darting around the room, around the kitchen. "Your father started losing track of what was important," she says. "Selfish. Isn't that why everyone leaves?"

If I'm not careful, I'll instigate one of her rambling rants, and I'm not sure if I'll ever have the guts to ask about my dad again. Carefully, I inch toward the table before lowering myself into the chair across from my mom.

"I'm not leaving," I remind her, and smile.

"No, you may look like him, but you're like me."

My mom loves comparing my best qualities to her, and the poor ones to my dad. I sometimes think it's a coping mechanism.

"Ma, this is very important for me to know, to understand. It'll help bring me closure."

She nods in agreement, with empathy, and I can sense she wants to tell me but isn't sure if she should. Glancing toward the door, she says, "This can't leave the house, you understand?" When I nod, she returns her focus on me. "Your father was a curious man. In fact, Flora reminds me of him, in many ways."

I cringe at the mention of Flora's name, but I swallow back the discomfort and continue listening to my mom's story.

"Your dad used to spend the evenings reading to you after dinner. Do you remember?"

I smile a sad grin. "Of course I do."

"He lived for you, which is why it bothered me when he started leaving after our family dinners to spend time with his friend Joe, instead. They started getting these crazy ideas about the—the—"

"The Wall," I finish for her.

"Yes, and The Other Side," she says. "I didn't understand their conspiracy theories, and I don't want to, but he grew obsessed. Maybe three months before he left, he stopped showing up for our family dinners altogether and was outwardly defiant against the laws here in Apollo. I kept telling him to forget it, that it wasn't worth him getting arrested and his son growing up without a father."

She stops at that last sentence, regretful for mentioning it. "I'm sorry," she says, trying to fight tears. "I shouldn't have said that to you."

I nod in encouragement, reaching out to take her hand, to let her know it's OK, that I want her to keep going, so she does.

"The night of the fight, he started telling me it was imperative for us to know the truth, that there was something much more, much *darker* than anything we could imagine going on. I told him I refused to endanger your safety, that the world we know is perfect—our family, our home, our friends, our garden; why can't he just accept it? But he wouldn't listen, said I didn't understand what was at stake. I cried myself to sleep, scared that we'd frightened you, and when I woke the next morning, he was gone."

She's somewhere else now. Her eyes are staring into nothingness, her hand encapsulated by mine. As I watch her drift away, disquiet creeps into my core, because I still have one more question to ask, but I'm terrified of what the answer could mean.

"Ma?" I say, and she levels her eyes to meet mine. "Do you think Dad left, or do you think he was taken?"

For a moment, all life stops: my breathing, the kitchen fan, my mother's nervous clicking of her fingers against the table. It's all suspended, waiting for her answer. And finally, she lets it out.

"I honestly don't know," she says. "And that's the truth."

Sophie

ANDREW

    I feel like a fish without gills, gasping for breath as blood boils through my skin, rushing to the center of a body that's growing hard, trapped, and desperate for release. Oh, what is a man to do when he hungers for sustenance, yet finds nothing but sand? When he thirsts for a warm body to quench the burning prick of lust, which in truth is but a shield for a plaguing contempt?

    I want to crawl out of my skin, escape from this cage, but I have nowhere to go. The shades of truth are becoming ever grayer to me, and I'm lost—like a mouse wandering through a maze for a spectator's entertainment. I've lost my one true anchor in this world, and it's my fault. I am to blame. Is it possible that she might be the only one I've ever truly loved, and yet, the only one I've never been able to have?

    Life is a cruel game of Russian roulette.

I place my pen down against the wooden desk in my room, shoving my hand onto my scalp. Drivel. It's nothing but drivel I'm scribbling into my journal, yet I can't escape this slimy sensation that's growing ever more prevalent since Flora shut me out and my mother revealed her truest fears about my father.

It's only been a day, and I feel like I'm sitting on a pile of dynamite.

That's when her name courses through my brain like a rocket: *Sophie.* The girl is nice; I know I shouldn't, but I think of Flora, of the way she was whispering against Don's ear in the library, and of the way she disregards my attempts to be something more, and my fingers reach for the phone.

***

We meet off a dirt road that opens into an expansive meadow. It's surprisingly private, as not many people hike through this area. This evening, the place is deserted. Good.

When I approach, Sophie is arching her back in the driver's seat of her car, obviously pretending to stretch with one intention only: drawing attention to those luscious breasts that are once again overflowing just for me. Blood begins pounding into my ears, now my stomach, and even lower.

"I just had to look into your eyes one more time," I tell her, lowering my elbows against her vacant window frame, and flashing my toothiest grin.

"On the phone, you sounded so..."

"In need?" I finish the sentence for her, and she's caught unaware, I can tell, and I watch as glistening lips painted rose gently part to reveal just the tip of an eager tongue. God, I'm itching to slip my hands under that snug bra; its yellow polka dots are already peeking from the square-cut neck of a fuzzy, maroon sweater.

"I want to help you, Andrew," she says, and reaches out to caress the hair above my ears.

"You can. You can help me right now." I pull away to open the car door and Sophie doesn't need to say another word.

I lean into her, warm and welcoming pillows softening against my hard chest, sweet lips that taste of watermelon opening into my mouth, against my neck. She pulls me in and I slip under her into the driver's seat. Her glasses fall off, my hands caress voluptuous curves: supple and yielding and willing.

We leave the door open and begin struggling like raging animals—me underneath, her spreading across my lap, the steering wheel pressed against the small of her back. She's tugging at my jeans, unzipping, slipping a soft palm underneath my boxers and caressing me with the delicacy of a feather, driving me into a fit of frustration.

I jerk my head against the chair and begin yanking up her skirt, pulling aside her underwear, burying my face into her collarbone. Now, now, I need it now. Hunger begins flowing through my veins, urgent and angry. Why is she being so careful, so soft?

"Please," is all I can manage, pulling her hips into me, guiding her teasing fingers to slip on the condom.

Finally, sweet salvation.

I thrust my hips into her, deeper and deeper and deeper, banging my way out of this lonely trap, forcing every thought and possibility and dangerous truth further and further into a dark hole, so I never need to fear them surfacing again.

And now I see it behind closed eyes: Don and Flora, whispering next to each other in that damned library. Her giggling like a schoolgirl, him stinking of smoke. I imagine them kissing, his slippery hands stealing the first-time exploration of her smooth body, his lips pressed against hers...

Nearly manic, I press my fingers deeper into Sophie's back, pumping even harder now, an unstoppable machine. God, why won't she want me? Why won't she—

"Flora!" I call out, and abruptly, the escape from reality stops.

"Flora?"

I open my eyes and look up into Sophie's stunned face, her skirt pulled up around her hips, her shirt jammed under her chin—half-naked and spread open and completely humiliated. I'm speechless and just sitting there, staring up at her, still hard and feverish and pent-up myself.

"Flora?" she repeats, and swings her legs off my lap, yanking down her skirt and covering her chest.

"Sophie, I'm sorry."

"Get out of my car," she says, and I watch as a tear makes its way down her cheek. "Get. Out."

I quickly shove myself back into my now-tight jeans and jump out of the driver's seat. My pants button still undone, I watch as Sophie kicks her car into gear and screeches off, a trail of dust flying from the rear in a cloud of desperation to escape.

To escape me.

I finish fastening my jeans and look back at my car. Everyone wants to escape me nowadays, it seems. And really, I can't blame them.

Government Class

ANDREW

LIGHT, TRUTH, AND KNOWLEDGE.

The words seem to mock me as they loom above my head, painted in bold, black letters upon the walls of the university. It's the first day back at school, the beginning of my sophomore year at the University of Apollo, and only now do I realize I'd never paid much attention to these words before. In fact, I had hardly noticed them painted along the eternal hallways of the university.

It's been three weeks since my encounter with Sophie, and I haven't heard from her. Then again, I haven't tried calling. More disturbingly, I haven't spoken a word to Flora. Inside, a part of me feels empty without her laughing smile and curious eyes. I know she's on campus today, and I am constantly looking over my shoulder, hoping to spot her.

I tell myself to hurry and pull my gaze from the four words and join the other students rushing past me to make their classes on time. My next period is Ethics and Philosophy in Government, a course I'd chosen to help me ponder deeper ideas for the novel I intend to write.

Gripping my backpack and pushing some rogue hairs away from my face, I yank my eyes away from the looming words, managing to push myself to class.

When I enter, an intrusive odor irritates my nostrils, pungent and immediate. I throw my backpack next to a desk toward the middle of the room and begin looking around, trying to decipher where it's coming from. It almost smells like, a skunk?

Not able to solve the mystery, I sit and take it, but as more students pile into the room, I watch as they crinkle their noses and look around in disgust, too. Finally, the professor waltzes in, a tall and slender middle-aged man with narrow glasses resting on a pointed nose. He doesn't waste any time.

"Did someone bring a pet skunk to class?" he asks. The class breaks into laughter, but when no one answers, he keeps pressing. "C'mon now, don't be shy."

From the back of the room, a student about my age stands with his head bowed in shame. "Sorry professor, that's me," he says, his voice broken from embarrassment.

A sea of heads turns around to glare at this poor, unfortunate soul.

"You have a pet skunk?" our teacher asks.

"No, they're female skunk pheromones."

"Pardon?"

The student takes a deep breath, and I wait for the story. "I sprayed female skunk pheromones on me," he says.

Our teacher looks perplexed and I can tell he wants to ask why, but doesn't want to humiliate the kid anymore.

"I got chased by a bear last weekend, OK?" the kid says, obviously sensing the overwhelming curiosity penetrating the room. "My father is a biologist, so he sprayed me with female skunk pheromones to deter the bear."

At this, the classroom breaks into another round of hysterics. I try to contain it—I honestly feel bad for this kid—but I can't help it either. The laughter pours from my core.

"And it obviously worked," my teacher says to the sulking student, "as you're alive and well with us today." He now turns to the rest of the class. "See, my humble students? It *is* possible to protect ourselves in a natural and environmentally friendly way. This is one of the great and many blessings of Apollo: *utility*."

The professor now launches into introduction. His name is Alister Wiggins. He holds a Juris Doctor from the University of Apollo, with undergraduate degrees in Philosophy and Political Science. He's worked as an advisor for some of Apollo's most esteemed senators during their election campaigns.

"Who here knows what utilitarianism is?" he asks, after thoroughly solidifying his intellectual significance into our brains.

We are all quiet. I've heard the term before, but was never quite sure how to define it. After several moments of silence, my professor continues.

"As defined by the dictionary, utilitarianism is 'the belief that a morally good action is one that helps the greatest number of people.' Can anyone provide an example of such an action?"

I'm surprised that he's initiating a lesson so soon, on the first day of school, but I enjoy his lively character. From the far right, a hand springs up, and Professor Wiggins calls on a girl.

"The Emancipation Proclamation," she says.

And another hand shoots up, accompanied by another idea: "Our universal healthcare system."

And another: "Taxes."

"Well," my professor cuts in, "I think one can debate the moral aptitude of paying taxes."

Once again, the class breaks into laughter, and my teacher waits for the giggles to calm before continuing.

"I find it intriguing that the examples you mention all stem from government," he says. "Utilitarianism has often been tied to democracy—such as we have here in

Apollo—although the two philosophies are not one and the same. Utilitarianism's success is determined by what *maximizes* utility. In order to do this, we need to determine what motivates us, as human beings, to contribute to society. Anyone want to take a guess at that ultimate motivation?"

This time, I have no doubt about the answer and raise my hand. When the professor points to me, I answer in one word:

"Happiness."

The professor's face breaks into a gratified grin. "Very good," he says, "*very good*. J. S. Mill, who was a famous British philosopher in the nineteenth century, called it desire. He said, 'The only proof of desirability, is desire.' If we are happy, we will make the best and most productive citizens. Therefore, whatever generates the most happiness for the most people, creates the most utility for a society."

"That sounds like the way Apollo works," another voice calls from the back of the room. Unable to identify the source of the voice, Professor Wiggins addresses the comment broadly.

"Yes indeed," he says. "Many of our laws in Apollo are based upon the utilitarian philosophy. We might be the leaders of truth and knowledge, but we cannot be the leaders of light without the *freedom* to pursue happiness."

Interesting concept, I think, but I also begin wondering: if utilitarianism caters to the needs and wants of the majority, then who will speak for the desires of the minority, for those whom society looks upon as outcasts?

I suppose that's something I have yet to learn. After all, we're only thirty minutes into the first class of the first semester.

The News

ANDREW

I'm sitting in the university's library, speaking into A-Search and researching this utilitarian J. S. Mill character for an assignment, when I feel a slight tap on my right shoulder.

When I turn around and peer up, my gaze connects with almond-shaped blue eyes, and the combination of familiarity and surprise knocks me off balance from my chair.

"You shouldn't trust technology so much," Flora says, looking over my shoulder into my A-Search results. "What are you studying, utilitarianism?"

I can barely find my voice, but when I do, I tell her it's for my Ethics and Philosophy in Government course. She doesn't look lifeless anymore; her eyes once again hold the faintest of sparks. God, she's beautiful, and the sudden urge to touch her overwhelms the nerves in my hands.

I want to ask how she's been, why hasn't she called, but I remind myself how she'd brushed me aside so easily only weeks ago, and that sense of caution returns.

"I know you're probably still mad at me," she continues, reading my mind, "and I'm so sorry I can't explain why things turned out so odd. I'm sorry I hurt you."

She pauses for a moment, and I want to accept her apology, but something stops me from speaking.

"I—uhh," she stutters, now shuffling her weight from one foot to the other. "I don't know how to say this, so I'll just say it. I'm sick, Andrew."

The words don't make sense at first. *Sick? What does she mean, sick?* It takes a moment for her message to register.

"What's wrong?" I ask. "You look better than when I last saw you. How can you be sick?"

"I started eating again since your visit to my house," she tells me. "But recently, I started having stomach pains and eating became harder, so I went to the doctor. And, well, the doctors, they say I have stomach cancer."

At this, the library drops away from under my feet. The chair, the computers, the books, the lively chatter surrounding me, every part vanishes, and all that remains is her and me, floating in some purgatory dimension, the only noise the echo of her confession. *Flora has stomach cancer?*

"Are – are they sure?" I ask.

Flora lowers her head, and I think she's trying not to cry. "Yes," she says, but I can barely hear her voice. "I have maybe a year."

The news strikes me like a storm, and it takes a moment to reorient myself. "What do you mean, you have *'maybe a year'*?"

"The doctors can't treat it," Flora tells me, avoiding eye contact. "With stomach cancer, I guess you don't feel symptoms in the earliest stages, which explains why I was eating OK for a while. But now that I started feeling the pain, it's too late."

I want to leap to my feet and embrace her until she melts into me, tell her I'm sorry I was such a dick earlier, beg for her forgiveness. But all I do—all I *can* do—is just sit here, mute and in denial, and stare at the ground.

"I dropped all my classes," Flora says, after a few minutes of silence. "I came here hoping to find you today. To tell you."

The earth's gravity grows stronger around me, pulling every muscle lower and lower until smiling is virtually impossible. "I don't understand," I tell her.

"Trust me, neither do I."

"I don't want to lose you." The words slip from my mouth through trembling lips, and Flora falls to her knees, collapsing into my shoulder.

"I don't want to leave," she says, her voice broken and muffled against my chest, her tears penetrating the cotton material of my T-shirt. "I'm so scared, Andrew. It's all my fault."

All her fault? I can't grasp how stomach cancer could possibly be her fault, but right now, I can't think. I can't make sense of this whole, crazy thing. Within two months, my life has turned upside down. Everything that was real is now false, and every awful illusion has morphed into a reality. So I hold Flora as she cries against my shoulder, trying to push back my own tears, and coming to the realization that within the next year, yet another person for whom I care so deeply will leave me, forever.

Death Sentence

FLORA

I've heard many stories of what people say, what they do, when they learn they're going to die.

When I found out, it was raining outside, swollen drops splashing against the window between the bed and the trees. I was at the Apollo Hospital for my yearly check-up, and that's all I heard: the pounding.

I kept thinking it can't be true, that I'm only nineteen years old and nineteen is too young. And then I thought of my parents, who I had yet to tell. They'd be left without a child, and I wondered what their faces would look like crying over my casket.

My casket.

That's when the nausea hit like a tornado; it wanted to suck me dry. The nurse caught me as I fell forward and heaved, her partner grabbing a nearby bucket as the vomit erupted onto the tiled floor beneath me.

As I purged, I saw Andrew's face behind my closed eyes. I'm not stupid; I know he could sweet talk any girl into bed, but he's told me many times that none of them... not one... could connect with and understand him like me. The thought of never seeing him again breaks my heart.

It's been about a week since the doctors delivered the news, and as devastated as I feel about my imminent doom, I also find it ironic: death makes me feel more alive. I've begun to realize how precious every moment is—the smile on my dad's face, the caress of warm water on my cheeks in the shower, the tickle of Ernest's tongue on my leg, the scent of sweet potato casserole baking in the oven.

Suddenly, everything is profound. Everything has a second meaning. If I could just hold onto this treasured moment a minute longer, maybe I'll never need to let go. And if I never need to let go, that means I'm immortal. And I *need* to feel immortal, because deep down, I'm actually terrified—terrified of not existing, of the blackness that'll consume me. I can't fathom not waking up the next morning, not experiencing another day. How is it possible that everything just goes... blank?

When I first broke the news to my parents, my mother fainted. My dad cried for maybe the fifth time in his life, and they weren't hysterical or desperate tears, but rather silent and reserved. Those types of tears are the worst, because they force you to feel guilty for dying, as if it's your choice. Nevertheless, you can't help feeling responsible for forcing your loved ones through something they don't deserve.

After telling my parents, the self-pity hit. I sat there and wondered, *what the heck did I do to deserve this?* And when I asked myself that question, the answer that slipped into my mind frightened me, like something inside KNEW:

You questioned the Wall. You questioned them.

Of course, I never vocalized it. But now, after telling Andrew about my fate and watching the life drain from his eyes once he realized I wasn't kidding, I can't deny it anymore.

I can't prove anything; it's intuition, that sixth sense which alerts mothers when their child is upset, or warns hikers of a nearby bear. It seems to make sense of the insensible, and this is what it's been telling me:

Your family doesn't have any history of stomach cancer, Flora. You have no risk factors.

Stomach cancer takes time to cultivate, and I know at my last checkup, I didn't have it. In early stages, I wouldn't have felt symptoms, and that's the excuse the doctors gave me: *You've probably been developing it over the past year, Flora, and didn't even know it.*

That nagging voice inside my head tells me not to listen, however, and reminds me that this thing is moving *fast*, much faster than normal. I'm already starting to feel fatigued.

I'd asked the doctors about chemo. They said there was no hope. I'd asked them how that is possible. Shouldn't we at least try? They said the cancer moved too quickly. They'd rather I live as much quality life as possible in the coming weeks, before the symptoms start hitting hard.

The coming weeks.

Sometimes I find myself panicked, and other times, life just goes on as it always has. I've concluded I experience these ups-and-downs because I'm in disbelief. Shock. It doesn't feel *real*—that I've been condemned.

The little voice inside my head sometimes whispers a name when I least expect it. *Joe,* it warns, and I know the voice is reminding me of the man who befriended Andrew's father, the man who died from a mysterious brain tumor. Somehow, his death is the missing piece to my puzzle. *What did he do,* I wonder, *and what did he know?*

Andrew begged to accompany me home for the night, but I told him no, and my heart sank as I watched his eyes lower to the ground like a lost puppy who'd been turned away by the kid he followed home. But I refuse to drag Andrew into this, to endanger his life, and he detests me for it.

I wish I could make him understand. I'm desperate to tell another soul. I fall asleep every night, reaching into the darkness, wishing to jump back into time and... and...

It's all your fault, Flora.

Now I'm lying in that darkness again, alone. My mom baked me a sweet potato casserole tonight, and despite feeling too sick at the thought of death to eat, I forced the food down my esophagus, because I know only so much time remains before I can no longer enjoy my favorite dishes.

My door creaks open and a sliver of light from the hallway pierces the blackness. I watch as the silhouette of my favorite golden retriever sneaks into my cave, and hops onto my bed with the grace of a ghost. Ernest never used to sleep with me at night, but I guess he knows his days with me are numbered, too.

***

I can't really say when the curiosity begins again, as the next days are a blur, but when the thought enters my brain, I find myself wandering to the Apollo Library. Perhaps it's the notion that I'm going to die—nothing can stop it—so I cease to care about anything else. Death has a way of killing the bullshit.

When I enter the library, I glance at the central statue of Apollo holding his torch of light into the sky, and I realize I've never asked A-Search about the Wall. I suddenly find myself frantic to know, coming to the conclusion I don't want to die without learning the truth.

I find an open computer and sit down; the bright blue light is blinking at me, waiting for me to talk. When I remain silent, it begins its famous, first question: "Hello, welcome to Apollo Library. What is your name?"

I pause for a moment, debating whether to say my name, fearing what *they* might do, but I grow angry. I'm tired of being tossed around like a used rag, of being the victim. *Throw it in Agent Jackson's face.*

"Flora," I say to the machine, my voice defiant.

"Hello, Flora. What can I do for you today?"

"I want to know everything about the history of the Wall."

"Most certainly. Please hold for a moment." The computer pauses, and I'm expecting it to draw a few links from the Internet, but instead, it begins talking.

"The Wall was first established in the year 2075, the year Apollo was founded," the computer tells me in its monotone, unisex voice. "Receiving an overwhelming ninety percent vote to build, it took workers two full years to complete it in the year 2077. At first, the Wall was often called The Great Protector, as its sole purpose was to shelter the citizens of Apollo from the evils of the outside world. It wasn't until the year 2080 that the first laws were created and executed to ban discussion of—and visitation to—the Wall. Lawmakers cited the need to preserve Apollo's moral value system. However, Senator Brookstein wrote an amendment to these new laws a year later, in 2081, citing interference in education, and thus allowing discussion of and research on the Wall to be conducted within the confines of a classroom."

After this explanation, the computerized voice stops. *Just stops.* I sit and wait for it to begin again, but nothing happens.

"A-Search, is that all the information you have on the history of the Wall?" I ask.

"Yes," the computer answers.

Frustrated and a little perplexed, I try another question. "Why was Apollo founded?"

Once again, the computer begins scanning its databases, talking in short, chunky sentences. "Apollo was founded to protect its citizens from the outside world. Apollo was to be the new leader of light, truth, and knowledge."

"Yes, but *why* do the citizens of Apollo need to be protected from the outside world?"

"Because the outside world is evil."

"But *why* is it evil?"

"Shhhh!" The annoyed voice comes from an older woman sitting nearby, and it startles me from my interrogation. "Keep it down over there, miss."

I look over my shoulder and apologize, just now realizing how loud my voice had been escalating. When I turn back to the computer, I see that it didn't answer my question. So I ask again, and still, the computer remains quiet.

"What's wrong with this thing?" I mutter, tapping it with my hand. However, the infamous blinking blue light of A-Search won't return, so I push to my feet and march to the librarian.

"Excuse me," I say, distracting her from a massive book organization she's undertaking. The librarian turns around, obviously annoyed, sighs and adjusts her glasses.

"May I help you?" she asks.

"Yes, that computer over there," I stop and point to the machine I'd just been using, "it's not working. The A-Search stopped operating."

She nods, dismissive. "We'll get someone to fix it; thank you for letting us know." She turns around and ignores me.

This place isn't going to offer me any help, I realize, so I leave.

Losing It

FLORA

As I'm riding my bike back home from the library, a wave of cramps slams through my stomach, like I'd eaten a bad piece of cheese. The seizing pain forces me to stop pedaling and wait for the cramps to pass.

I lean over the handles, holding my gut as I try to breathe my way through the moment. A couple of cars whiz past—I'm not too far from Apollo's Central Commerce Hub—and a looming billboard offers some shade. When I glance up, I see four words glaring down at me: LIGHT, TRUTH, AND KNOWLEDGE.

I want to spit on them.

Hunched over and hoping the cramps are almost done, I hear the gentle crackle of bicycle tires approach from behind me. Still holding my stomach, I turn to look over my shoulder, just in time to see another girl about my age staring at me. Her eyes look wild, like she'd just outrun a bear, and her dark hair is disheveled.

"Are you Flora?" she asks.

Unsure what this girl wants, I remain evasive. "Who's asking?"

When she offers no name, I tell her that yes, my name is Flora, and ask what can I do for her. At the confirmation of my name, the girl swings a leg off her bike, marches up to my huddled body, whisks back her hand, and slams it across my face. The sting is so strong, combined with the agony rattling my stomach, that I flop to the ground. Stunned, I hold myself against the concrete, before tasting blood from my upper lip.

"Who do you think you are, going around brainwashing the guys around here?" she says, her voice quivering. "It's always good girls like me that end up screwed, because of sluts like you."

I'm still on all fours, my knees digging into the hard ground. Slowly, I pull myself to a standing position and stare into her face. Tears are streaming down her cheeks, her mascara washing away with them.

"I don't know who you are, or what you're talking about," I say, defeated, "so just do me a favor and leave me alone."

"How do you do it?"

The nagging, the demands, the assumptions: they're all starting to swirl over my head in a funnel... pestering... badgering...

"Do *what*?" I ask.

"Make a man yell your name when he's in bed with someone else?!"

I glare at her and raise my voice this time, the frustration overwhelming any sense of sanity or fear of repercussions. "What are you talking about?"

The girl stops her accusations abruptly; I think she finally realizes that I'm clueless.

"Andrew," she says. "He yelled your name. Do you have any idea what it feels like to dream of caring for someone, of being the person he craves at night? And when your dreams are finally coming true, when you finally think he wants you, he calls out *another girl's name?*"

The realization whacks me like a rock to the head, and everything finally makes sense. I let out a long sigh, reach up, and touch the cut on my upper lip, flinching from the prick and warm blood that trickles onto my finger.

"Andrew did that?" I ask.

"What did you do to him?" The girl's voice has changed, no longer angry, but pleading. "I want to know your secret. Please. He's addicted to you."

I stare at the girl for another moment, my mouth bleeding, but shake my head before turning around to my bike and climbing aboard. I hear the girl calling after me, begging me to tell her.

Yet I keep pedaling. I just want to get home.

***

When I walk through the front door—cramps finally gone but sweat forming a "V" down my back—I hear hushed voices chattering in the other room. I'm out of breath and feeling discouraged, because usually, a simple bike ride to the library generates *more* energy for me.

I swing my leg off my bike and walk it into the house, leaning it against the wall near the door. As usual, Ernest trots up to greet me, his dopey tongue hanging from his mouth. I scratch his head and immediately begin heading toward my room. I just want to sleep, and forget.

"Flora!" my dad calls from around the corner. "Would you come in here for a moment?"

Normally I'd answer that I need some rest, but ever since The News, I can't find the strength to say "no" to my parents about anything. So I drag my feet through the hallway, following the voices, until I reach the kitchen.

My dad is standing and pacing from one end of the room to the other, waiting for me to arrive, and behind him are two people sitting at the kitchen table. One is my mother, and the other is...

"Agent Jackson?" I ask, my heart jumping into my throat.

"Yes," my dad answers. "We called him, sweetie. We thought maybe he could help." My dad pauses when he sees my face and kneels down, pulling me closer.

"What happened to your mouth?"

I dismiss it as nothing, telling him I fell off my bike when some stomach cramps hit. My mom stands and joins us now, rubbing my arm. I think she suspects another incident from a group of girls, but she pretends to believe me. Her face screams of sleep deprivation as she explains why Agent Jackson is visiting our house.

"He was such a gentleman at the station, handling everything so well," she says. "We just thought that perhaps he could sway the doctors at the hospital to try some treatments."

I stare at my parents. What else can I do? I'm sure I must look both spooked and hypnotized, and slowly, I turn my aimless gaze toward the stout, bald man sitting at *my* kitchen table, in *my* house. Like the cancer invading *my* body.

"Hello Flora," Agent Jackson says. "How are you feeling? Your parents tell me you developed stomach cancer?"

His voice drips with phony concern, and I swear I see the corner of his mouth curve up, into a smirk. *Bastard.*

I'm feeling smothered by his stench. It's crawling everywhere: under my shirt, into my ears, under my armpits, into my mouth. And there's nothing, absolutely nothing, I can do to stop it.

"Flora, Agent Jackson just asked you a question," my mother says.

I cross my arms and narrow my eyes at him. "I'm feeling *fine*," I tell him. "So, any luck with the doctors?"

That smirk grows even wider now. "Well, I was just telling your parents that I'd be more than happy to see what I can do. Of course, there's no guarantee. I'm sure the doctors are only doing what they believe is best for you."

"Maybe I *want* chemo," I say, and realize my teeth are gritted. "Maybe I'd rather *die* trying to *live*, than not live at all."

Did I just talk back to Agent Jackson? My words came out as chainsaws, ripping through those preaching billboards, those fake messages that everyone knows are false, but are too damned happy in their pitiful lives to admit it.

"Flora," my dad cuts in, "Sweetie, take it easy. Agent Jackson is just trying to help. He drove all the way here from ABI Headquarters after his day ended to talk with us about your situation. Look, why don't you go rest? I'm sure you're tired."

Agent Jackson smiles openly at me now. My parents think it's a sympathetic gesture, but I know better. "That's probably a good idea," he says. "Your dad has a point. You're going to need your rest, as much as you can get."

"Would you like to stay for dinner?" my mom asks Agent Jackson.

"No!" I catch myself in my immediate reaction, realizing I appear too alarmed. "I mean, Mom, I'm just tired and want some peace tonight, if that's OK?"

"She's right," Agent Jackson says. "Let her get her rest. I'll be on my way and see what progress I can make with the doctors."

I stand still as my parents walk up and shake this man's hand, *thanking him,* like he's a god who brought me back from the dead. Like they owe their freakin' *lives* to him. I'm trembling as I watch Agent Jackson leave my house.

The Phone Call

FLORA

The number reads "555-859-2111." It's scribbled in black ink, buried inside a folded, crinkled piece of paper.

If you ever find yourself caught in a trap, call this number. It's safe.

Don's words ripple through my mind as I stare at the line of digits on the paper I just pulled from my jeans pocket, wondering if I can trust it, if I can trust *him*. How much do I really know about Don? Would he try to hurt me, to trap me in some way? No, I'm being ridiculous; he's only a nineteen-year-old kid, like me.

But if I'm going to call, I'd better do it from a public payphone, and I'd better do it during the day when other people would use it. Calling too late at night, or too early in the morning, might seem odd.

Yes, I'll call tomorrow morning, about ten o'clock. I'll call and see what happens. I'll see who answers.

***

The payphone seems to tower over, mocking me. It's painted a faded maroon and plastered against an ancient gas station that's been abandoned for fifty years in Old Apollo, a few miles north of the train tracks. I chose it on purpose.

It's deserted.

I'm jiggling two coins in my right hand, the metal solid and cool against my skin. Anxiety distracts me from the crisp air, which bites my cheeks, and I hop from one foot to the other, feeling like a twitching cat covered in fleas. Taking a deep breath, I tell myself to grow a pair and I step forward, slipping one coin, then the other, into the tiny slot above the phone's receiver. I pick up the handset, hold it to my ear, and begin dialing.

The phone goes silent for a moment before the ringing starts. And continues. Ringing. Ringing. Ringing.

I swallow and contemplate hanging up—maybe this isn't such a good idea. *Ringing.* Yes, this is stupid, stupid! But do I have another choice? *Ringing.* That's it: I start pulling the handset from my ear, preparing to return it to the booth, when I hear a voice. "Hello?"

It's a male voice, and I try to speak, but the words become knotted in my throat.

"Who's there?" the voice says, a little more demanding this time.

I force a harsh gulp and remind myself to breathe. "Yes hi," I say in one breath. "Is this Don?"

"Yes," he says, his voice eerily monotonous. "Hi, Flora."

The echo of my name from the other line astonishes me. *How does he know I'm the one calling?* Thoughts zip through my head, but I find myself speechless, and my silence provokes Don to continue talking.

"Where are you calling from?" he asks.

"A payphone."

"Good. No one followed you?"

"Why would someone follow me?" I'm losing patience and realize my voice is starting to pitch in tone. "Look, *you* gave *me* this number, so I'm calling. Just help me, OK?"

"Help you do what?"

"I don't know!" I swing my head from side to side, checking to make sure no one is nearby, and when I confirm it's clear, I continue speaking. "You gave me this number, remember? Well, I'm trapped. I'm freakin' trapped and I'm ready to lose my mind. Just help me, *please.*"

I'm hoping Don may finally offer respite from this shithole situation I've been cornered into. No one—not one person—has been able to offer me any true relief. Perhaps the faith I've placed in Don is a fallacy, but I have to believe that he knows something I do not.

"I heard you're sick," he says, after a moment of silence.

"I am, but I don't want to talk about it."

Don shuffles around on the phone, and I hear clinking noises in the background. He breathes long and hard, as if he's made some arduous decision.

"Do you know where I live?" he asks.

I tell him no, I have no clue, so he gives me directions and instructs me to wait until after dark, then drive my car without headlights to his place around ten o'clock tomorrow night. "And bring a backpack with a survival kit," he says.

"Why will I need a survival kit?"

There's a long pause on the other line, and I hear Don breathe into the phone again. "I'm going to help you get answers, and that means getting out," he says. "Isn't that what you want?"

***

Don told me on the phone that leaving Apollo is the only way to learn what the Wall is hiding, the only way to satisfy my burning curiosity. *"It's not something I can tell you,"* he said. *"You have to see it for yourself."*

I'll be gone a week, but I'll need to give my parents an excuse for my absence. When I asked him why a week—why the need for lies—Don told me if I turn up missing, it would alert the authorities that something suspicious is afoot, and they'll question my family. The less they know the better. I'd asked him how we will get beyond the Wall, but he wouldn't tell me over the phone.

"I have my ways," is all he said.

Now, I have mere hours left before my nighttime trip to Don's house. Earlier today, I decided to tell my parents I want to take a final camping trip with Andrew at the Grand Canyon, while I still can. They'd both cried and my heart fell through my feet.

Then there's Andrew. I close my eyes and see that beautifully evocative look from two months ago, when we first stumbled upon the Wall together in the forest during our morning bike ride. I can hear his comforting voice, feel his fingers entwined with mine. Now everything is different. Convoluted.

Nonetheless, I have to protect him, so I'll give Andrew the same excuse I gave my parents, except I'll tell him we're traveling as a family to the Grand Canyon. I'm not ready to call him yet, not prepared to make everything so final. Instead, I delve into my closet and dig through the boxes I've stashed away, until I find it. *Our map.*

After my diagnosis, I buried the map among piles of junk, unable to bear the reminder of all the places I'll never discover with Andrew. Now, I trace the red lines and circles and Xs we marked together—navigating every cave, every building, every swimming hole, and every gulch.

A life and a friendship that I love so deeply, destined to fade into mist. I have to start letting him go.

I walk into the office and sit down at the computer, beginning to type Andrew's name and address onto a mailing label. I leave the return address blank, print the label, and press it onto an envelope. Now, I take a pen and turn to our map, pulling it close to kiss, and scribble a message at the very top:

What's knowledge without curiosity?

In a bittersweet moment, I fold the map with the care of a mother and place it into the envelope addressed to Andrew. Don is beginning to feel like the Angel of Death, coming to shepherd me away from the land of the living, away from my parents, from Ernest, and from Andrew.

I have only two stops remaining before I sneak to Don's place tonight: the sports store for a survival kit, and the post office.

Don's House

FLORA

I left my house around six o'clock, telling my parents I was staying the night at Andrew's place in preparation for an early start tomorrow. Lying to them made me feel worse than the slime stuck to the bottom of my shoe.

Afterwards, I drove into the middle of a deserted meadow that falls between the nearest two San Francisco Peaks, and there, I waited until after dark, munching on store-bought chips and brownies, slipping in and out of sleep, occasionally running into the forest because my stomach acted up.

Now, it's nearly ten o'clock, and I'm pulling into the dirt driveway of what looks like a deserted cabin in the middle of the forest, about seventy miles southeast of Apollo's Central Commerce Hub. Jagged broken glass windows litter the exterior of the place, and it smells of pine trees and mothballs.

It's too black outside for me to see much—I still have my car's headlights off—but I notice a soft, blue radiance glowing from inside the cabin. I climb from my car and close the door as quietly as possible, dragging my survival-kit-backpack behind me.

The air is growing crisp, and its cool edges sting my cheeks. The silence is deafening; I can hear nothing more than the gentle whistle of the breeze and the chirping of a few rogue crickets. My shoes crunch over twigs as I approach the door, and when I step onto the wooden deck, the floorboards creak underneath my soles. I find myself wondering if I've wandered onto the set of a horror movie.

As I lift my fist to knock on the crooked door, it scrapes open, and a single eye outlined in black makeup peers through the crack.

"I'm ready," I say, and the door slides open a little more. Don reaches out and grabs my elbow, yanking me into his lair.

The interior isn't much better than the outside. My eyes scan a few empty beer bottles, half-drunk glasses of water, dirty plates with food still crusted on top. A warm blaze is beckoning me from a cozy fireplace, and across the living room, there are rows and rows of computers and electronics, their screens flat with running numbers scrolling from device to device. Other machines are mere motherboards, connected to various contraptions that display blinking lights of assorted colors. There are routers and printers and modems.

Then, there are the maps, pinned all over the walls with circles and strings and pushpins and scribbles marking times and dates and places, as if from a lunatic's mind. Their haphazard arrangement draws my attention to a fridge, and the pitiful twin-sized mattress lying on the floor nearby.

Only now does it occur to me that this place is where Don lives—not some hideout, or a summer cabin, but his *day-to-day home*. No family, no garden out back, no pets. And I suddenly become sad. What kind of life is this?

"I, uh, apologize for the unkempt appearance of my place," he says, obviously observing the startled look on my face. As always, his eyes refuse to meet mine, instead fixating on the bruised, wooden floor beneath my feet.

"Where did you get all this stuff?" I ask, forgetting about my own predicament for the moment.

"Places."

I don't push for more details, but I start wandering around his home, in complete awe of the personal headquarters he's developed. One thing is noticeably absent, however: books.

"I thought you liked to read," I say, turning back to Don.

"What gave you that idea?"

"You're the one who let me borrow *1984*, remember? So, where are all your books?"

His eyes shoot over to a computer screen, but he says nothing. Instead, he walks toward and plops down next to the fire. "Come and get warm," he tells me. "And sleep. We leave before dawn tomorrow morning."

"I thought we were leaving tonight."

Don shakes his head and points to one of the maps tacked to his wall. "No, the cameras are still on tonight."

I drop my backpack on the floor and join Don next to the fire. The warmth feels good against my face and I let it blanket my hands. Relaxing me. Reassuring me. Allowing me just a moment to taste a sense of normalcy again, before asking my next question:

"Did you say there are cameras on the Wall?"

Don nods his head, but keeps staring at the fire. "Yes, on the outside. Different sections are shut down at different times, for maintenance. We can't have any physical evidence that you left, so we'll wait."

"But, won't the maintenance workers see me?"

"No," Don says, his voice still monotone. "They don't go on The Other Side—no one does. The cameras only shut down for thirty minutes, so we will need to move quickly."

I find myself lost in wonderment by all his knowledge. Don remains calm as he tells me everything, like he's talking about his breakfast or a movie he recently saw. I ask him how he knows so much.

"Just sleep," he tells me. "I'm going to bed now."

The Tunnel

FLORA

I don't sleep; I can't. Instead, I spend the night tossing and turning, my stomach twisting and rumbling, reminding me that my internal clock is ticking. Faster and faster.

I'm resting on a pile of blankets Don let me borrow, but I find myself craving my bed, craving Ernest and his warm fur snuggled next to my feet, wishing Andrew could stay the night and sleep on the pillow next to me. I think of my parents, of my dad's piano notes and my mom's famous sweet potato casserole cooking in the oven.

I begin wondering if leaving is the best idea—if maybe, I'd rather curl under my own covers with the ones I love most, and drift away forever. But that crazy, nagging curiosity returns: *I don't want to leave this earth without knowing. They may take my life, but they can't take this.*

For the bulk of the endless night, I float in-and-out of REM sleep, and just as I feel myself beginning to finally drift, a hand shakes my torso.

"Wake up," Don whispers. "It's time to go."

When I come to full consciousness, the sterile beeping from his processors carries me back to reality, and I rub my eyes while pushing myself to a sitting position. The fire has died, leaving the smell of ash and burnt bark behind. The only light that now remains is the soft, bluish glow of Don's computer screens.

"We leave in fifteen minutes," he tells me. "It's almost four-thirty in the morning."

I force myself up, the world spinning around my head, and walk to his bathroom. I figure this might be the last time I'm near a toilet for a while, so I'd better take advantage. Afterward, I strap on my backpack with its survival kit intact.

When we walk outside, I approach Don's car, but he shakes his head, instead motioning to a set of mountain bikes. "We ride," he says.

"But, it's so dark."

Without saying a word, Don tosses me a headlamp to strap onto my forehead. I stare at him as he secures his and begins illuminating the path in front of him. I follow suit.

The forest is black, except for the few yards of artificial light before me. I try to concentrate on Don's wheels, following them and hoping to avoid slamming into trees or slipping off cliffs. I had a few sips of water before I started, but I'm already beginning to break a slight sweat.

My bike's tires crack over twigs and branches, and I can hear my own breath panting in the early morning silence. The air is moist and cold, and my nose is beginning to run. *So different from my Saturday morning rides with Andrew*, I think.

Every five minutes or so, I ask Don to stop so I can catch my breath. I tell him I'm not usually like this, it must be the cancer. He's always quiet when I say this, but he's also patient, and we continue in silence.

I don't know if it's been an hour or two, but after a long time, Don stops his bike. "We're here," he tells me.

Semi-exhausted, I swing my leg off the bicycle—my muscles are shaking—and begin looking around. By now, my eyes have adjusted to the darkness, so I'm not sure if it's my sight, or if Don's crazy. But I don't see the Wall anywhere.

"Under there," Don says, pointing toward the undergrowth-littered ground a few meters away from my feet. "Careful."

I squat down and inch closer to the area where his hand is pointing. And now I see it: a hole or tunnel underneath a fallen tree.

"In there?" I ask.

"Your way out."

"A hole?" A wave of nervousness spreads like a spider web, tingling into my fingers and toes.

Don walks closer to me and places his hands on my shoulders, pressing down. "Sit," he says before plopping next to me. "Before you leave, we have some things to discuss."

***

Don lays it out for me, the entire plan, and only now do I begin realizing this is really it. I'm about to commit perhaps the greatest and most dangerous crime in Apollo. If they catch me, they could legally kill me.

"I built this tunnel," Don tells me. "You'll have to crawl under the Wall and come out on The Other Side. It'll take you about thirty minutes."

"You *built* this?" I ask, in disbelief. "Have you actually been to The Other Side?"

But Don ignores me, waiting to see if I understood his directions. I know time must be of the essence, so I drop the question, and nod in understanding. When he sees that I comprehend, he keeps talking.

"When you come out of the tunnel, you'll have exactly thirty minutes to get as far away from the Wall as possible. The cameras and motion sensors turn off at six-thirty, then come back on at seven o'clock. If you're too late, they'll catch you."

There are motion sensors, too?

Don stops talking for a moment, pulls a watch from his pocket, and hands it to me. "Keep this on your wrist, and *do not* leave the tunnel before six-thirty, understand?"

I tell him yes, I get it, and he continues. "Good. Because if you so much as slide a finger outside the tunnel too early, the cameras and motion sensors will catch it. They'll *see you*, and you don't want that.

"Now, moving on... about five miles southwest of here is the next touch point with scheduled maintenance. The site is marked on The Other Side with three Aspen branches formed in the shape of a triangle, surrounded by several river rocks. Meet me there exactly a week from today at five-thirty in the evening. That's your only window back into Apollo, undetected."

Everything is swirling in my head: times and dates and windows of opportunity. Confused, I stop Don and tell him to slow down, to let me absorb it. He pauses for a moment and gets impatient. "We don't have much time," he says. "So listen carefully, OK?"

I apologize and he sighs in frustration, pulling something else from his pocket and placing it into my palm: a piece of paper.

"Don't lose this," he tells me. "It's your transport ticket. When you make it to The Other Side, you'll keep heading straight south, through the forest. It's about a day's hike or so, maybe two, but then you'll hit a road. If you walk further south on the road, you'll come to a transport station. Wait there, and you can catch the transport."

"To where?" I ask.

"To the city."

City? For the first time, the magnitude of the unknown sweeps over me, and I come to understand just how vulnerable, how small, I truly am against this... this... *new world*. I've wondered for half my life what's on The Other Side, what the Wall is hiding. But not until this moment have I considered that, whatever it is, was dark enough to prompt a group of people to segment themselves away from everything and everyone. Or, perhaps, was it the other way around?

"Don," I say, stopping him for a moment. "The Other Side, is it safe?"

But Don just looks at me, pointing to the piece of paper in my hand. "That ticket is a round trip," he says. "If you lose it, you won't be able to get back, understand?"

I nod my head, but still press. "Is it safe?"

Don sighs. "If you follow my directions, you'll be fine."

I don't like his answer, and for a brief moment, I reconsider taking this trip. But I quickly push away the doubt, reminding myself this is my only shot. "If I do lose the ticket, I could just buy a new one, right?"

"No, you can't. Our money is no good on The Other Side."

Troubled at yet another revelation, I demand to know how I am supposed to eat. Where will I sleep? Don doesn't appear concerned, though. Emotionless, he reaches into his pocket once more, and hands me another piece of paper.

"Go to this address," he says. "Tell them I sent you. There, you'll find everything you need."

"Who are these people?" I ask, growing nervous. "How do I know I can trust them?"

Don places his palm over my fisted knuckles, and I realize this is a gesture of reassurance. "They're good people," he says. "You packed food for the trip, right?"

I'm annoyed that he's being so evasive, but I nod anyway, telling him about my bread, canned salmon, and granola bars. He's about to start explaining something else, but the anxiety of the unknown is welling inside of me, mixing with the cancer invading my body... building, building... and suddenly, I heave over.

Don jumps out of the way just as I throw up. Disgusted, I lift my head and glance at him, only to realize he's scared.

"What's wrong?" I ask, but when I follow his stare back toward the ground, I realize I'd just vomited blood. *The cancer*, I think. *It's progressing.*

"I think you'd better get moving," he says. "We're running out of time."

Don ushers me toward the hole and I unhook my backpack, dropping it into the blackness under the fallen tree. My stomach is still tight but at least starting to settle. I take a deep breath, my heart pumping through my hands and into my feet, and I glance up at Don.

"Oh well," I say, my arms trembling as they grip the tree trunk over the hole. "What's knowledge without curiosity, right?" And I let myself drop into darkness.

Part Two
The Other Side

The Scent of Freedom

FLORA

I have never been one to believe in God. In fact, most people in Apollo aren't religious; it's considered a thing of the past, an idea that some families may choose to still follow, but otherwise, an unnecessary aspect of our lives within the Wall.

However, as I'm dragging myself through the claustrophobic tunnel—elbows scraping against small pebbles that feel like needles against my skin—I find myself praying. Well, perhaps praying isn't the right term, more like talking. Asking. Maybe even bargaining.

I know I'm going to die, but please don't let it happen Out There.

I'll never challenge the ABI again. Just make this sacrifice worth the risk.

Please don't let my parents or Andrew find out. Keep them from talking to each other?

Whatever happens, I beg you: don't let my stomach act up in this tunnel.

I also find myself racking my brain to understand the message Don yelled, after I began crawling through the darkness. He'd called something to me after I left, but I was too far down the hole to decipher anything besides muffled noise. *I'm sure it wasn't important*, I think. *Probably just an afterthought.*

The tunnel seems endless, and I'm thankful I was never one of those crazy, claustrophobic people who turn into an ax murderer when trapped in a small room for more than five minutes. The tunnel is too narrow for me to wear my backpack, so I push it in front of me, thrusting forward with my body, constantly squirming, pushing my legs and knees and arms to move.

Still wearing my headlamp, I glance down at the watch on my wrist: six-twenty. *You'd better hurry, Flora.* I have no clue how close I am to the end, but I don't see an exit ahead. I continue slithering through this damp pathway, the air heavy and the smell of mildew and wet dirt filling my lungs so deeply, I'm beginning to taste rotten mud.

I wonder if the Wall is over me yet, if after all its might and supremacy and dominance, it still failed to keep one curious, nineteen-year-old girl trapped.

It takes another fifteen minutes before I finally see it: the orange glow that I know is the end, the breaking light of dawn peeking through my constrictive route to freedom. It's now after six-thirty, and my window to escape is quickly closing. So I throw myself forward with every ounce of strength I possess, skinning my elbows against the dirt until they bleed. The ground feels like sandpaper, but I revel in the sting.

When the opening reveals itself, I'm forced to arch my back as the tunnel elevates to a vertical angle. I push my backpack up to the surface, and with weak arms, pull myself behind it. The moment my face strikes fresh air, I feel a strong breeze against my skin.

Absorbing the moment, I close my eyes and breathe deeply, filling my lungs with the crisp, mountain air—the scent of freedom. When I open them, I stare straight ahead: all forest.

I strap my backpack onto my shoulders, continuing to grip the restraints as I turn around to look behind me. And there it stands, littered in cameras just as Don had promised, smirking.

The Wall.

"Looks like I won this time," I say. "Try to stop me now."

When I turn around to begin my trek forward, I notice the sky is glowing red from the sunrise, the same way it looks when the forest is ablaze. The wind whips tiny strands of hair against my face, and they feel like barbed wire. In my right hand, I'm gripping the transport ticket that Don gave me, like it's the key to life.

And that's when the realization hits, like a tsunami of déjà vu: *This is my dream, the one that's haunted me night after night.*

***

Even though I'm tired from the cycling and crawling, and the cancer has affected my stamina, I do my best to run through the Ponderosa pines before the cameras come back on. I alter between jogging and walking, sometimes pausing to catch my breath. My throat is burning from the cold air, and I find myself coughing from a constricted chest, but I fight forward. It's nearly seven o'clock, and I can't risk being caught within range of the Wall. I tell myself I'll stop for water and bread once I pass the time threshold. *Just a little longer. Just a little longer.*

The soles of my feet continue pounding the forest ground, and right as my exhaustion makes the world begin to spin before me, a loud, distant buzzing pierces the silence of the forest. I freeze mid-step and glance down at my watch. It's seven.

For a moment, I stand motionless, swallowing my heart and gripping my heaving chest. I take a small step. *No noise.* Another few steps. *I think I'm in the clear.*

When I turn around toward the Wall, I realize it's gone, completely hidden from sight. If I can't see it, then it can't see me. *I made it.* I can barely digest this monumental accomplishment, this incredible crime. I MADE IT. And now that I'm safe, I allow myself to collapse, falling to the ground. Frantic for water, I pull the pack off my back and fish out my canister, gulping down massive swells of water that burn like drifts of sand in my throat.

I spend some time resting and munching on bread, even though my stomach rolls with protest. "Shut up," I tell it, refusing to let it control me anymore. I must regain my strength to start the day's hike.

***

When I notice the sun starting to dwindle, and no road yet in sight, I begin to worry that perhaps I made a wrong turn somewhere. But Don's words replay in my head: *It's about a day's hike or so, maybe two.*

After all, I have been stopping consistently to munch on granola and sip water. I therefore decide to camp for the night. I find a nearby tree and drop down, whipping open my survival kit and pulling out a heavy-duty space blanket, followed by my sleeping bag. I clear a wide area around the tree and begin hunting for rocks to build a fire pit. I grab branches, dirt, whatever I can find. Even though my stomach is cramping again, I try to ignore the pain and keep working to set up a shelter for the night.

I lose track of the time but finally finish, sitting down on my blanket and wrapping myself like a burrito. I'd never realized how fast the cold grows in the forest at night. This type of chill slices one's cheeks, numbing the nose and toes, even when protected under two layers of socks and closed sneakers.

Loosening the blanket so I can continue prepping a fire, I toss some cotton balls I'd covered with petroleum jelly into the pit. I light a match, and BOOM. Heat.

Feeling begins returning to the tips of my fingers as I warm my hands by the fire and pull out a can of salmon. Halfway through eating it, my stomach jerks and I jet to a nearby tree. This sickness is progressing faster and faster, so I shove the thoughts plaguing my mind deep into some dark place where they won't surface until tomorrow. Or the next day. Or the day after that.

I fall asleep cocooned in my blanket and sleeping bag after smothering the smoldering flames with dirt.

The next morning's sunrise is like a razor to my corneas, piercing into the back of my head until I'm forced awake. Once again, I take a few sips of my remaining water, eat a few slices of bread, and rinse my mouth with mouthwash. I'm getting low on water. *Better move fast today, Flora.*

When I start trekking, a seed of fear again reveals itself—fear that I've wandered the wrong way and won't have enough food or water to survive in the wilderness. But about mid-morning, the Ponderosa pines begin to clear, and I see it.

The road.

Elated, I fly into a sprint toward the paved trail. Now I just need to head south on this thing until I reach the transport station. I'm almost there, and soon, I'll have the answers to my lifetime of questions.

The Transport

FLORA

The transport station is deserted and painted a drab steel gray—nothing but a metal bench and a sign which reads, "Transport Station." How creative. The thing doesn't even have an overhead awning to protect people from the sun.

While I was walking toward the station earlier, about a mile up the road, I'd come across a barrier in the middle of the street, a looming metal fence with a sign reading, "STOP. Government property beyond this point. DANGER. Enter at your own risk." The sign was facing south, thus halting traffic traveling north toward Apollo, which is another two days' hike from this point.

As a pedestrian, I was able to walk several yards off the road and detour around it. But no vehicle could pass it, and as I wandered off the street, I started asking myself: what's so dangerous about us—about Apollo?

The forest is gone completely now, not even visible over the horizon, and fields of chino grass blanket the hills with fur. I've been sitting on this bench maybe two hours, sipping the last remnants of my water and shielding my eyes from the daunting sun. Finally, in the distance, I see what looks like a speeding bus flying up the road. Like the station, it's also a boring gray, and I begin wondering if The Other Side even knows color.

As the transport nears, I'm expecting it to grow louder, but it doesn't. In fact, the thing is nearly as silent as a breeze. It glides to a swift stop in front of me at the station, whisking my hair back from my face. The doors drift open and, looking down, I step into the transport. It looks and feels exactly like a typical bus, exposing windows and all.

As I climb the two stairs inside, I glance up to greet the driver, only to find the front seat vacant. In fact, there is no front seat at all, not even a steering wheel. The entire transport is completely empty. Shocked, I open my mouth to call toward the back... maybe there's someone there?... when a monotone, computerized voice rumbles from over me.

"Your ticket," it says.

I jump backwards and almost fall out of the vehicle. "What?"

"Your ticket," the voice repeats, and it reminds me of A-Search. Not sure where to show the ticket, I merely raise it over my head. From the right corner behind me, a faint buzzing approaches and when I turn around, a flat computer screen the size of a wallet is protruding from the side of the transport. As I watch it linger in front of my ticket, I realize it's scanning the document.

"You may proceed," the voice instructs, and the screen retreats back in line with the wall. "Please take a seat and fasten your seatbelt. Destination: Phoenix. Estimated arrival time: three o'clock p.m."

Phoenix? If I recall correctly from the history books, Phoenix was the capital of the former state of Arizona, but I didn't think it existed anymore. Confused and shaken, I listen to the voice's instructions and glance down at my watch. It's currently two-fifteen.

Without warning, my head jerks against the back of my seat and the transport takes off, leaving my stomach a mile behind. I turn to look out the window, but the vehicle is racing down the road so fast that every tree and shrub and detail smears into a single brush stroke.

***

The transport travels down the deserted road, winding through mountains piled with basalt and igneous rocks, and vast desert mesas with bone-chilling drops. It stops a few times at various destinations: Montezuma's Castle, the old Verde Valley, the remains of the ancient Black Canyon City. Not once does anyone board the vehicle with me, and I must admit, I find myself disappointed. I was hoping to meet a citizen of The Other Side, to ask the questions that have been burning in my brain. To perhaps understand what it's like out here, how they think, how they *live*.

But my hopes are diminished, and as the transport promised, it arrives in Phoenix at exactly three o'clock. The A-Search voice instructs me to leave, and once I climb out of the vehicle, it disappears into a blur, like a mirage.

I'm left standing on a random concrete sidewalk, staring into the transport's trail, and only now does the heat slam into me, blasting against my face like an open oven. I've never felt heat this intense, choking me, suffocating in its thick grip. I snatch my pack from my shoulder and grab my water, but I have only sips left. I allow myself a few drops and wipe away the sweat forming over my eyebrows.

As I take in my surroundings, a small seed of dread begins to grow within my core. I'm surrounded by the tallest buildings I've ever seen, buildings towering so high they block the sun from reaching my face, buildings that surpass even the tallest of trees in the forest. But that's not what unnerves me.

It's *the silence.* And the stillness.

I thought I was supposed to be in a city. Yet here, the streets are vacant. I can hear the wind whistling between the buildings, I can smell the stench of sewers, but where is everyone? Where are the scores of tiny trilogies roaming the streets, licking ice-cream cones and laughing until tears stream down their faces? Where are the professional men and women dressed in suits and ties bustling between restaurants after work and sipping coffee? The buildings don't look deserted; in fact, I see a few lights illuminating empty rooms behind wide and open windows.

Yet, I could hear a pin drop out here.

Bewildered, even a little scared, I begin inching my way down the sidewalk, aimless as my eyes take in this unbelievable sight. The first few shops I pass are closed, their windows boarded and broken. I peer inside and see nothing but some floating napkins in the breeze and a few cockroaches creeping along the bruised floor.

I continue down the sidewalk, when I hear the distant motor of a car. A car! I turn around and watch as a singular vehicle approaches my location from down the road. *Finally, someone to ask,* I think, also realizing that I need to find this address that Don gave me, so that I can survive the week.

The car is coasting at a relaxed pace, and I step toward the edge of the street to wave my arms in hopes of flagging down the driver.

"Hello!" I call as it approaches, but the car isn't slowing. Frustrated, I grow more incessant with my signaling, hoping to talk to someone—*anyone*—and ask what the heck is going on. "Please! Can you help..."

But I can't finish my sentence. As the car reaches a closer distance, I begin to see it's just like the transport: no driver or steering wheel. *Nothing.*

In fact, all I catch is a glimpse of assorted breads in the back seat. The loaves are separated into various plastic bags marked with names. It must be a delivery car, I conclude. But *to whom* is it delivering?

Now the questions start firing through my mind like bullets. What happened to everyone? I know there must be people around here; I've seen signs of them, like the delivery breads and lights in buildings, but why won't they come outside? Is there some epidemic I don't know about? Martial law? Radiation from a nuclear bomb?

Panic swelling inside me, I jog down the road, trying to keep the car within sight. Maybe it will lead to a real, living human. Otherwise, in a city this deserted, how will I ever find the address Don left me? How will I survive? I would have been better off in the forest.

As I'm pounding the pavement, my eyes scan each and every building for a phone, a phone book, a hint of life, but there's *nothing.* Just as I'm about to give up following the car, it begins to slow down and my nose catches a whiff of spices.

My mouth starts watering from the aroma, and I can almost taste the thrilling thickness of fresh pumpkin bread melting against my tongue and sliding down my throat. I didn't realize how hungry I'd grown until just now.

I swallow, my throat sticky from thirst and my shirt soaked in sweat, and I make my way toward the shop where the car stopped. When I approach, I realize I was correct. A sign outside reads, "Barry's Bread."

Relieved, I wipe the sweat from my forehead and walk inside, letting out a sigh. A tiny bell rings as I push open the door, but there's no one behind the empty glass counter. The drift of cool air relieves my hot skin, but as my eyes absorb my surroundings, I notice the distinct absence of pastry displays, tables, and chairs. As I walk along the empty counter, I observe the lack of ovens, as well. *How odd.*

In the upper left corner of the shop, I notice a square-shaped device, which looks like a window. It's flat, like the screen I saw in the transport, but it's clear. An audio recording is playing in the background, like a T. V. , but I can't find an active screen anywhere—just this strange contraption in the corner.

"Suicide rates have increased two-point-three percent in the past month, according to a report released today by the United Council Institute of Mental Health," the audio says, and I presume it's a newscast. "United Council sociologists are concerned about this continuing trend, citing studies from Sector 2, where similar developments have coincided with an increase in mass shootings and bombing attempts."

That's freaky, I think. *I wonder if this has anything to do with the public's avoidance of the streets.*

Since no one has bothered to come out and greet me, I call into the back of the shop, "Hello! Is anyone back there?"

No response.

So I try again. "Excuse me! I'm looking for the owner of this bakery?"

Finally, a middle-aged man with a balding head and two sideburns that look like Velcro on his face waddles in from the back. He is so pale, he looks like a circus clown, minus the red nose and vibrant makeup. He must weigh three hundred pounds, and his skin hangs off his face in miserable wrinkles. His appearance makes me sad.

"Hi," I say, when I realize he isn't going to initiate the conversation. "You must be Barry, the owner?"

He refuses to look at me; rather, his gaze remains fixed on the ground. His mannerisms remind me of Don, but unlike my strange friend back home, this man refuses to answer.

"The owner?" I try again.

The man's eyes dart over to another flat screen sitting atop the front counter, similar to the squared appliance in the corner of the bakery. This screen, too, is clear and unresponsive, and I find myself wondering exactly what the weird devices are for.

When the man still doesn't answer, my nerves become more frazzled. "Sir, are you alright?" I ask, not sure if I want to know the answer. "Can you talk?"

At this, the man's eyes grow wide, and I detect a sense of fear... *about me*. His pupils dilate, and I watch as he cautiously backs away toward the vacant kitchen, and then disappears from sight.

All I can do is stand motionless, my mouth gaping open in pure disbelief. Because only now, for the first time since I started this whole, crazy quest, do I realize that perhaps I made a huge mistake.

The Black-and-White Leggings

FLORA

I left the bakery in a flutter, desperate to escape the tormenting smell of mystery spiced breads that I couldn't eat, my stomach curled with hunger. And I jog down the street, an occasional car devoid of human life passing by. *Everything is cement out here,* I think. *No trees, no grass, no wildflowers.*

As I wander the paved jungle, I realize it's starting to grow darker, and I glance at my watch: five-thirty. The shadows that threaten to consume the city worry me. Unlike Apollo, The Other Side offers no trees for shelter, no wood for fire and warmth. *Will I have to sleep on the street, exposed?*

I start racing from building to building, but even those with glowing windows are locked and cold. Several of the apartments and stores I pass display those odd screens from inside their windows, and as I'm wandering down the endless city corridors, I notice more of the clear screens, some erected high above the ground, like billboards.

I'm beginning to panic. I'll die out here. I'll starve to death, or pass out from dehydration.

Surely someone is willing to help a nineteen-year-old girl, right? Clinging to this hope, I start calling into the empty air, "Is there anyone out here?" Yet only my echo responds. I begin pounding on doors of apartments, asking if someone— anyone—could help me find my destination.

Finally, I see a young woman, maybe in her mid-twenties, wandering down the street and I nearly skip toward her, delighted to see another person of similar age. The woman is dashing: black-and-white leggings hug slender limbs, accented by a short, flared skirt and black, strappy pumps. Her top is bright pink, dark shades contrast against milky skin, and her lips are painted the red of rebels.

Fascinated, I slow my stride before approaching her, having never seen anyone dressed in such style before. "Excuse me," I say, and the girl slows down. "I'm so sorry to bother you like this, but I'm new in town and seem to be lost. Do you know where this address is?"

I reach into my jeans and pull out the piece of paper Don gave me, but when I look up, the girl is scurrying down the path, trying to escape me. A little perturbed by her lack of manners, I jog after her.

"Excuse me!" I call, this time more sternly. "Maybe I wasn't clear. I'm new in town and—"

But before I can say another word, she swings her purse around and slams it into my stomach, sending jolts of pain through my intestines as I fly backward from the blow. Stunned silent and holding my stomach, I watch as she takes off running, her black-and-white mass growing smaller as she lengthens the distance between us. *What's going on with the people here?*

Mystified, I continue wandering down the street in a whirl of uncertainty when two patrol cars approach. Relief sweeps over me; perhaps I'll finally get some help now. But when the officers emerge from the self-driving vehicles, a claw of horror grips my throat.

The officers aren't people; they're drones. Or robots. Or androids. I'm not sure what to call them, but as they roll toward me, I am petrified.

Both drones are stainless steel statues on wheels, slightly shorter than me, with clear screens resting atop their "bodies." They have no legs, but display two extensions, which act as arms and remind me of a sci-fi nightmare. The drone on the left remains still as it faces me. I have no idea what it's preparing to do, so I begin curling into myself and backing away.

Time suspends for the next moments as I await my fate, and the other drone wheels itself forward and speaks. "Please halt your movement and place your hands above your head," it says.

My heart thumping out of my ears, I listen to the instructions, but also decide to try and explain myself. "My name is Flora Loban," I tell it. "I am new in town and just need help finding an address."

"Do not speak," the drone instructs.

It rolls itself closer and a small scanner extends from its center, skimming my body from head to foot. Hysterics are coursing through my veins now, like millions of spiders, and I swallow over and over in an effort to stay calm, to hold back the outburst that quivers in my throat. *You'll get through this, Flora. Just stay calm. Just stay calm.*

"Where is your identification?" the drone asks.

"I don't have any."

"Why not?"

"I'm just visiting."

The drone pauses for a moment, and I consider running from it, dashing away in a dramatic escape. I remind myself that I don't know where to go, or whether this robot is armed.

"That is no excuse. Where is your identification?" the drone asks again.

"I told you, I don't have one."

The terror has now gripped every inch of my body and without warning, my legs give out and I collapse. My hands are shaking violently and I'm too upset to notice the drones approaching, closer and closer, until I feel their metal claws snap around my wrists, and I shriek.

"Remain calm," the drone says.

But I can't; I'm squirming and screaming and cursing, yet their herculean grips make it impossible for me to move. Before I can register another thought, I feel a pinch against my arm, and moments later... blackness.

Dr. Thompson

FLORA

When I awake, I'm lying in a bed on my back, and the first thing I notice is gentle beeping sounds coming from the corner of the room. The walls are white as snow, as is the ceiling, and I swallow, realizing my throat isn't sticky anymore.

My vision is somewhat blurry at first, and everything looks like convoluted blobs of color, but after a few blinks, the image that comes into focus is almost unbelievable.

A person. A real, living human.

It's a woman, skin the color of mocha, who looks like she might be in her forties or fifties, wearing a white lab coat. *A white lab coat.*

Slightly alarmed, I try to move and realize I'm secured to the bed, an IV connected to a vein in my arm. I try to talk, but all that materializes is a faint moan. The woman in the white lab coat turns around and is by my side almost instantaneously.

"It's OK, just breathe," she says, and her soft demeanor reminds me of my mother. "The drugs will make you feel a little heavy and it may be hard to talk at first. But it's perfectly normal."

I catch a glimpse of a glass of water behind her, resting on a table, and I moan again, motioning with my eyes toward the cup. She nods in acknowledgment and brings it to me.

There's a burning, sharp pain emanating from my stomach, and I groan from the discomfort. The woman in the lab coat lowers her head and looks at me sympathetically before placing a soft hand over my stomach.

"You'll feel a little uncomfortable, but don't worry, we fixed you up, OK?"

After taking a few more sips of water, I determine I can finally talk, however faint my voice might be.

"Where am I?" I ask.

"Oh, I'm sorry," the woman says. "I thought you remembered when they brought you in, but you were rather sedated. You're at Phoenix Psychiatric Hospital. We also perform medical procedures here; that's where I come in. I'm Dr. Thompson."

It takes a moment for it to register. "Psychiatric hospital?"

"Oh yes. You poor thing, so upset that you were driven to talk in public. We saw the recording of the whole thing. I'm really not supposed to be talking to you either, but I managed to convince the board that a case as severe as yours calls for interpersonal communication therapy."

I'm so confused at her response, I feel like I can't think. What is she talking about: a case as severe as mine? Talking in public? And what did she mean when she said, *Don't worry, we fixed you up?*

"I want to talk to someone in charge," I say, growing a little more alert, and therefore, a little bolder.

"That would be me," Dr. Thompson says. "I do have some very good news to report. We killed the stomach cancer."

I cough when I hear the words. *What did she just say?*

Obviously reading the disbelief on my face, Dr. Thompson continues. "You're lucky you made a spectacle of yourself out there, talking to bread shop owners and that girl you scared to death. We wouldn't have known you were wandering around with such a horrible disease, otherwise."

"You—you mean you were able to...?"

"Oh yes, we did." She pauses for a moment and grows serious, a little less soft. "Can I ask you something? Did you do it on purpose?"

I'm baffled by her question, and at the same time, I'm desperately trying to fight back tears of elation. *They cured me?*

"Did I do what on purpose?" I manage to ask.

"You know... *talk*... in public? Hoping maybe the government would pick up the bill to cure you?"

I don't know how to answer her, so all I do is just stare. She smiles, nods, and shakes her head, seemingly at herself.

"Listen, I'm sorry. You're right," she says. "You need to rest right now. The procedure will make you a little sore while the new cells are generating in your new stomach. You must excuse me; I don't get to practice the art of interpersonal communication on patients very often. Yours is a rare case, and I was dying to try it out. I'll let you rest. And oh, I think we can take these shackles off now, don't you?"

Dr. Thompson leans over my face and carefully frees my wrists and ankles from the bed. She gives my stomach another gentle pat and leaves the room. All I can do is stare at my IV.

***

After several minutes, I feel myself gather the strength to push to a sitting position. I'm wearing a white hospital garb, and all my clothes are gone. For a moment, I panic, because the address Don gave me and my transport ticket are both in my jeans. But I notice a vacuum-sealed plastic bag hanging on the far wall across from me and realize it's my clothes. Even though they've been condensed to the size of a shoebox, they look much cleaner. The hospital must have thrown them into the wash.

Thrown them into the wash.

Concern stiffens my muscles as I realize I still may have lost my two most important papers: most critically, the transport ticket. *No, no, no.*

I thrust to my feet and feel a pinch from the center of my arm. *The IV.* Remembering I'm still connected to machines, I shuffle over to the drip bag and wheel its stand with me toward my clothes. I unzip the vacuum pack and my garments balloon out. Searching, I yank out my underwear, my top, and finally my jeans. I reach into the first pocket.

Nothing.

Hoping I searched the wrong one, I reach into the other pocket and feel the sharp edges of folded paper. I pull it out and look. "The ticket!" I cry out in relief.

With less urgency now, I continue digging for the piece of paper from Don, the one with the address, but I can't find it anywhere. Is it possible I dropped it on the sidewalk when the patrols stopped me? Regardless, it's gone. If this place lets me go soon, my best bet is to simply head back toward Apollo, and play my odds in the woods. At least I have my survival pack, which doesn't do me much good in the city. I've been roaming through The Other Side for about a day now, and to be honest, I'm not a huge fan.

But—*but*—they did cure me.

I slip my hand beneath my hospital robe and feel the smooth skin over my stomach, and I smile. My hand runs over a knot of flesh—a small scar—which runs from below my belly button to the skin a few inches above it. *That must have been where they operated.*

How is it possible they cured me so quickly? I reach up toward my scalp, and realize I still have a full head of hair. No chemo? No radiation? What did they do?

A small part of me doesn't care. All that matters, in this little portion of my brain, is that I'm going to *live.* My parents will still have their daughter, I won't have to say goodbye to Andrew, I will still be able to cuddle with Ernest, and listen to my dad play the piano. I'll be able to wander through the towering shelves of the Apollo Library and read any book I want, and go to school, and get a degree. Andrew and I can still have many adventures together, and hold hands... the wistfulness returns as I find myself wishing for more, but I must not be greedy. All that matters is that we can continue to be in each other's lives.

I wish Dr. Thompson would come back. I want to fall to my knees and kiss her feet in gratitude. How can I show her how thankful I am for what she did?

Wanting to leave my room to see if I can find her, I inch toward the door, pulling my IV drip bag behind me. When I reach to turn the handle and open it, however, the knob won't rotate. I try again. Still nothing.

I look back into the room, over my shoulder, and notice another one of those blank, clear screens hanging from the ceiling; it's suspended above my bed. Staring at it, I remember I'm in a psychiatric hospital. Is it possible they locked me in my room?

"Hey!" I call out to the vacant screen. "Can you guys let me out of here? I need to stretch my legs."

But there is no response. Slowly, the unease returns, and I remember Dr. Thompson's reference to talking in public as if *it's a bad thing*. There was the bread shop owner, the girl on the street... I remind myself to stay calm. These people did save my life, after all. They're good guys. I need to be patient with them. Besides, they don't know I'm from Apollo yet. I just need to clear that up. Then they'll understand.

Yes, then they'll understand.

Diagnosis

FLORA

Dr. Thompson returns in a few hours with a plate of food for me. Passing the time has been mind-numbingly boring: nothing to watch, no board games to play. I wondered several times if this place has a library, as I could use a good book right now.

When she enters, Dr. Thompson smiles, but I notice she is accompanied by a man. He's young, probably in his early thirties, and wears a suit and tie. He carries with him an essence of arrogance, an air of superiority, further evident by the way he slicks his black hair from his face, revealing a sharp widow's peak. I chuckle to myself, figuring he must have spent a good hour this morning sculpting that mane.

Dr. Thompson isn't as talkative as before, and the man just looks at me. He's attractive, but something about him makes me uneasy. His eyes are cold, calculating.

I watch as Dr. Thompson places the tray of food before me. It's mostly soft: mashed potatoes, mashed carrots, pudding. Before she says anything, I catch her glance at the mysterious man, like she's asking permission for something. He gives her a slight nod, and she turns back to me.

"Flora, I brought you some lunch. You'll need to remain on soft foods for the next three days," she says, motioning to the plate. She stands and turns toward the man. "Also, I'd like you to meet Dr. Hauser. He's our resident psychiatrist. Think of him as my equivalent, only he specializes in the mind, rather than the body. Since I was the first doctor to have contact with you, I made the recommendation that we begin with interpersonal communication therapy. Dr. Hauser will take over from here, for the most part."

I look back toward the man—Dr. Hauser—and nod.

"I'll leave you two alone," Dr. Thompson says, and promptly leaves the room. I'm wishing I'd said something to thank her for curing me, but I was too distracted by the presence of this new doctor.

He closes the door behind him, and the walls seem to shrink with the clicking of the lock. This scenario is beginning to seem eerily familiar—a day in another white room, with another cold, calculating man, when I was wearing a different white outfit.

I shiver.

"Flora Loban," Dr. Hauser says, taking a seat before me and glancing over a handheld, miniature screen. "Approximately twenty years old. Stomach cancer.

Had a psychological event in public, generating two emergency calls: one from a bread shop owner, and another from a girl attacked on the street."

Attacked? The anger rushes through me like a gust of wind at this accusation. "I didn't hurt anybody," I say. "I *talked*. To a bread shop owner. And a girl. I just needed some directions. *She* hit *me*."

Dr. Hauser glares at me, but remains calm. He places the clear screen on his lap and leans forward. "Yet, that's all we have," he says, refusing to acknowledge my reaction. "No I.D. No place of origin. A mystery."

"I tried explaining to the patrol robots," I say. "But they told me to stop talking."

"Of course they did. Where are your contacts?"

Puzzled by his question, I can't find my voice for a moment. "I don't wear contacts," I finally say.

"Well, *everyone* wears the contacts, Flora. It's OK to admit you lost yours. But if that was the case, why didn't you immediately tell the patrols?"

I'm speechless. How can I possibly answer him?

"Look, Dr. Hauser," I say after a few minutes, "I have no idea what you're talking about. I've never needed to wear contacts or glasses. I don't have an I.D. because I'm only in town visiting."

"Then you should have an I.D. from your city of residence. The government issues I.D. s to everyone. You know that, right?"

I stare at him blankly, but don't say anything. I feel like we're speaking two completely different languages.

"That's OK," he finally says. "Why don't we start from the beginning? Are you willing to tell me a little about yourself? How old are you, and where do you live?"

Yes, this I can do. "As you know, my name is Flora Loban. I'm nineteen years old, and I live in Apollo. I was actually a student at the University of Apollo, until recently."

"Apollo," the doctor repeats, but I sense insincerity in his voice. "I see. And what about your parents? What are their names?"

"Randy and April Loban. My father is a pianist, and my mother is a journalist for the *Apollo Times* newspaper."

"Uh huh." Dr. Hauser takes notes with his eyes and punches various spots on his handheld screen with his index finger. "Can you tell me a little more about this Apollo? Where is it located?"

I shift in my bed now. Why am I getting the feeling that he doesn't believe me? I continue to answer his probing questions, anyway.

"Up north, in the mountains. It's a beautiful state, surrounded by Aspen and Ponderosa pines. The Central Commerce Hub is located where the old college town of Flagstaff used to be."

He looks up from his screen again. "In the nuclear waste dump?"

I feel like someone just threw me against the wall. What does he mean, *nuclear waste dump?* My heart palpitates and I find myself struggling to breathe. My palms grow slick with sweat.

"No," I manage to get out. "No nuclear waste dump."

Dr. Hauser places his screen down and walks over to me, taking a seat on the bed. His fingers slip to my wrist to feel my pulse, and he gently lifts my head and pulls down the lower lids of my eyes, looking into the whites.

The room is beginning to spin and I catch a glimpse of Dr. Hauser drawing lines in the air with his pointer fingers, making all sorts of strange gestures. He glances at the clear screen above my bed and nods. Within moments, two nurses rush through the door and lay me back onto the bed, positioning my legs into the shock position. My heart is racing like a speeding train ready to burst from my chest. One of the nurses changes the drip bag for my IV, time slips by, and I start to feel calm again. My heart rate returns to normal and my palms dry. When Dr. Hauser motions, the two nurses leave and close the door once more.

He returns to his seat across from me. "Flora, I'm going to tell you something that might be a little unsettling, so I want you to prepare yourself, OK?"

I simply nod, and he continues. "Newspapers and pianos have not existed for nearly one hundred years. Therefore, it's impossible for your mother to be a newspaper reporter, and your father a pianist. Do you understand what I'm telling you?"

"But—but that's impossible," I protest. "I mean, my father has a piano in our *house*, Dr. Hauser. I fall asleep every night listening to him play. You're going to tell me I've been imagining that my whole life? And as for newspapers: I could pull one of my mother's front-page articles from yesterday's edition and show you, if you want proof."

But the doctor is just staring at me, a sympathetic look sweeping over his features. I sense *pity*.

"I'm sorry, Flora." He sighs, punching again into his odd little screen. "I'm afraid you're very sick. The diagnostic program recommends I diagnose you with schizophrenia, and I'm going to agree. We'll have to commit you until you're no longer deemed a danger to yourself and others."

"A danger to... what did I do?"

"Talking in public, indecent exposure, disturbing the peace."

"Since when did talking to people become a crime?!"

"Since 2104," Dr. Hauser answers, to my utter disbelief. "The passage of the Indecent Verbal Act. Talking in public was deemed indecent exposure. Here's the bottom line: if you do not stay here, you *will* end up in jail. But you need treatment, not prison. Dr. Thompson and I will make the recommendation to the courts tomorrow morning."

I try to sit up all the way, but the moment I lift my head from the pillow, dizziness overtakes me in giant waves. The nurses must have given me some sort of sedative.

"You can't keep me here," I tell Dr. Hauser, trying to sound intimidating from my hospital bed. "This is unlawful imprisonment. I'm not crazy."

"No, you're not," he reassures. "You're just sick. But like we cured you of stomach cancer, we can cure you of this, too. It will all be alright, Flora. Rest now, OK?"

He looks back toward the large screen over my bed and makes another random gesture into the air. And as I fall into a deep, medicated sleep, I wonder if I'll ever see my family again.

The Contacts

FLORA

It's dark when I awake, and the IV is gone. My room has changed too—in fact, I might be in a different building altogether. I have no clue how long I've been asleep, and the remnants of the medication still cause extreme wooziness, tilting the world when I sit up straight.

Unlike before, this room has a window, and the gentle moonlight shines lazily through vertical blinds, caressing curves and corners, and creating sharp shadows that causes dread to well up in my healing stomach. *My stomach.* The cramps have vanished. *It's real*, I think. *They really did cure me.*

But now, I'm trapped. Will they release me in time to catch my transport back home? If I miss it, I have no way to communicate with Don and develop another plan for return. What will happen after my week is over, and Andrew and my parents realize I never returned from the Grand Canyon?

As the wooziness begins to subside, I push to my feet with care, ensuring I don't fall and hurt myself. I realize I'm no longer wearing the hospital robe, but instead, a white pant-and-top outfit the staff must have dressed me in. The fabric is loose and soft, like a mix of cotton and satin, and when my feet meet the floor, the tile is cold against my soles.

Of course, the first thought that crosses my mind is escape. My attention turns immediately to the window, but when I approach it, I see that bars adorn the exterior. This chamber resembles a cell more than a hospital room. It even lacks one of those mysterious, clear screens.

I start wandering around the space, gathering the rest of my surroundings. A little bathroom that looks like an oversized cube is embedded into the side wall, and in the corner, I notice a robot—like the patrols that arrested me on the street. The place reeks of sterile cleaner. I suppose on The Other Side, hospitals still smell like hospitals.

I don't bother trying to understand the door; it's completely void of an inside knob, therefore any attempt to open it is pointless. As I'm staring at the door, the lights flash on, and I'm suddenly swimming in bright, florescent beams. Within seconds, the robot comes alive, and I jump back into my bed, scared this one will trap me with its metal claws, too. I watch as it rolls toward me and stops.

"Hi, Flora," it says. "I see you woke up; how are you feeling?"

I refuse to answer it.

"My name is Justine. I'll be your nurse. If you need anything, you can let me know. Dr. Hauser ordered you a new pair of contacts and an ear bud. He asked that you put them on after you wake up. They are on the table next to your bed."

I glance over my shoulder, and just as the robot promised, an ear bud and pair of contacts are waiting for me. I turn back toward the robot.

"I don't wear contacts," I tell it.

"Dr. Hauser said if you refuse, we will sedate you again and force them into your eyes. I don't think you want that, and neither do we. If you put them in, we'll be one step closer to beginning your treatment."

What choice do I have? I walk over to the contacts, but stop before continuing. I glance over my shoulder at the robot.

"How do I put them in?" I ask.

The robot is quiet for a moment before beginning its answer, and instructs me to use the saline solution as a cleaner. I start following directions, but pause once more.

"I don't need treatment," I tell the robot, before turning around and looking down at the contacts. They're small, hard, half-cylinder pieces of glass. I clean one in the palm of my hand using the solution provided, and balance the tiny glass cylinder on the tip of my pointer finger.

I walk to the only mirror in the room and try to open my eye. Every time my finger draws close to my cornea, I wince involuntarily, and have to start the process over again. I cycle through this sequence for the next several minutes, my teeth gritted in frustration, until I finally succeed with one contact. It feels like forever before both contacts are secure in my eyes.

I wait a few moments before turning around to face the room again. When I do, I nearly lose my balance from shock. A three-dimensional screen appears in the upper, right-hand corner of my vision, and wherever I look, the floating screen follows me.

"What the hell?" I say, waving my arms and trying to shoo the screen away. When I realize I can't make it disappear, I try to touch it, but my hand glides through the image like a cloud. The screen is just... there.

"It's OK," I hear the robot say, and I swing around toward the android, noticing how the clear screen resting atop its body has come alive, like a television. The image is three-dimensional and a woman's face is protruding from the screen, staring at me. She's wearing a nurse's hat.

"Who are you?" I demand, falling onto my bed now.

She looks confused, but her gaze lowers to something below the screen's line of vision, and the robot speaks again.

"I'm Justine, your nurse."

"What *are* you?"

"I'm a person," it answers.

"You're not—like—artificial intelligence or anything?"

The nurse is starting to look really worried, and the robot tells me to put in my ear bud. Perplexed, I listen and position the small device comfortably above my right ear canal.

"There, isn't that better?" a normal, female voice says to me, and I flinch at the dialogue that seems to materialize from thin air. I look back toward the three-dimensional screen with the nurse's face, and I realize she's smiling at me.

"Is that you?" I ask, and she nods.

"That's me," she says.

"Where are you?"

"I'm in the hospital's main control room, so I can monitor all of my patients more efficiently."

This time, her lips move when she talks, whereas before, she must have been typing something for the robot to speak on her behalf. "What are these things?" I ask, pointing to my eyes.

"Those are your government-issued contacts. You're required to wear them; they act as your I.D."

"How do they work?"

"Well, if you need me, just say my name, and I'll be with you momentarily," she explains. "If there's someone you want to message, just say 'message,' and the person's name. Speak your note, then say 'send message.'"

I have so many questions, but I can tell Justine is preparing to leave me, so I ask only one more. "Do you have a library here?"

Her lips tighten when I ask this question, and she pauses before answering, uncertainty washing over her features. "What do you mean, 'a library'?"

My heart falls through my feet at her response, but I force myself to explain. "You know, a room where you keep books? Stories by Ernest Hemingway and Victor Hugo and Homer?"

"Oh, you mean a literary database," she says. "Yes, you can access it by saying, 'call literary database.'"

"If it's just a database, how do you read the books?"

Justine is quiet, looking at me like I'm mad. "Again, you speak in odd terms. What's a book?"

What's a book? I'm now convinced I've crossed some space-time continuum boundary and have fallen into an alternate universe, the yang to my yin. I return

Justine's stare, bewildered and unable to answer; how can I *possibly* explain a book to someone who doesn't understand the concept of a library? My silence prompts her to end the conversation though, and the robot closes down, wheeling itself back against the wall. Justine's face disappears from the screen.

My three-dimensional square remains in the upper right corner of my vision, and now, sprawled across it are the words, "What would you like to do?"

I lie down on my bed and stare at the white ceiling. These contacts are making me feel nauseous, like motion sickness, even though I'm not moving. I keep staring at the words: *What would you like to do?*

So I say, "Look up history of Phoenix."

***

The results are endless, infinite, exponential. Thousands of pages of links pop before my face, hanging in the air like a kite. I've never seen anything like this in my life. Not even in Apollo, with A-Search, would so many results be generated.

The first of many links is from the World Encyclopedia. I want to click on it, but how? I verbalize a command, but nothing happens, so I try swiping at the image. Still nothing.

Finally, I tap my temple in frustration, and the link highlights. Going with instinct, I double-tap the same spot on my head, and the web page opens. Curious, I begin reading the words floating above my head. They're now filling my line of vision.

Phoenix is a city in Sector 1 of the United Council. Current population: 2,435,671.

I stop reading for a moment and make a mental note to research "United Council," but only after I finish this.

Phoenix was first incorporated in 1881 under the former state of Arizona, which fell under the jurisdiction of the former United States of America. At the height of the former U.S., Phoenix was the capitol of Arizona. It relinquished that title in 2075 and became an official member of the United Council in 2076.

Twenty-seventy-five? That's the year Apollo was founded. I begin developing the sense that something momentous happened that year, something that...

How are your new contacts fitting?

The words startle me, popping into the corner of my vision, accompanied by a professional headshot of Dr. Hauser. It takes a moment for me to realize this must be a message, similar to what Justine had mentioned.

I want to answer back, but I'm stuck sitting on my bed for the moment, trying to recall how the contacts work. *If there's someone you want to message, just say 'message,' and the person's name.* Justine's instructions echo in my mind, and although I feel silly, I speak into the air, "Message Dr. Hauser."

At this, a blank window appears before my eyes, and I start speaking my response. "They are OK. I am getting used to them."

I instruct my contacts to send the message, and my note shoots onto the three-dimensional screen under Dr. Hauser's question. I notice I have a headshot too. When did they take this picture? I look like I belong in a mental institution. Maybe it's fitting.

Within moments, Dr. Hauser responds.

Good. We will continue with sessions of interpersonal communication therapy about once a week. In the meantime, I want you to get comfortable wearing your contacts again, OK? Dr. Thompson is on her way to bring you food.

Within seconds, his screen and his photo and his words are gone from my sight and my door opens. This must be Dr. Thompson with my dinner, I figure, so my research on the United Council will need to wait.

Socialization Hour

FLORA

I must admit, I'm beside myself to see Dr. Thompson. I hate being alone, and something about her demeanor reminds me of home. I'm half expecting her to waltz in with a tray of my mom's famous sweet potato casserole.

"How are you feeling today?" Dr. Thompson asks me, carrying my tray of nourishment. She's still smiling, but I notice a change in her conduct this time. She's become more... reserved.

"Hungry," I admit. "Dr. Thompson, can I ask you something?"

She places the tray of food on the table next to my bed and turns toward me. She's avoiding eye contact now, staring toward the ground. But she tells me to go ahead, so I do.

"How can I get out of this place?" I ask her. "What will make them release me?"

Dr. Thompson sighs. "You need to listen and work with Dr. Hauser."

"I don't like him," I say, and it feels good to tell someone. "I don't trust him."

Even though she's looking down, I notice Dr. Thompson's eyes grow sad. "I wish there was more I could do for you," she says, but her voice has become quiet.

"Oh, but you did! Dr. Thompson, you gave me back my *life*. I never thought I'd get to see my parents again."

This time, Dr. Thompson does glance up, and her eyes meet mine. As we hold each other's gaze the next few moments, I sense she's trying to tell me something. I lean in, straining to detect this discreet message, and I decode it, deep within her eyes: *You still may not see your parents again.* Dr. Thompson remains silent, and I suspect she's ready to cry for me.

"Eat," she says, and pulls her eyes from mine. "Socialization hour starts in five minutes."

And before I can ask her anything else, she walks out of the room, her white coat trailing behind mocha-colored arms, leaving me alone once again.

***

Although I was sad to see Dr. Thompson go, I was ecstatic to hear the words "socialization hour" come from *anyone* around here. I nearly inhale my food while trying to forget the message Dr. Thompson relayed. Maybe I misinterpreted it? Yes, of course I did. Of *course* I'll see my parents and Andrew again.

Just as Dr. Thompson promised, within five minutes, my screen changes color and the words, "socialization hour" materialize before me. I walk toward my door, anticipating it to open any moment, but it never moves. Instead, my vision changes, and I'm no longer able to see my room.

I yell, crippled by my sudden blindness, and stumble backwards, falling. A sharp pain shoots up my spine as I hear the *thunk* of my tailbone against hard tile. Stiffened from the sharp throbbing, I call out for help, but no one responds.

All I can do is sit where I am and wait, staring straight ahead, as a new line of vision materializes before my eyes. The image of another room forms around me, a larger room, encompassed by beige walls and hard, brown carpeting. As I strain to understand what's happening, I notice them: rows and rows of other robots, each one crowned with a screen that houses a different three-dimensional face.

It takes a moment for me to realize that these robots, with these faces, are *other patients.*

Am I a robot, too? My lower back still throbbing, I manage to find my balance and climb to my feet. When I turn my head to the right, my alternative line of vision also moves to the right. When I lean forward, I realize I'm strolling forward in this room. My breath quickens as I come to understand that this *is* my socialization hour—trapped in an android.

"You must be new," I hear, and I jerk my head to the left. The voice is female and came through my ear bud. Like I anticipated, a robot is waiting for me to answer. The face protruding from the screen is middle-aged and ragged. I wonder if this woman has ever known what it feels like to smile.

"Yes," I answer. "My name is Flora."

"Welcome to hell," she tells me.

"Why do you say that?"

"Because, just like hell, this place is eternal."

"Oh, but they can't hold us here forever."

"Honey," she says, her voice condescending, "they can do whatever they want. They get *paid* by the government for every mouth they feed. So as long as the money keeps rolling in, so will the diagnoses and treatments."

I'm about to say something, but the woman's face disappears and the screen goes clear. I watch as the android closes down and rolls back toward a corner. What happened to her? But as the reality of her words sink in, so does the dread. Can it really be that bad? Will they hold me here, like a prisoner of war, calling me crazy just to make a *profit*? What kind of place, of society, would do that, would allow that?

I peer into the ocean of robots now beginning to roll throughout the room, all of them storing different faces, different souls. Some are old, some young. Some are women, some men. They all look overweight. They all look *gray*, as if the white walls and florescent lights have sucked the life from them, until there's nothing left.

Is this merely a small window into The Other Side, into their world, their dementia?

I try to talk to other nameless faces, but many turn away, refusing to engage in conversation. Others can't speak well, their words staggered like broken gibberish, stumbling over consonants and vowels. They mumble some form of abbreviated acronyms, and I suddenly find myself sick, the disgust reaching all the way into my bones.

The hour feels like a vast desert, dry and desolate and endless, with no water—not even a mirage—in sight. But finally, it comes to an end, this torturous existence, and my screen vanishes, returning my vision to my present room.

My cell.

At this point, I begin to face the possibility of true loss of freedom. Is this what Apollo, and the ABI, have been protecting us from this entire time? Is this why they're willing to kill discreetly? No, I tell myself. There must be something more. There must be something even darker.

Therapy Session

FLORA

It's been a week, and I now know my damnation. I'm staring at my watch. I'm supposed to meet Don within the next two hours at our rendezvous outside the Wall. But instead, I'm stuck here, in this isolated hole.

They started giving me pills two days ago—called them "antipsychotic medication." My nurse, Justine, refused to close down her robot until she saw the capsule disappear into my mouth with a gulp of water. I had to think quickly the first time they ordered my ingestion of this poison. I knew if I didn't prove that I am, indeed, taking the medicine, they'd sedate me and force it through an IV.

Therefore, I've been popping the pill onto my tongue and holding it to the roof of my mouth as I down the water, shoving the pill into the pocket of my inner cheek when she asks for proof that I swallowed. After Justine is satisfied, and her face disintegrates from the robot screen, I spit out the pill and go to the bathroom, and flush it down the toilet.

Dr. Hauser said once they get my schizophrenic symptoms under control, he can begin psychosocial treatments. In the meantime, it's medication and a weekly interpersonal communication session—so he can *assess*.

That session is approaching soon, and frankly, I'm looking forward to it. I know this sounds crazy, but Dr. Hauser will be here in-person, and I'm sick of staring at screens of people's faces, or pop-up messages floating before my eyes. I'd even visited the literary database, thrilled to finally read a story and lose myself in the plot, only to discover nothing but holograms of words floating above my head that made my vision spin like a storm. I wanted to screech in aggravation, longing to hold a book again with binding and ink and pages that smell of knowledge. But books don't exist on The Other Side; it seems most people don't know an author until they research him or her through their contacts.

When Dr. Hauser walks through my room's door, he reminds me of a shark, and I begin to wonder why someone like him would go into a therapeutic field like psychiatry. "Hello Flora," he says, dressed, once again in a slick, black suit. "How are you feeling today?"

"Fine, thanks," I respond, losing my anticipation to engage in conversation with this man faster than lightning strikes a mountain.

"Any side effects from the medicine? Restlessness? Muscle cramps or spasms?"

I merely shake my head, and Dr. Hauser nods before spitting out his next set of questions.

"I'm curious to hear your thoughts on Apollo," he says, and I know immediately he's testing me to see if the medication has begun taking effect. I think of what Dr. Thompson told me: *You need to listen and work with Dr. Hauser.*

So I heed her advice, and answer the man.

"It's weird," I tell him. "A part of me feels like Apollo is some sort of dream that's become embedded in my mind. But I have to keep reminding myself that it IS just a dream, a dream that I want to believe. I need to believe."

"Why do you need to believe it?"

"Because, for my whole life, it's been my truth."

Dr. Hauser nods his head—he seems pleased—and begins punching into his little handheld screen. Unlike before, this time I can make out lines and words on the device, but they are not three-dimensional like the others. Therefore, I can't decipher what he's doing.

"What about your parents?" he asks. "What do they do?"

I'm clueless how to answer this one, so I decide to stick with my original story. My father is a pianist. My mother is a journalist. This time, Dr. Hauser shakes his head, obviously disappointed, before punching into his screen again. This man is easy to predict, but I have another question that's been burning in my brain, so I take the opportunity to ask it.

"I've been feeling kind of, you know, *lonely* sitting in this room by myself," I say. "Do you know when I'll actually be allowed outside, maybe get some fresh air and mingle with other people?"

Dr. Hauser gives me a long "hmmm," and I can't stand his condescending "I'm the parent; you're the child" tone. I try and swallow it, instead forcing a smile as he answers.

"Flora, you are here for rehabilitation. Part of my job is to ensure my patients are prepared to re-enter society."

My patients, as if he owns us. His words feel like worms slithering down my back. "I see," I say. "So how is all of this relevant?"

He appears confused by my question. "I'm not sure I understand. All we're doing is practicing socially acceptable behaviors."

"So you mean to tell me that talking through screens and living in solitary confinement is socially acceptable?"

He just stares at me, and I come to understand that this man—this psychiatrist—is actually expecting me to *agree* with him.

"I'm not sure I know what you mean by solitary confinement," he says after moments of silence. "You can talk to anyone you want, any time you want, and visit any place you want. In fact, we're more connected as a society now than we've ever been. Don't you think that's exciting, Flora? Don't you think that's something to be happy about?"

"The people here don't look too happy."

"Well, this is still a psychiatric hospital."

Something tells me, however, that what I'm witnessing is closer to normal than Dr. Hauser or Dr. Thompson or my nurse, Justine, want to admit. No, I take that back. I sense that Dr. Thompson *knows*; she just chooses to live in an ill-conceived state of denial. Taking a breath, I decide to play the dumb and crazy card for the next few minutes in an attempt to squeeze additional information from Dr. Hauser.

"In Apollo, in my dream, we have universal health care," I begin. "During socialization hour last week, a girl told me that this hospital gets money from the government to care for its patients. Why?"

Dr. Hauser is back to swiping and punching his screen before acknowledging my inquiry.

"That's a fair question," he says. "As well as that structure may work for Apollo, it doesn't work here. Money is everything, and health care is expensive. So to maintain order in society, the government has to pay us to ensure people like me can rehabilitate those who might otherwise become a danger to society, but can't afford their own treatment. And we can't work for free, now, can we?"

"I suppose not."

"Exactly. Let me explain something to you, Flora; you seem smart enough. Ideally, everyone would pay for their own care, but there's a chunk of people who are too lazy to work a decent-paying job, and therefore, they can't afford to fix their own problems. It's an issue we've had for decades." He pauses for a moment, appearing proud of his observation. "But if their disease goes untreated, the rest of society will suffer."

"And they pay you well to fix those people, huh?"

"Oh yes, very well."

I suspected feeding his ego would prompt Dr. Hauser to relax his doctor/patient boundaries for the moment, thereby revealing a clue, and I was right. I glance at his suit—a different one from our visit a week ago. His tie looks like it might be pure silk. In contrast, an image of Dr. Thompson's white lab coat flashes through my mind, and another one of her worn shoes. The instincts I inherited from my mother are beginning to kick in, and I find myself wondering just *how well* the government pays Dr. Hauser. Who does he know at a high level to have landed such a cushy deal for himself?

More patients, bigger payout.

"Well, I think we're finished for the day," Dr. Hauser says. "The nurse will be in momentarily to take your blood, then this week's socialization hour begins. Good to see you're improving, Flora. We'll keep you on the same dosage."

He stands up, and walks out.

The Patient

FLORA

I watch with dread as the words "socialization hour" appear and disintegrate before my eyes and, within moments, my world transforms. I'm back in that large, beige room with nothing but soul-trapping machines wandering aimlessly through space.

I imagine that if purgatory exists, this room—this world—embodies it.

Unlike the week before, I don't begin chatting with different patients; instead, I sit quietly, watching the scene play out via my clear screen. Maybe someone will talk to me, but really, I don't care.

I remember how Andrew once told me I could be too curious for my own good. Now, as I stare into the sea of androids, I finally begin to comprehend his warning. Was this truly worth it? Now that I know at least part of the story, do I even care?

Yet if I'd remained in Apollo, it would have been my death sentence.

"You look like a girl who knows how to think," a voice says from nearby. It's a deep, male voice, and when I turn to my right, a man's face is studying mine closely. He looks to be around my father's age, and his eyes and hair are dark and thick as night. Like everyone else in this room, he, too, looks sad. Yet there's something hidden underneath the surface, something I haven't seen in this place, but I can't quite decipher it.

"Some might say I know how to think a little *too* much," I respond.

"And who would say that to someone so full of life?"

I can't help it. His compliment triggers a smile, even though I know I look anything but lively. "Oh, just my best friend back home."

Something about this man's demeanor is different, and I realize I want to keep talking to him. "What are you here for?" I ask.

The hint of life within the man's eyes now fades at my mere mention of the psychiatric hospital, but he answers anyway. "Apparently, I'm delusional. Schizophrenic."

"That seems to be a rather popular diagnosis around here," I mutter. "Why did you say I look like someone who knows how to think?"

Now the man laughs, and some of that light returns to his face. When he smiles, I notice a five-o'clock shadow highlighting a once-strong jawline, softened from years in this hospital.

"Because that's a rare quality to find around here, someone who's inquisitive," he says.

"You mean in this hospital?"

"No, in this *world.*"

A little confused, I ask him what he means, and his smile grows wider.

"Gosh, it feels good to really *talk,*" he says, before continuing to answer my question. "Haven't you noticed that no one can think for themselves here? For example, before they threw me in this place, I worked in information technology—I.T. Part of working in I.T. is figuring out solutions to problems in a computer, right? Well, out here, the computers fix *themselves,* and the I.T. people just go along with the recommendations."

"I think I know what you mean," I say, and for the first time since I escaped the Wall, I forget that I'm trapped. "Dr. Hauser used some sort of program to diagnose me with schizophrenia. He just agreed with its recommendation."

"Ahhh, another fellow delusional," the man says. "Pleasure to make your acquaintance."

I can't help but imagine that, had we met in person rather than over a computer screen, this man would have swept my hand to his lips and placed a chivalrous kiss upon my knuckles.

"Yours too," I say.

"May I ask the young lady, for what is she diagnosed delusional?"

This man speaks exceedingly well, I notice, not like the other patients around here. The only others who converse like him are the two doctors, and even they sometimes appear uncomfortable speaking directly to me. But this man is different, and I find myself growing curious.

"Apparently, my home doesn't exist," I tell him. "And my parents' professions are not real. I've been living in a dream world my entire life."

When I mention this, the man grows serious. Not sad, but intense. "And where does this dream land reside?" he asks.

"It's called Apollo, and it's located up north, in the mountains, where the town of Flagstaff used to be."

I wait for the blow, closing my eyes and flinching in my seat on the bed, but the judgment never comes. When I open my eyes again, the man is staring at me, all sense of joy and playfulness wiped clean from his expression. And a single tear is slipping down his cheek.

"Oh my dear," he says, and I catch him swallowing hard, like he's trying to suppress a lifetime of pain. "I would never think such a thing. Tell me, what drove *you* to go beyond the Wall?"

I can't speak. I can't move. All I can hear, momentarily, is the thumping of my heart in my ears, as the rest of the room melts away. Is it possible? No, it can't be, it *can't* be.

"You are not the only one," the man continues. "I've met about six others."

Six others?

"H-how long have you been here?" I finally manage to ask.

"Too long. Eleven years."

My heart bleeds for him when I hear this, and panic overwhelms my body, right down to the bones. If this man has spent eleven years locked away in this nuthouse, what does that mean for *me*?

"I allowed my curiosity and my sense of dissent to become more important than those I loved most," he says. "I never could have imagined what it would cost me."

His voice trails off, and I find myself crying—crying for him, crying for us. "I know what you mean," I say after a few moments. "There are no words to describe it."

The man nods and we both remain silent for the next few moments. When he speaks again, his voice startles me.

"You know, back home, I have a son about your age," he says. "You remind me of him a lot, in fact: hungry for life, adventurous. I just realized, I never got your name."

"Flora," I tell him.

"Nice to meet you, Flora. My name is Andrew."

At the mention of his name, I nearly jump out of my skin. It takes a moment for the possibility to sink in, but when it does, all the pieces come flying together like a storm in my brain. *Gone eleven years. Son my age. Worked in I.T. Same name, same hair, same eyes.*

"Your son," I say, and realize my voice is quivering, "is his name also Andrew? Andrew Goldsmith?"

The man pauses for a moment, probing straight through the three-dimensional screen with slanted, black eyes. "How did you know that?" he asks.

I nearly scream as his face comes rushing back to my memory, now aged from our brief encounter when I was eight. He's barely recognizable, but it's him, and I break into hysterical tears—sorrow and elation and yearning all pouring from my core like a flooded river. Oh Andrew! I found him! I found him! And he loves you! *He loves you and never meant to leave for good.*

"You know how I'd mentioned my best friend back home?" I ask, fighting through tears.

The man responds with a "yes," and I can hear the anticipation welling in his voice. For a moment, I worry about the hospital workers overhearing our conversation, but I don't care. So I say it, and the words feel like life flowing from my lips:

"My best friend is your son."

Deceived

ANDREW

It's nearly midnight when my phone rings and startles me awake, sending my body jetting out of bed. For a moment, I can't comprehend what's going on, or what time it is, or why anyone would be calling me in the middle of the night during a *workweek*.

It could be Flora, but she was supposed to arrive back from her Grand Canyon trip tonight with her parents, and I doubt she's awake.

Without bothering to look at the number blinking on my cell screen, I grab the phone and answer it, my voice irritated and muffled from sleep. But when I hear Flora's mother on the other line, I perk up.

"Mrs. Loban?" I ask, and I can't help but notice the nervous hesitation in her voice when she first says my name. "What's going on? Is Flora OK?"

She practically snaps back, asking what I mean and saying she's calling *me* for that very reason. Now, of course, I'm confused out of my mind and not even sure I heard her correctly. So I ask her to repeat the question, and now I'm positive something is wrong.

"Didn't you arrive back tonight?" she asks me.

"Arrive back from where?"

There's a long pause on the other line before she says, "The Grand Canyon."

The floor swallows me when I hear this. "I was never at the Grand Canyon," I tell her. "Flora said she went there with *you*, and would be back tonight."

Flora's mother screams on the other end, and I hear scuffling over the phone. Silenced by the commotion, it slowly starts to dawn on me that Flora tricked us—all of us. She *never* traveled to the Grand Canyon, and wherever she went, she didn't come home tonight.

Worry grips every nerve and muscle and joint in my body until I'm held hostage in the frigid air. I hear Flora's dad begin talking through the phone's tiny ear piece. "Andrew, we'll have to call you back," he says.

But before he can hang up, I respond, "I'll be right over."

***

When I pull into their driveway, the house is already surrounded by the flashing lights of the authorities. *Like roaches*, I think. Squinting my eyes, I can barely make out the letters "ABI" printed on the side of a white car parked in their driveway.

That strikes me as odd. Since when does the ABI respond to missing person calls? Don't the local police handle those cases?

Regardless, I climb out of my car into the night's blackness and slam my door behind me. What the hell did Flora get herself into? I think of her naiveté at the beginning of summer, when she pranced around the fence of that mysterious building hidden along the cliffs of Oak Creek Canyon. I begin to worry that my deepest fear has come true:

The dogs finally attacked the innocent, white cat.

I enter the house without knocking, and the first thing I hear is the wailing of Mrs. Loban's voice, pleading with the authorities to find her daughter, telling them how's she's fatally ill with cancer and needs medical treatment.

Ernest is the first to notice me enter and comes trotting to my side. Even his furry face looks worried—poor dog. I scratch his ears until Mr. Loban sees me and races to my side.

"Andrew," he says, and his usually large, gentle eyes are glossy from tears. I always liked Flora's dad; he sort of became my surrogate father. Now, to see him teetering on the edge like this breaks my heart.

I just smile in response to his greeting and let him lead me into the living room. He invites me to sit on the couch, but not before asking if he can get me some water. *Always thinking of others.*

Flora's mom is lying on the floor, clearly in shock, a paramedic by her side, encouraging her to breathe slowly while they prepare sedatives. At the helm of all this, however, is a man I've never seen before, although he exudes an air of importance and dominance over the situation.

The man isn't that tall, and he's bald. He wears khaki pants and a simple, black button-down shirt. Yet, somehow, his demeanor is intimidating.

When Mr. Loban approaches me with a glass of water, I ask him who the man is, standing in the kitchen, watching everything go down.

"Oh, that's Agent Jackson," he tells me. "He works at the ABI and is in charge of the investigation. He'll probably want to talk to you."

"Why is the ABI involved?" I ask.

"Don't worry, kiddo. He's on our side. He wants to find Flora as much as we do."

After giving me a quick, reassuring pat on the back, Mr. Loban leaves my side as quickly as he appeared and begins chatting with two police officers and a reporter. I take a sip of my water and glance at the corner of the room. A piano rests innocently against the wall, and I think of the nights I'd joined Flora on this couch and listened to her dad play.

Where can she possibly be right now?

I start racking my brain, trying to recall event after event that occurred over the past few months. Did she leave any clues, any possible tracks, to her whereabouts?

Did she mention anything? She did seem off? Then again, who wouldn't, after learning they were doomed to die a slow and painful death?

"Andrew Goldsmith?"

The sound of my name startles me from my thoughts, and I glance up, only to find the bald man in khaki pants looming over me, a stale smile fixed on his face.

"Who's asking?" I say.

"Agent Jackson, of the ABI. Mind if I ask you some questions?"

Of course I have to say yes, because you *never* deny an ABI agent. It's one of those unwritten rules in Apollo—not official, not even a law. But if you don't cooperate... well, the bureau doesn't exactly make things easy for you.

"I understand you and Flora are friends," he says, after sitting down next to me on the couch, a little too close for comfort. I notice that his breath smells of old coffee disguised by spearmint gum. I try to hide my disdain, but I fear my face is completely readable. I'm starting to have a sneaking suspicion that the ABI had something to do with Flora's disappearance.

"We are," I say. "We've been friends for a long time."

"That's good. It's important to have close friends you can trust."

"Yes, it is." I pause for a moment, and growing somewhat impatient, I press on and say, "What are these questions you have for me?"

Agent Jackson starts asking about Flora: her likes and dislikes, her favorite pastimes. And now he's asking if she'd behaved strangely recently. At this question, I lie and say no, except for the part about her dying. Yes, she's acting differently, but no more than any other nineteen-year-old would, if they received the same death sentence.

I'm coasting through his questions when Agent Jackson says the thing that completely knocks me off the race track. "You're named after your father, Andrew Goldsmith Sr., aren't you?"

My voice falls away for a moment, and I'm trapped in my own silence like a wild animal in a net. I watch as the corner of Agent Jackson's mouth creeps up, into a smirk, and a feral rage begins brewing in my core.

"I'll take your silence as an affirmative," Agent Jackson says. "And he's been missing since you were eight years old, correct?"

"What does my father have to do with this?"

Agent Jackson takes a long, deep breath, as if deliberately prolonging his answer.

"Well," he begins, "before your father's disappearance, we had a classified interview with him. It's in our records. Let's just say your friend Flora and your father had many of the same... *fascinations*. And I find it intriguing that you're the common link."

Now I fly to my feet, infuriated at the innuendo. "I think this interview is done," I say, my teeth clenched. "My best friend has just gone missing, and you have the gall to imply that I somehow played a part in all of this, even my father's disappearance *when I was eight years old?* Do me a favor, Agent Jackson, if you ever have the pleasure of running into him, please inform him that his son has done his job for the past eleven years. And his return would be most welcome!"

At this, I grab my wallet and storm out of the house. As I climb back into my car, jamming the keys into the ignition over and over again with unsteady hands, the anger suddenly forces another face and name. And I know immediately who I need to ask about Flora.

I can already smell his stench of smoke.

The Mail

ANDREW

If only I knew where the little fucker lives.

Flora would gasp at my use of the term, but everything is starting to boil over now. I'm racing home in the night, the vague silhouettes of trees blanketed by darkness whizzing past my car's windows. I'm determined to find Don. Something tells me he knows the answer to this particular mystery.

When I arrive home and fly through the front door, my mom practically falls to my side, her eyes wide and swollen with tears.

"Where have you been?" she asks, her voice raw from crying.

"Ma, not now."

"Andrew!"

Her hysterical tone stops me mid-step, and I turn to look at her, *really* look at her. "It's Flora, isn't it?" she says.

My eyes skim my mother's ragged appearance. Without her makeup, she looks exhausted, and I suddenly feel awash in guilt for brushing her off in my fury. I turn to face her and lower my voice until I sound like a rational person. "How did you know?" I ask.

"You wouldn't leave the house in the middle of the night for any other reason."

My stomach drops when my mother says this. She knows me better than anyone, even better than I know myself. And she's right, *so right*. How could I have been so blind while this entire time, my mother always knew? She loves Flora, and now, after her words throw truth back into my face, I can no longer deny it.

I love Flora, too.

"She's missing, Ma," I say, and my legs grow weak at the mention of it, until I fall against the couch. "She's missing, just like Dad."

My mother looks at me with the weight of the world, and finally, the tears come. I can't hide them, can't stop them. They're bleeding out of me, all the fury and resentment and frustration and denial of all these years. *Everything*. Somehow, the events of tonight culminated the entirety of my life, and I can't hide anymore. I can't keep these burdens buried deep inside any longer.

So as I sit on the couch, defeated and drenched in my own tears, my mom comes and rests beside me. For the first time in many years, I feel like the child again. Relief overwhelms me as my mom pulls my head against her shoulder, gently stroking my cheeks, my head, and tells me that things usually have a way of working out.

We'll find Flora. She'll be OK. I'll see.

"She's always been so good to you," my mom says, as I begin to calm down. "That girl really cares about you, Andrew. A mother knows."

"She gets me."

"Yes, she does, much more than any of the others you've brought home over the years."

I chuckle at my mom's obvious disdain for my ex-girlfriends.

"You're very sensitive, just like your father," she continues. "I always worried that some girl would take advantage of you because of that. From the moment I laid eyes on Flora, when you were eight, I knew she was different."

Now I pull my head from my mom's shoulder and look into her eyes; they are warm, comforting, the eyes of a mother who loves her son more than she can express.

"Ma, I don't want to lose her," I say. "If I lose someone else, I think I'll go crazy."

My mom just smiles when I acknowledge this—a knowing, almost whimsical smile—and says, "Trust me sweetie; I know what you mean."

For the moment, I'd nearly forgotten my mom spent two weeks in a mental hospital when I was in high school. Maybe I'm more like her than I realize.

"Thanks, Ma," I say.

She pats me on the back and climbs to her feet, staggering into the kitchen. As I watch her walk away, I begin to understand the burden my mother has carried all these years, and I curse myself for not being a better son, for not being more patient with her, for only thinking of my feelings rather than hers.

You need to stop letting fear rule your life, Andrew, I tell myself. And you can start by going after Flora.

***

I'll have to wait until morning to search for Don at the university. I know I should be sleeping, but I can't. My mind is a broken record that won't shut up.

Defeated, I climb from my bed—where I've been staring at the empty ceiling in the darkness—and wander into the kitchen. My mom fell asleep hours ago, and I take a seat at our kitchen table. When I glance at the digital clock on the microwave, I see it's three-thirty in the morning.

I tap my fingers on the table. I stand up and grab a glass of water. I sip the water and let my stomach roll with anxiety. I stare at the clock some more. Only five minutes have passed. Why won't time move faster?

I finally begin shuffling through leftover mail scattered across the small table: bills, coupons, random advertisements from a local real estate agency. And now I see the envelope marked with my name in a simple font—no return address.

My mom and I usually check our mail every few days, so this letter must have come within the past week. Curious, I grab the envelope and flip it over. Blank.

When I rip through the envelope and pull out the piece of paper, I discover it's worn and crinkled, thick and heavy. As I begin to unfold it, I immediately recognize what's inside.

The map I made with Flora.

A lump the size of a baseball forms in my throat. Who sent this to me? How did they get it? My eyes skim the map hungrily as I trace my fingers over every crevice we've explored together, and I see the words, scribbled at the top in unmistakable handwriting:

What's knowledge without curiosity?

I catch my breath as I realize who mailed me the map, but why? What would possess Flora to send our map but leave the return address blank? I search the yellowed sheet of paper, front and back, desperately seeking some sort of note, of coded message, but there's nothing.

Antsy as hell, I spring to my feet with the map in hand, pacing back and forth in the kitchen. Why did she send this to me? What was she trying to tell me? I read her scribbled note at the top again. *What's knowledge without curiosity?*

And it hits me. How could I have been so oblivious? *Oh Flora*, I think. *You didn't.*

But I know she did.

The Meeting

ANDREW

I skip class the next day to find him. My vision feels disconnected from my body, hanging over my head like an apparition, and I know this sensation is from pure exhaustion. But I don't care. I'm waiting for him here in the university's library, a jaguar ready to pounce.

Tucked away, deep in the underbelly of my backpack, is our map. I'm not letting go this time.

"Andrew," a soft voice says from behind me, and I spin around, coming face-to-face with Sophie. She looks unsure of herself, wondering if she should say anything at all, but when her eyes take in my five o'clock shadow and lopsided baseball cap, she steps backward.

"Are you OK?" she asks, before I can respond. Wow, I must look like a schmuck.

"A rough night," I tell her.

"I see." She pauses and glances down, and I can tell she's toying with the idea of leaving, out of embarrassment or anger or both. The wave of guilt slams into me without warning, and I'm so ridden with the feeling, I know exactly what I need to do next... what I should have done weeks ago.

"Listen, Sophie," I begin, standing up and trying to meet her eyes, "I owe you a serious apology."

At this, her head shoots up, full of hope. I motion for her to sit down with me, and I take a deep breath. "What happened in the car, a few weeks ago: that was completely uncalled for. I've been going through some, *stuff*, and well—there's really no excuse for how I acted."

Now the hope fades from her eyes, and I begin wondering if I just made things worse.

"You mean, you didn't want to be with me?" she asks.

"No, that's not what I meant." I glance down and take her supple hands into mine, not sure how to phrase it. "You're a very smart, attractive girl. It's just that... I'm in love with someone else. And I was going through some stuff when you and I met. I should have never taken advantage of the situation."

I know I just let her down; I can tell by the rapid rise and fall of her chest, but I genuinely meant every word.

"Flora," she mutters, and yanks her hands from mine. Her eyes are growing glossy, and I watch the fight develop within her to keep tears from flowing freely.

She staggers backward a bit, conflict filling her face and body with tension. Can I blame her?

"I'm so stupid," she finally says, and her voice is broken.

"Sophie—"

"Don't," she interrupts. "Please, just don't." Her words shove me back into the chair, and all I can do is stare while the battle plays out before me, and she manages to collect her emotions.

"I have to go," she says before looking at me one more time. "Just tell Flora I'm sorry, OK?"

This catches me by surprise, but when I ask her why, she's already walking away, ignoring my questions and burying her face into her hands.

And that's it.

I'm wracked with even more guilt now, but I'm also stunned. What happened between Sophie and Flora? Before I can entertain the question any further, I see him, and all feelings of remorse or empathy or curiosity melt away faster than snow against fire.

Now, finally, to get some answers.

***

When I approach him, he's sitting quietly at a table, reading a book by Friedrich Nietzsche, his knee propped haphazardly against the slab of wood. I don't say anything at first. Instead, I loom over him until he notices my presence.

"What?" is all he says, as those raccoon eyes roll up to meet my face.

"How about you tell me," I say.

"Do I know you?"

I refuse to answer his question, instead grabbing a chair and positioning it across from him, jerking the legs against the hard floor, and I settle into the seat. "Oh, you bet you do. Can't remember me, huh?"

Don's eyes squint in examination, and recognition crosses his face as his black gaze drops toward the ground. "You're Flora's friend," he says.

"Yes, Andrew, and I want to know where you sent her."

His facial muscles stiffen, but he downright lies to me. "I don't know what you're talking about. So piss off. I'm reading."

His jagged words ignite something deep inside, and it's like someone pulled the pin from a grenade. How dare this little twerp withhold information from me—information that could save *my best friend!*

I lean over the table and slowly pull the book away from his hands, holding it to the wooden surface, piercing that smarmy little face with my stare.

"Don't lie to me," I say. "I know you know where she is. And I know you know she's missing."

Don rolls his eyes when I say this, and smirks. *Smirks!*

"First of all, I don't owe you anything," he says, reaching to reclaim his book. "And second of all, even if I did know where she went, your little mind couldn't possibly grasp the magnitude of it. So why don't you go back to your benign bubble and sweet talk some more girls into bed? Now, for the last time, leave me alone."

At this, the grenade explodes and I lurch forward, seizing the book from his icy hands and chucking it at the empty table next to us. The motion startles him, but I don't stop. I *can't* stop. Shoving the chair out from under my body, I lunge into him, gripping the collar of his shirt and pulling his face against mine, until we're nose-to-nose.

"I notice you don't like looking people in the eyes," I whisper against his face, and his stench of smoke makes me sick. "If you don't tell me what you know about Flora, so help me God, I'll catch you when you least expect it and redesign your face. Now, I'm going to give you one more chance before I drag your ass out of this library. *Where is she?*"

His right cheek begins to twitch, and those black eyes jet over his shoulder, ensuring no one is listening. I can feel his warm breath pulsating against my cheeks. My grip still tight on the collar of his shirt, I watch as Don collects himself and slowly loosens from my grasp.

"I'll tell you tonight," he finally says.

"No, tell me now."

This time, however, Don returns the strength of my clutch, squeezing his palms over my hands. "If you really want to find your friend and last more than a day doing it, we do this my way. I'll give you what you want, but we wait until tonight."

I release him when he says this, and watch as he reaches into his pocket and jots down an address before shoving it across the table. "Meet me here tonight, nine o'clock."

I look at the scribbles on the piece of paper, fold it, and thrust it into my pocket. "OK," I say, "we'll do it your way. But you better be there tonight, or else."

***

The moon is full tonight, but had the sky been pitch black, I'd still have known I'm walking through a pile of trash: broken windows, creaking wooden floors, a few empty beer bottles lingering outside the front doorstep. No pets or gardens or solar panels.

I've never seen such a dump in my life.

I find myself wondering what the hell Flora ever saw in this guy. Or, is it possible her interest was in something else?

A twinge of hope sweeps through me.

When I knock on the front door—I swear the thing looks crooked—it scrapes open to reveal Don sitting on the floor near a fire and working on a computer. In fact, the whole room is interconnected with wires and motherboards and modems and printers. And on the walls are maps, dozens of them, littered with times and dates. If I didn't know Don personally, I'd think he was some sort of spy.

"Hurry and close the door," he says without looking up from his computer screen. "You'll let in the cold air."

Confused, I close the door, but stare at the various broken windows sucking in the chill from outside. I stand in silence for the next few minutes, but Don doesn't acknowledge me further. Annoyed, I finally speak up.

"So?" I say.

"So, grab a seat."

My eyes scan the room, but all I see are carpets on the floor. I open my mouth to protest, but decide against it and plop down near the fire. "What are you doing on that computer?" I ask.

"Stuff."

Right, I think, and begin wondering if I'd made a mistake by agreeing to this ridiculous meeting. "Look, I don't have all night," I say, and it takes every ounce of strength to maintain my patience.

"Neither do I." Don closes down his computer screen and turns to face me on the floor, his legs crossed. He still doesn't meet my eyes. "You have a real grip."

"Only when someone I love is in trouble, and someone else is withholding vital information I need to help."

"The library isn't safe," he says. "But they can't track me here. That's why you needed to wait."

Puzzled, I ask who "they" refers to, but Don doesn't answer. Instead, he launches into some explanation about a research project Flora started over the summer, and how she bugged him for help until he was ready to rip his hair from the scalp, and agreed. Of course, I'm not surprised when I learn of the topic: The Other Side, the same obsession my father had.

I figure this was the reason Flora never told me about it. She's never kept secrets before, but now I realize she was also trying to protect me.

"Anyway, that's why she came to me," Don says, finishing his explanation.

"I don't understand."

"She needed to get beyond the Wall, to The Other Side."

He says it so abruptly, with such nonchalance, that I take a moment to catch my breath. Somehow, hearing the words spoken aloud, by someone else, makes it real, *too real*. As quickly as the shock smacks into me, the bitterness hits, as I come to understand what Don actually did.

"You selfish bastard," I say. "You let a sick girl, someone who's *dying* of *stomach cancer*, go out into that—that place? What did you charge her?"

"You seem like the type who'd judge," he says, but his voice is lower this time, not full of the defiance that resonated in the library. "I started thinking maybe you were different, but thanks for proving me wrong."

I'm getting ready to jump to my feet when I stop myself, trying to remember I need to keep my cool if I want to help Flora. So I sit back down. As my head clears and rational thought returns, it occurs to me that, based on Don's reaction and the sad look in his eyes, perhaps he *didn't* charge her. Maybe Don actually tried to help Flora, for free.

"Why did you do it?" I ask.

"I don't own her," Don says. "Neither do you. Neither does anybody. What right do I have to deny her dying wish? And besides, why should I care what she, or anyone else, does with their lives? It's none of my damn business."

I don't know how to respond to that statement, because the truth is, he couldn't be more right. Why do we somehow believe we possess control over the actions and decisions of our loved ones? Is it possible that I was trying to control Flora, simply because I care?

Speechless, I sit and stare at Don, wondering about him for the first time. Until now, I'd never thought much about *why* he's so weird. Don attends school with Flora and me, yet he lives alone. Every student I know still lives with his or her parents while attending the university.

"Why isn't she back yet?" I ask, pushing away my curiosity. "I'm assuming you helped devise the whole Grand Canyon scheme."

At this, Don shrugs his shoulders. "I don't know. She was supposed to be back a day ago. She never showed up at our meeting point."

"You don't know?" My voice is growing coarse with alarm now. "She never showed up?"

Don shakes his head, and I spring to my feet, jetting back and forth near the fire. "How can you be so calm? How do you know she wasn't *killed* out there, Don!"

"I doubt that."

"Oh, I bet you do!"

I pace the floor until my feet numb, and now my arms, and skin, and I can no longer feel the air surrounding me, or inhale oxygen into my lungs. *Shit, shit, shit. Oh Flora, what did you get yourself into?*

"You'd better sit down," Don says, but his voice is sounding further and further away. "I think you're hyperventilating."

With no recourse, I listen to him and collapse onto the floor, unable to think straight. I glance toward Don, who's shoving a paper bag into my face and instructing me to breathe. I obey blindly, desperate for this feeling to go away. It seems like an hour, but the clock says it's only been five minutes, when a sense of normalcy begins to return. For the moment, I push aside my pride and thank Don for his help, handing the bag back to him. He tells me to keep it.

"So, what do you think happened to her?" I ask after regaining my composure.

"I don't know," he says. "But when she was preparing to leave, I forgot to tell her something. I called after her into the tunnel, but I'm not sure if she heard me."

I press to know what he overlooked, and he's reluctant at first, but finally admits, "I forgot to tell her that talking in public is not allowed."

I almost laugh at the irony. Of all the things Don could have forgotten to tell Flora, he forgot this. "How could you forget such an important detail?" I ask.

Don stiffens. "She threw up. Blood. Right as I was getting ready to tell her. It kinda jarred me. Hearing she was sick was one thing, but seeing it? That's a different story. I remembered only after she started crawling out."

"Well," I pause and take a deep breath, "this finally makes some sense. What are your plans to help her?"

But Don tells me there's nothing he can do, and when I hear his words, the unrest brews again. "You got her into this, Don. Now it's your job to fix it."

"It's not my stupid problem!" The force of his voice sends me falling backwards. "It's not my fault she decided to act careless and ask questions about places no one is supposed to know. I'm not going to risk my own safety for her stupidity."

"How dare you call her stupid." Protectiveness rushes through me. "Naïve, yes, but she has more brains than you, or I, or anyone else in Apollo can ever *hope* to have."

I try to retain my composure, because it's become clear that in order to help Flora, I'm going to need Don. So I'd better play somewhat nice.

"I'll tell you what you're going to do," I continue, and for the first time since I arrived here, I catch Don looking straight at me. Do I spot a glint of remorse buried in those black holes?

"You're going to help me get past the Wall, just like you helped Flora, and then you're going to accompany me to The Other Side, and we're going to find her together."

Of course he begins protesting, telling me why he won't do it, why it's not possible for the next two months because of some maintenance schedule. I stop him mid-sentence and lower my face to his eye level.

"You are going to find a way," I repeat, "because if not, I'll hold true to my promise of finding you in the night, and redesigning your face. Got it?"

He must have seen something in my eyes, some driving force beyond my reasoning or his understanding, because without another protest, he agrees. Deep down, I think he knows he's bound to Flora now too, because of what he did, and what I plan to do. So I nod my head, tell him he has three days, and I leave.

Lunch Date

ANDREW

The next day is a Saturday, and I decide to spend it with my mom, because at some point in the coming weeks, I'll be leaving and I cannot begin to fathom what awaits me on The Other Side. I will break the news of my trip to her today. No matter how much she begs, I tell myself, I cannot reveal the truth of my destination. I cannot put her at risk because of me.

The Central Commerce Hub is alive today with small families rushing the sidewalks and businesses. The streets pulsate with laughter and sunshine, even as the air takes on its yearly September edge while autumn falls like a blanket around us. The open breeze smells of pines and promises of Halloween in the near future, and my mom smiles as we pass a rogue violinist performing on the street corner for spare change.

In the central square, a Saturday yoga class practices its warrior poses and sun salutations while children skip by licking ice-cream and calling for their parents. Flora likes to call the families "tiny trilogies."

My mom and I settle on a small sandwich and coffee shop for lunch. We ask for a table on the patio to enjoy the fresh air and nearby violin music from the street performer.

"He's pretty good," my mom says, referring to the musician. "Not sure why he needs to grow out his hair and beard to play. He could be in the Apollo Philharmonic, but to each his own."

"Ma, c'mon, don't judge," I say, but I know it's useless. My mother is in one of her sassy moods today. I enjoy her like this. It's like I'm out with a friend.

"Andrew, I'm just speaking the truth," she responds. "Is a mother not allowed to make observations anymore?"

"Observe away."

Within moments, the server approaches, and I order my usual cup of coffee with creamer and sugar; my mom does the same, and it dawns on me we like our coffee the same way. A slight brush of homesickness passes through me at this epiphany. Maybe it's because the thought of putting my mother through any more emotional trauma upsets me, but what can I do? I have to help Flora.

Or maybe it's because deep down, I fear once I leave, I may never see my mom again.

"I ran into Randy at the grocery store yesterday," she starts telling me.

"Oh, Flora's dad?"

"Yes, and things are not going well. Her poor mother has been sedated and Randy is trying to work with the authorities, but no one seems to have any clue. She just, *poof!...* disappears off the face of the earth, like a molecule. I am worried sick about that girl."

"Me too, Ma," I say, my voice quiet.

"I wish there was more we could do. The Lobans are such a nice family—they've done so much for us over the years—and I love reading April's columns in the paper. She once wrote about the importance of developing a stronger Apollo Hospital, and thanks to her, my friend from work, Pauline, survived breast cancer."

I watch my mom as she chatters away, and I think how alive, how *youthful*, she looks, talking with her son on a Saturday afternoon while sipping coffee on a patio. I imagine before my dad left, she was more like this, and the thought makes me happy. This is the woman my dad married: his wife, my mom.

"Hey Ma," I say, pausing before continuing with my question. "Why do you think the doctors were able to help your friend Pauline, but can't do anything for Flora?"

The question stumps her, and she stares at me with a blank expression. "That's a really good question," she says after a few minutes.

"Don't you think it's a little unusual?"

She begins nodding her head. "Yes, yes I do think it's odd. In fact, if Flora had been anyone else's daughter, April would have jumped on that story."

My mom pauses and lifts her coffee mug to her lips, takes a small sip, and catches my eyes. As we stare into one another's gaze, some sort of mother-son ESP sweeps over us, and we both think the same thought, right at the same moment. She doesn't voice it, and neither do I, but we can read each other's minds: the face of my dad's friend Joe, who died of the brain tumor. He never found help from the Apollo Hospital, either. And we both wonder if this was coincidence, or something more.

Now's the time to tell her, Andrew.

The server approaches again and asks if we're ready to order. I can't help but feel as though I'm caught in the midst of a suspenseful thriller movie, where the main character is preparing to reveal a critical point to the plot, but the waiter interrupts at the right moment, prolonging the suspense.

"Can I get a turkey sandwich on one of those delicious challah rolls you make here?" my mom asks. "Extra mayo."

I haven't looked at the menu yet, and I'm not sure if I'm even hungry, so I order the same meal as my mother. The server finishes writing our orders on an old, scratchy pad of paper, and leaves. I turn back to my mom, and she's staring at me. I think she knows I'm planning on telling her something important.

I stand from my chair and walk toward her side of the table, lowering myself into the chair beside her. This is not something obvious or apparent, but her eyes are begging me to speak, so I smile and lean close to her ear, like I'm telling an inside joke.

"I know where Flora is," I whisper, keeping the smile on my face. "Try to act like I'm telling you something funny."

My face is close enough to my mom's that I can feel her breath quicken, her pulse increase. "I can't tell you where she is, but she's in trouble, Ma."

I pull away from her ear and envelop her hands into my own. Still keeping my head tilted low, the smile on my face, I take a deep breath. My mom's eyes have fallen from me now, out onto the streams of families and groups of teenagers flowing through the Central Commerce Hub. She's somewhere else, probably anticipating what my next words will be, so I just say them, my voice still a whisper.

"I'll be going away for a while."

Her grip tightens against mine, and I can feel her palms growing slick with sweat. The smile I asked for never comes. Her eyes stay fixed to the aimless stare she's secured into nothingness.

"It might be a few days, or it might be a few weeks. Either way, I need you to be brave for me, Ma, for both of us."

Finally, her empty gaze drifts toward me, and for the first time, she appears to take in the magnitude of the news I relayed. She's remaining perfectly quiet, perhaps because she's afraid to cause a scene, but her eyes have grown shiny from tears.

"I love you so much," I tell her. "You've been my mother *and* my father. I promise I will be back, and you'll never have to be alone again."

At this moment, the server reappears with our food. And once again, just like in the movies, his timing is perfect.

The Way Out

ANDREW

I was so angry when I'd left Don's house that I'd forgotten to confirm *how* we'd reconnect. So I've spent the past few days hanging around the university's library between classes, hoping to catch him, but he hasn't showed. I know where the guy lives, but now I'm beginning to worry I made a huge mistake walking out of that dump in the middle of the forest without getting his phone number, at least.

Of course, I have no idea how we're going to pull off our stunt, so I started preparing for the only aspect I can predict: survival in the woods. I'd stopped by the store and bought a survivor's pack, talked to that kid in my Ethics and Philosophy in Government course and bought some female skunk pheromones to ward off bears.

However, it's been nearly a week, and now I'm growing impatient. All I can do is think of Flora every waking minute, wondering if she's dead, or alive, or being held against her will in some jail somewhere. But perhaps what frightens me the most, are the possibilities I *cannot* imagine.

This is why Don needs to hurry.

As I'm scribbling these thoughts in my journal, my phone vibrates. When I look down, a text message from a blocked number stares back.

Meet me in the meadow to the north of the Central Commerce Hub, 7 p.m. tonight.

I know immediately it's him, but how did he get my number? I never gave it to him, and we don't have a public phone book in Apollo. I think, and ponder, and although I never come to an answer, it dawns on me that the meadow is the same one where I met Sophie only months ago. I sigh at the thought.

Oh well. Looks like I'm returning to that same spot, only this time, for Flora.

***

The days are beginning to grow shorter, and the meadow at the bottom of the valley is already steeped in evening shadows—long and dark and ominous. Don is waiting in his rundown car when I arrive, the paint peeling from its roof and hood. One of his legs hangs from the driver's seat, his foot resting in the dirt.

I park my car and climb out, approaching him slowly. He appears to be fidgeting with some handheld device and doesn't notice me drawing near.

"For someone who flaunts caution, you really don't pay much attention to your surroundings, do you?" I say.

Don stops his fidgeting, but otherwise remains still. "And for someone who says he cares so much about helping his friend, you really don't pay much attention to the time," he responds.

I glance down at my watch and realize I'm ten minutes late. I didn't even realize...

"Climb into the back seat," he tells me. "Hurry."

I glance over my shoulder before hopping into the back of his car and I lean over the seats to examine the mystery mechanism on his lap.

"What's that thing?" I ask him.

"Our way out."

"Yeah, but what is it?"

Don sighs in annoyance, but answers me anyway. "It's a handheld EMP device."

I pause before peering at his face, which remains expressionless. "You mean, it sends an electromagnetic pulse?"

"Yes, to disarm the cameras on the Wall. You can't exactly run to the store and buy one at the cash register. It's not completely done, but I should have it finalized by the end of next week."

"You made that thing?" I ask, shocked.

He stops and turns his head in my direction, and I catch him rolling his eyes. "Who else would have made it? My imaginary brother?"

I want to laugh just as much as I want to punch him in the nose. So instead, some odd form of an agitated chuckle emerges, and Don's face contorts into a disgusted look.

"Well, that's great and all, but won't it cut off all the electricity in Apollo?" I ask.

"You said you didn't want to wait two months. You wanted to go now. Well, here is your answer. Will it kill Apollo's electricity? I don't know. I did my best to contain the pulse to a five-mile radius, but we won't know until we use it."

I take a deep breath and stare a little longer at the device. The thing is intricately wired and reminds me of an oversized, ancient console for video games, like I've seen in the history books. Brilliant, absolutely brilliant.

"Are you studying computer engineering or programming?" I ask him after a few moments of silence, genuinely curious. "You know, in school?"

"I'm undeclared," he says, and his voice is vacant, empty.

"You hacked into my phone, didn't you? Earlier today?"

Don doesn't answer my question, but instead changes the subject to something else: our escape.

"We are leaving after dark next Friday," he tells me. "Meet me at my house, ten o'clock p.m. Make sure no one follows you. And bring a survival pack. It's a two-day hike after we make it to The Other Side."

"And you're sure your EMP device will be ready?" I ask.

"Ten p.m.," he repeats. "And before we leave, I have a few things we'll need to discuss."

The Museum

FLORA

Andrew's father has been beside himself ever since we met. Day after day, I receive pop-up messages from him, asking about Andrew. What does he look like now? Is he attending college? What's his major? When I told him writing, Andrew's father messaged back saying, *I used to want to write, too. But my mother talked me into I.T. She said it was a better future. I'm so glad he's writing.*

Then one day, during the hospital's socialization hour, he asked the question I'd hoped would never arise: "Does Andrew hate me?"

I watched through the three-dimensional screen as soulful eyes, the same as my best friend's, searched my face—sad and hopeful and despondent. Of course, I didn't know how to answer that question, so I deflected the only way I knew how.

"You are so charming, I couldn't imagine anyone *not* liking you," I said.

Thankfully, it worked, perhaps because he was flattered, or perhaps because in truth, he wasn't ready to know. I haven't had a moment yet to ask Andrew's father what drove him beyond the Wall, nor the more pressing question about how he escaped Apollo. When Andrew's father left, Don was only eight years old, so I'm pretty sure he wasn't Andrew's father's underground smuggler, too.

Messaging with Andrew's dad on a daily basis, while confined to this empty cell, has prompted me to crave my father's presence and his beautiful piano notes. The hospital monitors our conversations, of course, and every so often, a nurse will intercede, but that never stops Andrew's father and me from continuing our conversations later. The staff members usually write it off as crazy talk.

Dr. Hauser tells me constantly that I have the world at my fingertips, that there's no need to feel lonely. He says I can message any of the hospital's patients through the directory. Our access to the World Wide Web has been limited—this is for our protection, apparently—but otherwise, I could participate in all the games and interactions I want.

Dr. Hauser also told me about select online "communities" that are available through the Internet. While not all are open to me, I have thousands I could join and therefore talk with people over the Web. I tried this once, but the people are nothing but names and photos and virtual avatars plastered to a three-dimensional screen floating above my face.

Everything feels hollow.

Plus, the people in these communities are often mean, anyway. Not just mean, but *malicious*, sick. They take pleasure in bragging about horrible thoughts, like disfiguring babies with knives and carving out a woman's genitals. They speak of things I never knew were possible—things that aren't fathomable in Apollo.

And as the time passes, I miss my father and his music even more.

I'm not sure what day it is—everything here is so repetitive and bland that it's easy to lose track—but I'm nauseated from homesickness tonight as I try to fall asleep. I'm staring into the desolate darkness, my sixth straight day without direct human contact, wishing I could hear my father's piano music as I drift off, just like back home.

Ridden with restlessness, I call Justine's name and message her, asking if we have anything available. When the question reaches her, however, she twists her face into a snarky expression and says, "You mean *real* piano music?"

"Yes," I say, irritated by her judgmental tone and unexpected condescendence, "*real* piano music."

"Well, that doesn't exist anymore," she tells me, and I feel a section of my heart die. "You can take a tour of the Museum of Musical Instruments and go visit the piano. They let our patients in for free, but otherwise, all we have is e-music."

"We're allowed to get out and visit the museum?" I ask, my voice piquing.

"Well, you can't leave, but you can take a tour."

The nothingness washes over me again when I hear this. I'm not sure what Justine's answer means, but I've come to the conclusion that I'm a prisoner of this hospital cell.

When I ask for more information on the e-music Justine mentioned, she merely rolls her eyes and uploads something into my earpiece. A contorted form of computerized, synthetic sounds jerk their way into my head, noises that resemble drums, and violins, and pianos, and guitars. Apparently, none of these instruments are crafted anymore. Wondering what happened, I command my government-issued contacts to look up the history of musical instruments.

Within moments, a string of answers appears before my eyes, hanging over my head in the darkness. Once again, I select the World Encyclopedia's explanation:

Digital musical instruments first came about in the early 21st century in the form of video games. However, they soon evolved into serious mediums for musical artists between the years 2040 and 2050. The development of professional digital musical instruments suppressed the need for the older, more traditional methods of composing music.

Due to the easy nature of composition via these digital models, everyday consumers began utilizing them on their computers and phones through simple commands. Catching onto trends, marketers soon began targeting all consumers with their products, coining the famous phrase, "Anyone can be a composer."

By the year 2063, the last acoustic musical instrument was crafted. Today, traditional musical instruments can only be found in museums, as the majority of them were destroyed in the year 2075, during the Virtual Revolution.

I stop reading. There's that year again, 2075—the year Apollo was founded. Why did we never learn about the Virtual Revolution in school? Why haven't I come across information about it on A-Search? This leads me to another, more disturbing question: if I never learned about the Virtual Revolution, what else was kept from me over the years?

A part of me yearns to know more, aches for the answer the way a widow longs for her husband's touch. But then the other side takes over, crushes the curiosity, and all I desire is comfort: Ernest's floppy ears nuzzled under my arms, Andrew's warm smile and penetrating gaze, my father's piano music.

"Justine!" I call into the darkness again. This time, however, she merely answers through a pop-up, her message one word:

What?

I speak my message and watch as words appear on the screen floating before my face: *When does the museum open?*

It's always open, she responds.

How do I get there?

After a momentary pause, Justine sends a link through the message window. When I open it, a repertoire of violins and pianos and trombones and guitars surround me. The words, *How may we help you?* linger in front of my eyes.

"I want to take a tour of your museum," I say aloud. Nothing happens at first, but then my information—name, age, government I.D. , place of residence—emerges, and a computerized voice asks, "Is this information correct?"

"Yes," I respond, and like socialization hour, my line of vision goes black, and a new one materializes. Towering glass walls line expansive hallways, and behind them, musical instruments rest in silence, on display. Each is accompanied by a virtual heading and description. I'm beginning to wonder if everything is automated when a harsh, female voice begins talking into my ear—very real, and very human. Her irritated tone heightens my awareness that it's also very late, possibly after midnight.

"Welcome to the Museum of Musical Instruments," she says. "I'm Eve, your tour guide."

I can't see her, so I merely sit on my bed as my line of vision begins to stroll past the endless corridors encased by glass. It occurs to me that, like socialization hour, I'm stuck inside a robot, once again.

"Can you hear me?" I ask my tour guide, as she begins explaining about the first instrument on display: a clarinet.

"Yeah," she responds. "What do ya need?"

The crudeness with which she speaks bothers me, but I ask her anyway. "What time is it?"

There's a long pause before she answers, "One in the mornin'."

"And you're working?"

"I'm always working." She pauses, and I hear her take an annoyed breath. "Do ya wanna go on, or should we become best friends?"

I ignore her patronizing tone and ask one more question. "I do, but first, where are you?"

"Where else would I be? I'm home, just like everyone else 'round here."

Home. She's doing this from home. At one o'clock in the morning.

"OK," I say. "Can you just take me to the piano?"

"Whatever the nuthouse wants."

Her words sting, not because of their content, but because of her attitude. She says this like she's talking about eating dinner, or taking her dog for a walk—like her emotions are disjointed, and it doesn't occur to her that calling a psychiatric patient "nuthouse" might be construed as cruel.

But I don't respond. I allow her to lead me toward the only piano the museum has on display. It's a magnificent Steinway made from carved cherry wood, the same model as my father's. As my line of vision approaches the stunning contraption, I can feel my eyes begin to burn and my chest grow heavy with bereavement, but all I can do is sit on my bed and stare, the piano's keys dusty and untouched for decades.

Eve begins talking about the piano's history, and I can hear background music swell over her voice. Anticipation rises in my chest—could it be? *Real* piano music, just a sense of back home, a taste?

But no, I soon come to realize that even the semi-familiar sounds which play in my ear bud aren't real: the notes bare and gray and digitized, just like the world that's threatening to consume me. *E-music.*

I find myself tuning out Eve's ragged, fragmented voice and instead longing for my father's beautiful notes, and my mother's soft smile, and Ernest's gentle greetings. I never realized I had the potential to miss anything so much.

Andrew.

His face flashes in my memory and I'm suddenly beginning to understand that I may never see him again. I'll have only his father for comfort in his eternal absence, which, in retrospect, may actually become more torturous. In the moment, I forget about the piano I'm passing by and close my eyes, picturing his dark, soulful face—the way he can see straight through me to a place buried so deep that I sometimes forget it exists.

I wish that I could lie down next to him in this lonely bed, that we could experience this monumental discovery, however gloomy it may be, together. Just like we'd always done, until now.

It's at this point I come to the conclusion that I no longer care to learn about The Other Side. I hold no curiosity about this United Council or Virtual Revolution anymore. I couldn't care less why everyone thinks Apollo is some nuclear waste dump. Instead, all I can recall are the words Andrew's father spoke to me when we first met:

"I allowed my curiosity and my sense of dissent to become more important than those I loved most. I never could have imagined what it would cost me."

Lockdown

FLORA

What is that?

I'm jerked awake from a deep sleep, adrenaline shooting through my body like heroin. It's early morning and the sun has barely begun to peek through the shades of my window.

What IS that?

Piercing, shrieking... *sirens.* Yes, they're sirens, or alarms. And they're blaring through the hallways of the Phoenix Psychiatric Hospital.

I jet to my feet, unaware that my pulse has doubled and my breath quickened so much that tiny droplets of sweat begin inching down my temples. *What is going on out there?*

Without warning, a violent jolt knocks me to the ground and I land on my palms against the solid tile, crunching my wrists and wincing from the pain that shoots up my arms. The floor continues vibrating through my nerves, and I can't be sure, but I think I heard an explosion when the ground jerked.

Screams. Terrifying screams, the sort that accompany nightmares or death. Holding my wrists, I scramble to my feet toward the door and push to my tiptoes, frantically peering out the window of my hospital cell into the hallways. I see quick flashes of white—nurses in their garb, perhaps?—racing past my window.

"What's going on?" I yell into the open air of my room, hoping that perhaps Justine will hear. But no one answers.

Pop-pop-pop. I realize the uproar is taking place on the floor below me. Smoke, I swear I'm smelling smoke now, but it's not the same comforting scent as a campfire in the woods. No, this smoke reeks of gunpowder and blood.

I could die, I think. *I need to get out of here.*

Before I can react, my vision turns red, and blindness stops me mid-step. The same blaring alarm penetrates through my ear piece and vibrates into my skull. I cry out from the pain, but also in surprise. I must have fallen asleep with my contacts in, because I didn't realize I'd been wearing them until now. A message painted in bold, black letters flashes before the redness invading my vision:

SHOOTING ALERT. LOCKDOWN SYSTEM ACTIVATED. REMAIN IN YOUR ROOM. AVOID WINDOWS.

It takes a moment for the severity of these words to register. As they do, unbridled panic and terror burst through me, firing from my extremities in electric shocks and choking the cry forming in my throat. *This can't be happening*, I tell myself. *No, this can't be real.*

The words soon dissipate and the redness dissolves back into my current room. The lights go out. Swimming in darkness now, I must rely on the spears of sunlight creeping through my window.

Petrified from fear and confusion, I hunch into the center of my room, eyes jetting from one corner to the next, always falling back to the door. The ceiling spins as blood pounds through my vessels, until I can hear nothing but thunder in my ears.

"Don't!" a lady screams from outside my room, and her voice sounds distant. "Pleeease!"

But I hear another pop, and a thump. *I'm going to die.* I think. *I'm not ready, I'm not ready.*

The door to my room whips open, and now the shriek comes, bloodcurdling and piercing.

"Flora! Shhh." It's a female voice, and as my eyes focus on the figure closing the door and lunging toward me, I recognize mocha-colored skin and that worn, white lab coat. Dr. Thompson!

Her fingers close with urgency around my bicep and she yanks me onto my feet, throwing me into the cube-sized bathroom in my room. She flies behind me, pulling both of us deep into the bathtub, and we huddle there together. I can feel her nervous breath pulsating against my scalp, her arms shaking as they cradle me against her torso.

"What's going on?" I whisper.

"Shhh," is her only answer.

I hear someone yelling outside my door now, a male voice filled with rage and homicidal mania. The smell of smoke grows stronger, and I curl into a fetal position, trying desperately to keep the tears at bay. The man screams incomprehensible threats while banging against my door, the blows forceful and frightening.

A deafening *boom!* rattles the walls and tub surrounding us, and I scream—another wave of fear rushes through me like a flash flood. The room trembles, but my ears are buzzing and I can barely hear the trays clanging to the ground just outside the bathroom.

And now, quiet.

I realize I'm coiled into a tight ball and holding my breath, my fingernails drawing blood from digging into my palms. The gentle beeping from Dr. Thompson's ear piece slowly lures me from my terror-induced trance, but nothing comes through mine yet.

Dr. Thompson pulls herself to a sitting position and looks around, paying keen attention to the message she's receiving. Her hand strokes my hair, and her breath begins to calm.

"It's all clear," she says after a few minutes.

I'm shaking with such angst, I can barely talk. But when I do, my voice sounds broken and fragmented. "How... do... you know?"

"The system says so."

I look up at Dr. Thompson. She's reclaimed that authoritative, yet calming demeanor I first met after waking in this hospital weeks ago.

"What just happened?" I ask.

"Mass shooting. They happen every day now."

"Here?"

"Everywhere," she tells me. "In all the Sectors. Are you OK?"

Before I can answer, Dr. Thompson stiffens when a new report begins buzzing through her ears. Her eyes narrow, and she shakes her head in disbelief.

I ask what happened, what did the message say, but Dr. Thompson won't tell me. From the tautness of her face, her knuckles white from gripping the nearby countertop, I can tell she's greatly affected—probably trying to hold it together for the patients.

"Please, you need to tell me," I say after a few minutes. "You need to tell *somebody*."

Dr. Thompson looks down at me, her eyes bleeding sorrow, and she gives in. "I just received a report of the damage." She pauses. "Twenty wounded, and fifty dead... including Dr. Hauser."

My stomach drops. I've never seen anything like this in my life—this sort of violence, of senseless murder.

"Who—who would do that?" I ask. "Why?"

Dr. Thompson shakes her head and looks defeated, placing her hand atop mine. "That's the world we live in, Flora. If it were up to me, I'd rather exist in your Apollo, even if it is a dream world."

Something about the tone in her voice touches a place deep inside me, a place that no one on this Other Side has been able to find. Maybe she felt I deserved a taste of the real her, after living through such a traumatizing event together. Maybe she said it for herself, for something to believe in, but whatever her reasoning, I'm happy she did it.

"I need to assess the rest of the damage now. Will you be OK?" Dr. Thompson looks at me with care.

I nod my head, but stop her before she walks out. "How did you know I needed help?"

"I didn't," she says. "The system did."

For some reason, her answer fills me with sorrow; I was hoping we'd shared a deeper connection than a computer. "The system told you to pull me into the bathroom?"

Dr. Thompson smiles at me. "Of course it did," she says. "How else would I have known what to do? Now rest up. Everything will be fine now."

***

I'm not allowed out of my room for hours. I can hear the police—a combination of robots and humans—mingling just outside my door, probably collecting evidence before their cleanup crew comes to sterilize the crime scene. Apparently, one of the gunmen died there, just on the other side of my room, and I shudder at the thought.

After everything is finished, my door opens and I'm allowed to roam freely among the hallway for the first time. Of course, barriers are placed at the ends of the corridor, and several nurses are present via their assigned androids, but I'm finally able to look upon the other patients in person; we're no longer trapped behind screens.

As I'm absorbing my moment of controlled freedom, I see Andrew's father, his room only a few doors from mine.

Our eyes meet—the moment seems surreal—and we run toward the other, falling into a deep embrace. I can't stop myself from bawling into his shoulder. It's been three weeks since anyone has hugged me, has shown empathy or caring or... *connection*. But now, in this moment of relief and survivor's guilt, I can release myself, closing my eyes against Andrew's father's soft and weathered shirt.

"It's OK, sweetheart," he tells me, and his voice is gentle. He sounds so much like my best friend, and I'm homesick beyond reason.

"Who—who would do that?" I mumble against his shoulder, still unable to control my tears and heaving breaths.

"It's a shock to see this, coming from our world. But I promise, you'll get used to it."

Get used to it?

I pull myself away from his chest and peer up into kind eyes. He looks so much like Andrew, but his comforting embrace reminds me of my father. It suddenly occurs to me that, much like I've yearned for home these past three weeks, Andrew's father has craved to feel like a parent these past eleven years.

I struggle to shake the feeling and refocus my thoughts on the sentence he just spoke. "What do you mean, 'get used to it'?"

Out of the corner of my vision, I'm vaguely aware of numerous pairs of eyes watching us, judging us.

"This has happened before," Andrew's father says.

"You mean, here? At the hospital?"

He nods his head. "Last attack was less than two years ago."

I'm speechless for a moment, shocked out of crying. "Why?"

"People are angry—disconnected and fed up. They just don't care."

A directive materializes in front of my eyes now, instructing me to return to my room. I don't have the opportunity to say goodbye to Andrew's father because the nurses begin shepherding everyone from the hallways via their strolling robots.

Already? But that was so short! Why even allow any interpersonal interaction for such a brief period of time? Is it because we were all traumatized from a shooting? Do they really believe a quick, five-minute fix would be all that we needed?

When I return to my room, the same sense of hollowness sweeps over me, so I lie down on my bed in the shock position, breathing through my nose and soothing myself.

"Turn on the news," I instruct my contacts, and within moments, a screen pops before my eyes, hanging in the air like a toy above a baby's cradle. Just as I expected, the newscast running is about the shooting at my hospital.

A mass shooting at Phoenix Psychiatric Hospital today killed fifty and wounded twenty. Authorities say ten of those wounded are considered in critical condition. Among the dead are several nurses, patients, and the presiding resident psychiatrist, Dr. Norman Hauser. According to reports by police, three armed gunmen entered the facility at six-forty-five this morning, forcing their way into the building with homemade bombs. Police sent in SWAT android units at six-fifty and successfully killed the three gunmen, one as he was preparing to forcibly enter a patient's room.

I know immediately the room they're referencing is mine, and a knot forms in my stomach.

This is the third mass shooting in Sector 1 in a month. Ironically, the United Council Institute of Mental Health published its September report today, indicating that suicide trends have not reversed as expected, but have actually increased by another one-point-two percent.

I begin tuning out the chatter from the newscaster, and instead, my eyes fall to a section below the broadcast; it looks like a place for people to leave comments on the story, most of them real-time videos, every voice and face debating at once. An icon indicates the news story has been shared more than one thousand times—whatever that means. The comments catch my attention, however, more than anything else.

The first is from a girl about my age, with beautiful olive colored skin and bright green eyes. Yet, despite such outward beauty, her eyebrows are furrowed in contempt, and her voice is filled with rage as she begins firing.

"Good, I'm glad someone got the guts to stick a bullet in that shitty-ass doctor and his bottom-feeding moocher patients. I heard that Dr. Hauser was one of *them*. If I knew how to make bombs, I'd have done it myself."

After her, I watch a man who looks like he's pushing fifty spill his venom into the camera. "If I had it my way, we'd round 'em up and stick 'em in camps and let 'em die off. These men are heroes!"

Commentary after commentary after commentary, screaming about a group of people called "The Upper Class," accusing Dr. Hauser of being "one of them," and calling the patients every name in the book while spouting off reasons we deserve to die. They all herald the gunmen as heroes, and wish they'd done it themselves. When it comes to the violence and death, there's not a single word of sympathy, from *anyone*.

I tell my contacts to close down the news, because all this hate is poisoning me. I'd never known humans are capable of such animosity. Of course, I'd been bullied in Apollo, but *this*? Never *this*.

Suddenly, the events of the day begin consuming me, and I grow exhausted. So I allow my eyes to drift shut, and my mind to fall into a deep sleep.

EMP

ANDREW

Something about the Wall has always terrified me, and it takes a *lot* to make me cower into a corner. Perhaps it's due to my father's fascination and disappearance, but whatever the reason, I find myself shocked that I'm not more scared right now.

The night has fallen into an eerie darkness, as if the trees are trying to warn us. It's barely after ten o'clock on Friday, and I'm sitting cross-legged on the wooden floor of Don's home. He's just finished telling me about a pair of contacts he packed, and how they're vital to our survival on The Other Side.

"Did you give Flora a pair?" I ask him.

"No."

"Why not?"

Don begins rummaging through scattered papers across the floor, and mutters, "Because, only the government can give them to you. This is the only pair I have."

"So how did *you* get them?"

He pauses his fidgeting and glances toward me, still refusing to meet my eyes. "I have my ways," he says before changing the subject. "We'll have to make a stop to get you a pair once we arrive in the city."

I'm growing frustrated with his refusal to share the details of our trip, so I keep pressing. "And how do you propose we do that?"

Don halts his incessant preparation, pushing his bag of crap to the side. "Look," he says, an edge to his voice I hadn't noticed before, "there's a lot of stuff that has to be done, and I don't have time to explain the philosophy of our world to you right now. You'll learn soon enough, so in the meantime, let me work."

I decide to let this slide—after all, he is helping to find Flora—so I shut my mouth. After sitting in excruciating silence for the next ten minutes, I ask Don if there's anything I can do. But he tells me "No, just wait another five minutes. Then we'll start cycling."

***

I never considered that riding a bicycle through the woods in pitch darkness would be this difficult. After all of my Saturday morning bike rides with Flora, I thought I knew the Apollo woods like my mother understands me. Yet here is Don, whizzing past trees and around branches like he's a cheetah in his element, hunting at night.

My legs are burning and my eyes are strained from navigating with nothing more than the small beam of light shining from my head. I feel like we've been riding all night when I hear him tell me to stop.

Panting, I prop my bike against a tree and begin looking around. I don't see the Wall anywhere. Certainly, the darkness wouldn't conceal a structure that large, would it?

"Where are we?" I ask him between breaths.

"On our way out," he says. "Sit down for a few minutes."

I plop onto the damp ground, and its coolness refreshes my body. I'm practically sweating from the workout, despite the chilled air. Don lowers himself nearby and begins laying out a laundry list of rules I need to follow.

Don't show my face outside the tunnel once we reach The Other Side, until he says it's clear

Don't talk on The Other Side. Let him conduct all communications.

Try not to look anyone in the eye.

"You mentioned a tunnel. Is that how we'll get past the Wall?" I ask.

Don turns his head toward a log a few feet from where I'm sitting and shines his overhead light on it. I follow his gaze, but see nothing. Don tells me to keep looking, so after further squinting my eyes, I make out a black hole under the fallen tree.

"I go first," Don says. "It's the only way we can use the EMP device."

I feel my muscles start to tighten, but I swallow the rising swell of doubt. *For Flora*, I tell myself. *For Flora.*

I nod my head, more from nervousness than anything else. "And... you're sure this EMP device will work?" I ask him.

Don looks me straight in the eyes. "I'm ninety-nine percent sure."

I pause before asking the next question, because part of me doesn't want to know the answer. "What about the other one percent?"

"Let's not think about that."

Wise idea. I take a deep breath and find myself laughing, so I let it roll through me like waves in a swimming pool. "Well, shall we?"

Without saying another word, Don scoots toward the tunnel, pushes his backpack through, and drops from sight. I'm past the point of contemplation now, so I don't think anymore; I just follow him and fall.

***

The damp dirt has the consistency of mud, and it slides across my forearms and belly as I drag myself through the endless tunnel. The air is heavy and I find myself struggling to breathe, but all I can think about is Flora. She managed to do this by herself? *With cancer?*

"How did you discover this thing?" I ask Don, as we're slithering our way through.

"I dug it."

It takes a moment for his words to register, so when I answer, it seems like a delayed reaction. "Wait, you actually built this tunnel?"

"That's what I said."

"How many times have you snuck out?"

Don refuses to acknowledge my question though, and remains silent. The curiosity is starting to drive me into madness, so I keep pressing. "Don, how many?"

I hear him sigh, and he stops slithering for a moment. The tunnel is too narrow for him to turn around and look at me, so he keeps staring straight ahead when he answers. "About once every year or so," he says.

I'm dead quiet, lying here underground, in complete shock. "Holy crap," I say, and Don begins moving again. "You slick son of a bitch. And no one has ever caught you?"

"No."

We continue pushing through the dank dirt for the next five minutes in silence, but I'm fascinated by Don's story. All this time, all this time...

"How?" I ask. "And why?"

"Look, I'm really not the type who likes to talk much," he says.

"C'mon. We might as well get to know each other. At least tell me how you pulled off a crazy stunt like that. I'm curious."

I hear Don's panting as he continues pushing his backpack in front of him. Deep under the ground like this, I can hear nothing but breathing, the scraping of skin against soil, and conversation. It reminds me of being underwater: peaceful, reclusive.

"I have a schedule of Apollo's Wall maintenance," Don says after a few minutes, breaking the deafening hush. "About once a year, they shut down the cameras closest to my house for thirty minutes to conduct maintenance—major system updates and such."

"How did you get that schedule?" I ask.

"I hacked Apollo's systems."

"You're crazy!"

But Don doesn't acknowledge my comment. He merely continues telling me about his regular escapes, how he waits for the scheduled maintenance, then uses the thirty-minute window to flee.

"That's how Flora escaped," I say when he's done explaining. "You gave up your window for her."

Don's voice grows much softer now. "Yes," he says.

"That's pretty brilliant and all, but why don't you just hack the Wall's system instead? Seems easier than all this planning."

"No, absolutely not." Don stops crawling again, and his voice grows harsh. "Hacking occasionally is OK, but doing it every time leaves evidence you were there—like a digital footprint. It could lead back to me. Waiting for the maintenance is better. It's safer."

I want to ask him why he goes through the trouble to escape at all. Why not just accept things the way they are back home, rather than risking so much year after year? But instead, I settle for a simpler question. "So, what's it like on The Other Side?"

Don grins when I ask; I can feel his smirk. "You'll see," he says. "Hey, slow down. I think we're coming to the end of the tunnel."

I stop behind him and keep staring straight ahead. Don unzips his backpack and fidgets through his arsenal of contraptions. I try to shine my headlamp over his shoulder, barely able to discern the handheld EMP device when he pulls it from the bottom of his pack.

"Is it ready to go?" I ask.

"In a few minutes. I need to charge it."

I listen as Don clicks something, and now I hear a soft, steady buzzing. I continue to lie quietly in the damp dirt, waiting for the next few minutes.

"OK," Don says. "Shield your eyes. It's going to be bright."

I listen to him, take a gulp of air and hold my breath. *Here goes nothing*, I think, and Don starts counting down. "Three... two... one."

The buzzing explodes into brilliant beams of light, and I hear Don yell from their intensity. I cover my face, the brightness penetrating through shut eyelids, and I grimace into my arms, digging my nose further and further into the dirt.

The lights keep shining, pulsating out of the device, and like a light switch, it suddenly goes dark.

"Holy crap," is all I can say. "Holy, holy crap."

I hear Don's rapid breathing, but he remains quiet, so I speak again. "Did it work?" I ask.

"I can't—can't know for sure. There's only one way to tell."

Don doesn't need to say any more. I know exactly what we need to do. I watch as he squirms forward, frantic and hurried. I follow, my heart rate elevating from adrenaline. Don pushes his pack up the vertical end of the tunnel and pushes out, and I do the same.

The night's cold chill slices across my cheeks the moment I reach fresh air, and I breathe in the welcomed mountain scents. I turn around and look over my shoulder, and just as Don had promised, the Wall is littered with cameras, watching me.

"Let's go!" I hear him yell.

No time to think, Andrew. Move your ass!

I snatch my pack and toss it across my back, pounding my feet into the moist forest ground and following Don blindly through the trees. I don't hear an alarm, or gunshots, or any other sound that might signify imminent death, so as the cold air begins burning in my throat, I can only assume we made it.

Don's device must have worked.

Hallway to Hell

ANDREW

I don't know what I expected on The Other Side—grimy air and rivers of people entombed in their own worlds of technology, perhaps?—but certainly not this: silence, stillness.

A dead city.

No cars. Clear air. A quiet so potent, you'd think you just stepped onto a nuclear wasteland. It's eerie, and my first impulse is to ask Don what the hell happened, but the moment my eyes fall upon him, he shoots me a look, a reminder: *don't talk.*

So I swallow my questions and continue following him down the street. We are supposed to be wandering through downtown Phoenix. I never knew this city still existed. Los Angeles, Chicago, New York, Denver—I thought they were all gone. History, like the former United States of America.

Yet, here I am.

A transport delivered us here, and I found the thing curious. Sad, even. Nothing like it exists in Apollo, and yet it retains this mysterious sense of nostalgia, as if recalling a time not so long ago when things were better. Happier. More colorful.

Now, only a shadow exists.

I can tell Don is beginning to grow somewhat weak. His stance is starting to slump like a hunchback's, and the pack adorning his back looks heavier and heavier with each passing minute. Yet, he keeps walking down the desolate sidewalk, staring toward the ground. I continue following him.

As we wind deeper into alleyways and leave the open streets behind, I notice some bodies lying on the sidewalk, and I can't tell if they're dead or alive. As we move closer, I can make out one person to be a woman, and the other a man. They're alive, I now realize, but worn and weary souls, possibly in their forties or fifties, but not older than sixty. Their faces are caked with mud and filth to such an extreme, they remind me of military figures in movies conducting secret missions in camouflage. But their bodies—the images evoke flashbacks of photos I've seen in history books of prisoners in Nazi concentration camps in World War II.

The man is sitting upright, sipping from a water bottle, but the woman, she's the one who catches my attention. The layers of grime emphasize her eyes and they remind me of a dying street cat's glare: hollow and *yellow.* Her fingernails, too, are the color of mustard. And her cheeks sink into her face like collapsed mines.

I want to ask Don what's wrong with her. Why isn't anyone outside helping this woman and man? The yellow tint is what worries me the most. I remember learning about that symptom from biology class: jaundice.

As we walk past the couple, I hear the woman moaning, obviously in pain, yet she refuses to acknowledge my presence. Something about her frail figure, along with those tortured and muffled cries, triggers some reflex deep inside of me, and I suddenly think of my mother.

"Ma'am," I say, and stop before her, even though I know it's against the rules. I lean down to offer my hand and am slapped with the stench of rotten eggs and urine. I fight the gag reflex and keep talking. "Do you need us to call someone for you?"

I don't have time to witness the woman's response, however. Don's fingernails scrape against my shoulder through my shirt, tearing me away from the couple. I try to turn back, but he yanks my arm, so I stop struggling.

Riled that he'd be so cold as to leave that woman dying on the street, I'm about to scold him, but the look in Don's eyes stops me: his glare is murder.

So I take a deep breath and let the air quiver out my lungs, trying to calm down. Don releases my arm and turns around, marching forward again. I allow him to get a few steps on me before I continue following. And I see it.

The woman and man aren't the only ones lying on the steaming concrete, wasting away in the shadows of the city's gutters. The further we continue around hidden corners, the more and more I see others like them. Some are missing patches of skin from their faces. Others have softballs growing out of their throats. And some just look like they're in agony.

I'm nauseated by it all: the smell, the scene. I can feel death teasing me at every corner, tickling under my arms, twitching at my feet, and I want to bolt from this scene, fearful that if I remain here any longer, death will entomb me as well.

I shake the sensation from my skin and try to ignore the hollow faces as I pass them. We're dragging ourselves along this hallway to hell for several more minutes before Don stops and lifts his hand, motioning for me to pause. He's standing outside an old, rundown building with broken wood panels that are splintering from the jagged threshold. Faded graffiti decorates the once-white brick, which is now a convoluted concoction of sand and feces.

I watch Don as he lifts his head and begins nodding, gesturing into the air with his hands and fingers.

"Don," I whisper, but he shoots me an angry glance, and I know to shut up immediately. He returns his focus to the blank wall. All I can do is stand here, and observe. After another few moments he stops his curious signals, jerks his pack further up his back, and I hear him grunt, even though he tries to hide it.

I approach him and take my place by his side, staring blankly at the old building, wondering what we're doing here. Right as I open my mouth to ask, the wall slides back into itself, revealing a dark pathway that leads into nothingness.

"Are you sure this is safe?" I ask Don, keeping my voice low so no one else will hear.

"Shut up and follow me," he says, and I can see his desperate attempt to keep his lips still as he whispers.

***

When I first meet Stone, he's nothing but a looming shadow at the end of a dark, vacant hallway. The first thing I notice about him is the power. It drips from every aspect of his being: his overwhelming physique, his movements, and when he eventually emerges from blackness, his glare. Even his tattoos intimidate—the skulls and fallen angels—and my initial instinct warns me that Stone is the type who kills when crossed.

Don motions for me to stop once Stone appears before us. The two of them seem to be having a silent conversation of some sort, their facial expressions changing as they nod heads and motion with their hands, and I catch Don smile.

Smile!

It occurs to me, when I see this, how unhappy Don must have been all these years. Not once have I seen his eyes lighten, or his eyebrows lift in delight. He always wears the skin along his face like rags, so much that I'd begun to wonder if he developed a permanent frown. I ask myself what on earth could have coaxed a genuine smile from Don, and it suddenly strikes me that these two know each other.

Don and Stone. But how, and more importantly, *why?*

"You don't have contacts?" The voice that speaks to me rumbles through the air, vibrating around my ears like a baritone from an opera. It takes a moment to realize this voice belongs to Stone.

Nervous and unsure of how to respond, I glance at Don, seeking direction. He nods before saying, "It's fine."

I turn back to Stone and answer, "No, I don't have any contacts." And I realize—now that I'm looking into his face—he's older than I initially thought, perhaps in his mid-thirties. A dark five o'clock shadow outlines a defined jaw.

"He says you're OK talking until you have contacts," Stone says, referring to Don.

"Yeah," I tell him. "Talking works."

Stone merely nods and instructs us to follow him, and we continue further down the endless corridor. I turn to Don, befuddled, but he's following Stone, so I do too. In another moment, an elevator shaft materializes from the hallway, dimly lit.

"Where are we going?" I ask, to no one in particular.

"To our headquarters," Stone says.

"And, who exactly are *you*?"

"They're hackers," Don answers. "Like me. Their organization is called HELL."

"Hell?" I ask, not sure if I heard correctly.

"Yes, HELL," Stone says. "Hackers for Ending Lawless Labor. It's a shitty acronym that some asshole developed years ago to spell out the real reason we're here."

"And why is that?"

"To break free of the crap cycle everyone is stuck living out there. This is the only way we can regain control of our lives."

I want to keep asking questions, but the elevator has already dropped several hundred feet, and I'm quite sure we just dove underground. When the elevator's doors open again, I'm shocked at what I see.

Stone wasn't joking when he had said "headquarters." The room is the size of two to three football fields, lined with row after row of hanging lights from a compacted ceiling, painting the spread below a sickly yellow. But what amazes me are the hundreds, no, *thousands* of black boxes littering the floor. Between them are dozens of hackers who must be part of HELL, looking like madmen as they swipe into thin air, and talk to ghosts.

"What are those?" I ask Stone as we step off the elevator, referring to the boxes.

"Quantum computers," he says. "Our job would not be possible without them."

"And what job is that?"

"OK," Don cuts in. "I think that's enough questions."

But Stone waves him off, annoyed that he tried to stop our conversation. "Let him. Besides, if he came from The Other Place—where you disappear to for years at a time—what threat could he pose, right?"

The Other Place? My legs fall numb when I hear Stone say it, and I stop walking, unable to move. Is it possible? Could that seriously be a reference to... to... *Apollo*?

"Sure, whatever man," Don says. "Do whatever the fuck you want."

I try to clear my mind and refocus on the current situation as Stone returns his attention to me. "Our job is to provide protection," he says.

I'm delayed in my answer; I know this because Stone keeps staring at me with that deer-in-the-headlights look, wondering when the next inquiry will come.

"Protection from what?" I finally ask. "For whom?"

"For whoever can pay our price, which is pretty impressive. Come, I'll give you the grand tour."

I notice he didn't answer my question about *what* they're protecting their clients *from*, and I'm starting to wonder if making this trip to HELL was worth it. Why do they hide like this? Stone doesn't appear to deem me a threat now, but what happens if he changes his mind?

We trek down a long flight of stairs, our shoes clanging against black metal, and Stone leads us into the ocean of quantum computers. Don allows me to wander in front of him, and his ease within these walls triggers my suspicion that he's been here before. Several times. HELL must be the place he visits whenever he sneaks out of Apollo.

"Our hackers are some of the best in Sector 1," Stone says.

"What's Sector 1?"

Don and Stone begin their telepathic communications again—they seem to know what the other is thinking—before Stone returns his glare to me and talks.

"We're Sector 1," he says. "Our whole fuckin' continent."

"Canada? Mexico?"

"What *used* to be Canada and Mexico. Overseas, where the cities of Paris and London are, that's Sector 2. We sometimes recruit from there, but otherwise, we mostly recruit from Sector 3."

"Think Russia," Don says from behind me. "And China."

"So that's it?" I ask. "No more countries?" I'm surprised by how numb I feel—how little this monumental revelation is affecting me.

"Countries?" Stone's voice roars into laughter, like I'd just cracked the most ridiculous joke. "The word 'countries' left our vocabulary in 2075. Now we just have the United Council."

When Stone mentions the year 2075, I'm jarred. *That's the year Apollo was established*, I think, and I'm suddenly aware that somehow, Apollo's fate and The Other Side's destiny are tied together inextricably.

"So who do you work for, then?" I ask. "Are you an arm of this United Council, or what?"

Stone stops walking when I ask this and grabs my shoulder with his brick of a hand. I can feel the calluses along his fingers rubbing against my skin from underneath my shirt.

"Now listen to me, you little shit," he says, and his voice grows lower, deeper. "I don't give a rat's ass who you are, or where you came from, or how well you might know little Jaron here, but *no one* gives me attitude in my own home! Do we understand each other?"

I swallow my breath and nearly hiccup from the warning splintering down my spine. "I'm sorry," I say to Stone. "I didn't mean to be disrespectful."

But Don cuts in, sounding mad. "Stone," he says, "I told you, *don't* call me Jaron anymore."

I'm still unnerved by Stone's reaction to my question, but he's starting to cool down, and it takes a moment for Don's response to sink in. Did I hear him correctly? I pull my gaze from Stone and look at my travel mate. "Your name's not Don?" I ask.

"Yes, it is," Don says. "I haven't gone by Jaron since I was eight."

His words smack me across the face and I feel like I'd been shot down a wormhole into another dimension. Stone struts past me, his massive body nudging mine to the side, and slings a gorilla's arm over Don's neck.

"You'll always be Jaron to me," he says, and now I'm *crazy* curious.

So I ask how the hell these two know each other, but neither says a word. Instead, Stone starts walking forward and continuing the tour of HELL's headquarters.

Jaron

ANDREW

When we approach the cubicle-sized room shoved into the back of HELL's command center, Stone points to a chair and tells me to sit. I listen, but keep glancing toward Don, who has taken a seat nearby and is staring into space like a zombie.

"What are you gawking at?" I ask, but he shushes me. His pupils move from left to right, like a printer cartridge in motion, and I'm beginning to suspect he's reading something.

"Let me see your eyes," Stone says, and he approaches me with a penetrating light that pierces into my corneas. I cringe and wave him off, but he catches my wrist midair and squeezes. My bones feel like twigs in his grip. "Do you want to cooperate, or not? Jaron tells me you have a friend in trouble out here. If you want to help her, you'll let me look at your eyes."

I don't know how Don relayed this information to Stone, but I keep my mouth shut for right now. It's also driving me nuts that he keeps referring to Don as Jaron. Then again, that kid has never been the sort to share.

I lose my sight as the light flashes through my eyes and redness blankets my vision before it returns to normal. Stone nods in satisfaction before switching his attention to a smaller black box in the opposite corner of the room. I'm assuming it must be another quantum computer.

"I'm going to print you a pair of contacts," Stone says.

"What do you mean, 'print me a pair?'" I ask. "Don't you mean you'll make them?"

"No," he says, "I mean print."

He goes to work swiping into the air before him, tapping a clear screen protruding from the black box, and fidgeting with an industrial-looking device resting next to the computer. The air's heaviness is beginning to affect me now. I'm not sure how far underground we are, but my lungs warn that oxygen feels scarce. Every breath takes effort.

"She's not there," Don says from my side. When I ask what he's talking about, he continues staring straight ahead. "Flora. I thought maybe she got arrested by talking in public, but I just checked the jail's incarceration records, and she's nowhere to be found."

"That's what you were doing just now?" I ask. "Hacking into police records?"

Don nods his head and tells me he's sorry; he was almost positive we'd find Flora in one of the jails out here, but he was wrong. Frustrated, I ask him where else she could be, and he tells me there's one more place we can check after we leave HELL. Too anxious to sit and wait in silence, I decide to ask him about something unrelated.

"Why did you change your name?" I say.

"I didn't," he answers. "They did."

"Who's they?"

But Don doesn't respond. Instead, his gaze wanders to Stone, whose back is facing us, and when I glance down, I notice his hands are starting to twitch. *He's scared to answer*, I realize.

"He's referring to that place you come from," Stone says, without turning around. "No matter how many times I've pressured him to give me that place's name, he's never told me."

"If I gave you the name—" Don starts to say, but Stone cuts him off.

"I'd be able to finally get the hell out of this shithole. But you don't want to share, so that's fine." Stone directs his conversation back to me. *"They're* the ones who changed his name, though."

I'm confused as to why Stone's knowledge of Apollo's name would be so dangerous, but I decide not to push it. Don looks like an abused kid terrified of his father, so instead, I ask the other question that's been bugging me.

"How do you know all of this about Don?" I ask. "How do you know his name used to be Jaron?"

Stone breathes deeply, like he's held his breath for half his life, and turns around to face me directly.

"He's my little brother," he says, and for the first time since I've met this man, I watch as his black eyes soften and fill with sorrow.

***

The next few minutes are a blur, and exactly what I imagine time travel would feel like. Movements fuse together in slow motion, then burst into lightning: first it's Don cussing, now Stone yelling, back and forth they go, accusing the other of leaving, condemning the other for giving no choice.

Finally, I can't take the racket anymore, and I scream for them to shut up. They both stop their arguing and rotate their heads toward me, like they'd forgotten I was in the room.

"Can one of you *please* tell me what's going on?" I say. "My best friend is out there, in a world she doesn't understand, and for all we know, she could be *dead*. Don, you brought us here, you told me to trust you. I think it's time you did the same, and explain yourself before we go any further."

For the first time since we left Apollo, I feel like I have the upper hand; I have the authority. Because deep down, both Stone and Don know I'm right. I see it in their faces.

"Sit down," Stone says, and I didn't even realize I'd stood in the midst of the chaos. "You too, Jaron."

I lower myself back into the chair, allowing my breath to calm, and the two brothers begin telling me everything.

Stone was fifteen years old when Don was born here, on The Other Side—same mother, different father. "My dad already died," Stone tells me, "and Jaron was an accident later in our mom's life. She was already getting old."

The notion of a woman growing old while still able to bear children seems odd to me, but when they clarify their mom was forty, I feel stumped with shock. "That's not old," I say, but Don explains the average person only lives to about fifty on The Other Side. I want to keep asking questions, but I allow the brothers to continue telling their story.

Don's mother was already struggling to raise Stone when he was born. She worked nearly sixteen hours per day and barely made enough to afford rent and food. "That's life out here for most people," Don tells me, "unless you're part of The Upper Class: the richest of the rich—born into money."

Therefore, when Don came along, their mother told Stone he needed to get a job. Stone was preparing to work soon anyway, but he'd hoped to save enough money to afford college. Anything less ensured one a life of misery on the streets. At least with college, Stone says, he could've paid for a roof over his head.

Instead, with Don's arrival, Stone's future became clear. "I was doomed to a life of poverty," he says. "Every penny I made would go to Jaron's care, which meant I could kiss college good-bye. No matter how hard I worked, I began to realize my future would never change. It felt like slavery, and I fucking *hated* it. I asked myself, why should only The Upper Class have the type of money that buys freedom? Why should only they have access to the education, health care, and legal backing that ensures prosperity? And in the midst of my anger and desperation, I came up with HELL."

Both Don and Stone pause for a moment, and I'm suspended in eagerness, awaiting the remainder of the story. But as I'm waiting, an epiphany hits me.

"Your clients are The Upper Class," I say to Stone. "That's how you can afford all of this."

Stone nods his head slowly, a look of surprise sweeping across his face. "You're a smart kid."

"But you still never answered my question," I say. "You said you provide protection. What are you protecting your clients *from*?"

"He's protecting their privacy," Don says. "Their bank accounts, their government I.D.s, their age, their marital status, their whereabouts."

I don't understand, and Don must sense it, because he keeps talking. "Everything and everyone is connected out here, Andrew. You'll understand when you put on the contacts. Because of this interconnection, it's fair game for anyone who wants a bite: the government, an ex-lover seeking revenge, organized crime. If you're a girl who lives alone, a man can track you, know when you're alone and sleeping, then attack you."

Disgust rises in my throat as I start piecing the clues together in my head. Yes, this world is making sense now, and I'm beginning to understand the type of "protection" HELL offers its clients.

"What happens if someone can't pay?" I ask Stone.

"Then they're fair game for us to target, too."

"That's sick!"

"That's the world we live in, Andrew. It's them, or it's me, and if things were turned around, they'd do the *exact* same thing."

I spring to my feet, unable to understand how someone could be so malicious. "What if someone did that to your mother, huh? Would you still think that way?"

When the words slip from my mouth, Stone and Don drop their eyes to the ground, refusing to look at anything—even one another. I'm left in utter confusion before Don speaks up.

"It did," he says, "when I was six. She was attacked, and didn't make it."

I regret my words immediately, but an apology won't do anything, not here, and especially not with Stone. Instead, I sink back into my seat.

"That's when I started taking care of him full-time," Stone tells me. "Teaching him how to hack into computers, how to protect them. He was a cute kid, quantum computer for a brain. Learned like a sponge."

"But something happened when you were eight," I say, directing my attention back to Don. "Obviously you somehow ended up *elsewhere*."

Don's face grows bright red now, and he's bearing into Stone with the force of a bulldozer.

"You wanna know why I left?" he says, his voice shaking, his stare unflinching. He orders his brother to hurry and finish printing my contacts so I can see.

Stunned, I watch as the industrial contraption transforms into life, flicking gadgets every way, and within moments, a new pair of contacts materializes before me. Stone was right: he *printed* them, and I'm again struck speechless.

"Here," Stone says, handing me the contacts, and I notice they feel warm. "Your name is Corbin, you're twenty years old, and you were born in Los Angeles. You moved to Phoenix three years ago for a job in programming."

"A fake I.D.?" I ask.

"Put them on," Don orders. "And I'll show you why I left, and how."

HELL's Hole

ANDREW

Years ago, before my dad left, we used to watch old movies together on Saturday nights, usually as my mom rolled her eyes, secretly loving it. These movies were *old* too, like *ancient*, like before-Apollo-times. My dad had a fascination with the late twentieth and early twenty-first centuries.

One Saturday, he played a sci-fi movie for me about fusing together the digital and physical worlds, and I couldn't stop laughing when I saw how people eighty years ago envisioned the future. I suppose back then, it was cool, and I have to admit, I loved the storyline.

Anyway, as I struggle to place the contacts into my eyes now, the way Don showed me, that movie surfaces in my memory and I imagine this is how the protagonist saw the world: digital and data-ridden, all fused with reality, like a dream stuck in purgatory.

I turn to Stone first and my contacts scan his face, plastering words and numbers and information before my eyes: his date of birth, his age, his place of residence, his genetic makeup, his estimated years to live, his criminal record full of computer crimes.

"Tell it to give you my mood," Stone says.

"How?"

"Just say it."

"Tell me Stone's mood," I say, and within milliseconds, new data hangs before my vision, informing me that Stone's heart rate is currently elevated, perspiration is prevalent, and his respiratory rate is twenty-two breaths per minute—all indicating feelings of anxiousness.

"What are you worried about?" I ask him.

"Works perfect," Don says from behind me. "Do me a favor, stare at the blank wall for a minute, and tell me what happens."

When I follow Don's request, the information about Stone disappears and my vision returns to normal, or so I think. As I start moving my head, I notice a three-dimensional screen with the words, "What would you like to do?" that appears in the upper, right-hand corner of my vision. I try to shake it away, but the screen follows me.

"What's this weird box?" I ask, annoyed and somewhat creeped out.

"That's your control center, your home screen," Stone says. "You can visit any place in the world from there. You can also message anyone. Usually, these contacts come with an earpiece, but we didn't have time to print one."

"What does that mean for me?"

"Just continue to keep quiet outside," Don tells me. "We don't want to get arrested for talking in public."

His dismissive statement reminds me of Flora's situation, and how he forgot—so easily—to tell her this one, simple-but-critical rule. Suddenly angry, I'm about to turn around and lash out, "Just like what happened to *her*," but before I can say anything, Don jumps in.

"Don't be so damned pissed all the time."

I open my mouth to demand to know how he knows what I'm feeling, but remember how my contacts scanned Stone and fed me every bit of private information available. As I swallow my words back into my throat, I begin to understand why HELL is such a hot commodity: these contacts turn every stranger into a mind reader.

"Can *everyone* see the type of information I do?" I ask.

"Yes," Stone says. "Unless someone pays us. Then, only the authorities can see this, and only when it's necessary. That's why the government can't stand what we do. They can't track those who can pay."

"Keep looking at the wall," Don instructs, cutting off my conversation with Stone, "and tell your contacts to show you HELL's hole."

"Don't," Stone cautions. I detect his tone is not so much a warning, as a pleading.

***

When my vision changes, transferring into another room, I fall backwards from surprise. Don catches me and pushes my body back to a standing position, instructing me to continue facing the wall. "You're still standing in the same room," he says. "Think of it like watching a movie."

I force myself to breathe through my nose, trying to calm the shot of adrenaline that sliced through my vessels. As I focus my eyes ahead and struggle to orient myself, I realize I'm staring into a ditch. Nervous at first, I allow my eyes to absorb my virtual surroundings, and I observe desert landscape, gritty dirt, nearby cacti, and even an anthill. Everything looks so real, as if I'm *there*, that I swear I feel a warm breeze sweep across my face.

"What is this place?" I ask Don.

"This is HELL's hole."

I don't know why we're staring at some empty gap in the ground, but he presses me to keep watching, so I glare into this trench for another two or three minutes before two men approach. I step back, unsure if they can see me, but Don reassures me they can't. One man looks exhausted, his eyes swollen like pillows, and I realize he's been crying. I can't hear anything—I assume that's because I don't have an earpiece—but the man with swollen eyes appears to be speaking to the second man. The second man dismisses his words and takes a stance behind him. The man with swollen eyes moves his lips frantically, like a movie on fast forward.

And now I see the gun.

It rises from the second man's hand and aligns against the back of Swollen Eyes' head. Swollen Eyes falls to his knees, shaking his head while silent words fly from racing lips. Tears begin pouring down his cheeks, and I come to realize I'm about to witness an execution.

"Stop!" I call out. "What is he doing? Stop him!"

But before I can speak another word, the gun fires and chunks of brain matter spray across the ground on the opposite side of the ditch. Swollen Eyes tumbles into the trench below.

I scream for Don and Stone to get me out of here, to release me from this horrible movie, and I fall to the ground, lines from Edgar Allan Poe's "Dream Within a Dream" racing through my head: *O God! Can I not save, one from the pitiless wave? Is all that we see or seem, but a dream within a dream?*

Somewhere from the room which I can no longer see, I hear Don calling to me, telling me to speak the word, "return," and I allow it to float from my lips, lost and defeated and sickened. Within moments, my vision returns to the blank wall before me and I curl into a fetal position on the ground, disgust slipping under my shirt, into my spine, and clogging my throat. I've never seen someone shot before, let alone so senselessly.

Moments pass and I work to collect myself again, lifting my head to peer at Stone and Don, who are both staring down at me. Their data readings jam my line of vision. "What the *hell* was that?" I ask them.

"That," Don says, "is the reason I left."

"You mean, that just happened, as I watched it?"

"It's *necessary*," Stone says. "You were never able to understand, Jaron."

"How can you expect me to understand murder?" he snaps. "You killed my mentor!"

My head swings toward Don when he says this: *You killed my mentor.* I thought this drama couldn't grow more intense, but I was wrong, and for the first time since I've met Don, I find myself empathizing with him. All these months, I've assumed he was a grease ball who wore women's makeup to piss off the world, but now I'm beginning to understand that he's not much different from me.

"I *had* to kill him, Jaron. He was going to turn us in," Stone says, his voice growing in authority. "People can't leave HELL. There's only one outcome for that, and we'd all suffer the consequences, even you."

Still sitting on the floor, I watch as Don breaks down now, unbridled emotion punching away until the kid I met, who Flora met, is no longer present. I imagine who I'm seeing now is Jaron.

"He was the one who took care of me when you were busy, Stone," he says through tears. "And you wasted him *in front* of me."

"You walked in. You weren't supposed to see that."

"You still killed him!"

At this, Don grabs my arm and starts dragging me from the room. "C'mon, we're leaving," he says. "We got what we came here for. We have another stop to make if you want to find your friend."

Stone doesn't try to follow us when we climb the metal stairs again, back toward the elevator. Just like Don feels guilty for Flora's fate, it's becoming clear to me that Stone feels guilty for his brother's destiny, too.

The Real City

ANDREW

As we fly toward the world above, safely within the confines of the elevator doors, I demand to know what just happened. Don is gripping the handles inside the elevator like his last hope for salvation, and my contacts tell me he's in danger of passing out from hyperventilation. Torn between feeling confused and sorry for him, I try to calm Don's nerves.

"Look man, it'll be OK," I say, unsure if he's even listening. "I know what anger feels like, and trust me, it will pass. We're almost out of here."

The elevator comes to an abrupt stop. The doors open to reveal the same dark hallway through which we first wandered to learn about HELL and its disgusting hole. I lean in and link my arm with Don's elbow, helping him into the blackness. He leans his body's weight against me—I feel the weakness of his knees—and I never realized how deeply despair can affect someone. I thought I'd seen it all with my mother, but not in my wildest dreams could I have invented a story like that of Don and Stone.

"You grew up without a father," Don says, as we make our way toward the main doors.

"Yeah," I respond. "He left when I was eight. Didn't leave a note or anything."

"Do you ever wonder why?"

We stop walking for a moment and I push down the heaviness rising from my gut. "Almost daily," I tell him. "Can I ask you something?"

My contacts inform me Don is beginning to calm, and he regains control of his own weight. "Go ahead," he says.

"Do people out here even know about—" I stop before saying Apollo's name, unsure if anyone can track us, but Don seems to understand my question. He shakes his head and tells me no, they don't.

"So then, how did you end up living there?" I ask. "And why does Stone want its name?"

"When I was eight, I met a man, a history professor. His name is Dr. Hollister Wesson. He's the one I told Flora to visit. We're going to go see him next."

Don begins walking toward the main doors, continuing to talk as he moves. "Dr. Hollister Wesson is the reason I was able to leave here, but that alerted Stone that another place existed, a better place. His systems can access anything, you see; it's just a huge risk and takes a lot of manpower. If he knew our home's name, it might be the final piece to the puzzle for him."

Somewhat confused, I stop Don from walking any further. "And why would that be a problem?" I ask.

Don shakes his head, like he's disappointed in me. "I thought you could see more," he says. "Once a monster, always a monster."

We approach the towering metal doors that open to the outside, but before we leave HELL, I slide in front of Don, forcing us to pause before leaving. "Is it *really* bad out there, the way your brother made it seem?"

Don lowers his head. "Worse."

"And people live like this?"

"People have no choice." He sighs and glances toward me, but doesn't look into my eyes. "Don't try to message anyone when we're in public. Let me do all the communicating. Just be ready, because you'll see a whole new world when you wander outside this time."

He leans over and bangs three times on the interior steel doors, and I watch as they open.

***

This time, things *are* different, very different. I notice it first when we walk past the scores of homeless and sick people lining the alleys leading away from HELL. As I pass each person, my contacts send readings across my line of vision, giving me their diagnoses, their names, their ages, even their freakin' life stories. One man in his forties has AIDS. Another woman, slightly younger, is dying of syphilis, which she contracted after being raped in her home. As I pass her, I want to cry when I see her staring into space, murmuring to some apparition that her mind made real.

I know, from my contacts' readings, that none of these people were born into The Upper Class. Yet nearly all of them hold some college degree: computer science, history, marketing, sociology.

How is it possible upstanding citizens like them wound up here, dying on the streets?

We emerge from that grimy corridor, and I'm relieved to be free of the death which encompassed it. Guilt consumes me for admitting I feel relief, but the truth is, I can't help those poor souls, and I couldn't stand helplessly watching any longer.

The moment we walk into open space, Don was right: the world comes alive. Phoenix, this dead city, is no longer sleeping. Instead, around every corner, jumping off previously clear and blank screens, are faces and products and words. *Advertisements*, I realize after a few moments.

The first one slams into me like a sly ex-girlfriend. *Come play with us, Corbin*, it reads before my eyes, and I forget in the moment that I'm Corbin out here, on The Other Side. I want to ask about the meaning of the message, but within seconds, my question is answered.

Dozens of women surround me—seductive and topless and slithering against one another—right on the street. Torn between tormenting arousal and insane embarrassment, I stop walking and gape at these temptresses, like stumbling across the set of a porno. *We love to pleasure young programmers. Only fifty units for the sensation of a lifetime. Our program feels as good as the real thing.*

My pants grow tighter against my crotch, but just as quickly as they appeared, the women dissipate into thin air, and I realize they were holograms. Now, a new vision takes over. *Tired of sitting at your desk? Our platform will get you walking, even after a 12-hour workday!* Images of young men sporting six packs and blinding white teeth smile and point at me. *The ladies will love you for it. BUY NOW.*

Another ad pops after that one, pushing energy drinks. Now another for a software program to help organize my work life. And another, and another, attacking me like a swarm of bees—all of them speaking to my name, my age, my career.

I want to shout for everything to stop. How do people function amongst such assaults every day? To keep myself from screaming in frustration, I slap my hand over my mouth, and silently thank Don and Stone for not printing me ear buds. I think I'd lose my mind if I couldn't turn off the voices, too.

A message pops into my line of vision as I'm fighting through the tornado of ads, and next to it, a picture of Don.

Try to ignore the ads, it reads. *There's no getting around them. Just concentrate on me. We'll be there soon.*

I don't know how to answer without talking, so I just nod my head and try to focus my attention on Don's back. As we pass towering apartment buildings, my curiosity draws my sight upward, and though I cannot see inside, my contacts scan each residence and feed me information about the people within.

All of them are working like madmen, from their homes. Most are alone, and their ages range drastically: from sixteen to twenty-five to forty, but only a few are in their sixties. Just as Don and Stone promised, on The Other Side, sixty is old, and now I see why.

More than eighty percent of the residents in this building are diagnosed with clinical depression. Their cholesterol levels are higher than the mountains, and many are morbidly obese. I can't help but notice the stark contrast of this reality to the waves of advertisements that bombarded me.

The world is miserable, I realize. *Overworked, isolated, sick, and miserable.* For the first time in my life, I think of the Wall and rather than anger, I feel a sense of gratitude.

We walk another block before Don holds out his hands and motions for me to pause. We're standing in front of an old apartment building made of drywall, and I allow Don to quietly communicate with whoever lives inside. I suspect we've arrived at the home of Dr. Hollister Wesson, the history professor.

A pop-up message from Don soon confirms my suspicions, and the doors open for us to enter. I have a feeling this professor may hold the answer to what happened in the world, and maybe, what happened to Flora.

Dr. Hollister Wesson

ANDREW

His apartment rests high above the city, on the fifteenth floor of the building. The elevator creaked from lack of use when it went up, and now, I'm staring at an old, dying man. He's sitting at his desk when we enter, obviously working. My contacts inform me he's nearing the end, due to a heart condition. The man is one of the few who made it to sixty.

"Yes, the test looks good," he says to a clear screen when we first enter, and it takes me a moment to realize there's a face—that of a younger male—protruding from the screen. "Please upload it on Friday for the class."

"Yes, Dr. Wesson. Will I be grading them, or will you?" the face asks.

"You grade them. I have to go now. I have visitors."

"You mean another call?"

Dr. Hollister Wesson pauses and smiles before he answers the young man on the other side of the screen. "No, I mean actual visitors. A rare treat."

With that, the face disappears and the professor turns in his chair to study us. Like Don, his eyes don't meet mine, but his smile is wide enough to fit a plate. He's silent, but Don soon returns the grin before walking over to give the man a long hug. Dr. Hollister Wesson stiffens at the gesture, but I watch as he forces his arms to return the physical contact, awkward in his motions. I don't understand his hesitation, but I remind myself of the isolation I witnessed while walking to his home. I remember how talking in public is *illegal*, and that helps it to make sense—the discomfort of human contact, even something as benign as a hug.

You must be Andrew? a pop-up message asks, and next to it is the professor's picture and name. I freeze at first, unsure how to respond, but quickly I remember to give the verbal command for messaging. I don't know how Don can communicate without speaking, but I don't have that ability, so I tell my contacts to message the professor.

"I don't mind talking," Dr. Hollister Wesson says after hearing my verbal command. "These contacts are hard to learn."

I glance at him in surprise. "My name is Corbin," I say.

But Don cuts into the conversation and tells me I can relax, he already told the professor about me and how I'm wearing a fake I.D. The professor struggles to stand, and once he finds his balance, he steps toward me on unsteady legs.

"Another Apolloan," he says, and his eyes search me like I carry the key to

Heaven. "Healthy and vibrant, just as I imagined. Brilliant, absolutely brilliant. This confirms my theory."

I'm astounded. How is it possible this man knows about Apollo, when everyone else appears to have no clue? The astonishment must be apparent on my face, because Don tells me to sit down, and I allow my body to collapse onto the only couch in the apartment.

Dr. Hollister Wesson's living quarters aren't very big. In fact, the place is just one large box, about six hundred square feet, with a couch, a bed, a kitchenette, a bathroom, and a working space. I glance back toward the professor and notice he's extremely pale, and it occurs to me the man rarely leaves his apartment.

"Andrew was born and raised in Apollo," Don tells the professor. "He came with me today because we need your help. One of our friends is in trouble."

Reaching for a nearby cane, Dr. Hollister Wesson leans the full weight of his body on the stick as he lowers himself back onto his desk chair.

"It's my fault," Don says. "She wanted to know what was on the other side of the Wall."

"And you let her?" the professor says. "Jaron, you should know better: the consequences that could result from such a shock."

"So, she hasn't been here," I say. "You haven't seen her, Flora?"

The professor shakes his head. "No, afraid not. I'm sorry."

I sink into the couch now, letting it suck me into a hole of despair. I'm beginning to think the worst, and my mind can't bear the possibility. I'll go crazy if I can't find her. Even if she died, I need to know. I need to bring her body back with me, to allow her family to bury her, to say goodbye. I *need* to say goodbye.

Don and the professor continue talking, something about where Don sent Flora, how he forgot to tell her about the Indecent Verbal Act, but I'm not paying attention anymore. Let them chatter. I don't care. Flora is gone. SHE'S GONE. I close my eyes and picture her soft waves of sunshine, that contagious smile full of hope and exploration and innocence. *What's knowledge without curiosity?*

I might never be curious about anything again, I realize. Not if I can't share it with her.

"Andrew?" It's Don's voice that breaks me out of my black hole. "Did you hear what Dr. Wesson said?"

I shake my head, so the professor repeats himself. "Did you try the mental hospital?" he asks.

Confused, I shake my head again, trying to make sense of this odd suggestion. "Flora isn't mentally ill," I say. "Why would we need to check the mental institution?"

"Jaron tells me she might have talked. If she was talking in public, she would be considered crazy, no different than a man running around the street naked."

I look to Don, and he's smiling at me. He agrees, I can tell from his expression. We might have found our answer. A sense of excitement begins to brew deep in my core again, and little by little, the blackness fades away. The mental hospital, of course! The answer is so simple, it was practically impossible to consider.

"Can we go back to HELL to scan the hospital records?" I ask Don.

At the mention of HELL, the professor stands as fast as his broken body will allow, and reaches over to grab Don's arm. "You didn't go back there, did you?"

"I *had* to, Dr. Wesson. I can't come to visit and not see my brother."

"He's not a good man," the professor says, and his voice is beginning to tremble. "I brought you to Apollo to save you from that life."

"Wait," I say, my voice stiff from shock. "You actually *took him* to Apollo?"

Don told me Dr. Hollister Wesson was the reason he lived in Apollo, but this revelation is more than I expected.

The professor nods his head and falls back into his chair. "Yes. I caught Jaron trying to steal my bank account information for his brother. He was only eight at the time. I learned a few hacking tricks myself when I was younger, so I turned the tables and sought him out. When I found him, I learned he was an orphan, and I wanted to help."

The professor turns toward Don and smiles, and Don returns the warm gesture before Dr. Hollister Wesson continues.

"For my doctorate dissertation, I'd proposed researching an elusive mythological state, a supposed utopian society formed nearly a century ago during the Virtual Revolution of 2075. Of course, this mystery state was much like the Lost City of Atlantis; no one really believed it existed, and the only ones who knew of the stories were other history scholars like myself. I was therefore told to change my topic. I listened, but in secret, I continued my research.

"Some of my peers who knew of my research called me crazy, said I was wasting my time, but something inside told me I needed to keep searching. Maybe it was the hope that a place still existed where happiness and health and prosperity were possible, where stimulation of the mind through education and critical thinking was not so difficult to achieve, where families lived and loved together, where neighbors cared for neighbors and strangers helped strangers, where the mind was still free to roam and imagine other worlds—whether through music, literature, or art. Perhaps I needed to believe this, because amidst my own decaying world, these hopes were not possible, not anymore.

"Then one day, my research revealed a surprising possibility. If this state did exist, its most likely location was right here, within a two-hour drive north of Phoenix. I told no one of this discovery of course, but then I met Jaron.

"He was a wreck when I found him: terrified and sick with anxiety. When I asked what happened, he stuttered about an unspeakable act committed by his brother against his mentor. That's when I asked him if he'd like to leave this world forever. Jaron didn't want to go at first. He was scared of leaving what he knew, just as any eight-year-old child would be. But within the month, he found me and said he changed his mind. Before we left, I told Jaron to take out his contacts, and I'd remove mine. We couldn't allow ourselves to be tracked.

"When we first began our journey north, I had no idea what I would find. I didn't know where exactly this society existed, or if it existed at all. We always faced the possibility of running into nothing but a nuclear wasteland, exposing ourselves to radiation poisoning, but that was a risk I was willing to take. If we did find it, I had no idea whether they would take Jaron, or kill us on site. They risked much by losing their secrecy, you see.

"The journey took us a full week, some of those days traveling by foot through the Ponderosa pine forest. Then, one day, we came upon a Wall. It towered over us, taller than some of the pines surrounding it, and the structure was littered with cameras. I grew exceedingly excited at this discovery, as something inside told me we made it. But I didn't know what to do, so I approached the Wall and waved at the cameras.

"I waited until nightfall with Jaron, but nothing happened. We camped overnight, and the next morning, I decided to try something else. I gave Jaron most of our remaining food and water, and told him to stay by the Wall. I was going to leave, and would return in twenty-four hours. My theory was this: if the society did operate under the utopian principles I'd researched, they would never leave a child alone to die. Perhaps my presence was preventing them from revealing themselves.

"I felt horrible, as Jaron started crying when I left, but I reassured him I wasn't going far, just out of sight. The next day, I returned toward evening, and Jaron was gone. At first, I panicked, terrified that perhaps an animal attacked, but his tent, backpack and food were gone too. The only reasonable conclusion I came to was that They took him into Their arms.

"For years I hoped and hoped, until one day, about five years after our trip, Jaron appeared at my door. He was thirteen years old and said he found a way to sneak out. He came to visit me, to thank me, and to tell me he was well. And of course, he began feeding me information about life within the Dream, including its name: Apollo."

I'm speechless after Dr. Hollister Wesson stops talking. My mind continues telling me it's a lie, but I ask myself, how else did Don end up in Apollo? How would all of this make sense, otherwise?

"You have to understand," Don says, after several moments, "I couldn't say *anything*. They took me in as one of their own, but I had to take an oath, under penalty of *death*, that I would never reveal what was beyond the Wall. I was never to speak of The Other Side, nor visit it. They changed my name to something more fitting of Apolloan society, and in return for my silence, I'd have everything I ever needed."

I spring to my feet now and begin pacing the boxed apartment, filled with energy at these new revelations. "But over time, you grew restless," I say. "You missed your brother, and Dr. Wesson, right?"

Don nods his head. "I started seeing how much they control, in order to keep their perfect little society." Confused, I ask Don what he means by "control," and he spits out the answer, spite ripping through his teeth: "Information," he says. "They control information. The saying, 'Innocence is bliss' exists for a reason, Andrew."

His words prompt the lessons I learned on utilitarianism to reverberate through my head: *whatever generates the most happiness for the most people, creates the most utility for a society.* Yes, everything is beginning to make sense now. Not just what happened to Don, or Stone, or even to Flora, but *everything*.

"Flora knew something," I say, my voice elevating in anticipation. "They grew terrified she'd reveal whatever she learned, so they made her sick to silence her. It's just like the case of Alexander Litvinenko."

The professor's eyes light up when I mention this name. "Smart young man!" he says.

I nod and respond to the professor's comment. "Alexander was an officer of the former KGB—back when it existed in the twentieth century—who fled from Russia and found asylum in the United Kingdom. Nevertheless, Russia sent a member of its Federal Protective Service to poison him with radiation. He didn't even know *how* they did it. He died in 2013."

I turn and look at Don. "They say history is the best teacher. You suspected it, didn't you? That's why you helped Flora get out."

When I spin toward Dr. Hollister Wesson, a look of pride is sweeping across his face, as if he'd just discovered some rare jewel at the bottom of the ocean. "Amazing," he says. "Their education system truly does produce independent-thinking citizens. Do you know how long I've dreamed of seeing a pupil like you, Andrew?"

I ignore his question though; my mind is on fire, and I cannot stop the freight train. "What happened in 2075, professor?" I ask. "You spoke of a Virtual Revolution.

That's the same year Apollo was founded. *Something* happened that year, something that changed the fate of this world. I need to know."

The professor nods his head, tells me to sit down, and begins explaining everything.

The Virtual Revolution

ANDREW

I listen with fervor as Dr. Hollister Wesson begins his history lesson of The Other Side. The changes began with the dawn of the Digital Age in the early 2000s, he tells me. Social media, smart phones, apps, wearable devices: the equivalent of the Industrial Revolution in the eighteenth and nineteenth centuries.

"Unfortunately, society was so naïve back then, no one considered what might lay beyond these technological advancements," he says.

When I ask what he means, Dr. Wesson speaks of the greatest cost being the death of investigative and enterprise journalism. The Digital Age, he explains, drove away the need for print magazines, newspapers, and eventually, even books. As these entities lost revenue, they began thinning their reporting staff until eventually, some publications closed their doors completely.

"As journalists became outnumbered by public relations professionals, the line between journalism and propaganda was blurred," Dr. Hollister Wesson says. "This change becomes dangerous for any functioning democracy. It allows private entities or individuals the ability to sway public opinion more effectively. This, as you can imagine, begins to affect elections, which in turn affects the laws of the land."

The Great Recession, which began in 2008, combined with the growing competitiveness of globalization, caused many repercussions throughout the former United States. Forever changing the job market, these two forces prompted the average citizen to work longer hours—sometimes for less money—and to do so without complaint for fear of losing one's job. As the populace worked longer and harder, it cared less and less about the happenings of the nation's capital.

"Apathy, combined with lack of watchdog ability, is a dangerous combination," Dr. Wesson says.

People grew restless and angry. Some would not sit quietly and they took action, as exemplified in the historical Arab Spring. But it was not enough. By 2045, the cost of an education became so unattainable, many took to the Internet to learn what they otherwise could not afford in school. The World Wide Web began to represent freedom of information—the only salvation many had while suffering through a life of growing economic slavery. Within a few years, these issues had spread globally. The world, now in competition with itself, was screaming for a change.

"Now, you need to remember that the generations of these times, both old and young, differed from their parents and grandparents in that they grew up in the

Digital Age," Dr. Wesson explains. "Most had learned to use a computer or tablet device before they could speak, sometimes before they could crawl. They were drawn to the computer screen more than to a person's face, and they therefore trusted the virtual world more than the physical. Online documents offered free education, free information. But print newspapers, books, and traditional journalism? Well, that represented control.

"What these generations failed to recognize, however, is that *money* was the true controller, and as globalization grew, so did the gap between the very rich, and everyone else," he says.

By the year 2072, those who held the most sway on public opinion—the wealthiest of the wealthy, also known as The Privileged—saw an opportunity to seize ultimate control. They knew force would not be the most effective approach to gain power. But winning public opinion through propaganda would. People needed a common enemy, something that would unite them in their hate. It worked for Adolf Hitler against the Jews; it worked for Radovan Karadžić against the Bosniaks; now it would work for The Privileged against the world. Only this time, their target would not be a group of humans.

It would be an idea.

Regardless of their country, every person on this planet shared a commonality: they were born and raised in the Digital Age. They felt the same love for freedom of information through the Internet. And many believed that anything of the old world represented control. *This* idea is what The Privileged would use to gain their ultimate power.

"It seems silly at first, I know," the professor says. "But never underestimate the power of propaganda."

The Privileged spent the next three years pouring billions of dollars into campaigns demonizing individual governments for oppressing their citizens using the old, non-digital ways—a claim easily believable due to most people's living conditions. With the development of quantum computer technology, The Privileged bombarded millions of individuals with personalized messages based on their demographics, interests, and even desires. They could reach them in their homes, at work and in public, and they targeted every major country throughout the world: The United States, England, France, China, Russia, Israel, Iran. No one escaped.

These attempts began affecting elections around the world. Uprisings formed against dictatorships, and everything culminated in the year 2075.

"This, Andrew, is what we now call the Virtual Revolution," Dr. Hollister Wesson tells me. "By this time, The Privileged had the entire world calling for an end to global competition, begging to be united under one central government that would lead them into a virtual future of prosperity for all."

I listen as he paints the picture of protests sweeping across the U.S. , and in smaller countries, riots breaking out in the streets. Mobs burned books and sometimes musical instruments—anything that represented the old world they viewed as the enemy—in public bonfires. These images filtered across the planet within seconds via the Internet, therefore igniting new anger, new calls for change, and new public demonstrations.

The world's countries could no longer ignore the cries of their people. Their leaders realized if they did not meet to discuss the demands of their populace, the world would fall into chaos, and every government would lose its standing. They therefore met during the historical World Summit of 2075, which took place (ironically) on the Ides of March.

I smile when the professor mentions this. "March 15," I say. "The death and betrayal of Caesar."

"Precisely," Dr. Wesson says, returning my grin.

He continues explaining what happened next. Through recent elections, many who belonged to The Privileged served as high-level advisors to the world's various leaders. Together, they forged an unbreakable strength of persuasion during the World Summit, and by the end, the world's leaders decided to relinquish their individual governments in favor of establishing a new world order. *For the peace of mankind*, they had said, and decided to call it the "United Council."

When the announcement was made of this monumental change, the world erupted into celebration. Upon the encouragement of The Privileged—many who had now gained impeccable public favor—a ceremonial purging was to be conducted across the planet. Everything of the old world was to be burned: books, records, C.D.s, newspapers, pens, musical instruments. The only paper records people were allowed to keep were old family photographs. Governments were allowed to retain certain historical documents, such as the United States Constitution, but they were required to be housed in a museum. The goal was to rid the world of anything that represented control of information. People took part in this purging with zeal. The scene was one of climactic exuberance.

It was, in every sense of the phrase, a Virtual Revolution.

When Dr. Hollister Wesson stops talking, I realize I'd been holding my breath. I stare at him, at Don, in stunned silence. How should one respond to such an account? I feel numb, unsure of what to say, how to react.

"What happened to The Privileged?" I finally ask the professor, allowing the magnitude of the story to permeate.

"Since many of them already served as elected officials and helped gain public trust, those same individuals played an integral role in the development of this new United Council," he says. "They worked to strip countries of their names, and instead, segment off various portions of the world as 'sectors.' We therefore now have Sector 1, Sector 2, and so on.

"Over time, the gap between the wealthy and everyone else grew larger, contrary to what the people had hoped. The Privileged used their new power to generate more revenue for themselves. Many owned businesses and began contracting with the United Council: everything from defense and data security, to police, education, and health care. Their profit bases soared, as they were no longer limited to certain countries, and many therefore became the world's primary employers—the ultimate control."

I glance over to Don and realize he'd fallen asleep in his chair. I want to ask how he could sleep through such an incredible history lesson, but I remind myself he already knows. I turn back to the professor.

"The Upper Class," I say, "they're what became of The Privileged, aren't they?"

The professor nods his head. "Correct again. In the seventy-five years since the Virtual Revolution, The Privileged formed an entire new class of society. They are the ones Jaron's brother targets with HELL, and they are the ones who control almost everything across the world. Money equals access, access equals knowledge, and knowledge equals power."

I recall what Stone said about the Upper Class holding the key to the best education, the best lawyers, the best health care, and therefore the ability to prosper. I remember the solemn look on his face, combined with rage, when he described his reasoning and decision to create HELL.

As I ponder these thoughts, along with the lessons from Dr. Hollister Wesson, I suddenly feel isolated. Is it possible Apollo remains the only place on this planet that still uses newspapers, and books, and musical instruments? Are we the only ones left who live as an equal society?

"I still don't understand how Apollo fits into this story, how it came to be," I tell the professor.

"Neither do I," he says, and his answer shocks me. "In fact, I was hoping perhaps you might know the answer, Andrew."

Somehow, I believed that Dr. Wesson was preparing to share Apollo's history with me, so when he says this, I drop my eyes toward the ground. "I'm sorry to disappoint you, Dr. Wesson," I say. "But thank you for sharing everything else with me."

"My pleasure."

At this, a computerized voice materializes from the air surrounding us and instructs the professor that it is time to begin preparing for bed. *Brush your teeth and change into pajamas.* The voice awakens Don from his snoring slumber, too.

"That is my cue to start turning in," Dr. Hollister Wesson says. "Boys, please stay the night here. You can have the couch and the floor. It's too dangerous to be wandering the streets now."

Don agrees, as do I, once I realize my brain can't take another single thought, and I'm about to fall into a coma. Before I can thank the professor for his generosity, I pop out my contacts and collapse.

Return to HELL

The next morning, the professor allows us to use his shower, and the water feels like rainclouds on my skin. I haven't washed in three days, between the two-day hike to the transport station, and our arrival on The Other Side.

This feels like a dream, I keep thinking as water drizzles down the tender spot between my shoulder blades. *At some point, I'll wake up, and everything will return to normal.*

Don is hustling me toward the door by nine o'clock in the morning, and Dr. Hollister Wesson is already planted in the chair before his clear screen, wired into work. My contacts reveal his elevated heart rate; the man has only months to live.

I glance over to Don—the shower washed away the raccoon makeup, revealing much softer, kinder eyes—and for the second time since we've left Apollo, a tear streaks down his cheek, like torture. He must know the professor's fate, too.

"Dr. Wesson," he says, but the professor lifts a hand, instructing us to remain silent for the moment as he completes some intricate task. We allow him to finish, and Don approaches his chair. "I know you're not one for hugs, but I grew fond of them, living in Apollo."

The professor pulls his earpiece and places it on the desk before looking up at Don. "You must know by now, that this is goodbye," he says.

Don nods, the motion filled with heaviness and despair. Staring at the professor in silence, he drops to his knees and falls into the man's arms. "I will miss you," he says.

Once again, Dr. Hollister Wesson stiffens from the contact, but forces himself to return the embrace. After Don pulls away, the professor looks directly into his eyes. "You gave me the greatest gift," he says. "You allowed me a glimpse into Eden. You proved I wasn't crazy. Thank you for that."

Don merely nods, unable to speak, and the professor says something else. "Take care of yourself, Jaron. Always remember, the goodness of man still exists, no matter how far gone hope may seem. Wherever darkness lingers, so too, does light."

With that, we nod and leave the professor to live the remainder of his life locked away in that box. And we move forward, reentering the hurricane of advertisements on the streets... back to HELL.

***

As I'm fighting my way through the storm of commercials again, the professor's words keep playing over and over in my head. I know they were meant for Don, but I can't help but search for some hidden meaning that I'm meant to decipher. I wonder what Don thought of Dr. Wesson's message, his last words to the orphan he helped long ago.

When we arrive at HELL's headquarters, Stone appears unaffected by our return: not surprised, nor joyful, nor burdened. He's just indifferent, his only words of welcome sent via message: *the little brother returns.*

With the washing away of Don's makeup, his edge seems to have eroded as well, leaving behind a vulnerability that worries me. That makeup, I realize, was his shield, his armor—it's what transformed him into a soldier. Without it, he's a struggling veteran straining to heal from the war of life.

The heaviness of HELL's atmosphere is choking me once again, its mugginess suffocating. Stone is not speaking to us either. Instead, I find myself witnessing a virtual conversation between the two brothers that plays out before my eyes. I don't know how to join, so I settle on the notion that they at least found me vital enough to include.

U went 2 see him, didn't u? Stone says.

It's none of ur business.

It IS my biz. Ur my bro; it was always my job 2 watch after u.

Right... some job u did.

I can't help but notice the abbreviations, and perhaps it's my training in English, but it drives me mad. I tell myself this is not the time to ask, though, and I continue watching the conversation unfold.

We're back bec we need ur help, Don says.

Depends what I get in return.

I need access 2 HELL's system again, 4 the mental hospital. We think our friend might be there.

WHAT do I get?

UR MY BROTHER, Don says, and I sense this must be the equivalent of yelling. *That should be enuf.*

Being my bro got u access 1 time. We're running a biz here, not charity.

When Don doesn't answer, I realize he's out of ideas, and defeat is written across every crevice of his face. Maybe it's my turn to try, I decide.

"What do *you* want, Stone?" I ask, because I don't know how to silently message like they do.

Stone turns to me and stares toward my hands—refusing to meet my eyes—but shock seals his mouth shut.

"You keep asking what you get, so I'm asking what you want," I continue, an idea forming in my head. "Where I come from, we still have books, and newspapers, and printed photographs. We have recordings of real music, like from the piano or violin. Heck, we have old movies. In this world, those artifacts are probably worth a fortune, and Don can bring you anything you want on his next visit."

The intrigue spills from Stone's eyes like a prowling tiger, and I know I've hooked him.

"You said printed photographs?" he asks, and I nod my head to confirm. "You've got yourself a deal."

Don's eyes jet toward me in pure disbelief.

"If you really do have old cameras and printed photographs, here's what I want," Stone continues. "Get me a picture of that nameless place Jaron sneaks off to every year. I want to *see* what makes it so great, with my own eyes."

This must be some kind of trap, I think. *No way* that negotiation with Stone could be this easy. Why didn't he demand Apollo's name? But a message from Don pops up before I can take another breath, agreeing to the deal.

***

We're back in that cell of a room, where Stone printed my contacts and I witnessed the execution. I feel unnerved sitting here again, but I try to ward away the discomfort, reminding myself this is necessary. *For Flora.*

Don is leaning against the wall, his eyes scanning left to right. When I ask him what he sees, he shushes me. The impatience is rushing from my core like the release of a champagne cork from its bottle, so when he finally speaks, it's like my first breath of oxygen after nearly drowning.

"I found her," he says.

His words blast through my head and render me helpless with relief. I open my mouth to speak, but no phrases formulate. Don must read my reaction as one of concern, because he immediately tells me she's OK.

"She's at Phoenix Psychiatric Hospital. Dr. Wesson was right," he says. "It looks like she's been there for more than a month."

I can't bear to ask the question which rushes through my head next, but I force the words anyway, my voice stuttering. "Did – did they hurt her?"

"I don't know," Don says, and his voice hints at empathy. "The files only indicate who's been admitted, not their medical records."

I want to leave right now... what are we waiting for?... but Don instructs me to sit down. The old anger rises from within and I start growing defiant, reminding him that Flora has only months left to live. She deserves to spend her remaining days with her mom, her dad, Ernest, *me*. Of course Don isn't ready to leap forward into rescue mode—why should he care anything for her fate? He's merely here because I threatened to beat his ass if he didn't help.

"You really think that's the only reason I'm here?" he asks.

"You didn't care about *shit* until I said something... so yeah, I do."

At this, an impeding presence rises before our eyes, a simple sentence reminding us both of the massive hurdle we still must face, but have not yet addressed.

How do u plan 2 break her out?

Of course, it's Stone, writing in his abbreviations. He's not in the room with us, but he knows what we're doing, saying, *thinking*. I spin around, jetting my eyes from corner to corner inside the room: no cameras.

Do u really think u can just walk up, sign a form, & take her home? he continues. *The hospital won't give up profits that easily.*

"So what do you propose we do, huh, Stone?" I call into the open air. "You obviously don't intend on handing out charity, as you call it. So why even speak up?"

Tell me the name, he responds.

My heart stops. And now I come to realize why Stone never asked about Apollo before. This whole time, he was merely biding his time until the golden ticket revealed itself.

I want out of this hell hole. So tell me the name, he says again.

I glance over to Don, who is staring at me in desperation. I read his pleading eyes and keep quiet, trusting his instinct.

U know we can't do that, Stone, he writes.

The only way 2 get her out, is 2 hack in. U know this, little bro. U know I'm right. I want the name.

The Name

ANDREW

I've sometimes wondered how I would react if robbed at gunpoint. I've never held a gun in my life—couldn't tell you if the trigger feels rough or smooth—and so it's possible I might do whatever the gun-bearer instructs. I might lose all ability to think rationally, or even scream like a scared, little girl.

Essentially, that's what's happening now: Stone is holding a gun to my head.

Don's eyes meet mine, and we frantically exchange looks, terrified to swap silent messages for fear Stone would learn our secrets. *How do we answer? Could we pull this off alone?*

I'm scared to utter a sound. Deep down, I know Don and I could never execute an ingenious hacking stunt of this magnitude on our own. We will need the assistance of HELL, of Stone. But to give up Apollo? To give Stone the missing key, the only piece of information he needs to successfully pull off the hack of all hacks and discover Apollo's secrets?

Stone may be Don's brother, and he may have a sad story, but the nature of his unfortunate childhood turned him into an unpredictable monster. Would Apollo ever be safe if we allowed it to fall into the grasp of HELL's embrace?

"If we give you the name, will you help us get our friend from the hospital?" I ask, and Don nearly punches me for speaking.

Stone responds with one simple word, *yes*, and before I can even think what I'm about to do, I answer.

"The name of my home is Zeus," I say, "named after the Greek god leader of all other gods, just as we hope to be the new leader in this fractured world."

Don is staring at me—just *staring*—his jaw gaping in disbelief. Yes, I know the gamble, and I'm well aware of the danger I created should Stone learn I lied. Immediately after my response, he looks to Don for confirmation, and dutifully, Don backs my story.

I can tell Stone isn't convinced at first, and he probes further, so I school him on the history of "Zeus." It was established in 2075 with the intent of free education, free health care, and societal equality. I go so far to tell him about the Wall, but when Stone asks for the location of this "utopia," Don stops him.

I think you've heard enough, he writes. *The location of Zeus wasn't part of the deal; just the name.*

At this, Stone appears from behind the wall separating us from the rest of HELL's operating headquarters.

"Fair enough," he says. "Let's get to work."

***

The table is white and bare and round, emanating a sickly yellow aura, much like the rest of HELL, and the three of us sit around it. Stone had called another two of his best hackers, but they joined remotely, appearing as nothing more than holograms.

It's weird, this fusion of the virtual and physical, like a walk through time.

Here's how it's going to work, I learn: HELL will conduct a series of mini hacks into the hospital's records, locating Flora's living quarters and deciphering the building's layout. Then, they'll execute the main attack into the hospital's primary server, and upload a virus. The virus will filter into the other servers and disable the hospital's mainframe, therefore taking its security system offline. No one will be able to track us, or stop us. Once the system is down, Don and I will enter the hospital, pull Flora from her room, and get out.

I keep thinking this sounds good in theory, but the whole plan comes across a little too perfect.

"Do you *really* think they'll allow us to just wander in, take their patient, and leave?" I ask. No one answers, and as I glare around the room, observing both bodies and holograms, I realize from the various facial expressions that yes, they do expect this.

"In case you haven't figured this out yet," Stone tells me, "no one can function around here without the system."

"He's right," Don says. "Their security consists of nothing but droids—robots— that are operated remotely. Once the mainframe goes down, everyone will be rendered helpless."

Frustrated, I tell them I get it, but what about doctors, nurses, phlebotomists, for God's sake? Do they really believe no one will try and stop us?

"People don't know how to make decisions without a machine telling them what to do," Stone tells me. "Everyone has grown up wearing their contacts since they were babies. The system tells them when to wake, when to sleep, when to eat, *what* to eat. We'll render everyone at the hospital blind when we take down their system."

I consider Stone's words for a few minutes, and think back to the night I'd spent with Dr. Hollister Wesson. I do recall computerized voices telling him when to wrap up the night, but it never occurred to me that society grew so dependent on technology, it became the ultimate Achilles' heel.

I'm still skeptical, but I let it go for now, and we continue chatting through the details of our plan. As we're talking, Don scans further into the records of the hospital. That's how we learn about Dr. Hauser.

"He was the chief psychiatrist there," Don tells us, "killed a few weeks ago in a mass shooting." He looks around the room, laughs, and tells us that life has a fucked-up way of executing poetic justice. "Dr. Hauser's family owns the psychiatric hospital."

"You mean, he was part of The Upper Class?" I ask.

Stone and Don nod their heads, telling me the guy raked in a fortune as a government contractor administering behavioral health services to the poorest of the poor: those deemed a danger to society. Every patient equaled massive amounts of cash, all compliments of the United Council.

"I'm glad he died," Stone says. "Pathetic waste of human existence."

An overwhelming wave of desire to leave this place and return home to Apollo—with Flora—rushes through my body when I hear Stone utter these words. I want to run and crawl into a dark hole, where no one will ever be able to find me again.

Anxious to get the plan moving, I ask, "So, how are we going to let Flora know we're coming?"

At this, Stone smiles.

Part Three

The Escape

Poison Ivy

FLORA

Today is my two-month anniversary in this place. I wouldn't have known about my special anniversary, had a congratulatory message not popped up. I wasn't sure what to be excited about, so I had lain down on my bed, stared toward the ceiling, and accessed my own, personal calendar—which I recently learned is tied into my medical records, my arrest record, and every other possible public record one could imagine. This calendar reminds me when to take my medicine and when I have appointments with the doctor. It learns my daily, bodily schedules, and instructs me when to sleep, when to eat, when to exercise. It even told me yesterday I had to urinate.

As I stared at this calendar, I saw it—the date circled perfectly in a scripted font that's supposed to look handwritten, except the circumference is too perfect. Inside the calendar, my contacts left me a reminder: "two-month anniversary: hospital admission."

I've allowed them to medicate me. The pills send me into a blissful coma for hours at a time, and the days pass more quickly that way. The more I'm awake, the more I long for my mom, my dad, Ernest, and Andrew, and it sometimes tortures me into a hurricane of hysteria.

Since Dr. Hauser died, I have been spending more time with Dr. Thompson. In the beginning, I felt safe around her, but now, I've become indifferent, even if she did save my life. Dr. Thompson is the only human face I have eye-to-eye contact with anymore. Everyone else remains trapped behind a screen.

When I last saw her a week ago, she told me the hospital hired a new psychiatrist, another man, and I'd be meeting him soon. "Joy," I told her, the sarcasm raw on my tongue. Apparently, my time to meet this new psychiatrist has come today; my little calendar tells me our appointment is an hour from now.

In the meantime, I decide to log into the hospital's literary database. Reading in this virtual age makes me dizzy, and my fingers crave to crinkle paper, but the closest I can come is to the words floating above my face. And so my vision transforms into a room full of holograms—endless shelves of books (romance, literary, historical, biographies). Each shelf is a folder, and each book a computer file.

It's here that I wander, like a ghost between slopes of purgatory, the same way I used to drift within the Apollo Library.

And suddenly, I see her, staring at me through parallel shelves with eyes the color of poison ivy. Her face is new to me, unknown, yet she's staring through my mind like she's searched for me for eternities.

"Flora?" she asks, her voice both commanding and questioning.

I don't answer, but my eyes do not lie, because she continues. "I must be quick. Right now, only you can see me, but soon, they will too."

"Who?" I ask.

"Everyone," the stranger answers. "Listen to me carefully. We don't have much time. A rescue team is being assembled to come for you."

"A rescue team?"

But she shushes me, tells me not to talk—just listen. "They are developing a plan. Deployment will take place a week from now."

I want to ask what all of this means. Who is this woman? How does she know my name? But I remain silent, petrified of the unknown.

"Right now, this message is to put you on notice," the stranger says. "Stay alert. I will be back with more details as they become available."

I open my mouth, beg her to wait, but before my eyes, she disintegrates like mist into nothingness. I'm befuddled, staring into the vacant, virtual space where only moments ago, this cryptic woman stood speaking to me.

It takes a moment before the heaviness of her words strikes me like hail stones from the sky: *a rescue team.*

***

I don't take my medicine. For the first time in weeks, I *want* to remain alert. Hope—scared and cautious—brims under my skin, barely revealing itself. I feel like Pi when he found his floating island, after weeks drifting at sea. Or Pip, when the anonymous benefactor awards him with unlimited funds to become a gentleman in London.

Hope: what a beautiful, terrifying thing.

I fly through my first meeting with the new psychiatrist—I can't remember his name. And by evening, when Justine's robot brings my meds, I'm deceiving my caretakers again, slipping the pills to the roof of my mouth and then flushing them down the toilet.

And I wait, for Poison Ivy to return.

***

She appears in the newscast, three days later. This time, all I can see is her face, those eyes piercing through mine with the might of a monsoon.

"It will happen three days from now," she tells me, her voice and presence overriding the broadcaster's pearly whites and practiced speech. "At night. Around eleven o'clock."

"Who are you?" I ask again.

"A messenger," she says.

"What's your name?"

"You must be ready," she tells me, her voice growing more commanding, more insistent. "Bring nothing. Wear your hospital robe and slippers. Clothes will be provided after you leave."

"Who should I look for?"

But she doesn't answer that question. Rather, she continues talking. "The system will be down for about ten minutes. You won't have much time. Be ready by the door of your room. Someone will be there to take you away. Follow his lead."

"There are others," I tell her, and she looks at me, those slanted, green eyes hollow. When she doesn't respond, I speak again. "Did you hear me? There are others here from Apollo. We cannot leave them."

"I am out of time," she says, infuriating me with her indifference. "I must leave now."

"But the others!" I shout, and realize I must watch myself; I don't want to draw attention. "Four of them are on my floor."

I cannot finish. She fades away and the newscast returns. I swallow my heart back into my chest and tell myself to calm down. I think of Andrew's father, only three doors down from me. This might be my only chance to reunite them. I cannot leave him behind.

The Surprise

FLORA

Three days later, I awake an hour before my calendar rouses me. The adrenaline is pumping through my veins like an angry ocean. Not until I wake unprompted do I realize how much I've come to rely on these contacts. And it's only been two months.

Tonight, I think.

"Time to brush your teeth," my contacts say, and I stagger into the bathroom without thought and grab my toothbrush.

"Your bowels need to empty," the contacts tell me next.

"Duh, I know," I mumble under my breath as my stomach churns. When I finish using the bathroom, my contacts remind me to wash my hands.

For the past few weeks, I'd stopped caring about the small, stupid prompts, but now they're beginning to irritate me. I wonder how people don't rip out their hair and tear off their clothes in pure frustration. Once my morning ritual—teeth, bathroom, and shower—is complete, I plop on my bed and stare toward the ceiling.

"Message Andrew," I say, and wait for the conversation bubble to emerge. "Hi Andrew, I have a cool surprise tonight around eleven o'clock. I'll send you the link. Just be by your door to make sure you receive it."

I watch as the words appear before my eyes, right next to my ridiculous photo. "Send message," I instruct, and within moments, Andrew's father responds.

A surprise? Well, that sounds like a treat. Why must I be by the door?

I'm nervous about sounding too suspicious, so I hesitate until I can decide what to say. "Message Andrew: If I told you, it wouldn't be a surprise. Just be ready. Send message."

After a few short moments, a response materializes under my note. *If Miss Flora insists, ready I shall be.*

***

Socialization hour cannot approach fast enough. Once a dreadful experience, I'm now anticipating it like a kid going out for ice-cream. I spend the first hour of my day pacing back and forth, literally working up a sweat. When my feet grow numb, I stop and stare at my bed, and the white ceiling, with its white lights, and the white walls, and my white robe.

How the hell did Andrew's father tolerate this for eleven years?

I close my eyes and envision Apollo's towering Ponderosa pines, air that smells of freedom, and mountains that promise adventure. I can feel Ernest's soft, floppy ears against the nerves on my fingertips, and can taste my mom's sweet potato casserole. Yes, I can even hear my dad's piano music—*real music!*

And I can anticipate Andrew's warm, comforting embrace.

My grin spreads wide when I think of Andrew. Of course I miss him, but that's not why I'm smiling. I'm imagining the look on his face when he sees his dad, when he realizes what kept him away, when he understands that *he's still loved.* To be whole again—that's all Andrew has ever wanted.

I ask my contacts for the time, and realize only ten minutes have passed. Socialization hour is still two hours away.

***

When my vision finally transforms into the vast, open room I've come to associate with socialization hour, I nearly fall off my bed in exhilaration. I'm going to tell the others from Apollo about the cool "surprise" happening at eleven o'clock tonight, in hopes I might be able to snatch them up on the way out. I know the hospital's security monitors our conversations during socialization hour, which is why I must be vigilant. Patients are encouraged to share links and messages with one another. I therefore doubt—and hope—they will think anything of it.

As always, the first to approach me is Andrew's father, his welcoming face and soft eyes protruding from the three-dimensional screen atop the strolling robot. He smiles when he sees me, and tries to pry the intriguing "surprise" from my brain. I play it off by teasing that he's ruining the point of a good-humored surprise. Soon, the other six patients from Apollo join us.

I've spoken with them in the past, but shortly after Andrew's father introduced us, I began allowing the meds to take over my mind. This kept me from truly getting to know them. I was never lucid or alert, and probably looked similar to the other poor souls rolling around in a trance. Now that I'm feeling myself again, I come to realize I never learned how these six citizens of Apollo escaped, or *why* they were driven to leave. I do believe one of them is a mother, and she cries almost daily for her child, who she claims is probably finished with college by now.

I'm about to give them the same story I fed to Andrew's father, but I stop short. Glancing around the room, I begin to wonder if perhaps it might seem suspicious to those who monitor our interactions that I'm telling patients with the same "delusions" as me to be ready for a surprise by their door tonight.

Don't screw this up, Flora.

Reunion

FLORA

Justine's robot delivers me dinner, so I know it's about six o'clock in the evening. The food is factory-driven in this place, as bland as the walls and people. Andrew's dad told me they "print" it. Almost nothing is baked or cooked anymore. I could not understand what he meant until I saw it with my own eyes, when he sent me the link to a live video feed of a bakery at work. I was expecting to see ovens and dough and spots of flour all over countertops... but instead, I witnessed an exotic device that appeared to build the food, layer by layer, until finally, something edible materialized.

When I saw this, I thought of the bakery I came across when I first entered The Other Side. At the time, I couldn't understand its lack of ovens, but now the vacant kitchen makes sense.

I force the so-called food down my throat and gulp it away, constantly keeping my eyes on my contacts' virtual clock. Every minute feels like an hour, and every hour like a day. This must be what Einstein meant when he said time is relative.

Eventually, ten o'clock rolls around, and the nurses begin shutting down the hallway lights outside of my room. Justine's robot turns off, and I know she has headed home for a few hours to sleep. She'll be back to watch over me at six o'clock tomorrow morning... only this time, I won't be here.

I pace my room as ten-thirty nears, wondering if Poison Ivy was really a hoax. How can I trust her? How was she able to weave into my contacts? How do I know she's not some vision my mind created to cope with the idea of remaining trapped in this place for the remainder of my days?

At ten-forty-five, my vision turns red, and I screech, falling back into my bed. Unsure, all I can do is jet my eyes from one end of the room to the other, yet I see nothing but all-consuming red.

"Flora Loban," a voice speaks into my ear, and its eerie, computerized tone sends electric shocks down my spine.

"Yes," I whisper, unable to do more.

"Prepare, Flora Loban."

My room returns in a second, the red having dissipated. I glance down and realize my knuckles are white from gripping the bed sheets, and I've been holding my breath. I let the air escape from my lungs and gasp for more oxygen, rubbing the sweat from my palms onto the bed. I try to collect myself, remembering what Poison Ivy said: *Bring nothing. Wear your hospital robe and slippers.*

I climb to my feet and search my room for slippers. Where did I last leave them? By the bed? Near the door? I soon find them in the bathroom and jam my feet into the fluffy pillows.

This is really happening. Breathe, just breathe.

"Show clock," I say, and the time appears before my eyes. It's almost eleven. I'm getting warm, even though the room's temperature hasn't changed. That stupid, cliché pit forms in my stomach, and the thing is growing faster than a weed.

"Flora," a voice speaks into my earpiece again, and though I cannot see anyone, I recognize it. Poison Ivy.

"Yes?" I ask aloud.

"Flora, they are here."

"Who?"

Her green eyes flash before my face, piercing in their force, and everything goes black. *Everything.* The lights, the quiet buzzing from the hallway, and the floating screen in the corner of my vision.

It's gone.

I hear wails of fear seeping into the hallway from the other rooms, and I instruct my contacts to find out what's happening. They don't respond. I try again, this time demanding in my tone, but nothing happens. Frantic, I look around the room, wondering if it's eleven o'clock yet, wondering who will come to take me away. But I'm cut off.

I stand by the door to my room, but no one shows. I wish I knew the time. Poison Ivy said I would have barely ten minutes. I tap my foot, waiting, waiting, the panic rising into my throat and threatening to choke me. A loud knock.

"Flora!"

My heart leaps from my throat when I hear the voice, and I can barely answer. I'd recognize it anywhere.

"Andrew!" I call out, breaking into hysterical tears. "Andrew!"

New footsteps fast approaching, and quick whispers. I hear someone start a countdown, "Three, two, one, lift!" And, like the parting waters of the Red Sea... freedom.

Andrew is standing before me encased in darkness, his eager eyes reflecting moonlight. I want to soar out of my skin in jubilation at the sight of him, and I fall from my room into his embrace, the tears flowing freely. He's warm and comforting and *home.*

"I never thought I'd see you again," I say against his shoulder.

He grips me back, but another voice breaks the moment. "C'mon, we gotta move."

When I pull away from Andrew and turn to look over my shoulder, I see Don standing there, and I'm overwhelmed with joy at the sight of him—working side by side with Andrew—but I remind myself I don't have time for emotions now.

"There are others," I tell them, fighting to come down from the high, and turn my head toward Andrew's face. "Andrew, we can't leave yet."

"We have to," he says.

But I protest, grabbing his hand and yanking with every ounce of strength I own, dragging him three doors down, despite his opposition. "Open it," I demand.

When they refuse to listen, I turn around in a rage, bend my knees, and slip my hands under the giant block of metal, screaming as I lift with all my might. Watching me struggle, Andrew and Don jump to my rescue and help me pry the door up.

On the other side, staring at me with bewildered eyes, is Andrew's father.

Andrew grabs my hand and begins pulling me away when recognition crosses his face, even in the darkness. He pauses mid-step, turns back around, and I feel his palm grow slick with sweat. His hand drops mine. With eyes glued to the face of his father, Andrew takes a careful step forward.

"Dad?" he asks, his voice suddenly small.

This question, so simple, was all the confirmation needed. Without a word, his father surges past the threshold and scoops Andrew into his arms, a lifetime of tears and regret and redemption flowing from starving eyes.

Andrew, hesitant and shaken at first, lets go after a few seconds, returning his father's embrace. But I can see the stiffness crossing his face: disbelief, and also the sudden realization that his dad was held against his will this entire time.

"Later," Don says, urging Andrew and his father to hurry up. "We need to move."

I tear myself from the emotional scene, and grab Don's shoulder. "There are six others trapped here from Apollo," I tell him. "Four are right here, on my floor."

"Flora, we are running out of time. I can get us another five minutes, *maybe*, but we can't take everyone."

"Then let's take whoever we can."

I turn back to the reunited father and son, and my heart fills with gratitude at the sight of Andrew with his dad. "Think of the other parents and children separated," I tell them. "Think of the other reunions we can guarantee."

"If they catch us," Don says, "we will never see Apollo again. None of us."

Right as Don finishes, a faint beeping echoes from his earpiece, and Andrew jumps at the sound. I ask them what it means, and Don tells me the noise is our five-minute warning.

"If we don't leave right now, this second, we won't leave at all," he says.

At this, Andrew steps away from his dad and approaches Don. "You know

Stone can pull off another ten minutes," he says. "Call it in. We're not leaving anyone behind."

Getting Out

FLORA

I have no clue who Stone is, or how he managed to take down the hospital's system, but I don't ask questions. *Later*, I tell myself. *You'll find out later.*

All I know at this moment, is we have another ten minutes—lifeblood—and we cannot waste them.

Earlier today, I made a mental note of where the other six patients from Apollo are housed. Don, Andrew, his father, and I sprint from room to room, lifting with the adrenaline-fueled strength of Hercules, and yanking some confused people from their quarters.

"Take out your contacts," Don instructs each one after we race away, onto the next room. "They'll track you otherwise, after you leave the hospital."

Each patient asks the same questions: "Who are you? Where are we going?"

And each time, I step forward after they ask. "Home," I tell them. I ask Andrew for the time after we finish with my floor, and he says we're down to another five minutes before the warning goes off. "Why isn't anyone trying to stop us?" I ask, while we're treading down flights of stairs to the floor below, where the final two patients from Apollo remain trapped.

"Because," Don says, his voice winded, "look behind you."

I glance over my shoulder, where Andrew's dad and four patients are following us, and I suddenly understand. They're terrified, constantly asking what to do next, where to go. Andrew keeps slowing his stride to coax them, reassuring that it's OK. They worry they'll trip, or puncture their feet. Andrew tells them to look down—there's nothing on the ground. But they don't believe their own eyes.

Without their contacts, their technology, they are blind.

It occurs to me, right now, of the immensity of this society's vulnerability. These are people from Apollo, like me. If they are struggling this much after a decade or less of relying on technology, what's it like for everyone else?

We sprint from the stairwell onto the ground floor, running toward the final two rooms. We split up, each team grabbing one of the last Apollo patients. Andrew and his father accompany me, and as we're lifting, and grabbing, and coaxing, that faint beeping returns from Don's earpiece.

I stop for a moment, frozen in fear, and look to Andrew. His eyes mirror my own.

"Let's go!" he yells, and I swing around toward the exit of the hospital, but something stops me. A face. A dark face, with mocha-colored skin cloaked in a rundown, white lab coat.

"Dr. Thompson," I say, realizing she's standing by the door, staring at me. I glance around, a full three hundred and sixty degrees, and notice everyone is watching us. Some patients are peering through their windows, while third-shift nurses are staring from their monitoring stations. But no one—not a single person—makes an effort to stop us.

"Where are you going?" Dr. Thompson asks, and the question shocks me. I was expecting something else, like a demand to return to my quarters.

"Home," I tell her. "We're all going home."

She's quiet for a moment, just staring, and I hear Don yell my name, but his voice seems far off, like in a dream.

"You're going back to your Apollo," Dr. Thompson says, and I hear the sadness in her voice.

I'm struck speechless. "You're not here to stop us?" I ask after a moment.

Andrew leaps to my side, and I can feel the impatience flooding from him. The beeping continues in the background, reminding us moment after moment that doom is impending. Andrew links his arm with mine and urges that we need to leave.

But my gaze remains glued to Dr. Thompson—the woman who saved my life, twice, and brought me the closest comfort I felt to home in this place. Overtaken, I jerk my arm away from Andrew, dive forward, and swing my arms around Dr. Thompson.

"Thank you," I whisper into her shoulder. "Thank you for everything. I will never forget you."

I feel her hands return my embrace, and next to my ear, she whispers something. "I believe you, Flora. Go, and be happy."

With that, I pull away, and Andrew tugs me toward the door. Don calls for me to discard my contacts, so I toss them onto the floor of the hospital, next to the threshold of the entrance. And I re-enter the vast world of The Other Side.

***

"We have three minutes to get as far away as possible," Don tells us as we're sprinting through the silent darkness of the city. The other six patients from Apollo are struggling to keep up. In the hospital, they rarely gave us room to exercise. We had more than enough time, of course, but never the equipment, or the drive. It cost me some of my stamina, as well.

Through heavy breaths, I ask Don where we're going, but he doesn't answer. So I just keep following. The beeps continue to echo from his earpiece, and I see him nodding his head and muttering, "I know, I know."

Andrew and his father remain side by side.

We soon come to an alleyway, a slim corridor between two towering buildings, and the rescue team demands everyone huddle into the shadows as quickly as possible. We listen, filing into the claustrophobic space one-by-one. After we're smashed inside, Andrew turns to me.

"You need to change," he says, his voice hushed. "We brought you clothes."

"What about everyone else?" I ask. The other patients are dressed in their winter garb from the hospital: sweatpants and sweatshirts, along with odd shoes that are a cross between sandals and slippers.

"We had no idea they were coming."

"But I told her."

Don turns to look over his shoulder, and for the first time, I realize he's not wearing black eyeliner anymore. Without it, he looks younger, more vulnerable.

"You told who?" he whispers.

"The girl," I say. "The one with eyes like poison ivy."

Don shakes his head, annoyed. "That wasn't a girl," he tells me. "That was a computer program, a virus. It was not meant to retrieve information, only deliver it."

Don snatches his head back toward the street, and I see him nodding again. He must be communicating with someone, I gather, someone who is calling the shots. He continues making motions, and I watch carefully as he turns back around to all of us again.

"Listen up," he says, his voice still quiet. "I'm taking out my contacts, and we're going offline. The hospital system is back up, and the authorities have been notified. We have to lay low for the next few hours."

"But won't they be able to find us?" one of the patients asks. "They can detect heart rate, thought patterns..."

"That's why you removed your contacts," Don says. "Now they can't trace you. An escape vehicle will be sent to this location three hours from now, to transport us to a safe house. Until then, we have to remain very, very quiet."

I turn and look toward Andrew, and anxiety is dripping from his face. I reach down and take his hand in mine, and he looks at me and smiles. Slowly, I begin changing into the clothes Don and Andrew brought for me, taking special care not to make much noise. Through the slim corridor of the alleyway, I can see law enforcement drones beginning to patrol the streets and sky, while searchlights sprinkle the sidewalks. I know this will either be the end, or a new beginning.

The Safe House

FLORA

The combination of exhaustion, the city's desert heat rising from concrete, and ten nervous bodies smashed into an alleyway like sardines is beginning to take its toll. I can smell nothing but dirt and sweat and discarded food, and something else I can't quite identify. After much contemplation, I realize the mystery smell is fear.

I don't know the time, but it feels like we've been crouching in the shadows for hours. No one has said a word; in fact, everyone seems to be concentrating on controlling their breathing to remain silent.

The first hour was terrifying, as droids and air drones swept the streets, and we had to shuffle further into the alleyway. At one point, Don instructed us to jump into the surrounding garbage bins just in time, before a law enforcement droid shone its searchlight into our hiding place. I held my breath, unable to bear the stench of rotting food and discarded cleaning wipes.

We stayed like this for several minutes, then slowly started filtering back onto the concrete. Now, finally, the streets have begun quieting. The searches have spread out, further away from ground zero. And I'm hoping our escape vehicle will show any moment. Thirst is beginning to dry my throat.

Throughout it all, I can't help but smile every time I look at Andrew and his father. They can't talk, but they're speaking through their eyes. Andrew asking how this happened—why did he leave?—his father answering with patience, "In time." He leans toward Andrew, always taking him into his arms, and holds his boy close, as if he's eight years old again.

Watching them, I realize I still don't know why Andrew's father left, and I wonder.

In the distance, a slight humming pricks the night's silence. Don perks up at the noise, and Andrew follows suit. They both slide toward the front of the group, waving the rest of us back. As the humming grows louder, Don nods and Andrew rounds us up.

"This is our ride," he whispers, motioning for us to huddle close. "We've gotta move fast, OK?"

The vehicle stops before our alleyway, all lights off, and its side door slides open. Don and Andrew herd us into the vehicle, packing us in like cattle, and slip behind as the door shuts. They instruct us to lie as low as possible, and the vehicle starts moving. It's larger than a car, but smaller than a bus. In fact, I realize, I've never seen anything like it. "Who's driving?" I ask.

Don turns around and looks at me from the front of the vehicle. "No one's driving, Flora," he says. "I thought you knew this by now."

***

By the time we arrive at our safe house, I figure it's probably close to dawn. Once we climb from the vehicle, I recognize that we've traveled further north, closer to Apollo. We're nowhere near the base forest of the San Francisco Peaks, but the air has grown cooler, crisper. The landscape surrounding us still screams of desert, however: cacti and shrubs and dirt—all silhouetted against the moonlight.

The house is abandoned in the middle of what used to be a lively ranch, filled with horses and goats and chickens, I'm sure. But now, it's deserted. I wonder what happened out here. The home's doors are falling apart in splintered pieces, its windows broken and jagged. Don leads us through the entryway before herding us into the structure's basement.

Once we're all safely inside, the vehicle leaves, and Don turns around to face us.

"We made it past the most dangerous part," he tells us. "I've gotta get back online and secure a connection, now. We'll remain here until nightfall tomorrow. Feel free to talk again."

A unilateral sigh of relief echoes from the room, and we all exchange glances. Three of the patients from Apollo don't bother talking, but instead, lie down and fall asleep within moments.

***

When I awake, slivers of splintered light are shining into my eyes, and my stomach grinds and complains of hunger. I glance down and realize a blanket is covering my body as I rest on the basement's dirt floor. The other patients from Apollo are scattered around the room, some sleeping, some lying awake and staring toward the ceiling. From the nearby corner, I hear whispers, and quickly recognize the voices as Andrew and his father.

"She hasn't been doing well," Andrew says.

"This is my fault. I never meant to leave you two like this."

"But you did." I cringe at the anger in Andrew's voice. "Eleven years, Dad. Were you there when they threw her into the mental institution? Or when she had her crisis events? I was left taking care of her, doing *your* job, by myself."

"I should have been there."

"Yes. Yes, you should have."

There's a long silence after Andrew's words, and his father's regret is filling every corner of the room. I begin stirring from the uncomfortable silence, but his father starts talking again, prompting me to remain still and listen.

"What if I told you the reason I left was to save you?" Andrew's father asks.

At this, Andrew doesn't respond, but I glance up and catch him staring at his father in disbelief. A sickening sensation overwhelms my gut, too, and I realize Andrew's dad probably faced the same antagonist as me, back home. I close my eyes as the image washes over my memory: a man with a bald head, who wears khaki pants, and whose breath smells of old coffee disguised by spearmint gum.

"When I worked in Internet Technology for the Apollo government, I accidentally stumbled across classified files one day while doing my job," his father says, and I pretend to keep sleeping.

"I was researching an issue with one of the servers, and while pulling up encrypted files, I somehow found this. I wasn't sure what it was, but the files referenced certain types of technology that didn't exist—I mean, these terms weren't even in the dictionary. They also referenced something called the United Council."

I hear Andrew gasp, but his father keeps going.

"I should have just closed the files and left everything alone, but I grew curious. I never stole the files, or accessed them again, but I began doing my own research with my friend, Joe. Do you remember Joe, Andrew? He used to come over and—"

"Yes, I remember him," Andrew says, and his voice is heavy with sadness. He doesn't break the news of Joe's death to his father, and I silently praise him for that. Now's not the time.

"Well anyway, Joe and I began tinkering with our own technology, trying to research what was beyond the Wall. When your mother found out, she got angry, told me to stop it, said it wasn't worth the risk of going to jail. I should have listened to her, Andrew. I should have, but my curiosity overtook any rationale.

"I began piecing the puzzle together over the next few months, realizing that another world existed outside of Apollo: a world with advanced medicine and technology. And I started realizing that Apollo was feeding us lies. I grew angry, wanted to know why, and that's when he found me."

"Who?" Andrew asks.

"Agent Jackson."

I nearly scream when I hear the name, anxiety rushing up my back and choking my vocal cords. I breathe through my nose, and my mouth, trying desperately to calm my hypersensitive nerves.

"He gave me a warning. He said if I didn't stop my research, he would kill my child—you."

At this, I spring upright, unable to continue pretending anymore. "He tried to kill me too!" I say, and the tears start flowing uncontrollably. I'm heaving, hysterical, all the fear and frustration and anger pouring from the hidden place I'd kept it trapped for so long. And for the first time in months, I feel relief.

I turn toward Andrew, who's staring at me in astonishment. "That's what I couldn't tell you back in Apollo, Andrew. I'm so sorry. Agent Jackson knew about my visit to the building in Oak Creek Canyon. He's the one who made me sick."

Before I can say another word, Andrew is by my side, wrapping the blanket around my shoulders, holding me and offering comfort. He reassures me it's OK, that I'll get to spend my last days with him, and my parents, and Ernest. I won't be alone anymore. As he's saying this, I remember Andrew still thinks I have cancer.

I pull away from him, turning to face eyes that speak of home. "They fixed me," I tell him. "I almost forgot that you didn't know. Dr. Thompson, at the hospital—she killed off the cancer and gave me a new stomach. It was incredible."

Andrew's jaw drops, like in the movies, and his eyes begin filling with tears. "You're serious?" he asks.

"I'm serious."

Andrew turns back toward his dad with a smile growing so radiant, he could light the night's forest.

"Like I said," his dad says, "The Other Side has medicine which far surpasses our limits in Apollo. And I wanted to know why."

"I don't get it," Andrew says, refusing to let go of me. "What's so imperative about keeping the outside world's advancements away from Apollo?"

His dad shrugs, tells us he doesn't know. "But when Agent Jackson threatened your life," he says, "I knew we had to leave... all of us—you, your mother, and me. It was the only way I could ensure your safety, so I decided to make a test run as a scout. I developed a handheld EMP device to shut down any technology they used along the Wall, and built a contraption to help me climb over it from a nearby tree."

"An EMP device?" Andrew's voice quivers with excitement and realization, and he shoves a hand through that thick, black mane which I've always adored. "The newspaper brief. I saw it when I was going through the morgue in the Apollo Library. The day after you disappeared, the paper published a brief about a power outage the night before. They couldn't determine the cause."

Andrew's dad chuckles, says that was him, and praises his son for being so smart. But Andrew grows serious again. "So, you always meant to come back for us," he says.

His father leans over—I can tell he wants to reach for his boy, but Andrew is sitting too far away—and smiles. "Kiddo, it was always my intent to return for you and your mom. I just needed to make sure it was safe to leave. I never could have guessed that talking in public was illegal out here. I never could have imagined the type of world that existed only one hundred miles away. I hated myself after they picked me up and locked me in that hospital. I thought of you, of your mother, *every day*, and then one afternoon eleven years later, I meet a girl named Flora."

Andrew is in tears again—I've never seen him so emotional—and he turns to look at me. "What's knowledge without curiosity, right?" he says, and his voice bleeds gratitude.

I nod and return his smile. "Right," I say.

"I have my father back because of you, Flora. God, I love you so much."

The words shock me: so honest, so raw. No more games, no more hiding. I search his face and find nothing but adoration. Something has changed in Andrew since I last saw him, something dramatic. The flirtatious boy with lines of poetry is gone, and a protector stands in his place—a man who knows what he wants, and who he needs to be.

Soaring with happiness and hope and dreams of a future I almost lost, I reach up to smooth the skin along his cheek, and I tell Andrew how much I love him too.

The Plan

FLORA

We spend the day locked down in the basement. Don told us he'd secured a line of communication with Stone, and was given directions to a food printer buried outside. A few of the patients from Apollo join Don and Andrew as they uncover the machine, and within the hour, we're all eating the so-called food and gulping down water.

Andrew can't stop beaming as he watches me eat without pain.

As the afternoon lingers further, I approach Don—who's sitting in a far corner alone—and take a seat next to him. He looks naked without that eye makeup, and I can't help but feel sorry for him.

"I want to thank you," I tell him after sitting down, "for coming out here with Andrew, to get me. I have a feeling you were the brains behind this whole rescue mission."

"Yeah well, you're welcome, I guess."

I pause and chuckle to myself. "You know, you don't have to keep up the act," I say.

"What act?"

"The one where you don't give a shit. I think you proved that big, bad, mysterious Don actually *does* care. And it's OK. In fact, I appreciate it."

Now he pulls his eyes from the ground and looks at me directly. He doesn't say anything, but for a moment, I witness a lost, little boy who finally found acceptance. Overwhelmed with gratitude, I want to lean into Don, wrap my arms around that frail body, and press my lips to his frosty cheek. I wish I could show him that he's not alone in this world, but instead, I say, "Listen, do you wanna tell me about this guy named Stone?"

He pulls his eyes from mine when I mention Stone's name, and I cringe, wishing I'd kept my mouth shut. But Don says something that surprises me.

"I guess it's time to fill you in."

***

I'm overcome with disbelief when Don finishes his story. But when Andrew corroborates everything, I force myself out of denial. While in the hospital, I'd researched the United Council, and the Virtual Revolution, but I had no idea—*no idea*—what all of that really meant. After hearing Don's story, I'm sick with anguish.

"Is it really that bad for everyone out here?" I ask, and Don nods. In an effort to lighten the mood, I smirk and nudge him on the shoulder. "I like the name Jaron. You should have kept it."

But my playfulness quickly dissipates. "It wasn't my choice to change it," Don says, and that dark chill shudders down my back again. A new reality is beginning to surface, and I fear this danger may far surpass the one we've narrowly escaped.

"What are we going to do about Agent Jackson?" I ask. "We're bringing back eight people, including myself, who have been missing from Apollo, some for years. Do you really think there won't be questions?"

Andrew sighs from behind me. "She's right, Don. We haven't thought this far ahead yet, but we need to."

Don stands and begins pacing around his corner, rubbing his forehead as he thinks. "Agent Jackson is a psychotic man," he says. "I don't trust him. But if there's one thing I've learned, it's that he puts Apollo and its ideals above all else."

Andrew steps forward. "Including the *perception* of Apollo," he says. "He'll do anything to protect Apollo's reputation among its citizens. If the public doesn't question, Apollo's secrets are safe. We need to force Agent Jackson to keep us alive using the public."

I'd always known Andrew was smart, but watching him in action now, I can't help but feel lightheaded with giddiness. He's absolutely brilliant, and I know exactly what he's planning.

"We're the answer," I say. "Not the three of us, but everyone here. If we can sneak them back to their homes, it'll make news headlines in less than a day. Agent Jackson will be forced to come up with a story to explain this mysterious re-appearance of missing people. As long as we're part of that, we're untouchable."

Andrew leaps forward and throws his arms around me, hugging me so close I can hardly breathe. "You're beautiful and ingenious," he says, and a surge of girly silliness flutters through me at his compliment.

"Let's do it," Don says. "We move out tonight. Start spreading the word. Everyone needs to rest up. We have a long trip ahead of us."

***

I can't sleep, even with Andrew holding me against his shoulder. The sky has grown dark and I know we'll be moving soon. I tell Andrew about Agent Jackson, how he threatened my mother, the look on his face when he visited my house after I'd become sick. "His voice is the thing of nightmares," I tell Andrew.

"He's still just a man."

"I can't stand up to him," I say. "Of everyone who's ever bullied me, he's the worst. If I couldn't stand up to them, what makes you think I can beat Agent Jackson?"

Andrew sighs, and I can tell he's looking for the right words. "You already *did* stand up to him, Flora, just by defying him. Look at how far we've come. You've given me a renewed sense of hope, and because of your actions, I got my father back."

I pull away from Andrew's arms and turn to face him, the moonlight illuminating his jaw's outline. "You've never had to deal with this man like I have," I tell him. "He's sick, sociopathic, like Don said. I know he comes across as normal, but underneath that surface, something repulsive is rotting away. He *will* kill."

At this, Andrew sits up, and I sense impatience, even frustration, emanating from him. "Let me tell you something," he says, his voice stiff. "When I learned you'd left—and where you'd gone—I became infuriated. I found Don and accused him of tricking you into leaving. But really, I was angry at you, Flora. I thought you'd left me, like my father did, and chased your selfish curiosity into oblivion. I thought you'd lost sight of what really mattered. But that was *before*."

Confused, I ask him before what, and Andrew draws closer until I can hear his gentle breath panting against the cool night's air.

"Before all of this," he whispers, and catches my gaze in his. "Before your escapade cured you of cancer, and freed my father. When I look back at the events of the past few months, I realize something. All of this, it happened for a reason. Yes, I have my father back now, but other children will have their parents back too. Because of your defiance, your *curiosity*, many lives will now change for the better."

"What are you saying?" I ask.

"I'm saying you already won. And we've come this far unharmed, so we'll finish the journey safely."

Nearby, Don begins to stir and I hear him waking the rest of our crew. The time has come, and a tourniquet clenches my gut. I want to cuddle with Ernest in my own bed again, fall asleep to my father's piano music, but instead, thoughts of Agent Jackson invade my mind. I'm beginning to fear he'll haunt me until I die.

"I'm scared," I whisper to Andrew.

He looks at me with the weight of the universe when I say this, and before my mind can dedicate another thought to the man who clouds my head, the warmth of Andrew's lips press against mine, and all doubt melts away. My eyes drift shut as my breath merges with his, and I linger in this place between dreams and reality and space and time, where nothing but promise and possibility exist. I fall into this world with Andrew, his lips reassuring but restrained, and a deep longing rises from inside—a hunger I've never known.

When Andrew pulls away, he leaves me struggling to breathe, tracing his fingers along the sensitive skin of my cheek and sending frantic waves of desire through my body.

"Kissing you is like kissing a dream," Andrew says, his voice low. "You give me strength, Flora. Take that with you."

I will, I think, as we begin preparation to leave. *Oh God, I will*. And for the first time since our escape, I forget that Agent Jackson even exists.

Hacking War

ANDREW

My body feels like a freakin' grenade, and I'm desperate to pull the pin. Flora's lips tasted like honeysuckle, and her flavor lingers with me now as I join Don to organize the trip. I glance down and realize a small bucket of water is resting near my feet. Don is jabbering in my ear, but I can't register a single sentence. Instead, I drop to my knees and splash my face with cool water, trying to calm down.

"What is wrong with you?" Don asks, grabbing my arm and yanking me back to my feet.

I turn to look at him with the eyes of a forlorn and hypnotized man. When I answer his question with silence, he scoffs and rolls his eyes, returning to his business.

My dad and Flora are chattering toward the back of the group, and I watch them with a full heart. I have not felt this type of fulfillment since I was eight. For the first time in more than a decade, I have a family. *A complete family.*

I also have a future wife. I'm going to marry Flora, and I'm going to spend the rest of my life protecting her, caring for her, supporting her. I'm not scared to admit it anymore.

I join Don in shooting off commands and gathering food for the trip. As I'm mid-sentence, a middle-aged woman, still in her hospital sweats, approaches me and places her palm on my shoulder.

"You're Andrew?" she asks.

I turn to face her and offer a gentle smile. "Yes ma'am," I say.

"Don says you're the reason this rescue mission happened. I want to thank you." She pauses for a moment, shuffling in her place before brushing graying, auburn hair from her eyes. "I have a daughter back home, maybe a little younger than you. I haven't seen her in five years."

The woman has not removed her hand from my shoulder, and I offer comfort by placing my hand atop hers.

"Her name is Hannah," she continues, "after my mother, who died of breast cancer when I was only twenty. My name is Georgette, by the way."

"Pleasure to meet you," I say, nodding my head. "I haven't seen my father in eleven years, so I can imagine the exhilaration your daughter will feel when she sees you."

The woman lowers her head and forces a sad smile. "I hope she doesn't hate me."

When I hear these words, something erupts from deep within, and I brush the woman's hand from my shoulder, turning to face her completely now. I lift her chin, raising her head to look into my eyes, and I see my mother.

"She *will not* hate you," I say. "She might be angry in the beginning, but show her that you care. She needs to know you never stopped loving her."

The woman smiles a genuine grin, and thanks me. As I glance around the room, I come to the sudden understanding that many of these people don't view me as some nineteen-year-old college kid. They're looking for me to *lead them*.

Don's voice calling my name interrupts my thoughts, and when I turn to answer, distress is drenching his face. Concerned, I jog to his side and he motions for me to follow him outside, away from everyone. After we've left the basement, I glance toward the road and see a transport outlined by moonlight, waiting to carry us north.

"Stone knows," Don says, his voice shaken.

"Knows what?" I ask.

"He knows you lied about Apollo's name. He figured it out."

A swell of dread begins to build in my gut. "He knows about Apollo?"

Don shakes his head. "No, but he knows its name isn't Zeus, so I can almost guarantee he's researching possibilities."

"What should we do?"

Don pulls me further from the old house. "We need to leave now. Not thirty minutes from now, not five minutes. *Now*."

"Why so—"

But he cuts me off. "Stone knows we're here. He could be sending his guys. They could arrive any moment, and who knows what he'll do if we don't give up Apollo."

Flora. Without saying another word, I turn and jet back toward the house, but Don grabs me. "He bugged the transport, Andrew. I'm going to have to hack into its system, take it offline, and drive it manually. It's the only way Stone can't track us."

I nod in understanding, then turn and run.

***

Everyone asks the same question: "Why the hurry?" I decide it isn't the time to sugarcoat anything. I tell them about Stone, and HELL, and what might await us if we don't hustle. The mere thought of being held hostage again is enough to send some of our group over the edge, and they burst from the house in a ravenous rage for freedom.

When we approach the transport, Don is caught in the middle of an epic virtual battle—a hacker war with his own brother. I watch as the muscles strain in Don's back, his desperation to disconnect us dripping from his face, but Stone refuses to let his brother go. Don knows he's at a disadvantage, and I'm helpless, able to do nothing more than sit and watch, and hope.

"You think it's OK to lie to your own *brother?*" I hear Stone's voice roar over the transport's intercom.

"You're not coming with me," Don says aloud, and he's motioning into the air, frantic in his movements. "You can't be trusted, Stone."

"We're of the same blood, little bro. You speak blasphemy."

"I speak the truth."

"You speak nothing!" There's a brief silence as Don continues to struggle against his brother's power. "I refuse to remain banished to this black hole any longer," Stone says. "We're almost to your safe house. Give us the name and I'll call them off."

Don denies his brother a response, and infuriated, Stone grows more demanding. I can feel my heart pounding in my ears. With each passing second, Don appears to shrink further into himself, wasting away into nothing against his brother's might, when from the back of the transport, my father stands and walks toward Don.

"Need help, kiddo?" he asks, and Don glances toward my dad, a look of surprise sweeping his face.

"I used to work in I.T., you know."

I'm fascinated as I watch my father dive in to help Don, offering advice, pointing out vulnerabilities. With his support, Don regains confidence, even as Stone's voice continues to rumble overhead, demanding answers and growing more enraged each time Don ignores his requests. And from one moment to the next, his voice stops.

Time seems to pause as Don realizes he beat his brother—the connection is severed—and I yell for him to step on it.

Don taps the control screen of the old transport, flooring the engine and sending several members of our group flying into their seats. The vehicle takes off. I close my eyes and pray that we'll make it, that we'll escape the claws of Stone's HELL.

The Light

ANDREW

The road is dark, void of streetlights, and Don is struggling to operate the transport around the mountainous curves and ledges.

"Andrew!" he calls from the front, and I strain to make my way toward his side. "Take the lead," he tells me.

Alarmed, I ask him what he's talking about, but he grabs my hands and shoves them before a touchscreen that resembles tablet devices we use back home. "Run... the... transport," he says.

"But, I don't know how. I've never driven one of these things before. There's no steering wheel, no accelerator—"

"Listen," he cuts me off, "Stone is trying to hack back online. If he does, he'll know exactly where we're going. I need to keep him off. I can't do two things at once."

Shadows whiz past the oversized windows of the transport—rocks and cliffs and shrubs. The moonlight blurs into reflective streaks, and I know we must be moving at ninety miles per hour, if not more. *I'll kill us,* I think, frantic and overwhelmed at the command center before me. *I'll drive us off a cliff.*

But Don dismisses my worries and starts explaining how to run the transport. "Press here to slow down. Press here to speed up. This button turns to the right, and this one to the left."

I'm forcing my mind into sharp concentration, trying to retain everything Don throws my way. Each tidbit of information counts, I tell myself. There's no room for error.

"Got it?" he asks when he's done explaining.

I nod my head, take a deep breath, and Don switches operations to me before rejoining my father in an effort to keep Stone at bay. Don turned off the headlights and the transport is running off night vision instead. I imagine he did this to avoid detection. The problem is, I've never driven this way before—through a screen.

"I'll help you," a voice says from behind me. "You don't have to do this alone, Andrew."

Flora. Her voice calms my heart and numbs my mind of worries. I don't have the luxury of lifting my eyes to meet hers, but I can feel her presence behind me, comforting and soothing. *I can do this. I can pull this off.* Flora drops to her knees and joins my gaze at the command center.

"Curve right," she says. "You have a ledge approaching." She places her hand on my arm, the touch of faith. "I'll slow down the transport, so it's easier to drive."

I nod my head in response, and she reaches toward the screen and decreases the speed. As the transport slows, I feel myself regain control and confidence. Don and my father are working furiously nearby to make sure Stone cannot return online.

"Do you think we'll make it?" I ask Flora.

"In your words," she tells me, "'we've come this far unharmed,' so yes, I believe we'll finish the journey safely."

***

An hour into our trip, I catch my dad and Don hugging from the corner of my eye. When I ask them what happened, Don tells me we've made it. We're far enough north that we've escaped HELL's reach.

The transport's night vision is starting to reveal sporadic Ponderosa pines scattered among chino grass hills, and I know we're approaching the point where the transport will stop. Soon, we'll break for a nap, then continue on foot, hiking for two days before coming to the Wall. Don still has his EMP device stashed in the bottom of his backpack, but concerns of reaching the tunnel before the cameras spot us start to fog my mind. I motion for Don to join me.

"How are we going to filter ten people under the Wall before they see us?" I ask him.

Jubilant in the defeat of his brother, Don just shrugs and laughs. "We'll cross that bridge when we get there," he says. "Slow down, we're approaching the fence."

Up ahead, I see it: the barrier forbidding vehicles to travel further, its sign warning, "STOP. Government property beyond this point. DANGER. Enter at your own risk." When we left Apollo and I saw this sign, I wondered what it meant, why it was planted here. Now I understand. This is an attempt to paint Apollo as a nuclear waste dump. But one question still jabs at my brain.

"Tell me something," I say to Don, keeping my voice low as the transport stops. I lift my eyes from the command screen and scan the vehicle behind me. Everyone is sleeping like they haven't rested in years. "I need you to be one hundred percent truthful. Do you know *what* Apollo is? Why it was established?"

I turn to look at him, his eyes swollen with exhaustion, and Don returns my stare. He's grown serious now, all playfulness gone from his gaze.

"I do not," he says. "I think the 'why' is obvious, but the 'what,' well, I'm not sure Agent Jackson even knows that answer."

I take a deep breath and gaze through the transport's endless windows into the blackness of the night's forest. "Flora is terrified of that man," I say.

Don nods his head. "I am too. This world, it's a fucked-up place."

When he says this, I feel sorry for Don, remembering that he has no family to welcome him upon our return to Apollo. Instead, he'll resume his life in that shack of a cabin, lost in the middle of the forest.

"You know, maybe you could stay with my family for a while, when we get back," I say. "It's the least I could do, after everything I put you through."

Don takes a step back from surprise when I make the offer. "You didn't put me through anything," he says. "I wanted to help. Flora is the first person in Apollo to treat me like a normal human being. This whole situation was my fault, and I didn't want to abandon her."

"Thank you for helping us," I say.

Don glances over his shoulder, notices that Flora and my dad have moved toward the back of the transport, and turns to me again.

"You're lucky to have her," he says.

His words shock me, and after a moment, the realization dawns: Don *cares* about Flora, the same way I do. He had suppressed his feelings this entire time, probably knowing he didn't have a chance. I'm at a loss of words, so I just look at Don, speechless.

"Listen, take good care of her," he continues. "You're a good guy, and she loves you. Do you remember what Dr. Hollister Wesson said to me, before we left his home?"

I shrug. "Maybe a little."

"He said, 'Always remember, the goodness of man still exists, no matter how far gone hope may seem. Wherever darkness lingers, so too, does light.'" Don pauses for a moment and extends a hand. I look down, stunned, and return the handshake.

"People like you and Flora are the light," he tells me. "Thanks for the offer to stay with your family, but I do better alone."

At this, he pulls his hand from mine and walks toward the back of the stopped transport, lies down, and falls asleep to get some rest before we begin the hike. And I'm left standing in awe.

Moment of Truth

ANDREW

I would kill for a shower right now. It's the next day and we're hiking uphill, back through the Ponderosa pine forest toward Apollo, and I'm counting the days since my last shower. This is the third. I'm sticky with sweat, but the crisp breeze cools my skin. We're officially in autumn now, and the air promises of Thanksgiving.

What I would give for some soap, though.

Still in their hospital sweats, several of the patients from Apollo remain close together, rubbing their arms and encouraging each other. *Keep going, we'll be home soon... Just a little longer and you'll be with your wife again.*

I feel at fault for not supplying them with warmer clothes, but how was I supposed to know they'd be here? My dad is chilly too, and tonight, I'll need to sleep close so he doesn't freeze.

By the time night falls, Flora is complaining that her legs are shaking from exhaustion. She's hardly been active these past two months, and now the sudden hiking is killing her muscles. Don and I build a fire pit with the help of others in our group, tossing in our remaining petroleum-jelly-covered cotton balls to launch some flames. The warmth is immediate relief from the dropping temperature, which seems to decline more each minute.

"I bet snow is only a month away," my dad says, a wide grin spreading across his face. "I haven't seen snow in eleven years. Summer never ends in the desert."

Everyone huddles around the fire, rubbing their arms and curling into balls to retain warmth. I thought I'd hear more talking amongst our group; the silence surprises me. Instead, tension bounces from person to person, its prevalence surrounding us in our fogs of breath, in our voiceless stares.

Tomorrow we'll reach the Wall. Nobody wants to say it, but we're all thinking it: after sneaking back into Apollo, will we even make it home?

***

The night seemed to stretch the length of the universe, exponential in its reach. By the time sunrise approached, most of us realized we'd hardly slept. A few in our group had developed a cough.

"We don't have much time left," I told Don, and he merely nodded in agreement.

Now we're hiking through the trees again, munching on granola bars that Don printed for us before we left the safe house. The mountain air and fresh creeks have heightened my senses. Apollo is near—I can feel it.

Hours pass, and the sun switches from overhead to angular in the sky. We have three remaining water canteens, and our group passes them among one another. My throat is growing sticky from thirst, but I allow the others to drink first.

As I sense evening drawing near, Don shoots up his hand, motioning for us to stop. We do, and Don turns toward me, pointing at three Aspen branches formed in the shape of a triangle, surrounded by several river rocks.

"This is the spot," he says, and looks over my shoulder until he sees Flora. "Remember what I told you about this spot, Flora?"

Confused, she jogs to the front of the group, her wavy blond hair now flat and stringy, but her cheeks still rosy and full of life. After all of this, I can't believe how gracefully she continues to move.

"Oh my gosh," Flora says when her gaze falls to the branches and rocks. I watch her eyes fill with tears, and she slaps a hand over her mouth before breaking into fits of laughter. "You've got to be kidding me!"

"What?" I ask, both worried and curious.

I catch Don smirking at Flora, and she falls against his shoulder, cackling in disbelief. Somewhere inside, that old anger surfaces when I see them together, but I push it away, reminding myself I have no reason to feel jealous.

"This," Flora says to me, "is the meeting spot Don told me about; I was supposed to find him here after I returned from The Other Side, two months ago. He'd marked it with three Aspen branches in a triangle, surrounded by river rocks."

Don keeps smiling at Flora, radiant in the afterglow of her delight. "This is what started everything," he says.

I force a smile and laugh with them, but realize Don and Flora now share a connection which doesn't include me. I fight away the discomfort, reminding myself to stop behaving like an insecure high school student.

After the moment passes, Don grows focused again. "We cannot move past this point without risking detection by the Wall's cameras," he tells us. "We'll wait until nightfall, and I'll attempt to disarm the cameras using my EMP device."

Don explains we'll have only minutes to run toward the tunnel and make it underground once the cameras turn off, so we'd better get some rest. We're moving out in a few hours.

***

With nightfall, an ominous blanket settles over our group, the moment of truth fast approaching. "I feel a little like Odysseus," Flora says to me. "You know, from The Odyssey."

"Well, we're not being thrust into the unknown, possibly facing death," I tell her.

Flora looks at me, the softness of her blue eyes glowing in moonlight. "Aren't we?"

Her question, jarring in its simplicity, silences any response I might have offered. Don's voice rouses us, tells us it's time, and I pull Flora's forehead against mine. My eyes drift shut near hers, allowing the warmth of her breath to calm my nerves.

"Let's go home," I whisper, before we fall into a tight embrace, forcing the fear from our minds and gaining the courage for what comes next.

"Are you kiddos ready?" The voice startles us from the moment, and I lift my head to see my father standing over us. As I pull away from Flora, he places a hand on my shoulder. My dad doesn't need to say anything; the tightness of his grip speaks volumes—*I don't want to lose you again.*

Don calls for us to get down, and brilliant beams of light blind our vision, accompanied by a perpetuating buzz. With my arms, I shield my eyes and fall to the damp ground, counting the seconds until the EMP device finishes. Flora murmurs something, but I can't understand what she says.

And from one moment to the next, blackness. Don yells for us to run.

I sprint from my spot, grabbing Flora's arm and yanking her with me. My dad, fueled by adrenaline, paces my stride. I can hear his heaving breaths as he struggles to stay near, but I know he won't allow himself to fall behind. We have no lights to illuminate our paths, no running shoes to protect our ankles, but we fly through the night's forest, dodging trees as our legs carry us to freedom or ruin. The cold air burns into my throat, and Don calls to our group, encouraging us to keep going, we're almost there.

Up ahead, a menacing shadow appears in the distance, dark and gaping in its presence. I have no doubt it's the Wall.

Unable to see much, I hear Don commanding us to stop. He has us form a line and explains how we'll drop into a tunnel that runs underneath the Wall. I hear a couple of cries from behind, followed by concerns of claustrophobia.

"You don't understand," one girl says, "I become hysterical."

But Don tells her it's the only way, and he won't leave her side. Pushing the girl toward the back of the line, he kneels and helps the first of our group to drop underground, then the next, and the next. Within moments, it's my turn. I tell Flora to go first, and my dad will follow me. She nods and swings herself into the hole, dropping into nothingness.

When I follow, I hear Don urging us to move, we don't have much time, and I release myself into blackness, my hands landing in nothing but gritty mud.

"Flora?" I call.

"Up ahead," she says, and I follow her voice, squirming my way forward on my stomach, feeling the heaviness of the earth above and below me. The air is dense and smells of old rainwater, making breathing difficult, but I remind myself I've done this once already. Another body drops from behind me—my dad. I call to him, and he follows my voice forward.

One after another, we begin trickling into the tunnel, crawling our way back home—back to our families, and cooked meals, and books, and fresh air, and *living*.

The claustrophobic girl cries every few minutes, paralyzed from fear, and Don reassures. Ahead of me, others cough and struggle to breathe as the air grows thicker around us. Flora jumps to the rescue this time, offering support and encouragement.

I figure we must be under the Wall by now, and I can't help but picture the look on my mom's face when I return home with my father at my side.

Heck, I'll spend the first night at Flora's house, allowing my parents the privacy to reunite.

Minute after minute, and inch-by-inch, we make our way through the tunnel. I'm positive that within moments, we'll climb our way back into the fresh air, and reunite with Apollo.

The Return

ANDREW

My first gasp of air beyond the tunnel is like tasting sugar for the first time: I want more, until my lungs are ready to explode.

Flora is crying as I approach her, and when I ask what's wrong, she shakes her head and buries her face into my chest. "I never thought I'd see home again," she says.

My dad, smeared with dirt, is shaking when he pulls himself from underground. He does not cry, but the overwhelming emotion brims under his skin. I walk away with Flora and let him have a moment.

We linger in this spot, now within the borders of Apollo, and wait for the last of our party—Don and the claustrophobic girl—to surface. Flora and I fall against the Wall, the moonlight outlining our figures amongst surrounding trees. She collects herself, and I brush the hair away from her face.

"Remember the day we found this thing?" I ask her. "It was during one of our Saturday morning bike rides."

She doesn't say anything, but merely chuckles through tears. I continue brushing her hair from her eyes, clearing the mud from her face with the care of a surgeon's touch. For a moment, it's just Flora and me again, floating through the forest during one of our discovery journeys, out to mark our map. How I wish we could jump back in time to those days.

But Don's voice jerks me into reality, and I take Flora's hand as we walk toward the group. He is conducting a head count to make sure everyone surfaced, and now he calls my name. When I respond, he asks me to come forward, so I smile at Flora, let go of her hand, and join him at the front.

"Listen up," Don tells our group. "We're about seventy miles southeast of the Central Commerce Hub right now. I have an old vehicle hidden an hour's hike from here, on a deserted road. I'm going to turn your attention to Andrew, who will explain our plan. This is vital to our freedom, and possibly our survival."

Don looks at me and nods his head before stepping back. And I begin talking.

"How many of you here know about Agent Jackson?" I pause for a moment and watch as every person, nervous and insecure, raises a hand.

"That's what I thought," I say, after a minute. "The key to getting back our lives, is bypassing Agent Jackson. So here's the plan: once we reach the vehicle, we'll drive to Apollo's Central Commerce Hub and begin dropping you off at your homes. Your families will be thrilled to see you, but they'll also want to know where you've been.

You *cannot* tell them, not at first. We're anticipating our returns will make the news like wildfire. But Agent Jackson needs to develop the story to explain what happened. Do you understand?"

The crowd is quiet for a moment, followed by a wave of mumbles.

"So, we can't tell anyone we were on The Other Side?" one man asks.

"No," I say. "Absolutely not. Our stories will need to coincide with Agent Jackson's spin. That will be our shield, our protection. I know this will be hard, but we need to stay strong. Any other questions?"

When no one responds, we move out.

***

The night is almost over when we arrive at Apollo's Central Commerce Hub. Don had installed night vision into his car years ago, and was therefore able to drive us through the darkness without headlights. I'm sure this is how he avoided detection all these years.

The town is sleeping when our car rolls in; even the birds are nestled into dreamland. No lights, no distractions. The wind has quieted, leaving the trees still in the shadow of Apollo. Don slows the car, helping us to drift in silence down the slumbering streets. As we push further into town, we're greeted by two towering statues of Apollo holding his torch of light toward the sky. As always, the sculptures are encircled by the words, "LIGHT, TRUTH, AND KNOWLEDGE."

Next to me, the girl who'd complained of claustrophobia breaks down into tears. And the woman named Georgette, who had told me about her daughter, joins the girl. We're smashed into the car together—room for eight holding ten—but I do my best to twist around and look at my father. He's not crying, but a hand covers his mouth in disbelief as he gazes out the window, taking everything in.

Don reaches into his back pocket, pulls a crinkled piece of paper, and hands it to me. "Can you open it?" he says.

As I unfold the note, I see a list of names, followed by addresses. I don't understand at first, but soon I see Flora's name, and mine, and my father's. *Our party*, I realize. Don created a list of everyone's residence. I hand the paper back to him, and he turns down a side road that winds toward a hill capped by a small cabin nestled between several Ponderosas. As he slows the car to a stop, the claustrophobic girl lets out a small cry. In the moment, I can't tell if it's fear or despair, but when she bounds from the car toward the house, I realize she cried out in elation.

This is her home.

Don launches himself from the car to stop her, though, reaching for her shoulder. "Remember what Andrew said," he tells her. The girl merely nods, and runs toward her house.

I want to see what will happen, but Don rolls the car away, driving back downhill. "We can't let anyone see us," he says.

We begin making our way all over town, driving as far as the northern base of the San Francisco Peaks. Person by person, our load begins to lighten, and soon, the sun peeks over the eastern horizon, warning that we'd better hurry.

Don speeds the car to our final destination before we're free to return home. Other than the four of us, the mother named Georgette is the only one left. Don stops the car in front of her house. She starts climbing out, but stops and turns around.

"I can't thank you enough," she says to Don and me. "You gave me back my life, and my daughter."

With that, she shuts the door and walks to the front of her house. I'm expecting her to begin calling out her daughter's name, but instead, like a stranger hoping to use the phone, she rings the doorbell. Before I can watch anything else, Don turns the car and leaves.

"Andrew, you're next," he says to me.

But I shake my head, adamant in my demand. "No," I tell him. "Flora first."

The sun is now reflecting golden off the street, and I urge Don to hurry. Flora's hand grips my arm.

"Can you imagine the looks on my parents' faces?" she says, and I meet her hopeful gaze as Don powers down the street toward the south side of Apollo, where Flora lives.

"Your parents will never let you out of their sight again," I joke.

She smiles and nudges my arm, and I try to forget how the sun continues to rise faster than our car can travel.

***

The turnoff to Flora's street is up ahead, and Don floors the car toward the corner. Next to me, Flora bounces on her seat, unable to keep still from the anticipation of returning home. As we approach the curve, he slows the vehicle and swings into a sharp right, sending the four of us flying into the car's corner.

Flora, ecstatic in her approaching moment, lets out a small shriek. I'm ready to join her when I realize Don has stopped the car suddenly. Confused, I ask him why we're not moving, but he doesn't answer. Instead, he's staring straight ahead.

I look to my side and realize my dad is doing the same, and when I finally turn my gaze to join theirs, I see it: four white cars with the letters "ABI" printed in bold, blocking the street to Flora's house. I can see her cabin just beyond the cars, only a few yards away, but we cannot pass.

The color drains from Flora's face when she realizes what's happening, and she turns to open the car door. Frantic, I grab her.

"No!" I say. "You don't know if they're armed. Stay here."

But Flora is growing hysterical, and it's all I can do to wrap my arms around her body and try to calm and contain her.

"Let me take care of this," my dad says, but I yell at him, telling him to sit still. When he refuses, I reach over and grab his arm.

"Do you want me to lose my father all over again?" My dad must read the pleading in my eyes, because he falls back into his seat. Don remains still, staring out the front windshield, managing to appear unaffected. But I know deep down, he's swimming in fear.

A man climbs from the car closest to us, a bullhorn in hand, and flashes his badge. "ABI," he says, his voice commanding. "Come out of your car slowly, with your hands above your head, and no one will get hurt."

Flora turns toward me, her face swollen with tears and masked in terror, and she shakes her head. "I can't do this," she says. "Andrew, I can't do this."

Panicked myself, I caress her face in my hands and draw her near. "Yes, you can, my love," I tell her. "You're stronger than you think. Just remember how much I love you."

A hand grabs my shoulder and whips me around. I can barely comprehend what's happening when my father starts to speak.

"Listen to me, kiddo," he says, and I allow my eyes to focus on the fury that's taken over his face. "Don't say *anything* to them unless I'm there, by your side... understand?"

I just nod, fear choking the speech from me, and my dad pulls me into his arms until I can't breathe. "I love you more than anything, Andrew," he whispers.

The man outside grows more insistent and warns us one final time to surrender. Don turns around and looks over his shoulder, taking us in with those black eyes. No more makeup, no more darkness. I'm expecting him to say something, but he turns around and opens his door, stepping outside with his hands over his head.

Five other men appear from behind their vehicles, guns drawn and aimed at Don. Flora, my dad and I look at each other, then open our doors and do the same. Within moments, more guns are trained on us.

"On the ground," the man with the badge instructs. "Nose to the dirt."

As I lower my face, I can smell the morning dew mixed with the scent of a nearby skunk. Someone approaches me from behind and forces my hands into cuffs. A cloth slips over my face, consuming me in blackness. And as I'm pried to my feet, blind and bound, I hear Flora scream.

The Little Stunt

FLORA

They threw me into the car alone. I called for Andrew, for his father, for Don, but only a deep, foreboding voice responded. *"You'll be lucky if you ever see them again."*

Now, I'm chained to a chair somewhere, in a brick room that resembles a cell. I can't tell if an hour has passed, or three. Sporadic lights dangle from the ceiling like Halloween decorations, painting the room yellow, and it's all I can do to fight back the vomit that threatens to explode from my stomach. My hands, bound, are trembling. I can't fathom what will happen next.

My upper lip burns from the blow of the ground when they arrested me and threw me against it. After they slipped the black cloth over my head, I remember tasting blood.

I'm going to die, I realize. *I'll never see my parents again.*

The cell's door opens as these thoughts cross my mind, the creaks piercing my ears, and a shadow enters the room. I hold my breath in preparation, watching as the figure scrapes a chair against the hard floor, and I cringe from the earsplitting sound. The shadow steps forward into the sickly light, revealing its face to be none other than Agent Jackson.

"So, we meet again, my dear," he says, and I swallow my voice into my stomach, straining against the chains around my wrists. "This time, I do fear, under slightly differing circumstances. Extenuating, I might call them."

I open my mouth to speak, but no words form yet. Agent Jackson must see the terror written across my face, and the corner of his mouth tilts up. "Do you mind if I take a seat?"

He swings the chair before him and sits down, facing me. We're only a few feet apart.

"Where are Don, Andrew, and his father?" I manage to ask, wincing when I realize my voice shook.

"They're around," he says, and sighs. "You never learn, do you Flora? I always win. *We—the ABI—always win.* To resist us is... futile."

"You tried to kill me. *You* gave me cancer."

"I did what was necessary for the protection of Apollo."

I can do nothing but respond with a gaping jaw. What can one say to such an acknowledgment of attempted murder through such a devious, disturbing manner?

"First it was the water bottle," Agent Jackson continues. "Now, it was the beam of light on the other side of the Wall. Do you think I don't know an EMP device when I see one?"

"How did you know it was us?" I ask.

"I'll be perfectly honest with you, my dear. I never expected to run into Andrew, or his father. And Don—well, he is perhaps the greatest tragedy: the orphan who stabs his protector in the back. No, I was not expecting Don. It was *you*. I knew you were behind this, Flora. You, with your defiant little attitude and spoiled-rotten sense of entitlement."

His words are daggers to my psyche, and I am desperate to keep myself from breaking into tears. Me, spoiled? Entitled? I can't understand how fighting for your right to live translates into those attributes.

"So now you leave me in a difficult situation," Agent Jackson says. "Regardless of what you think, Flora, I am not a murderer. I take life only when necessary—when it maximizes utility for the sake of Apollo."

When he says this, I realize Agent Jackson doesn't know yet about the others we returned to their homes. For a brief moment, I allow myself to drift from this cell and beg the media—my mother—to hurry and cover the story. *Please discover our group. Please hustle and report.*

A loud knock on the door stops Agent Jackson from his discussion. He stands to open the door, peaks his head outside, and peers over his shoulder, back at me.

"You'll need to excuse me for a moment," he says, and leaves the room. His empty chair stares at me, and I wonder what is being whispered in the cornered shadows of this jail.

***

As I wait for Agent Jackson's return, I assess my surroundings in more detail. Upon further inspection, I realize the bricks aren't just old, but *red*, like the sandstone surrounding Oak Creek Canyon. The room is square in shape, as well. I close my eyes and try to recall how long the drive took to reach this place. I was blindfolded and therefore could not see the route, but I estimate we traveled about an hour, maybe more.

Could it be? Is it possible this building, in which I'm being held, is the same one Andrew and I discovered months ago, hidden away amongst the rocks above the canyon? Is this the place that started *everything*?

I hear footsteps approaching outside my door, stampeding down the hall, and demanding voices. A loud bang knocks me from my chair, but the chains still restrain me, and the door swings open. Three shadows fly into my room, followed by a fourth.

"Move up!" a voice demands.

The three figures step forward, and I realize their heads are covered in black cloths. The guard standing behind them yanks the covers from their faces, and Don, Andrew, and Andrew's father nearly collapse when they see me.

"Flora!" Andrew calls, and runs over. His hands are bound behind his back, but he drops to his knees before me and examines my face. "Did they hurt you?"

"No," I say, frenzied laughter rising from within. I don't know if I'm happy to see them, or just hysterical. "You?"

Andrew shakes his head, but I catch an open wound above his right eyebrow. I glance past Andrew's shoulder and see Don standing there, a look of defeat blanketing his face. He's not looking at me, or Andrew, or anywhere within the room. Instead, he's staring off into space, existing in his own world.

"Are you OK?" I ask Don, but Andrew shakes his head.

"He hasn't said a word since we were captured," he tells me.

Andrew's father leans down to us, a look of confusion crossing his face. "Something is off," he whispers. "Agent Jackson hasn't aged since I last saw him. In fact, he looks *younger*."

Before I can react, the door opens again, and this time, Agent Jackson returns. His demeanor has changed—more commanding, even angry—and I suspect the news of our group's homecoming has hit the airwaves. Agent Jackson is accompanied by three guards, who form a curved perimeter behind him.

"So, you decided to pull a little stunt," he says to us. "Smart, very smart. I must admit, I did not see that one coming."

All four of us remain silent, watching Agent Jackson as he begins pacing the room. He instructs his guards to unchain me from the chair, but keep my hands bound.

"Apparently, you don't understand the damage you caused, all of you," he says. "So now, I'm going to fill you in, and you're going to help me correct this mess. You are going to pay for this assault upon our Great State of Apollo."

Lymphocytes

FLORA

The transformation of Agent Jackson is fascinating to watch. Like a light switch, he turns from fury to calm, and back to lunacy. He seems to battle something inside, some inner voice or conscience that drives his actions and decisions and views. After a few minutes of this bipolar behavior, he returns to his composed demeanor, and turns to face the four of us again.

"Do you know about the lymphocyte cells in the human body?" he asks, aiming his question toward me.

"Yes," I answer.

"What do they do?"

"They are the cells within the immune system responsible for killing cancer cells."

"And what happens when a lymphocyte kills one of those cancer cells?"

I pause. "The lymphocyte dies," I say after a few moments.

Agent Jackson smiles. "Very good," he says. "The Apollo educational system has done well."

"I don't see what this has to do with us," Andrew says, cutting into the conversation. His voice is impatient, frustrated.

"I'm glad you asked," Agent Jackson says. "The human body is the epitome of a utilitarian society. Every cell has its purpose to keep the body functioning, and that purpose overrides anything else. In order to maximize their utility, lymphocytes sacrifice themselves for the greater good. What would happen if several lymphocytes decided they didn't want to die to destroy cancer cells?"

"The cancer would kill you," Andrew says.

"Precisely. Everyone loses." Agent Jackson seems pleased with himself. "Our bodies use utilitarianism to keep us alive, and we—as individuals—use it to keep society alive."

He's beginning to sound more and more like a madman. "I don't understand," I tell him.

"You will," Agent Jackson assures. "Apollo is like the human body—a work of art, a beautiful, precious life. But like any person, it can quickly die when its own cells begin to mutate, and turn against it."

Slowly, Agent Jackson is beginning to make sense. And I feel a sickness form deep inside.

"What you witnessed outside the Wall is the cancer," he continues, his voice growing harsher. "It's crept inside Apollo, through you, and through all these... *people*... you've brought back. And me—my department—we are the lymphocytes."

My fingers, toes, cheeks—they are tingling with fear. I'd never known terror like this before, never understood the depth of psychopathy in this man, until now. And I realize our fate hangs on the whim of a lunatic.

"So you're going to kill yourselves to take us down?" The defiant, angry voice shocks us, and in unison, we turn toward the corner of the room. It's Don, and he's staring at Agent Jackson like death itself.

"*You*, more than anyone, should understand what I'm talking about," Agent Jackson says, approaching Don with the fury of a defied god. "You *lived* Out There. Don't you understand what you have done by pulling this stunt?"

"We haven't done anything other than return exiled people to their families," Andrew's father says. "They just want to live their lives in peace."

Agent Jackson shakes his head and approaches Andrew's father in slow, ominous strides. "You opened the window for the public to ask questions. It's *imperative* they never know what is beyond that Wall!"

"Why?" I finally cry, infuriated. I'm sick and tired of these psychological games, of these *secrets*. They've ruined my life, and I'm done playing.

Agent Jackson turns toward me now, moving away from Andrew's father. "Tell me Flora, what did you witness on The Other Side?"

I pause before speaking, unsure of the right answer. "People weren't allowed to talk in public," I say, and Agent Jackson nods his head. "There was violence, a lot of it. Nothing was original: no books, no music. Everyone was stuck behind a screen, isolated, and miserable."

Now he looks to Andrew. "And you, valiant hero? I know you saw *much* more."

Andrew looks like he wants to tear through Agent Jackson's face with his teeth. "It doesn't matter what I saw," he says.

At this, Agent Jackson's eyes bulge, and I feel him slide behind me. Without warning, his arm snakes around my neck, pressing against my windpipe, and my body surges in adrenaline. A cold, metal barrel presses against my head, and panic grips every muscle when I realize I can't breathe. Bound and gagging, I thrash against Agent Jackson, but it's useless.

"Answer me, Andrew," he warns, but I can barely comprehend his words. My lungs are burning, desperate for air, and I feel like I'm swallowing my tongue. I look to Andrew for help, and he lunges forward, shouting, "No! I'll tell you, just let her go."

The arm releases me and I collapse to the ground, coughing and choking as I gulp down air through my throbbing throat, shaking in violent jolts against the floor. I hear Andrew spill his guts to Agent Jackson, speaking of an underground group called HELL, of starvation and death on the streets, of class separation that predisposes people to a life of either slavery or opportunity. "Everyone is a target, unless you can buy your safety," he finishes.

Agent Jackson nods his head in satisfaction. "Would you want to live in that world?" he asks.

Andrew shakes his head and lowers his eyes to the ground. "Not in a million years."

Agent Jackson radiates triumph. "That's what I thought," he says. "Here in Apollo, we live with families, and have community, and enjoy the freedom to express ourselves through music and art and literature. No one fears dying on the streets, or being denied an education. People are *happy* in Apollo. It is a paradise, a utopia, a piece of Heaven in this disgusting, rat-infested world surrounding us. And there is only one way to ensure that doesn't change."

None of us ask, but instead stare at Agent Jackson, waiting for him to answer. "Control of information," he says.

At this, an epiphany overwhelms me, momentarily pushing away the fear. Still on my knees, I lift my head toward Agent Jackson. "An intranet," I say. "That's where we are, why you tried to kill me when you thought I came close to discovering what was in here."

Agent Jackson doesn't answer, but I see Andrew's father nod from the corner of my eye, and I know I'm right. "A-Search, our so-called Internet," I continue, "none of it is real. This building is the intranet that runs Apollo."

I hear Don start to laugh, a borderline hysterical sound, and he steps forward from his corner, both infuriated and elated at my conclusion. His eyes are fixed on Agent Jackson.

"So tell me," he says, "how can you call Apollo the leader of light, truth, and knowledge, when our society is based on control of information? That is the most hypocritical bullshit I've ever heard."

Agent Jackson begins to concentrate on Don alone. In slow, calculated movements, he moves toward him, tilting his head as he approaches.

"How do you think The Other Side got to its current state, *Jaron?*" he says. "The more people who had access to information and technological advancements, the more they abused their knowledge. Companies used it to force employees to work longer hours. Politicians and special interests used it to blur the line between news reporting and propaganda. Criminals used it to invade privacy and attack their victims. If we open that window here in Apollo, we will lose *everything* we've worked to establish since 2075."

"So you're telling us," Andrew says, "it's either we suffer Out There but know the truth, or we live happily and free in Apollo, but exist in the dark?"

Agent Jackson nods his head and kneels before Andrew, looking him straight in the eyes. "Which would you choose?"

Secrets

FLORA

Something about the depth of Agent Jackson's knowledge seems strange, and the words of Andrew's father haunt me, too: *Agent Jackson hasn't aged since I last saw him. In fact, he looks younger.* There is more to this story than meets the eye.

"How do you know so much?" I ask, emboldened by the anger sparked by Agent Jackson when he choked me. Climbing to my feet, my hands still bound, I stare Agent Jackson straight in the eyes. "You're spouting off this information, but how can we trust you? Even if you were to let us go, who's to say you won't kill us quietly down the road—like you tried with me?"

Agent Jackson wasn't expecting this; I see it in his face. The man is slowly beginning to lose control, and it terrifies him.

"How do I know so much?" he says, and starts to laugh. I watch him, emotionless, but inside wonder if I just made a mistake. "Flora, your sense of curiosity never ceases to amaze me. How do *I* know so much? My great-grandfather was a founder of Apollo."

Andrew's father murmurs something, but I can't understand him.

"Do you think they recruit just anybody into the ABI to protect Apollo and its secrets?" he continues. "Only the bloodlines of the founders are bestowed with that honor, my dear."

The murmuring grows louder, and Andrew's father snaps up his head. "The bloodlines," he says, his voice growing stronger with realization. "It wasn't you I met eleven years ago. It was your *father.*"

Agent Jackson nods his head. "A great man, may he rest in peace. I learned from the best."

The revelation smacks me across the face, and I'm beginning to understand how far the story reaches. This didn't start with Agent Jackson; it stretches back for generations. To Agent Jackson, Apollo is more than a mere community that lives by a shared ideology. To him, Apollo is family.

"How is that possible?" The question comes from Andrew, who I can tell still doesn't trust the explanation.

Agent Jackson pauses for a moment, pondering if he should reveal more. After a moment of thought, he speaks. "My great-grandfather was part of The Privileged, which eventually became The Upper Class."

A thump from behind startles me, and I turn around to see Don collapsed on the floor. I run to his side, asking if he's OK. He nods and instead of answering, he asks, "The Upper Class?"

To my surprise, Agent Jackson answers. "In 2075, during the Virtual Revolution, a small group of individuals from The Privileged did not agree with the agenda being executed around the world. My great-grandfather was among them. Together, they combined their money and influence to negotiate with the newly formed United Council and demand an agreement for their own plot of land, to establish their own state. They'd collect a populace of like-minded individuals—some with families, some alone—and establish a better way of life. In return, my great-grand-father and his allies would not incite an uprising against the new powers-that-be. That state, was Apollo."

We're all quiet for a moment, a silence breathing disbelief, but I know Agent Jackson is telling the truth. The story is too real.

"The sign on the road," Andrew says, breaking the quiet, "and the stories about Apollo being a nuclear waste dump. That was part of the agreement to keep everyone away?"

Agent Jackson confirms Andrew's theory by nodding his head, turning to face us all.

"Now you see the grave problem you caused, so here's what we're going to tell the public: The Other Side sent a spy into Apollo to infiltrate our system. They out-smarted us for years, even kidnapped several of our citizens. Once discovered, the ABI sought some of its best, young hackers and sent a rescue team beyond the Wall to bring back our citizens. The team was successful; they not only accomplished the rescue mission, but they also flushed out the spy."

The four of us exchange glances, wondering who will be this mysterious spy. As I latch onto a brief gaze with Don, a loud *pop!* echoes in the vacant room, and I watch my friend curl into himself, and collapse. Before I can register what happened, a red stain spreads across his white shirt, along his chest. When I smell something burning, I peer over my shoulder to Agent Jackson and see a smoking gun in his hand.

"What did you do?" I yell, suddenly frantic, and I rush to Don's side, calling his name. "Stay with me! Please stay with me." My hands are useless against the cuffs, no matter how hard I tear my skin on the metal. I'm stuck, bound and helpless, so I drop to my knees and rest my face close to his, no longer able to conceal the tidal wave of tears rupturing from beneath. I can smell nothing but deteriorating flesh and blood.

Within seconds, Andrew and his father join me, and we're surrounding Don, talking to him, reassuring him. But he convulses against the struggle to breathe, choking up blood, his hands remaining bound behind his back. The guards just stand there and watch.

"Someone always has to die," Agent Jackson says from behind. "Consider it redemption for your betrayal of Apollo, Jaron. You're finally serving your purpose for the greater good. Congratulations."

Don's eyes narrow, and he seems lost without his dark shield of makeup, a vulnerable puppy fighting to survive in a harsh world. His lips form to say something, but he can't speak, and through clouded tears, I tell him to hush—I'm here. But he shakes his head, blood bubbling through his lips, and with his eyes, he begs me to lean closer.

As I lower my ear to his mouth, I hear his faint breath striving to shape a phrase. I tell him to try, I'm listening. With every ounce of strength, Don manages to formulate three words.

"Be... the... light."

I don't know what he means, but before I can respond, his last breath whispers away, and Don's once-intent stare falls into oblivion. I'm left staring at his lifeless body, telling myself to wake up, this can't be happening, but when Agent Jackson orders his guards to take Don away, I begin screaming.

Andrew begs me to calm down, but I'm thrashing, furious and desolate, desperate to break free of these chains imposed by Apollo and The Other Side and Agent Jackson and *the world*. My voice has exhausted, but my breath continues to heave, and somewhere from beyond, I hear Andrew's pleading, mingled with threats against the guards.

Hands grip my legs and shoulders, pinning me to the ground against my insanity, and I feel a sharp piercing in my right arm. I yank against the pain, but can't fight it anymore, and I drift into blissful oblivion.

The Choice

FLORA

When I awake, I find myself lost between two worlds, unsure if I'm back in the psychiatric hospital or still locked in the ABI's cell. The bed feels the same, and my head throbs with vigor. My hands no longer bound, I push myself to a sitting position, grimacing from the invasive fluorescent lights above. I swallow and realize my mouth feels like one giant cotton ball.

"Andrew?" I say, barely above a whisper. But there is only silence.

I almost call Don's name next, stopping myself mid-breath and retracting back into a bubble of despair.

The room is made of bricks, and I therefore conclude I have not left the ABI intranet building. As I climb to my feet, I begin circling the room, studying each corner, and I notice a camera. It looks identical to the ones I saw on the Wall.

I peer into its lens and narrow my eyes. "I know you're on the other side of that screen," I say. "And I know you're watching me, just like you did with A-Search."

The drugs they fed me still have an effect, because I tumble to my side, suddenly woozy. I catch myself against the bed, and the door to my room opens. I'm expecting Agent Jackson to emerge, but instead, it's Andrew. His eyes are swollen from tears and anguish. I fly into his arms.

"You're OK," I say, relief spilling over as his arms encircle me. Andrew grips my waist like a raft after shipwreck, and I cry against his shoulder. "He didn't deserve to die," I say.

"No, he didn't."

When I pull away and we both calm down, Andrew guides me to the bed and gestures for me to sit. Exhausted and weak, I do, and he rests next to me.

"We can't let them win," I say after a few minutes.

I'm expecting Andrew to agree, to unite with me in defiance for Don, but instead, he's quiet. I wait for an answer, but when it doesn't come, I grow annoyed.

"Andrew, we *can't* let them win."

I watch as he jams his hands into his thick mane of hair and rubs his forehead, and I begin to understand he actually thinks I'm wrong.

"They will never let us go," he says after a minute. "Not you, not me, not my father. Your parents will be left wondering what happened to their daughter for the remainder of their days. My mom will be alone in the world."

"Unless?" I ask.

Andrew sighs. "Unless we agree to go along with Agent Jackson's story."

"Never," I say.

"Flora, it's a truce from the ABI, signed and sealed. They will *never* go after us, our families, or our loved ones—including those we rescued—as long as we remain true to the story and safeguard Apollo."

When he says this, I understand why Andrew is so adamant about joining the ABI in its public lies. This truce is not an offer of peace. It's a threat in disguise.

"If we decline, Don's death would have been in vain," he continues. "He did this so you could return to Apollo and reunite with your family. Refusing to sign will mean no one wins, except them."

Fury fumes beneath the surface, ready to explode, but I force myself to take a deep breath and try to think. *Rationalize, Flora. Rationalize.* I close my eyes and allow my thoughts to drift back home: my mom working on her newspaper columns locked away in the office, my dad playing his piano in the living room as a fire burns nearby, Ernest curled on a rug near the couch.

I could go back to that life again. We could be safe. They could be safe.

When I open my eyes, Andrew is staring at me with anticipation. I lower my eyes and reach for his hand. Our fingers lock, and I take another deep breath.

"OK," I say. "Where are the papers?"

***

They told us we'd re-emerge into the public as heroes, as superstars. The media would engulf us in a frenzy, so before we were released to our families, they gave us showers and new clothes and haircuts. They fed us and gave us a few nights of rest and made sure we were ready.

"One week after you return home, we will hold a press conference," Agent Jackson told us. "Your answers to the press will be general. I'll handle the details."

They were right, about everything. The ABI car drives down my street, and I can see the cabin—*my* cabin—up ahead. The sidewalks are streaming with reporters and spectators carrying point-and-shoot cameras. People are holding signs with messages like, "Welcome home, Flora!" and "You're a hero!"

I stare at everything in a haze, their faces and words whizzing by my window in a blur. And I feel like I did months ago, after my first meeting with Agent Jackson, when my parents praised him as I sank into the backseat of the car.

We pull into the driveway of my house, and as I climb from my seat, I see the cabin's front door open. A ball of fur jets through the threshold, barking like the world's about to end, and tackles me. I fall against the car, covered in dog saliva and smothered by overjoyed yelps.

"Hey boy," I say to Ernest, and I'm overwhelmed by a sudden wave of homesickness. I nuzzle my face against his soft, golden coat, seeking solace in such unconditional love, and force away the tears that threaten to erupt.

When I lift my face, my parents are standing before me. I hear the surrounding cameras clicking like a chorus, but that doesn't matter. Everything falls away, and in this moment, it's just me, my mother, and my dad. They're looking at me like I returned from the dead.

"Oh sweetie," my dad says, and swings forward, scooping me into his arms and breaking into tears against my shoulder. "I thought we'd never see you again."

My mom, unable to control herself, starts sobbing hysterically and joins the embrace with my dad and me. The three of us stand here, holding onto one another like life itself, and for the first time in months, the sickness in my soul slips away, and I feel nothing but security.

I'm home. I'm finally home.

Home

FLORA

The next days are filled with home-cooked sweet potato casserole, cheerful piano music, and even a family camping trip. I ask my dad if we could travel further north, away from Oak Creek Canyon. His eyes inquire why, but he says nothing and grants my wish. Over campfires, we cook beans and sing songs and cuddle with Ernest, who looks like the happiest dog on Earth.

When I nuzzle under the covers in my own bed, I think back to the countless nights I spent locked away, dreaming of these moments. At times, I never thought I'd see home again. But then I think of Don, how he never had the luxury of returning to his bed, and guilt consumes me.

The only time I talk to Andrew throughout the first two weeks is during our press conference. He tells me his mother had one of her events when she saw his dad again, but has since returned to normal.

"She believes the story," he says. "I'm her hero, now." I detect sadness in his voice when he says this, but his face beams when he talks of his parents' reunion. "I never thought I could feel like this again."

"Like what?" I ask.

"Complete."

The press conference is different, though. I'm sitting in a pressure cooker throughout the whole event. When one television reporter asks me a question, I nearly burst.

"Flora, I understand you befriended Don. How did you discover he was a spy for The Other Side, and did you know this before you became friends?"

I freeze, anger brimming from inside my chest at the scrutiny bleeding from everyone's eyes—judging Don, the *real* hero.

Not sure how to answer, I glance toward Agent Jackson. He widens his eyes at me, and I look back to the reporter, her face impatient and waiting for my answer. I swallow, never feeling so vulnerable.

"Well," I say, "when I met Don, I didn't know he was a spy. In fact, our friendship started genuine. He was a great person, smart, perceptive, and he struck me as the type who'd risk his safety for a friend." I pause and take a deep breath, hating myself for what I must say next.

"As we spent more time together, aspects of his reclusive life began to seem odd. I pulled together the puzzle pieces, and that's how I learned his true identity. I want to make this clear, though: what happened needed to be done for the protection of Apollo and its citizens. Don's actions were unfortunate, but they *do not* represent him, as a whole. In my opinion, Don was the tragedy of the evil on The Other Side."

Andrew reaches over and takes my hand. Lowering my eyes from the crowd, I fight back tears, but feel consolation in knowing I spoke the truth about Don's fate— he *was* the tragedy. When Agent Jackson nods his head at me, I know I did well.

***

My mom and dad mention nothing of my absence those first two weeks, but with each passing day, the unease of anticipation expands in my belly. On a snowy Sunday beginning my third week home, my mom breaks the muzzle.

"Your father and I don't believe the news stories," she says, as we're sitting around the table eating dinner. I wonder why she picked now to bring it up, and my stomach clenches from anxiety.

"What do you mean?" I ask. "Why not?"

"It doesn't add up," my dad says. "We're worried the ABI did something to you, sweetie, and we want you to feel comfortable telling us. We'll protect you."

Panic surges when he says this, and I fly from my chair, dropping my fork, and it clangs on the ground. "No!" I say. "Everything happened just as Agent Jackson described it."

"Then how did you recover from the stomach cancer?" my mom asks. "Why didn't the ABI inform us when they recruited you, so we wouldn't worry? Why did Agent Jackson come to our house after you disappeared, acting like the ABI was looking for you?"

I stare at my parents' faces and realize nothing I say will convince them to believe otherwise. Yet telling the truth is out of the question. How can I make them understand I'm trying to protect them, to protect *us*?

"I—I can't tell you what really happened," I say after moments of screaming silence. "I signed a contract, and that's all I can reveal. But please, you *cannot*, under any circumstance, let these words leave this room. What really happened doesn't matter. I'm back home now. We're all safe, and we have a future ahead."

I sit down again, re-joining my parents at the table. They're looking at me miserably, helpless to do any more than offer general comfort.

"Maybe I can leak a few leads to my colleagues at the paper," my mom says.

I shake my head in frustration, dropping my face into my arms. "No Mom, *please hear me*," I say. "That would be disastrous for everyone. Not just you, or Dad, but for Andrew and his family, and all the people who came back."

My parents continue staring at me like I'm crazy, their faces ridden with concern. "Trust me," I say. "I want to have a normal life again, but I can't without your support."

My parents look at each other, communicating silently. I find this moment ironic: it reminds me of The Other Side.

"OK sweetie," my dad says. "We support you, and we love you, and all we want is for you to be safe. We'll stick to the story from Agent Jackson."

Be the Light

FLORA

January has always been one of my favorite months, because it represents beginning anew. In the past, everything looked fresher to me: the people more excited, the air crisper, the vibe hopeful. But now, I struggle to find that sparkle—an orphan staring through a window into a home that is no longer hers.

The forecast promised snow today, and I'm enjoying the sting of cold against my cheeks as I sip coffee outside of La Experiencia Maya, waiting for Andrew. It's a little after eight o'clock in the morning on Saturday, and Apollo is beginning to rouse. A few cyclists breeze past me, and I admire them for exercising in this cold. A line forms nearby for coffee, and I can hear people talking and laughing.

The sound of life.

"Flora?" The female voice comes from behind, and when I turn around, a girl my age is staring at me, her auburn hair framing a voluptuous face with full lips and thick glasses.

"Yes?" I ask. Something about this girl seems familiar, but I can't quite place it.

She chuckles nervously. "You probably don't remember me, but I just want to tell you I'm sorry. I saw your story on the news. You didn't deserve what I did to you."

I rack my brain, trying to recall the mystery crime this girl committed against me, but I'm at a loss. "I'm sorry, but who are you? A lot has happened these past few months. My memory isn't the best."

The girl rubs her forehead and seems to curse herself before looking at me again. "My name is Sophie," she says. "I was the one who hit you a few months ago, because of what Andrew said."

Recognition sweeps over me now, and I remember everything. At the time, Sophie's action was one of several catalysts that drove me from Apollo, but now—after everything I've witnessed—it seems so insignificant.

"Oh, right," I say, and stand to meet her eye-to-eye. "It's OK, don't give it another thought, but thanks for the apology. I appreciate it."

Sophie smiles, nods, and walks away to order coffee. I watch as she interacts with the barista, so innocent, so naïve. I find myself thinking how differently Sophie might view the world, how she might interact, if she knew *the truth.*

Minutes pass, and Sophie leaves. I take another sip and realize my coffee is growing cold. I begin to wonder where Andrew is; we were supposed to have met a while ago.

Just as I start to contemplate leaving, I see him laughing with his parents in the distance, walking down the sidewalk. His father swings an arm over his mother's shoulder, pulling her close, while he whispers something intimate in her ear. She giggles, pulls away, and slaps him across the chest. He delights in her playfulness, reaching for her again. Andrew turns around and says something to them. He is radiant.

I signal as they approach, and Andrew sees me waving. When his father notices me too, his face lightens even more.

"Hey kiddo," he says. "How are you holding up?"

For some reason, his question causes a surge of anguish, and I nearly break into tears. I force a smile, but sensing my quiet desperation to leave, Andrew tells his parents we're going to take a walk. Deep inside, I thank him, as I can't bear to remain around people right now.

**

"I thought returning home would be easier," I tell Andrew once we've walked away. "Everyone else seems to be reintegrating so well, but not me."

"Do you really think it's easy?" he asks.

I shrug. "Look at you: your father, your mother. You all look so *happy*. I've run into some of the people we rescued, and they're ecstatic."

I stop talking for a moment, and we sit on a nearby bench positioned under two Ponderosa pine trees. I reach down and snatch a pine cone, playing with it in my gloved hand. "All I wanted, for months, was for life to return to normal. Now that it has, wherever I look, all I can think about are Don's words."

Andrew's eyes grow soft with concern. "Which were?" he asks.

I sigh and look toward the ground. "The world is a fucked-up place."

I hear Andrew sigh, and he reaches for me, running his fingers under my chin, gently lifting so my eyes meet his.

"You know what I think?" he asks. "When I was in Microphysics, studying the work of Stephen Hawking, my professor told us about these subatomic particles that suddenly appear in the universe, clash into each other, and then disappear. The particles always oppose each other, and at the same time, attract each other. My professor said to think of them as Yin and Yang."

I smile, grateful for Andrew's obvious attempt at distracting me, but I can't understand what this has to do with my statement. When I ask him, he continues.

"During my first few weeks home, I was beyond exhilarated to have my father back, yet I couldn't bring myself to leave bed. That's when I remembered my professor's lesson, and I realized something."

"What?" I ask him, now genuinely curious. "What did you realize?"

"Wherever there is good, there is evil. Wherever there is hot, there is cold. Our entire universe, down to its subatomic particles, is filled with opposing forces. If this is a universal truth, then the idea of peace—even within ourselves—is a fallacy."

I can do nothing more than stare at Andrew after he reveals this conclusion to me. I'm dumbfounded, and at the same time, I realize he's right.

"No peace?" I ask.

"No peace," he says. "So all we can do is cope, and we have each other for that."

Andrew stands from the bench and reaches into his back pocket. From it, he pulls out our map. I haven't seen it since I mailed it to him before I left for The Other Side. Andrew sits down again and stares at the crumpled paper before handing it to me.

"The adventure never has to end for us," he tells me. "As long as we stick together, we'll be OK, no matter what life throws our way."

I slowly unfold the map and my eyes fall to the words scrawled at the top, in my own handwriting: *What's knowledge without curiosity?*

I turn to Andrew, and his eyes are filling with tears. I find myself starting to laugh, but not from joy. I feel jaded, cynical, a slave to fate.

An earthquake rattles from inside and when I look down, my hands are shaking from the struggle, and I drop the map. Andrew dives for it, saving it from falling into slush. As he pulls his hand from the snow, I reach down and grab his wrist, my fingers gripping him like a wrench.

"Andrew," I say, my voice trembling, "his death was my fault."

The confession rushes from a place somewhere so deep, not even my consciousness was aware it existed. I fall against Andrew and he lets me cry on his shoulder, stroking my hair until I begin to calm down.

"Don wouldn't want to see you this way," Andrew says. "You couldn't have stopped this from happening any more than you could prevent a monsoon." He pauses for a moment, and I feel the rise and fall of his chest. "Let me tell you something. Before we hacked into the hospital, Don and I visited a history professor, the man who brought Don to Apollo. His name was Dr. Hollister Wesson. And as we were leaving, he said something to Don that was very profound."

I pull myself from Andrew and turn to face him. "What did he say?"

"He said, 'Always remember, the goodness of man still exists, no matter how far gone hope may seem. Wherever darkness lingers, so too, does light.'" Andrew pauses and leans into me, pressing his lips against mine and I breathe in his warmth, all worries falling from my mind. When he pulls away, he takes my hands into his, and I tremble.

"*We* need to be the light, Flora," he says. "That's what Don was trying to tell you. We need to be the light wherever darkness lingers."

Confused, I pull my gaze from Andrew's and look toward the sky, watching birds fly from one tree to the next, and a snowflake drifts from the painted heavens—like serenity—and lands atop my cheek. I close my eyes and lift my face as another falls, and another, and another, each one whispering against my skin. I'd forgotten how much I love the snow, how its scent loiters in the air, mingled with pine. As the flakes begin to float down in greater numbers, I turn back to Andrew, his hair now sprinkled with white.

"How?" I ask. "After everything we learned, after all we've seen, after the lies we've told, how can we possibly be the light?"

Andrew shakes his head, and I know he feels as lost as I do. "I don't know," he says, and he lifts his hand, placing our map back into my palm. "But I suppose that's for us to figure out. At least, through it all, we can do it together."

A Note to My Readers

Thank you for supporting an indie author! While you're here, would you take five minutes to jump onto Amazon and leave a quick review of *The Apollo Illusion*? This is my debut novel, and Amazon reviews will help *The Apollo Illusion* find new readers and become successful. Also, if you use Goodreads, reviews are helpful there, too.

Sign Up for My Readers Club!

If you like my writing, don't miss my next book or story! Sign up for my Readers Club email list, available on my website at www.ShariLopatin.com. Readers Club subscribers are always the first to know about new stories, fun giveaways, cover reveals, and my book recommendations with "Shari's Pick."

I'm also on social media:
- Instagram (@sharilopatin)
- Facebook (Facebook.com/ShariLopatin)
- Goodreads

About the Author

Shari Lopatin tells stories that matter. An award-winning journalist in her earlier years, she now writes complex and stimulating suspense novels that tie into modern-day social issues. Shari has worked as a newspaper reporter, magazine writer, public relations professional, social media manager, and earned the title of "Cat Mom of the Year."

Learn more about Shari, her work, and how to connect, by visiting www.ShariLopatin.com.

www.ingramcontent.com/pod-product-compliance
Lightning Source LLC
Chambersburg PA
CBHW031219120726
47905CB00002B/401